THE
MOONLIT
WORLD

DAW BOOKS PROUDLY PRESENTS
THE NOVELS
OF EDWARD WILLETT

WORLDSHAPERS
WORLDSHAPER *(Book One)*
MASTER OF THE WORLD *(Book Two)*
THE MOONLIT WORLD *(Book Three)*

THE CITYBORN

THE HELIX WAR
MARSEGURO *(Book One)*
TERRA INSEGURA *(Book Two)*

LOST IN TRANSLATION

THE MOONLIT WORLD

Worldshapers: Book Three

EDWARD WILLETT

DAW BOOKS, INC.
DONALD A. WOLLHEIM, FOUNDER
1745 Broadway, New York, NY 10019
ELIZABETH R. WOLLHEIM
SHEILA E. GILBERT
PUBLISHERS
www.dawbooks.com

First Printing, September 2020
1 2 3 4 5 6 7 8 9

DAW TRADEMARK REGISTERED
U.S. PAT. AND TM. OFF. AND FOREIGN COUNTRIES
—MARCA REGISTRADA
HECHO EN U.S.A.

PRINTED IN THE U.S.A.

For my best friend in high school, John "Scrawney" Smith, in memory of all those after-school writing sessions.

ACKNOWLEDGMENTS

ANOTHER BOOK, ANOTHER round of acknowledgements!

First, the usual suspects:

Thanks to my wife, Margaret Anne Hodges, and daughter, Alice, for putting up with a husband and father who spends as much time thinking about fictional worlds as the real one. (Shadowpaw, our black Siberian cat, doesn't seem concerned one way or the other, as long as he is fed regularly and petted on demand.)

Thanks to my editor and publisher, Sheila Gilbert at DAW Books, for, as always, finding the flaws and asking the questions and providing the suggestions that help me make the book better.

Thanks to everyone else who is part of the family of DAW Books, which is, if I might paraphrase Pangloss, "the best of all possible publishers."

Thanks to my agent, Ethan Ellenberg, for his support and efforts on my behalf.

A special thanks to the Saskatoon Public Library. Much of *The Moonlit World* was written while I was writer-in-residence there, and even if the latter part of the residency ended up with me as writer-in-residence in my own residence, providing writing advice virtually, I thoroughly enjoyed my time working with Saskatoon writers. The writer-in-residence program is an invaluable service not only to local authors but to the writers chosen for it, since it provides substantial support for a period of time as they work on their own projects. I was honored to be chosen.

And finally, thanks to you, dear reader, for following Shawna Keys' adventures in the Labyrinth to this point. I hope you've enjoyed the ride!

PROLOGUE

THE SILVER CANISTER gleamed inside its glass-walled cabinet like a precious artifact in a great museum.

The thought gave the Adversary some slight amusement—as much amusement as he allowed himself. Any thief who might think it valuable and spirit it away would be sorely disappointed. The canister held nothing of intrinsic value in this world, but something of immeasurable importance to the Adversary: a bloodstained shirt, immersed in liquid nitrogen.

Any thief who spirited it away would also die, painfully, over as long a period of time as the Adversary could arrange. Ordinarily, he found torturing a citizen of a world he could Shape a pointless exercise because the Shaped weren't real human beings, merely simulacrums of people of the First World. Since the primary purpose of torture was to elicit information, and it was far easier to simply Shape someone to tell him what he wanted to know, why go through the mess and bother and waste of time of inflicting pain on them? (It was different, of course, for denizens of the First World, who could not be Shaped.)

However, the Adversary would have been the first to admit—had there been anyone to admit it to—that when it came to matters related to Shawna Keys (whose world this had once been), the thrice-damned Karl Yatsar, emissary of the criminal who called herself Ygrair, and Ygrair herself, his emotions were unprofessionally engaged. Yatsar had not only helped Shawna escape this world, he had destroyed the Portals: the one leading to the world into which Shawna had fled, and the one leading back to the last world the Adversary had seized, which had been modeled on the work of a human playwright called Shakespeare.

The shirt in the shining canister, stained with Karl Yatsar's blood, offered The Adversary his only hope of someday opening a new Portal and continuing his advance through the Labyrinth of Shaped Worlds to bring Ygrair to justice. And so, should anyone interfere with that, he would take what catharsis he could find in their slow, brutal punishment, Shaped creature or not.

The Adversary turned from his contemplation of the cylinder to the empty laboratory surrounding it. In the morning, the members of the team he had assembled—and Shaped—to reverse engineer the nanomites contained in the blood on the deep-frozen shirt would arrive and begin their research.

It would take time: months at the least, possibly years or decades. Shawna Keys' version of Earth boasted the same technological know-how as the Earth of the First World—which, from the Adversary's view, and that of the Shurak, the once galaxy-ruling race to which he belonged (and from which the nanomites had originated, in the distant and interdicted past), was but a baby step up from stone knives and bearskins. Unfortunately, he could not simply Shape the level of technology he wanted into existence because he hadn't a clue how the technology *worked*. He was just a . . . he supposed "cop" was the closest word English offered for his profession.

What he *could* do—and had—was Shape the brightest minds of this world to focus on the problem. Eventually, they would crack it. Eventually, they would provide him with the technology the criminal Ygrair, a Shurak like him—though, like him, currently trapped in a human-like body, with all the limitations that imposed—had given to Karl Yatsar: the technology to open new Portals.

Once he had that technology, he would no longer be limited, as he had been at first, to following Yatsar from world to world. Instead, he would blaze his own path through the Labyrinth, moving ever closer toward its center—toward Ygrair.

And once he had *her*, and the stolen Shurak technology that had opened the Labyrinth to her, all these worlds would crumble back into the quantum foam from which they should never have arisen in the first place.

He returned his gaze to the gleaming cylinder. No, he would no longer *have* to follow Karl Yatsar. In fact, he would backtrack to the world he had first Shaped himself and force the second Portal out of it into a world he had not yet visited. But should his path intersect with that of Karl Yatsar and Shawna Keys somewhere along the way, he would very much enjoy visiting upon them some version of the torture he had already imagined for the hypothetical thief.

He turned away from the canister and walked to the exit. Research would begin in earnest in the morning. Shawna Keys and Karl Yatsar had won themselves a reprieve from his attentions, nothing more.

He turned off the lights, plunging the bloody shirt in its gleaming cylinder into darkness, went out, and closed the door behind him.

ONE

THE NEW EXPERIENCES travel offers are said to broaden the mind. I'd had rather more new experiences (and more mind-broadening) than I really cared for since exiting my own world, pursued not by a bear but by the Adversary, and I'd just added a new one I could have done without: being shaken awake in the dark inside a ruined thatched-roof cottage and told, "I think we're going to have visitors from the castle."

I admit, I didn't immediately know a) who was shaking me awake, b) why I was lying fully dressed between far-too-thin blankets on a cold wooden floor, or c) what castle? But it all came rushing back in a moment. In order, a) was Karl Yatsar, the mysterious stranger who first revealed to me that the world I used to live in was one I'd Shaped into existence (though I didn't remember doing it) and told me I had to flee it due to the encroachment of the aforementioned Adversary (who killed my best friend and would have killed me if I hadn't instinctively reShaped the world to save myself); b) was because, just a few hours previously, we had entered this world from the Jules Verne-inspired one we had just left, sealing the Portal behind us, and this cottage had been close at hand and offered at least a modicum of shelter; and c) was the castle across the valley, around whose towers we had seen mysterious winged things flying. "Visitors" from that castle seemed unlikely to be good news.

Unless . . .

"Is the Shaper in the castle?" I asked Karl. "Maybe he or she sensed our arrival. Maybe we should just let ourselves be captured. Or walk over there and knock on the gate."

Karl—in the dimness, just a dark form bending over me, outlined against the stars shining through the hole in the roof—straightened and turned away. "I do not know."

It was so rare for Karl to admit he didn't know something I almost stammered my response. "You . . . you don't know if . . . if we should let them capture us, or you don't . . . ?"

"I do not know if the Shaper is in the castle." His silhouette against the stars changed shape as he turned back toward me. "I cannot tell."

"I thought you said you could always sense the Shaper's whereabouts when you entered a new world."

"I always *have*. This time I cannot."

I sat up, emitting only a minor, ladylike groan. "So what does that mean?"

"I do not know."

Two times in a single conversation. Utterly amazing.

"So why do you think we're going to have 'visitors'?"

"The flying things have been patrolling. One of them flew over, then turned and flew over again, lower. Then screamed and flew back toward the castle."

"That doesn't sound good," I had to admit.

"No. There could be more of them at any moment."

"Right, then." I got to my feet. I hadn't slept nearly enough, soundly enough, on a soft-enough surface, or with enough covers. But I'd slept, and our journey to the Portal in the world we had just left had been a leisurely one, so I felt I could function. I quickly rolled up my bedroll and tied it to the top of the backpack I'd brought with me from the last world. (It was nice to enter a world with clean clothes, food, and water, not to mention a good sharp knife and, at the very bottom of the pack, a pistol and ammunition, instead of arriving with nothing, like I had in the last one.)

We hurried out of the cottage. The road to the castle, covered with crushed, pale-white stone, shone in the moonlight.

Wait. What? I blinked up at said moon. It hung, full, and bright, in exactly the same spot in the sky it had been when we'd first entered this world, hours ago. *That's weird.*

And that wasn't the only thing that was weird. That moon was *huge.* Way bigger than it should have been. The way the moon looks when it's rising or setting, except that's an optical illusion. This one looked that big even though it wasn't too far off the zenith.

"We must not stay on the road," Karl said. "If that flying thing returns with reinforcements, they will see us for sure."

The overgrown fields associated with the cottage lay on the side toward the castle. In the direction we turned rose a ridge, covered with a forest of towering pines whose tops glimmered in the moonlight but at whose roots pooled darkness, into which the white road plunged and vanished.

The forest did *not* look like the sort of place I wanted to be forcing my way through in the middle of the night. "If we leave the road, we'll be lost in no time," I pointed out.

"Are you saying we are not lost now? Do *you* know where we are?"

A fair point. I sighed. "All right. I guess the forest it is."

Fortunately, it wasn't as dark in the forest as it had looked before we entered it. The moon, shining between the spindly trunks, painted the needle-strewn floor with long streaks of silvery light, enough to show us our way. And although it's true we didn't know *exactly* where we were going, the direction we needed to take was abundantly clear—away from whatever might come out of the castle.

The ridge, though not terribly steep, was not *not* steep, either. I concentrated on putting one foot in front of the other and not turning my ankle on one of the fallen branches or loose, flat stones that littered our path, hearing Karl's steady breathing behind me. I remembered how much more out of breath than him I'd been while climbing a mountain pass back in my own world. Clearly, a few weeks of healthy outdoor activities like running for my life and being shot at had toughened me up.

I'd had no way of knowing, when we'd begun our journey, what time it was. "Middle of the night" seemed to cover it. But clearly it was more like "very early morning," because almost without my being aware of it, the forest became less black around us, the first hint of the coming dawn—though that full moon continued to shine, in exactly the same place in the sky.

Geostationary orbit? I thought. But that made no sense, for something the size of the moon. What would that do to tides?

Unless, in this Shaped world, the moon was much smaller . . . say, the size of the Death Star. (Not that I had any idea off the top of my head just how big the Death Star was supposed to be or how big it would look if it were in geostationary orbit. Once again, I missed the Internet.) But even then, weren't geostationary orbits only possible at the equator? Were we at the equator? Since I was distinctly chilled, I thought not. But this wasn't the real world, it was a Shaped world. So anything was possible . . . wasn't it?

A world lit by an extra-large moon hanging motionless in the sky sounded crazy. But so did the idea of a world based on the works of Jules Verne—a world where you could literally journey to the moon in a spacecraft launched from a giant cannon—and I'd just come from such a place.

The trees thinned and the light continued to slowly wax as we approached the top of the ridge. By unspoken agreement, we then paused and looked back down the way we had come . . . just in time to see four winged creatures alight in the yard of the cottage we had fled. Enough light now finally filled the sky that I could see them clearly. Though it was taking its own sweet time about making an appearance, dawn couldn't be far off.

My eyes widened as the creatures folded their wings and changed shape. Suddenly, four people stood by the cottage, all naked: three men and a woman. One of the men had dark skin, the others were pale. Two of the men disappeared into the cottage. The dark-skinned man and the woman stared up the ridge in our direction.

The snowy peaks on the far side of the valley to the west suddenly turned bright orange, as though set on fire. The sunlight had touched them, but it still had to crawl down them and across the valley floor before the sun itself rose above the peaks shadowing us to the east.

The men emerged from the cottage. A discussion ensued. Faces turned toward the sunlit peaks across the valley, then turned in our direction, looking up the ridge. *They can't see us*, I told myself. *Not in this light. We're too low on the ridge to be silhouetted against the sky.*

But I still got chills. "They can't see us, right?" I asked Karl, seeking reassurance.

"Humans couldn't," he said, which didn't exactly provide it, because although the naked quartet down there currently looked human, minutes ago they'd all been winged and furred.

"Can Shapers Shape intelligent nonhumans?" I demanded.

"Of course they can. I told you about the elves and dwarves I have encountered. And remember the giant wolf you saw when you first opened the Portal."

I wasn't likely to forget that monster running toward me along the white-stone road, eyes glowing red.

"You thought it was a werewolf," Karl said.

"Those things down there aren't werewolves."

"No. But if within this world there is one nonhuman, intelligent race—werewolves—there may very well be . . ." His voice trailed off as the woman broke into a run in our general direction and leaped into the air, body reshaping itself in an instant into one of the bat-like creatures, arrowing toward us.

"Run," suggested Karl, and I didn't argue.

When we had entered this world the night before, we had sought shelter immediately in part because of a weird, winged thing in the sky, whose chilling, wailing cry had echoed across the valley. Now we heard that cry again, from the weird, winged thing pursuing us. That keening call stabbed itself into my brainstem, the limbic system, the "lizard brain," and would have sent me scrambling away and up the slope even without Karl's urging.

I knew the instant the thing flew overhead. We were screened from the sky by trees, but I still felt the terror of its passing, a brief surge of unreasoning fear that would have driven me to my knees to hide my head beneath my arms if it had gone on a moment longer. As it was, my heart pounded. If this world had seemed more Tolkienish, I would have guessed it was a Nazgul.

And then . . . it was gone. The sky felt empty . . . clean. "Why didn't it land and attack?" I gasped out to Karl as we hurried on through the forest. "And what was it?"

"I do not know," he said.

That, I thought, *is becoming tiresome.*

We topped another ridge. Looking back, I could no longer see the cottage where we had spent the night. Four winged creatures were hurrying away from us in the direction of the castle, the highest tower of which the sun chose that moment to limn with gold. "Maybe it's the sun." I blinked. "Whoa. Winged bat-like things that don't like the light, in a world where werewolves are real . . . are you thinking what I'm thinking?"

"I am not a mind reader," Karl said.

"I'm thinking vampires."

Karl shrugged. "Anything is possible." He turned away from the castle. "In any event, since whatever they are, they do not seem to like the sun, I suggest we make the most of the day, and get as far away from the castle and whatever those were as we can while the sun shines."

"We have to find the Shaper," I said. "Can you tell where she or he is yet?"

"No," Karl said shortly. "I cannot sense anything."

"Why not?"

"I do not know," he said again. "Nor do I have a clue *why* I do not know."

He started down the slope. I followed a few steps behind. *Great*, I thought. *Last world I entered, my all-knowing guide was missing. This time I've got him, and it turns out he's not all-knowing after all.*

"I've got a bad feeling about this," I muttered.

TWO

EVENTUALLY, THE SUN rose above the eastern peaks.

The sky turned blue.

The moon stayed right where it was.

After descending the ridge, we hurried on through thinning trees, trying to put as much distance as possible between us and the patrol from the castle. Just because we couldn't see them didn't mean they weren't following. We entered cleared land, though it was so overgrown it was obvious no crops had been planted there for years. We passed more ruined cottages. We didn't talk much because what was there to say?

And still, as the morning passed, and the sun climbed, the moon didn't move. It hung in exactly the same spot in the sky where it had hung all night: pale, washed out, but visible. "What's with that?" I finally asked Karl, when we paused to eat some of the dried meat and fruit and drink some of the water we'd brought from the last world. It wouldn't last long, but I'd already seen several streams and larger bodies of water, and with snow-capped mountains surrounding us on every side, it seemed unlikely water was going to be a problem going forward.

What *would* be a problem going forward, of course, was figuring out what the hell was going on in this world. It looked not all that different from parts of Montana—a fertile valley nestled among mountains, although these mountains put the Rockies to shame—

but in my world, and presumably in the First World, the moon rose and set.

"I do not know," Karl said, looking up at the pale sphere in the bright blue sky.

Stop it, I thought.

"Clearly it is something the Shaper wanted," he continued.

"Well, duh," I said. And then I suddenly felt like an idiot. "Of course! This *must* be a werewolf world. Werewolves can only change when the moon is full, so the Shaper made this a world where the moon is *always* full."

"Perhaps," Karl said. "A reasonable supposition, at least."

Thanks, professor. "Still no hint of where the Shaper is?"

"I do not have a clue," he replied, which at least made a nice change from "I don't know."

He lowered his eyes from the moon to the valley, peering into the distance. I followed his gaze. There was nothing to be seen we hadn't already seen: more ruined cottages, more abandoned farms, more overgrown fields. "What do you think did all this?" I said.

"War, perhaps. Or, simply, time."

"I've been meaning to ask you about that."

"About what?"

"Time." We were resting in the shade of a tree at the edge of a farmyard. Like the cottage where we had spent our interrupted night, the farmhouse had only three walls. The roof had collapsed. Weeds grew all around it. An old wagon, one wheel missing, slumped against a split rail fence, itself on the verge of falling flat. "None of these Shaped worlds are more than about a hundred years old, from what you've told me."

"A hundred years in the First World," Karl said. "Yes."

"So if time did all this," I gestured at the ruins, "it was *fake* time. Something the Shaper included to give the appearance of age."

"Did not your world contain antiquities?" he said. "And yet, in First World terms, it was no more than ten years old. You copied your antiquities from the First World, but you could also have simply willed them into being."

"And they would have seemed ancient no matter what tests archaeologists performed on them?"

"Within the context of your world, they *were* ancient." Karl spread his hands. "You didn't just Shape physical objects when you Shaped your world. You Shaped your world's *history*. Your world *was* as old as it appeared to be. The time within it was no less real than the objects within it. The people you knew who were fifty or sixty years old *were* fifty or sixty years old. Not in the time of the First World, but in the time of your world, Shaped into existence just as the world itself was Shaped."

Appearance of age. I remembered thinking, in the last world, about how creationists argued that the scientifically accepted age of the Earth meant nothing because God could have created it with the *appearance* of age. It might have been created in seven days just a few thousand years ago, like the Bible said, but appear far, far older.

What hadn't occurred to me until just then was that, if God created the universe with the *appearance* of being billions of years old, how was that any different from it actually *being* billions of years ago and aging through all that time? God was, presumably, outside time: like space, it was just another bit of clay He spun on His potter's wheel to make the universe.

I shook my head. "And yet you say Shapers aren't gods."

"Nor are they," Karl said. "God created the First World out of nothing—*ex nihilo*. Shapers are only shaping imitations of it, making variations, like a pianist improvising upon a theme."

"I didn't say you said Shapers aren't *God*. I said you said Shapers aren't *gods*. Small 'g.' But within their worlds, aren't they?" I gestured vaguely back in the direction from which we'd come. "Robur styled himself as one. He Shaped his world's religion to make his people worship him."

"I am no pagan, to believe in multiple gods," Karl said shortly.

I cocked my head at him. "Does that mean you believe in *one* God?"

He said nothing, continuing to gaze down the valley. A few miles away rose a massive ridge, much larger than the last one we had crossed, an outthrust shoulder of the eastern mountains that we would soon either have to climb or go around, but I didn't think he was planning our route. "I think I do," he said at last.

"A First Shaper for the First World?" I said.

"If you like." He looked back at me. "You must have figured out by now that I left the First World a long time ago."

"I *have* noticed you're not exactly up to date on pop culture," I said dryly.

He nodded. "I was last in the First World in 1910."

Even though I'd expected something like that, his flat statement came as a shock. "How is that possible?"

"People of the First World," he said, "do not age in a Shaped world."

I blinked. "What?"

"I thought what I said was quite clear."

"But that means . . . you're . . ."

"One hundred and sixty-one years old. More or less. It is difficult to count birthdays when you visit worlds with wildly different calendars."

"But . . . but I was getting older in *my* world!"

He shrugged. "An illusion. To the Shaped of your world, you would have seemed whatever age you were supposed to be. But you yourself would never have felt the effects of aging. Nor would you have died of old age." He snorted. "Which, considering you forgot you were a Shaper, would eventually have caused considerable consternation."

My mind was officially blown. Again. But I hadn't forgotten the question I'd asked that had taken us down this rabbit hole. "Okay, so, you're from the nineteenth century. What does that have to do with my question about you believing in God?"

"I was raised in a religious family," he said. "In fact, my father was a preacher for, and elder of, a church in Kansas. I believed in God without question when I was growing up. Later . . . I had doubts. But the more I travel the Labyrinth, the more I am convinced that He . . . or at least, a Supreme Being of some sort . . . must exist."

I opened my mouth to ask why—and then, suddenly, I knew. " 'So God created man in His own image, in the image of God created He him; male and female created He them,' " I quoted from Sunday School memories. "You believe the fact Shapers are capable of Shaping worlds is proof that they partake in the creative spirit of God—that being creative is part of being created in the image of God."

Karl's eyes actually widened. "I am . . . impressed," he said after a moment. "I did not expect you to make that leap without my guidance."

I ignored the compliment . . . if it *was* a compliment . . . because I'd thought of something else. "Back in my shop, when we first met, you said creativity arose alongside intelligence—'however it came about, evolution or God.' Now you say it's God?"

"You asked me what I believe," he said. "That is what I believe. I do not expect or ask you to believe it."

"Fair enough." I fell silent. I'd just learned more about Karl Yatsar's personal background in five minutes than I'd learned in the past two worlds we'd been in. His father had been a preacher? *"The only one who could ever move me was the son of a preacher man,"* sang through my mind. Karl didn't move me *that* way. But it was still nice to know a bit more about the companion with whom I was theoretically going to boldly continue to explore strange new worlds and seek out new life and new civilizations, for who knew how long.

A five-year mission? I shuddered. *God, I hope not.*

God. Did I believe in Him/Her/It?

Sunday School God? I didn't think so. But Karl had a point. I'd thought of J. R. R. Tolkien earlier. He'd called the act of making stories "sub-creation," and surely the act of Shaping worlds was an even greater example of that. The fact we had this capacity to sub-create, the fact it was an innate part of human nature . . . did that speak merely to some evolutionary benefit, or to something far greater?

I scrambled to my feet. "Let's get moving. All this thinking is giving me a headache."

"I have noticed you have an aversion to it," Karl said, rising. As he led the way toward the ridge looming ahead of us, I followed a few steps back, wondering if I had just heard that rarest of things: a Karl Yatsar joke.

The afternoon passed. The sun crossed from left to right, which meant (presumably, unless the Shaper was just messing with us) that we were heading south. The mighty ridge ahead of us rose higher and higher, but before we reached it, the sun slipped behind the western peaks.

"That winged thing from the castle could appear again any time," I said as the light began to fade.

"There is another ruined farmhouse up ahead. We will take shelter there."

And so we did. Or, rather, we took it in the stone barn, which stood right where the slope of the ridge began. Unlike the previous night's lodgings, it had an intact roof, although a hole in its back wall looked big enough to accommodate a bear, which I rather wished I hadn't thought just before bedding down.

We dared not light a fire, lovely though it would have been to ward off the night chill . . . not to mention a clammy mist that rose from the ground and flowed over and around things as though it came from a dry-ice fog machine on a Broadway stage. When I'd first gazed into this world through the Portal from the last one, I had thought it looked straight out of an old horror movie. That impression was growing stronger all the time.

We heard a howl in the distance as night became full, echoed by another. Then the weird wail of the thing that had winged its way over us just before dawn—or another just like it—once more shivered across the sky. "Werewolves and vampires," I said to Karl. "Has to be."

"You may be right. But it is still just a guess."

"I'd rather keep it as a guess if proving it means either disembowelment or exsanguination," I said. "But it seems to fit the situation. Which means we're probably looking at a Shaper inspired by horror movies or books."

"If a Shaper still remains in this world," Karl muttered. He sounded more peeved than I'd ever before heard him. "I still sense nothing. Nor do I sense the location of the next Portal."

Come to think of it, neither did I. I reached out with my mysterious Spidey . . . um, Shaper-sense. *Nada.* "What does that mean?" I said, then answered before he did. "Never mind. I know what you're going to say: 'I do not know.'"

"If you knew what I would say," he grumbled, "why did you ask?"

"Just making conversation."

He snorted. "I suggest getting some sleep instead. I'll keep watch."

"Fine," I said.

"Fine."

I closed my eyes and tried to make myself comfortable on the dirt floor. My bedroll provided little padding, and my backpack made a lumpy pillow, but the effects of a long day of hiking after a short night and an early start did the trick, and I dozed off . . .

. . . only to awaken, yet again, to Karl shaking me, which was another thing I was getting tired of. "Our friends are back," he whispered. "By the farmhouse."

I sat up abruptly. "What do we do?" I whispered back.

"Flee. Out that hole in the back wall."

I scrambled up and bent toward my bedroll and pack, but he grabbed my arm. "No time!"

I followed him, on hands and knees, through the aforementioned hole, glad now it had been there, despite my earlier worry about nocturnal bears. We scrambled upslope in the dark. I didn't look back until I had to take a break to catch my breath. Then, I saw in the moonlight, down at the abandoned farm, four naked people, three men (one dark-skinned) and a woman—if not the same as those who had pursued us the evening before, indistinguishable from them at this distance. Two went into the barn where, I knew, my pack and bedroll remained, proof we weren't far away.

Hell, my blankets are probably still warm. Blood-warm.

Considering what I suspected those things were, that thought gave me the impetus I needed to catch up to Karl, who had never stopped climbing. I suddenly realized he wasn't wearing his pack, either. In just two nights, we'd managed to lose all the supplies from the previous world I'd felt so smug about having, including the pistol. We weren't literally naked like the things chasing us, but we certainly were metaphorically: naked *and* defenseless.

We clawed our way up a near-vertical rock face, and at the top of it, paused and looked back. I could just make out the naked quartet, congregated behind the barn, clearly discussing matters. In a moment they'd be winging their way up to us . . .

And then the howls we'd heard earlier repeated, but they were no longer distant. Instead, they came from directly below us, ululating, bone-chilling, and bloodthirsty, as four giant wolves with glowing red eyes, like the one I'd seen the first time I'd looked into this world, burst out of the trees and leaped at our pursuers.

Karl grabbed my arm. "Run!" he shouted. Turning from the melee that had erupted below, we scrambled up the slope.

Vampires and werewolves and Shapers, oh my, a corner of my brain insisted on chanting.

You're not helping, I told it, and then concentrated on escaping with my life.

THREE

SNARLS AND HOWLS and bloodcurdling shrieks pursued us up the steep, shale-strewn slope, which I guess was better than being pursued by the things *making* the snarls and howls and bloodcurdling shrieks . . . although I was pretty sure they *would* be pursuing in short order.

My breath came in short gasps as I struggled uphill in Karl's wake. The trees were sparse and the flat black rocks shifted and slid beneath us, sliding downhill with an almighty racket that ensured the creatures below knew we were above them.

The sounds of battle dwindled to nothing. Silence reigned behind us. It wasn't as comforting as you might think.

At least there's moonlight, I thought, glancing up. *Here, there's always moonlight.* The stars around the moon looked normal, the constellations the ones I knew from my world, presumably the same as those in the First World. Though from what Karl had said, these stars weren't really stars at all, just a very-large-scale stage backdrop to give this pocket universe, this cosmological cul-de-sac, the illusion of infinity.

My thoughts returned abruptly to Earth . . . this version of it, anyway . . . as a rather large boulder dislodged by Karl came bounding toward me. "My apologies," he said over his shoulder.

"No worries," I said, with a *soupçon*, perhaps even a dash, of sarcasm. The rock leaped and crashed down the slope behind us for a good fifteen seconds.

And then, suddenly, the slope eased. Ahead of me, Karl straightened, walked a few paces, and stopped. I scrambled up onto the level ground where he stood. Together, we looked at what lay beyond the ridge.

"Wow," I said at last.

"Succinctly put."

We stood just a few feet from a sharp drop-off. Spread out before us was more of the valley—a *lot* more of the valley. It stretched as far as I could see, which was pretty far in the omnipresent moonlight. Fields, forest, rivers, ponds, and hills tumbled away into the indistinct distance.

Directly below us lay a lake, smooth as glass, reflecting the brightest stars and the moon back at us as though it were a mirror. Fields surrounded it and, unlike most of those we'd passed through, appeared cultivated. We could only see half of the lake from our vantage point—we'd have to get closer to the edge to see the rest.

Karl reached for my hand, which surprised me; and I took it, which surprised me even more. "For safety," he said.

"I'm all for safety."

Together, we edged forward until we stood at the lip of a cliff that might not have been perfectly sheer but was within spitting distance of it, although said spit would fall a long, gut-clenching distance before it hit anything. Directly below us, on the near shore of the lake, stood a village, a cluster of buildings surrounded by a wall of pale stone that shone in the moonlight. A few yellow lights burned here and there.

Other than the castle, it was the first inhabited place we'd seen since entering this world, and considering what had come out of the castle, I thought it reasonable to worry about what might live in the village.

But a howl sounded behind us, answered by one of those weird, blood-chilling screams. The werewolves and maybe-vampires were still abroad, and they had to know we'd climbed the ridge. The village had a wall around it. Behind a wall sounded exactly like where I wanted to be. So . . .

"There is a path," Karl said. I glanced at him. He wasn't looking at the village, and following his gaze, I saw what he had seen: two wooden posts, with a gap between them and, sure enough, what looked like the beginning of a trail.

He released my hand and walked carefully over to the posts. I followed. He held on to one post, and I held on to the other, and together, we peered over the edge.

The path descended a couple of hundred feet, switched back, descended another hundred or so, and continued in that fashion on down the rock face. Trees rose between the switchbacks. It looked steep, but not too terrifying.

Another howl.

At least, no more terrifying than whatever was coming up the slope behind us.

"I think we should take our chances with the village below," Karl said. "Do you agree?"

"Fervently."

We started down.

You might think, if you have never been pursued through the mountains by monsters, that going down a hill is easier than going up one. You would be *almost* right. It's less wear and tear on the heart and lungs and more wear and tear on the legs, which start to ache in short order, and keep on aching. It turns out holding your body back to keep from tumbling headlong is hard work. But that's what we had to do, because the slope of the path we followed definitely did not adhere to building-code requirements for a wheelchair ramp.

After ten minutes, I would have welcomed a mountainside to climb. After fifteen, I would have welcomed a sharp blow to the head to put me out of my misery. But the path went on and on . . . and on. Every once in a while, a howl or a shriek rent the air, but they were far enough in the distance that they were only mildly alarming, as opposed to breathtakingly terrifying.

Not long after we began the descent, I realized it wasn't as dark as it had been, that the sky had begun to lighten and the stars to dim. On the one hand, that was a relief, because as day began, based on the previous night's experience, the maybe-vampires would disappear. If the howling things were werewolves, presumably they'd run off as well.

Of course, if they weren't werewolves, but just regular (if somewhat oversized and glowing-eyed) wolves, they might actually *prefer* the light, in which case, we were about to be exposed to everyone— or everything—in the valley.

Including whoever was in the walled village. Smoke now rose from buildings inside the walls, one of which had the unmistakable cruciform shape, not to mention the tall bell tower, of a church. Which was interesting. Did this world have Christian churches?

I hope so, I thought. In the last world, Robur, the Shaper, had set up a religion that worshipped the Shaper . . . which was all kinds of ick, for my taste.

However, Robur was not only merely dead but really most sincerely dead, so it wasn't like *pretending* to be a god had translated into *actual* godhood. In my world, I'd copied over all the religions of the First World. I myself had grown up going to Sunday School. If this world had some version of Christianity, I'd feel right at home.

Also, a village with a church seemed unlikely to be friendly to either undead bloodsuckers or flesh-eating lycanthropes, so there was that.

We paused to rest our aching . . . or at least, my aching . . . legs. I looked back the way I'd come. Nothing. I looked down at the village. "They're stirring down there," I said. Traditionally, people seen from a height are said to look like ants, but we weren't quite that high, so I thought they looked more like cockroaches as they moved through the streets and the village square. There was no sign they had seen us.

Karl looked up at the brightening sky. "Between the devil and the deep blue sea," he said, almost to himself.

"Rock and a hard place," I put in. "Out of the frying pan, into the fire. Torn between two lovers . . ."

Karl gave me a look I was becoming accustomed to: equal parts annoyance and . . . well, annoyance. A touch of amusement would have been a nice change, but I suppose the last of my examples, though it predated my birth, had postdated him by decades. "Since we're pretty sure the things chasing us are on the side of the devil," I hurried on, "I suggest we opt for the deep blue sea. Or at least the smooth black lake." I pointed down.

A bloodcurdling shriek came from behind us . . . and above us. I twisted my head around.

Two of the winged things burst into sight, black cutouts of giant bats against the pale sky. "Run!" Karl shouted, leaping to his feet.

Below us, I heard faint shouts: the cockroaches—villagers—had obviously spotted the vampires, too, if that's what they were. Karl and I charged down the trail, or charged as fast as we could without tumbling head over heels and either breaking our necks or plunging to our deaths. Unfortunately, that wasn't very fast at all. Certainly not fast *enough*.

Another shriek, almost on top of us. Karl glanced up. His eyes widened. Then he twisted, grabbed me, and pushed me off the ledge.

For a horrifying instant I thought he had murdered me. I screamed as I plunged to . . .

. . . a relatively soft landing on my back in the thick, leafy branches of a tree that thrust out from the slope, maybe eight feet below. Staring up wide-eyed, heart pounding, I saw the flying things swoop down on Karl, grab his arms—they had arms themselves, as well as wings, and legs, too, and didn't that make them six-limbed?—and pull him into the sky. I saw his pale face staring down at me as, without a word, he dwindled away and vanished along with his captors over the top of the cliff, in the direction of the castle.

I thrashed, struggling to pull free of the branches that had snagged me, but they gave alarmingly and dropped me another couple of feet, bringing my heart into my throat. I gasped, quit struggling, and hung there, helpless as a fly in a spider's web. I had nowhere to look but back up the side of the rock face we had so laboriously descended, and just then, at the very top, I saw, staring down at me, one of the wolves, both like and unlike the one that I *had* seen when I opened the Portal the first time: unlike, in that it was smaller and slenderer; like, in that its eyes glowed the baleful red of hellfire.

I gulped. It stared down at me for a long . . . very long . . . nearly eternal . . . moment . . .

. . . and then it started loping down the path toward me.

My heart had not exactly settled from the falling-off-a-cliff surge of adrenaline and now it redoubled its efforts to break free of my rib cage. I stared up at the wall of stone. I couldn't see the wolf on the switchbacks leading down to me, which was actually worse than if I *had* been able to see it because I knew I'd have no warning before . . .

The wolf's head suddenly thrust out over the edge of the path. It glared at me with burning red eyes, aglow from within. It crouched and inched closer, until its front claws hung over the edge—still several feet above me, but all it had to do was leap and I'd be puppy chow.

Except suddenly it startled, head snapping up and looking to its left, my right. It yelped and scrambled back onto the path, turned to run—and I heard a meaty *thunk*. The wolf screamed, a disquieting howl of agony that suddenly became a hundred times more disquieting as it morphed into a human scream, as the creature reared on its hind legs and transformed into a naked girl, clawing at the crossbow bolt in her side, blood pouring down her pale flank and hip and thigh.

And then she collapsed, falling out of my sight.

I gasped, and realized I'd been holding my breath. A moment later, I heard the thud of running, booted feet. Two new figures appeared above me, a man and a boy, dressed in leather and long black cloaks, both carrying crossbows, both wearing silver crosses around their necks. The man looked over the side at me, and his eyes widened. The boy, though, stood staring down, presumably at the wolf-girl, whom I could no longer see. He dropped his crossbow, and his hand went to his mouth. Then he turned away from me, vanishing as he fell to his knees. The sound of retching filled the still morning air.

The man gave the boy what I judged to be a compassionate look, but then turned back to me with what I judged to be an aggressively noncompassionate one. He leveled his crossbow at me. Like the cross around his neck, the head of the bolt glinted silver in the dawn light.

"What are you?" he growled. He either spoke English or there was something to my thought, back in the previous world, that I would hear English in all Shaped worlds, that there was a kind of universal translator/TARDIS effect. In any event, I could both understand his words and intuitively grasp the unspoken threat that if I answered wrong, a silver-tipped crossbow bolt might fatally sprout from my anatomy, too.

"Human?" I said tentatively. It wasn't that I was unsure I was human—heck, as a Shaper, born in the First World, I could have said I was more human than they were (although I didn't). I was only unsure about whether "human" was the right thing to say to keep me from becoming a very dead pincushion.

"We will wait," he said.

For what? I wondered. "For what?" I said out loud.

"For the sun to touch you." He kept the crossbow aimed squarely at my chest but glanced over his shoulder. "Eric," he said, his tone considerably softer than the one he'd used with me. "Are you all right?"

"Yes, Father Thomas," said the boy's voice. He stood, bringing his upper body back into my view, then leaned over to pick up his crossbow. He cocked it and reloaded it as he stared down at me. "I didn't . . . know . . . it would be like that." He glanced to his right, where the body must lie, then resolutely averted his eyes, returning his gaze to me. I pegged him at no more than fifteen.

"I'm sorry, son," said the man—Father Thomas—a priest, presumably? "But you saw her in her true form. A monster. A moment later, and she would have leaped at this one, and likely devoured her."

I swallowed, then called, "Thanks, Eric."

He ignored me. Again his eyes flicked right; again he averted them. "But now she looks so human," he said to Father Thomas. "And so young. She looks . . . my age."

"And there lies the danger," Thomas said. "In human form, they and the vampires can lie and seduce and twist men's minds. This one," he, too, glanced to where the wolf-girl must lie, "is beautiful. And now you see her in human form, naked and alluring, and you cannot help but feel sorrow at what you have done. But suppose you had come upon her in this form, and had given her your cloak, and brought her into the village, thinking she was human. What would have happened?"

"Tonight she would change and kill as many of us as she could," Eric said. "Starting with me."

"Starting with you," Thomas said. "Or, worse, she would not kill you. She would change you, and you would become the monster she was . . . and she *was* a monster, Eric. You saw it. You saw the beast hiding beneath that fair skin."

Eric nodded miserably. "I know, Father. But . . . to kill something that looks so human feels so *wrong*."

"It's the world that is wrong, Eric," the priest said heavily. "It has been wrong since the Pact collapsed. All we can do is God's will, to the best of our poor ability. The rest is in His hands."

Well, I thought, *presumably* he's *not the Shaper* . . .

The branches shifted beneath me, and I grabbed the nearest with a squeak. "How much longer?" I called up, a little breathlessly.

Neither the priest nor the boy answered. They simply stared down at me, silent, morose—and armed.

The sun finally touched the peaks on the far side of the valley, and slowly swept down them and across the fields and forest of the valley floor. Very, very slowly. An interminable amount of time passed before the sun cleared the eastern mountains and its full rays found me in my birdlike perch—although birds usually perch more gracefully. I was more like a cat who had climbed too high and was now clinging to the top of a bendy tree, mewing piteously. Not that I was mewing piteously at the moment, but if Father Thomas and Eric didn't do something to get me out of that tree pretty damn quick, I was going to start.

As soon as the sun touched my face—I blinked in the light—Father Thomas grunted and lowered his crossbow at last, handing it to Eric. He took the boy by the shoulders, turned him, and lifted his cloak to uncover a leather backpack. From it, he pulled a coil of rope. He turned back toward me and tossed down one end. "Take it."

I didn't need to be asked . . . okay, told . . . twice. I grabbed on as tightly as I could, and with that support, was able to find my feet on the branches and then scramble up the side of the cliff and back onto the path I had so precipitously departed (with Karl's help).

I came over the edge on my hands and knees and found myself staring into the dead eyes of the naked wolf-girl, lying on her back with her head turned in my direction, the feathered end of the crossbow bolt protruding from her other side, blood pooled beneath her. I suddenly found it hard to breathe. I had seen her in wolf form, looming over me, eyes glowing red—but now, she just looked like a young girl. Her eyes seemed to be accusing me. I was glad to be hauled to my feet.

Father Thomas turned me to face up the path—I resolutely looked over the girl's body—and held me there. "Bind her," he said to Eric.

I didn't see where it came from, but in short order my wrists were wrapped with what felt like rawhide cord. "I will finish your testing at the church," Father Thomas said, now turning me around to face down the slope. "Walk."

"Testing? For what?"

"Walk," Father Thomas repeated, and pushed me forward. Eric led the way.

"What about . . . ?" I half glanced over my shoulder.

"I will send a burial party," Father Thomas said.

In silence, we descended, and in that silence, I had time to ask myself the most pressing question on my mind: where was Karl?

Dead? My mind shied from that possibility. I could open Portals myself now, but I still hadn't taken the *hokhmah* from a Shaper in whatever way I was intended to. I'd only received the *hokhmah* belonging to Robur, the self-styled master of the Jules Verne-themed world we'd been in . . . mind-bogglingly, just the day before yesterday . . . because I'd been standing next to him when he died. Based on that single data point, if I killed the Shaper of this world while standing next to her or him, his or her *hokhmah* would automatically flow into me—but I had no intention of becoming a serial killer of Shapers. That was the Adversary's approach.

My goal—our goal, Karl's and mine—was to peaceably take the

hokhmah of this world's Shaper: first, so it would be unavailable to the Adversary if he ever found his way into this world (we hoped we'd stopped him from doing so, but we couldn't be certain), and second, so I could convey it to Ygrair, the mysterious woman at the center of the Labyrinth of Shaped Worlds, the one who had placed me and all the other Shapers here to begin with. According to Karl, if I brought the *hokhmah* of enough worlds to her, she would be able to use that gathered knowledge to protect all the worlds from the Adversary and drive him out of the Labyrinth for good.

It sounded like the plot of a straight-to-StreamPix sci-fi series, but that's where I found myself. And if Karl were dead, I wasn't sure I could do any of that.

I also didn't want Karl to be dead because he was my friend.

I thought.

Sort of.

Although he *had* said, if anything happened to me, he'd just find another powerful Shaper to take my place. *Bully for him.* The trouble was, if something happened to *him*, I was *extremely* unlikely to find another alien-technology-enabled guide-to-the-Labyrinth to take *his*.

Now that I was no longer holding on to the tree for dear life, I had leisure to feel the scrapes and bruises from my plunge into it. Just what had Karl thought he was accomplishing? What if he'd misjudged, and I'd broken through the branches and plunged to my death? What if a bit of sticking-up branch had impaled or disemboweled me? What if I'd lost an eye? *It's only fun until someone loses an eye.*

All the same, I hoped I'd have the opportunity to complain about his cavalier treatment of my person in person, and that he wasn't currently being drained of blood or devoured in some unspeakable fashion . . . as I had apparently been mere moments from being devoured myself, if not for the timely arrival of the priest and the boy.

A priest, I thought. *A kindly village priest, who, once convinced I am purely human, will no doubt apologize for my rough treatment, bind my wounds, and give me food and water and a safe place to sleep. Just the ticket.*

Trouble was, I wasn't getting a lot of kindly-village-priest vibes from the good father, which left open the possibility he might actually be more of a Spanish-Inquisition-type priest dedicated to rooting out infidels and/or witches and burning them at the stake.

I sighed. In the last world, I'd been briefly accused of being a witch and threatened with being tossed from an airship. At the making of good first impressions, I clearly had a long way to go. *I wonder if there's a world based entirely on sweetness and light? That would be nice.*

But as we reached the bottom of the path at last and started along the broader road to the gates of the village, the lake glistening beyond a thin line of trees to our left, I saw the silver-tipped spikes topping the walls, the hinged pots clearly meant for boiling oil, and the crosses incised in every brick. In this world, clearly, as in the last—as in mine, for that matter, after the Adversary got hold of it—sweetness and light were in short supply.

Who would Shape a world plagued by werewolves and vampires? And why?

We passed through the gate. Ahead loomed the spire of what I was now certain was a church, where Father Thomas would decide my fate.

I wonder who's deciding Karl's?

FOUR

THE COLD PREDAWN air whistled past Karl's ears and tugged at his clothes, a gale-strength blast that made it hard to breathe but still failed to blow away the rank smell of the bat-things that had him in their grip, an unsettling mixture of animal musk and decaying flesh. His shoulders ached and his eyes watered, but despite his discomfort, the wind of their passage impressed him. They were flying at an amazing speed.

To his left, across the valley, the sun had set the peaks ablaze and was crawling down the mountain slopes. As it did so, his captors flew lower and lower, until he feared he would be scraped from their grasp by the daggerlike tips of the pine trees below.

Within his chest, his heart pounded. His mistress, Ygrair, might have opened the Labyrinth, placed all the Shapers within it, and lived at its center in her own Shaped world, but she had no magical power to ensure his survival in the face of the multiple hazards every world contained. If the bat-things—vampires?—released him, he would plunge to his death in the forests below.

Still, they had held him aloft now for many minutes. Why bother if they intended to kill him? Clearly, they wanted to take him somewhere, and equally clearly, that somewhere was the castle he and Shawna had seen the moment they had entered this world. So quickly had they flown, covering the distance he and Shawna had taken a full day to walk within the space of perhaps half an hour, that already it swelled in size ahead of him, on its crag across from the cottage where the Portal had opened, and he and Shawna had spent their first night in this world.

As they swept up to the castle wall, the creatures conveying him almost bashed his skull against the battlements, so desperate did they seem to avoid the sun. Ahead loomed a tower. The sun had already lit its roof and was crawling down its stony sides. They rose a few yards. Karl saw a balcony, open French doors behind it. His captors swept up and over the railing and let go, and he dropped, hit the floor, and rolled, banging against the doorframe. Gasping, he scrambled up, went to the railing, and stared down into the castle courtyard as both winged creatures landed on its cobblestones.

The sun reached his balcony, lighting him like a spotlight. The courtyard remained in shadow, so it was hard to see clearly, but he saw well enough that the two winged creatures who had flown him to the castle suddenly became a man and a woman, both naked, the man dark-skinned, the woman light, though there had been no difference in pigmentation between them in their bat forms. Black-robed figures appeared and handed cloaks to the nude couple. They donned them unhurriedly, as if unconcerned with modesty but feeling slightly chilled, and then they and the guards disappeared from his sight as the sun continued its slow ascent and the shadows of the castle wall retreated across the flagstones below.

Karl turned from the suddenly deserted courtyard to look at the room beyond the balcony door, rubbing his sore shoulders and bruised upper arms.

The circular chamber boasted tapestried walls (the tapestries depicting hunters on horseback chasing badly rendered foxes); a four-poster bed curtained with burgundy drapes of heavy velvet; a massive wardrobe of dark wood; a fireplace in which a fire crackled cheerfully against the chill of the mountain air; two chairs arranged on either side of a round table, on which rested a covered platter; a comfortable-looking armchair by the fire, upholstered in the same deep burgundy as the bed drapes; and, next to it, a small side table holding a glass and two crystal carafes, one containing wine, the other water (or a clear liquid, at least, but it seemed unlikely to be gin or vodka). The room did not look like a prison, but when Karl crossed it to test the only door, that door was, of course, locked.

He sighed and went to the table with the covered platter. Opening it revealed bread and butter, jam and honey, a few rashers of bacon, and a wedge of hard, yellow cheese. A knife was provided, but it was far too blunt to serve as a weapon . . . not that it mattered since he still wore his own much more substantial knife at his belt. Which was curious. Why had they left him armed?

Because they don't think I'm a threat, even with a knife, he thought, which, in its own way, was concerning. What was the traditional way of dealing with vampires? He'd read Bram Stoker's *Dracula*, but a long time ago; something about garlic, crosses, a stake through the heart? But a wooden stake, not a knife.

He might be armed, yet still defenseless, if this was indeed a world Shaped to contain werewolves and vampires.

Who would Shape such a world? he wondered. *And why can't I sense him or her?*

Perhaps the Shaper was dead. Robur's fate in the previous world was proof enough if any were needed—it hadn't been for him because he already knew it, but perhaps it was a lesson Shawna needed to learn—that a Shaped world did not necessarily protect its Shaper. He could imagine a Shaper creating a world full of monsters, spurred perhaps by a childish infatuation with tales featuring such creatures, only to fall prey to them once they became incarnate.

If that were the case, Shawna would have no one from whom to take the *hokhmah* of this world, and their time here was a waste that could be better spent in the next world . . .

. . . assuming he could find the Portal to it. For the moment, he could not even sense *that*, or, rather, the Shurak technology that provided him an awareness of such things could not. It seemed confused. Uncertain. It was still there, in his blood, in his brain; he could feel it, but it was not providing him with the information it normally did.

Which meant what?

He did not know.

He spread honey on a piece of bread and took a bite. For the moment, he was stymied, a prisoner in a strange castle that might or might not be home to the Shaper of this world. All he could do was wait for someone to come for him.

It won't be long, he thought. *The lord or lady of this castle must even now be talking to the ones who brought me. No doubt I will be summoned before long. I'm sure of it.*

He sat in the comfortable chair by the fire and focused on breakfast.

Father Thomas and Eric led me through the gates of the walled village. The houses inside looked like mini-fortresses. Only a few were built of wood. Most were of stone or brick. All those I could see had multiple crosses of metal beaten into their walls, and every door boasted a cross that ran from top to bottom and side to side. A few window shutters had been thrown open by now, and men and women and children looked out at me suspiciously.

Father Thomas took me to a brick building not far from the gate. It contained a long table with benches on either side and a fireplace against one wall. It appeared to be a place for guards to take their coffee—or whatever they drank around here—breaks. On the mantelpiece, a tiny, intricately made clock gleamed inside a glass bell jar. "What's that?" I asked, pointing to it.

"A clock," Father Thomas said. "It chimes to announce real dawn, and real sunset, every day as the seasons come and go."

"Real dawn? Real sunset?"

"When the sun would appear over the horizon, or vanish behind it, if there were no mountains," Father Thomas said impatiently. "Now, sit. Wait." He glanced at Eric. "Guard her."

He went out, presumably to organize the burial party he'd spoken of. I studied the boy. He studied me. He looked unhappy, still upset about shooting the werewolf. I remembered him retching on the path above me, and I couldn't blame him for that. She had looked so human in death . . . but I hadn't imagined the red-eyed wolf staring down at me.

"Thank you," I ventured. "For saving my life."

He said nothing.

"Lucky for me you were there," I continued.

"It wasn't luck," he said, the first words he'd said directly to me. "We send out two-man patrols every morning just before dawn, to ensure no monsters are lurking near the village. We'd seen movement on the path, so Father Thomas decided he and I should check it out. Turns out he was right."

"You've never found anything before?" I said.

Eric shook his head. "Not me, but another patrol once caught a vampire hiding out in an old farmhouse, planning to pass himself off as a human and come inside the village during the day."

"What happened to him?" I said, then realized how stupid that must sound, considering I'd just witnessed what happened to the werewolf on the path.

"Stake," Eric said, with admirable conciseness.

The conversation flagged at that point.

"My name's Shawna," I said, after a long silence. I tried a smile. "And you're Eric."

Nothing.

"How old are you, Eric?"

"Fifteen," he said. "Sixteen in a month. How old are you?"

Rude, but I couldn't help but smile. I remembered my own irritation at being asked that question when I was his age. "Twenty-seven," I said. "Any family?"

He gave me a sullen-teenager look. He was very good at it. "Why are you asking all these questions?"

"I'm not a monster," I said. "I'm human. And I'm grateful to be in a village full of humans. I'd like to get to know them, that's all." *Also,* I thought about adding, but didn't, *have you had any hints one of them might be the person who Shaped this horror-movie world?*

"Father Thomas is my only family," Eric said. "I'm an orphan. Left on the church steps as a baby."

"So you live with Father Thomas?"

"No, I live in the orphanage." There was more than a hint of how-stupid-can-you-be in that reply: teenagers, apparently, were the same yesterday, today, and forever, in whatever world you visited.

"But he's raised you?"

"Father Thomas is training me to be a priest. Like him."

Training which apparently included, in this world, how to shoot werewolves with a crossbow.

I would have asked more questions, but Father Thomas chose that moment to return. "Let's go," was all he said from the open doorway. Eric, between me and the door, stepped to one side, but kept his crossbow leveled. I got up from the bench and followed Father Thomas out into the street.

He escorted me down it toward a square fronted by shops and the church. Villagers stepped aside and regarded me with suspicion, muttering to each other, as I passed. They looked like they belonged in the opening number of *Beauty and the Beast.* I half-expected someone to yell, "Marie! The baguettes! Hurry up!"

With Eric following us, Father Thomas led me to the church, but not up the steps to the big front doors. Instead, he took me down one side. I saw gravestones ahead, through a roofed gateway in a wall extending out from the church wall. The lych-gate, some part of my mind supplied.

We turned right and went through a small back door in the church into a narrow, stone-walled and flagstone-floored hallway. "Take her into the south side-chapel," Father Thomas told Eric. "I will join you momentarily."

The priest turned left through a side door, closing it behind him. "Keep going," Eric said, and I continued through the door at the end of the hall, emerging into the main part of the church. I glanced back at Eric. "Side-chapel," he said, jerking his crossbow to the right. I followed orders, and a moment later stood before a very plain marble baptismal font, beneath a rather spectacular stained-glass window showing the crucified Christ, in the aisle between four rows of wooden pews, the nave behind me.

Father Thomas joined us a few minutes later. He now wore a white cassock and a golden stole trimmed in red.

"We haven't been properly introduced," I said to him. "My name is Shawna Keys."

He frowned at that. "An odd name."

"And you are . . . ?" I prompted.

His eyes narrowed. "Thomas Hauptman, priest of the village and parish of Zarozje." (I found out how to spell it later—to me it sounded like Za-rose-yeh.) "You are remarkably calm, Shawna Keys, for one whose life hangs in the balance."

"Guess you could say I'm trying to put my finger on that balance," I said. "I'm not a threat, Father Thomas."

"Simply saying you are not a threat is not proof you are not. A monster would say the same."

"A moment ago, we were in the sun," I pointed out. "I didn't burst into flames or crumble into dust."

Father Thomas frowned. "Why would you?"

Oops. "Isn't that what vampires do when the sun touches them?"

His frown deepened. "Of course not. They simply turn into ordinary human beings, like you, until the sun sets again."

Who Shaped this? I thought indignantly. *That's all wrong!* "Okay, but I was *already* an ordinary human being. Even *before* the sun touched me."

"And as I already pointed out, merely making that claim proves nothing."

"At least you know I'm not a werewolf," I pressed on. "I was human even before the sun came up, while the werewolf you shot was still a wolf."

"Again, your defense is meaningless," Father Thomas said. "Werewolves can control if or when they change during the moonlit night. You could have chosen to remain unchanged last night, or you could have changed back to human and dressed yourself well before dawn, in order to deceive us this morning. You may have had a plan to appear to be threatened by the monster Eric shot, to make us trust you, a plan thwarted only by Eric's good aim. Perhaps she was supposed to run off, we were to rescue you and bring you inside the walls, and tonight you would have opened the gates and with her ravaged the village."

I grimaced, while a part of me puffed up in outrage. Werewolves here could *control* their change, even beneath a full moon? Vampires merely became ordinary humans in the light of the sun? How *dare* a Shaper play with established folklore like this? How was I supposed to navigate their world if I couldn't count on what I thought I knew?

Just like the Jules Verne-inspired world, filled with things Verne never wrote about, I reminded myself. I was beginning to sense a trend.

"And so," Father Thomas said, "I must test you. Which is why we are here, in this holy place."

I sighed. "Fine. Bring it," I said, then belatedly thought, *Wait. Is "test" a euphemism for "torture?" Is there a kind of Spanish Inquisition in effect around here after all?* I wasn't expecting it, but then, I wouldn't, would I?

Father Thomas continued to frown. "Your way of speech is as odd as your name."

"I'm not from around here," I understated.

"There is nowhere but here to be from. If you are human, your lies do you no credit. If you are not human, they will do you no good. Silver and holy water will settle the issue."

"I love silver, and I can take a bath in holy water if you want. I'm human."

His frown deepened to a scowl. "Bathing in holy water would be sacrilegious."

Crap again. "Sorry. I'm not Catholic."

"You're not what?" He shook his head. "Never mind. Eric, hold her."

Eric lowered his crossbow for pretty much the first time since he'd seen me, set it on one of the pews, and gripped my arm tightly. "Ow," I said, giving him a dirty look. He met my gaze and squeezed even harder.

Scowling, I faced Father Thomas.

"You remember your lessons in this matter," the priest said over my shoulder to Eric.

"Yes, Father."

"And the tests are?" Father Thomas asked. Apparently, I was part of the priestly equivalent of a teaching hospital's bedside visit by a physician.

"First, holy water," Eric said. "The priest must draw a cross upon the forehead with a forefinger wetted with holy water, while praying the Prayer of Discernment."

Thomas removed the bronze lid from the font and crossed himself. Then he dipped his hand in the water, turned, and while loudly reciting something in Latin—*They have Latin here?* ran through my mind—drew a damp cross on my forehead, finishing with "Amen."

I resisted the suicidal impulse to scream and thrash, and instead merely smiled at him. "Cold," I said. "But refreshing."

He frowned, but addressed Eric, not me. "What does this indicate?"

"That is the definitive test for a vampire," he said behind me. "She is not one."

"Could I even stand before a stained-glass window depicting Christ on the *cross*," I emphasized the word, "if I were a vampire?"

Father Thomas looked at me again, as though, whether or not I was evil, I was definitely dim. "During the day? Of course you could."

"But not at night."

"No."

"Yet, even during the day, I could not stand the touch of holy water."

"Of course not."

"How about garlic?"

"Opinions differ. It may depend upon how it is used."

"Do vampires cast reflections?"

"During the day, yes. At night, no." He shook his head irritably. "Enough of this. Be quiet and stand still."

Another world where I can't trust anything I think I know, I thought. *Great.* "Why?" I said out loud. "I just passed your test."

"For being a vampire, yes," he said. "But not for being a werewolf."

He turned away and took something from the chapel's altar. When he turned back, he was holding what looked like a sewing needle. He grabbed my arm, and without a word of warning, scratched my wrist with the needle's point.

I flinched. "Hey!" I looked down in outrage at the little spots of blood forming along the scratch. "What was that for? And was that pin sterile?"

"I do not know what that means," he said, "except in the sense of infertility, and that would not seem to be applicable to an inanimate object."

"Great," I muttered.

"It was silver," he went on. "Were you a werewolf, you would be howling in agony right now." He nodded to Eric. "Release her," he said, and just like that, I was free.

Eric drew a deep breath, and I glanced at him in surprise. He seemed almost as relieved as I was. *He was afraid he'd have to shoot me, too.* I was glad that at least he hadn't been looking forward to it.

I turned from him to Father Thomas and gave him my best glare. "If I get blood poisoning . . ."

Father Thomas considered me a moment longer, then told Eric, "You may go, son."

"Are you sure, Father?" Eric said.

"She is human, not demon," Thomas said. "Neither vampire nor werewolf, as I have just proved. Whatever her purpose here, I do not think she will somehow overpower me."

I would have felt hurt if not for the fact he stood at least six-foot-two and his broad shoulders strained the corners of his cassock. I figured he could pick me up like a rag doll if he wanted to.

Might be fun, my libido, which had been sadly underused these past few weeks, commented. I told it to shut up.

Father Thomas stepped past me and put his hands on Eric's shoulders. "I know how difficult this morning has been for you," he said softly. "You did what had to be done. Cling to that thought. Do not dwell on the girl on the path. Remember instead the monster she was when you shot her. Remember this one," he nodded toward me, "who now lives because of your quick action."

"Yes, Father," the boy murmured.

Father Thomas squeezed his shoulders. "We will talk later." He released Eric, who gave me a final inscrutable look, and then picked up his crossbow and walked away, toward the main doors of the church. Rather than go through them, though, he disappeared through a side door, leaving me alone with Father Thomas.

The priest led me from the side-chapel into the dim, incense-scented nave, motioned me to sit on the front pew, and then sat beside me.

I looked around at the Gothic interior. "Nice church," I said. "Is it old?"

"Several centuries," he said. "It was built two hundred years before the Great Cataclysm."

That gave me two things to think about. First, it wasn't nearly that old, really, of course. No Shaped world could be older than Ygrair's academy for Shapers, and it had only been around a century and a bit. Karl, from what he said, was somewhat older than that, and Ygrair, being an alien and all, was presumably considerably older.

But that conversation I'd had with Karl about God and time came to mind. If a world were Shaped with the appearance of age, how was that different from it actually *being* that age? Time, once it has passed, is not something you can travel back into, *Doctor Who*, H. G. Wells, and various episodes of *Star Trek* notwithstanding. We live in the moment, as actors like to say, one eternal present moment, the past existing only as our memories of it. A church Shaped to be "several centuries" old would be absolutely identical to one that, in the First World, had actually *passed* through those several centuries.

For all I knew, I had just been created, and everything I thought

I had experienced up to this moment . . . or this moment . . . or *this* moment . . . were memories just now inserted in my mind by some *über*-Shaper.

My brain hurt again.

Second, and of more immediate interest: what on Earth, or whatever this world was called, was the Great Cataclysm?

"What on Earth was the Great Cataclysm?" I repeated out loud, since I seemed more likely to get an answer that way.

Father Thomas looked at me, again, as though I were either crazy or irredeemably dim. I didn't take it personally. I'd gotten that look a lot in recent weeks, starting with the moment Karl Yatsar discovered I had no memory of being at Ygrair's school and didn't even know I had Shaped the world I thought I'd grown up in, and continuing through several encounters in the aforementioned Jules Verne-inspired world. For example, Athelia, who had replaced Robur (the Shaper) as ruler of the Republic of Weldon after his death, had given me exactly that look when I'd tried to explain the musical *Cats* to her.

"How could you not know of the Great Cataclysm?" Thomas said.

"I'm not from around here," I said, again. Some people need reminding. "I'm from . . . outside this valley."

His expression went from confusion to flat-out rejection. "I have already told you; your lies are useless. No one lives outside the Valley. Not anymore."

"What?" That startled me. "In the whole world?"

"That is what the Great Cataclysm *was*," he said. "The cleansing of the world by God, the wiping away of sinful humanity everywhere but in this valley, this new ark for a new generation of the righteous."

"That's just what you think," I said, still trying to salvage my story. "Not *everyone* was wiped away. My people survived. Our land has grown and prospered, and now we are exploring the world. We came into this valley . . ."

"Stop!" Father Thomas cried. "Have you no shame? Would you blaspheme in the very house of the Lord?"

Blaspheme? Claiming God didn't kill everyone outside this valley a few hundred years ago was blasphemy?

No one actually died, I reminded myself. *It's all just fictional backstory. And God had nothing to do with it. This is all the work of the Shaper.*

But why?

It was, after all, a rather disturbing thing to build into the fabric of the world. The story of Noah's Ark had always terrified me in Sunday School. Sure, God promised he would never again destroy the entire world with a *flood*—"Never again will all life be destroyed by the waters of a flood; never again will there be a flood to destroy the earth," the Bible said, a sentiment so nice, God said it twice—but eight-year-old me couldn't help but notice that there was nothing in that promise about never again destroying all life using some *other* method: "the fire next time," as the saying went.

"Did God kill the animals, too?" I said.

Thomas looked like I was giving him either whiplash or, possibly, a stroke. "What?"

"In the flood, God killed humans and animals, but had Noah save a pair of every animal in order to repopulate the Earth. Did God fill the valley with animals?"

"No," Thomas said impatiently. "The animals were unaffected by the Great Cataclysm. They have the run of the Earth outside this valley, untroubled by humanity."

Good for them. "I don't know what to tell you, Father," I said, trying for humility. (A stretch, I know.) "I entered this valley only two nights ago." I stuck to first-person singular: I figured I'd work my way around to mentioning the missing Karl later. "Before that,

I was in a very different place. Clearly, not the world outside this valley, but . . . somewhere else." *Okay*, I thought. *Let's see him interpret that. Is there room for another heaven and earth in his Shaper-dreamt philosophy?*

To my surprise (and relief, since I still didn't know where the Church in this Shaped valley stood on the whole burn-the-heretic thing), it appeared there was. The doubt and suspicion that had been his primary responses to me thus far suddenly gave way to a wide-eyed look of wonder. "'S'truth?" he said, a marvelously medieval turn of phrase I'd never before heard someone use in actual conversation.

"You've . . . heard of other worlds?" I said cautiously.

"Of course," he said. "Did not Jesus say, 'And other sheep I have, which are not of this fold: them also I must bring, and they shall hear my voice; and there shall be one fold, and one shepherd.'?"

"That's in your version of the Bible?" In my world . . . or at least in my Sunday School . . . that was usually taken to be a reference to Gentiles since Jesus had said it to Jews. But in this Shaped world, that apparently wasn't the standard interpretation.

Oh, there was that "are-you-crazy-or-just-dim?" look again.

"Version of the Bible? There are no 'versions' of the Bible. There is only the Bible."

I thought about asking if it was the King James Version, but I suspected the question would make no sense, so for once I shut up. Anyway, the scripture he'd quoted had definitely been the King James Version, so maybe he'd already answered it.

"No," Thomas continued. "The many-worlds hypothesis is a matter of metaphysical speculation."

Many-worlds hypothesis? The phrase was so incongruously modern I almost laughed out loud. "Metaphysical speculation?" I said, instead.

He nodded seriously. "The Mother Church's seminary—where

I and all priests of the Valley once studied and took our vows—has long maintained an intellectual order devoted to research and thought on the subject of the nature of the universe. There has been a long-standing debate between the 'one-world' and 'many-worlds' factions. The former believe that God only created one world, and we who dwell in the Valley, having escaped the Great Cataclysm, are therefore the only humans who still exist.

"However, there are many equally devout and devoted scholars who maintain that the creation of worlds is a defining part of God's nature, and thus to claim that He only ever created one is hubristic, a narrow, limiting conception of God—in support of which, they quote John 10:16, as I have just done. They believe that, if God created one world with humans upon it, He may well have created many more. There may be worlds, they suggest, where humanity did not fall, where Eve did not eat of the fruit of the Tree of the Knowledge of Good and Evil and give it to Adam, who ate it in turn; where humanity still lives in innocence and ease within the Garden."

Innocence and ease and perpetual nudity, I thought. "Not . . . the kind of world I came from," I said, understating things again by a considerable amount. C. S. Lewis had played with that idea, though. I wondered if I'd find myself in a version of Perelandra at some point, if—admittedly a big "if"—I survived my quest long enough to visit a sizable number of Shaped worlds.

Or maybe Narnia. Talking animals would make a nice change, provided someone had already dealt with the White Witch.

"Of course not," Thomas said. "Those who dwell in such a world would never leave it. But that does not preclude the possibility of many other worlds, an infinitude of worlds, perhaps, where history has taken a different path than in our own—since in each, humanity would have free will to follow or fall away from the will of God, and every time a man or woman made one choice, another world would be born where he or she made the other choice. And if there are an infinitude of worlds, then it stands to reason that, however rare may be the occurrence, those who dwell in one may sometimes find a way to journey to another."

I personally wasn't sure reason had anything to do with such a belief. But it offered me a way to account for my arrival here, so . . . "That does seem to explain why I find myself in a world I know nothing about," I said cautiously.

"But this is marvelous!" Thomas exclaimed, beaming. "Your presence . . . this will settle a metaphysical argument that has raged for centuries. Once Mother Church knows . . ." But then his face fell. "If she still stands."

"Why wouldn't she?"

"Nothing has been heard from her for almost ten years," Thomas said. "Since the breaking of the Pact. Riders once came regularly to every church in the valley, once a month, bearing words of encouragement, news, instruction. Neither I nor any of the remaining priests I have managed to exchange messages with has seen a rider from Mother Church since the Pact collapsed."

The Pact? I didn't have a clue what that was, but I set that question aside for later. "Hasn't anyone tried to reach it . . . um, her?" I said.

"Of course," Father Thomas said. "Armed expeditions have been sent. None have returned."

"That doesn't sound good." And it didn't, not only because of what it implied about the state of this world, but because it could very well be that the Shaper had been part of—maybe even the head of—Mother Church and something, potentially something fatal, had happened to him or her.

What I needed to find out first, though, was what had happened/ was likely to happen to Karl. After that, I could worry about finding the Shaper. To achieve either goal, I needed more information.

"So, if you believe me now, will you tell me more about your world? As if I've never been here before? Because I haven't."

"Of course," Thomas said. "If you will also tell me of yours."

"Of course," I said, though I wondered what he would make of it. "But first, I must tell you . . . I did not enter this world alone."

He frowned. "You had companions? What happened to them?"

"Just one companion, a man named Karl Yatsar. And what happened to him, happened last night. Before the werewolf—and you—showed up." I told him how we had been pursued by vampires from the castle, and how, just as it began to get light, Karl had been seized and borne away. "Can you tell me what his fate is likely to be?"

"Nothing good," Father Thomas said heavily. "I am very sorry, but if he has been taken by the vampires there are only two possible outcomes. Either they will feed on him and discard his blood-drained body, or, worse . . ."

"There's a *worse*?" I said, horrified.

"They will turn him into one of themselves." He shook his head. "I grieve to tell you this, Shawna Keys, but if you see your friend again, he will no longer be your friend. He will be a soulless demon. He is either dead or undead . . . and yes, the latter is much, *much* worse."

FIVE

MY MIND TOYED with the idea of Karl Yatsar as a vampire, then rejected it. That wasn't going to happen.

Could it happen, to someone of the First World?

On further reflection, I had a horrible feeling it could. Robur, self-styled Master of the World, had thought his world would not let him die. He had been proved wrong by a "fulgurator," a super-missile that had very *thoroughly* slain him and had come terrifyingly close to slaying me at the same time.

If even the Shaper of a world was subject to the physical laws that defined it, then any visitor to that world must be, as well. In this world, apparently, from everything we had seen, it was a physical law that those bitten by a vampire could be turned into a vampire—and, presumably, those bitten by a werewolf would turn into a werewolf.

Maybe if Karl gets turned into a vampire, he'll be more a brooding-vampire-with-a-soul than soulless evil monster, I thought. "Who leads the vampires?"

"Queen Patricia," Thomas said.

"And the werewolves?"

"Queen Stephanie."

Two queens, both alike in dignity. Two prime candidates for Shaper. But which would it be . . . if it were one of them? "And the humans?"

He looked grim. "We merely try to survive since the Pact failed and the war began."

"There's a war?"

Thomas stood abruptly. "Let us repair elsewhere to continue this conversation. I would not profane this holy space with talk of such evil."

I stood, too. I took a quick look at where he'd scratched me with the silver pin. It had scabbed over, but it didn't look angrily red and I didn't have crimson streaks running from it up my arm, so I hoped I'd survive. *Well, that's a relief. This world apparently offers much more interesting ways to die than boring old sepsis.*

I followed Thomas out of the church and back into the church-yard. At the far end of it, I now saw, up against the wall, a thatched-roof, half-timbered cottage with walls covered with white stucco, and a smaller, separate structure of plain wood I took to be an outhouse. The priest led me to the cottage, weaving between the tombstones. I took a quick glance at one: *Hester Amos Obergranz, 378-451. May the next world treat her better than this.*

"What do the dates measure?" I asked.

Father Thomas glanced at me. "Years since the Great Cataclysm, of course. Dates are divided into AC—after—and BC—before." He strode on toward the cottage, where he opened the green-painted door—adorned with a cross made of tarnished silver nails—and ushered me in.

Beyond the door lay a cozy dining/kitchen area, with a wood-burning cast-iron stove (I was surprised to see even that level of "technology"); a small, round table surrounded by four chairs; and two cabinets, one tall, one short enough for its top to serve as a food-preparation space. Through a door to my left, I could see the Father's bedroom: a narrow cot, a wardrobe, another chair and table, a bookshelf with maybe twenty books in it, and a crucifix on the wall.

"Have a seat," Father Thomas said, indicating the table.

I obeyed, and the priest busied himself with stoking the stove, filling a kettle from a hand pump in the corner, placing the filled kettle on the stove, retrieving two mugs, spooning dried leaves into each, and pouring water into them once it had boiled—in short, making tea, although this world was strange enough I watched him narrowly for some time, in case he was actually crafting some magical potion for nefarious purposes. I only knew he thought of it as tea because he said, "Tea," when he placed my mug in front of me. It certainly wasn't *tea* tea—it was some sort of herbal infusion. It could hardly be otherwise, if all of humanity were restricted to this one valley, which was definitely not located in the tea-growing clime of this weird world.

So it could be some nefarious potion after all, I thought, but after the first sip, I didn't get sick, my skin didn't turn green, and I didn't turn into anything inhuman, so I took another sip. Nope, definitely not tea . . . but also, not half bad. In fact, it was quite soothing to my understandably frazzled psyche.

Father Thomas also placed some bread and jam on the table, which was even more welcome than the tea, since I hadn't yet eaten that day. "I need to know the history of this world," I said to Father Thomas, as I spread a thick swath of raspberry jam on a hunk of crusty brown bread. "In detail."

He sat down across from me and cupped his hands around his own steaming mug. "Can you read?"

I blinked. "Of course, I can read." I took a bite of the jam and bread. Heavenly.

"No 'of course' about it. Most people cannot. They have no use for the ability."

The notion that most people had no use for the ability to read gobsmacked me enough I didn't reply, though that was also partly because my mouth was full.

"If you can read," Father Thomas continued, "then you can educate yourself." He rose from the table and went into his bedroom. He knelt by the bookshelf I had glimpsed, selected a tome, and brought it back. He placed it before me. "Can you read the title?"

I looked down at the book. For a moment the letters looked strange, then they swam into English. "Yes, I can," I said. I read out loud, "*Annals of the Valley of the Select, Deduced from the First Origins of the World, the Chronicle of Vampiric and Lycanthropic Matters Together Produced from the Beginning of Historical Time Up to the Great Cataclysm and Beyond*, by Archbishop James Ussher."

Then I frowned. *Archbishop Ussher . . .* The name sounded familiar. Although why it had a second "s" in it, I hadn't a clue . . .

Wait. He's the guy who dated the creation of the world to . . . was it 4004 BC?

I remembered now. Ussher was a favorite of the young-Earth creationists. Based on what scientists thought in my world, he would have been off by billions of years.

Of course, as it turned out, scientists in *my* world were the ones who were wrong, since my world was really only ten years old. There—and here, too—Ussher was only off by four millennia. The scientists were off by billions (billennia?).

My head was hurting again. "This will tell me what I want to know?" I said.

"Some of it," the priest said. "There are some additional writings which might interest you in the church library. I will show you when I return."

I blinked at him. "Return? Return from where?"

"Mass, of course," he said. "We celebrate it morning and evening, and the morning Mass is within the hour." He indicated the kettle, which he had taken off the stove when it began to sing. "Help yourself to more tea and eat as much bread and jam as you'd like. I will return anon."

He went out, presumably heading to the vestry, while I marveled at the fact I had heard both "'S'truth" and "anon" used in conversation in the same morning.

It wasn't the sort of thing one could marvel about very long, though. I made a second mug of tea, smeared jam on a second hunk of bread, and turned my attention to the book he had left me.

While I had never read Archbishop Ussher's chronicle of the world's history in my own world, I was pretty sure this version had a much higher quotient of vampires and werewolves. I felt like I was reading one of those "British-classic-with-added-monsters" books that became inexplicably popular a few years ago in my world—*Wuthering Heights and Werewolves* and *Great Expectations and Goblins* were the two I remembered best.

As Ussher told it, after God created the heavens and the Earth (on Wednesday, October 23, 4004 BC), he went on, within the next seven days, to create Adam and Eve in the garden of Eden. They, in turn, proceeded to eat of the fruit of the Tree of the Knowledge of Good and Evil, resulting in them being expelled from the garden before they could also eat of the fruit of the Tree of Life and live forever. Angel, flaming sword, etc., etc.

After that, history was a version of what I knew from my own world. The ancient civilizations, as far as I could tell with my less-than-comprehensive knowledge, played more-or-less their accustomed roles—Egypt, Greece, Rome—right up until Jesus was born. After that, the Christian church arose . . . though here, it never became the *Roman Catholic* church. There was no split between the Eastern and Western rites. Jews remained a separate people and lived peaceably in Israel. Jesus' disciples really did go into all the world and preach the gospel, and the world accepted it. The Chinese, the world's aboriginal peoples, the Polynesians, the great civilizations of South America—all converted. Islam never even arose.

Christianity for the win!

But while all this was going on, the world was also dealing with the reality of vampires and werewolves. Though not mentioned in the Bible (but then, neither are cats or potatoes), they appeared in the real world about the time of ancient Babylon, their origin unknown (there were many theories, of course, usually involving magical artifacts discovered, ancient rites revived, deals with demons, things man was never meant to know, etc., etc.). Over the ages, werewolves and vampires, though small in number relative to humans, had been a real and constant threat, showing up in history in surprising (to me) places. In this world, for example, Alexander the Great did not die of a mysterious fever but was killed battling a vampire that had infiltrated his camp, and Richard the Lionheart, rather than dying from gangrene after being struck by a lucky crossbow shot from the walls of a castle he was besieging, was instead torn apart in his tent by a vengeful werewolf whose family the king had killed.

The Great Cataclysm began in 1347, a date that tickled something in the back of my head. It took a few minutes to come to me, then I remembered: in my world, and presumably the First, that was the year of the Black Death, the plague that killed more than half the population of Europe, and something I mostly knew about from having read and loved Connie Willis' 1992 science-fiction novel *Doomsday Book*, about a time traveler accidentally plunked down in the middle of it. (Since the book long predated the ten-year lifespan of my Shaped world, I presume it was a real thing that also existed in the First World.)

The Great Cataclysm, though, was far more thorough, far neater, and yet even more horrifying than the Black Death. It was a wave of destruction that rolled outward from the Middle East . . . from, the church believed, the long-hidden Garden of Eden itself . . . at the pace of a walking man. Entire villages and cities disappeared overnight, vanishing as though they had never been, replaced by apparently untouched wilderness.

People fled, of course, but the pace was relentless. Refugees flooded into coastal towns that were swallowed up in their turn, taking with them the desperate multitudes who could not find ships to board. Eyewitnesses who saw settlements or individuals disappear reported no pyrotechnics or fanfare—they simply evaporated into thin air, building by building, person by person, leaving nothing behind, not even dust. Plants and animals, however, were unaffected. A slaughterhouse would vanish, taking all dead animals with it—but the cows who had been waiting their turn to die simply fell to grazing in the meadow they now found themselves in. The Cataclysm was aimed only at humanity—humanity, and the vampires and the werewolves who had longed preyed on humans and whom they feared and fought.

The Great Cataclysm brought an end to that endless battle. Humans saw vampires and werewolves as demons in human skins, and yet, it was through them that God saved the remnant that now dwelt in the Valley.

This time, God sent no prophet to the humans. Instead, He sent a prophet each to the vampires and the werewolves. According to Ussher, a vampire named Barnabas Ross and a werewolf named Remus Gailbraith, filled with the spirit of God, urged those in their communities to follow them to a place of safety. They set out on a long journey, proclaiming their vision and picking up many followers along the way, until eventually, after many hardships, they reached this remote valley, already inhabited by humans who until their arrival knew nothing of the Cataclysm taking place outside. The humans were, of course, terrified, but Barnabas and Remus told them there was no need to fear: God had decreed that humans, vampires, and werewolves should all live in peace within this sacred sanctuary, which would remain untouched by the disaster.

At a meeting in the great monastery set in the westernmost cliff of a side valley snaking away to the west of the main valley, the monastery that became Father Thomas' Mother Church once all churches outside the valley had vanished (Rome itself, of course, had been gone for years), Barnabas and Remus, now styling themselves King of the Vampires and King of the Werewolves, respectively, signed a Pact with . . .

I paused, reread the passage, and then laughed out loud. I'd almost been suckered into thinking this was real history, but there was clearly a Shaper's hand at work in what I had just read, though it had taken a few moments to sink in.

First of all, Barnabas and Remus? Barnabas was a famous vampire from the *Dark Shadows* TV series, which aired thirty years before I was born but I had watched on StreamPix during my *Buffy* phase, when all things vampiric had fascinated me. Remus, of course, was the name of a werewolf character in the *Harry Potter* books. I should have twigged the moment I saw *their* names, but it was the name of the leader of the monastery that was the real giveaway.

The Pact, you see, had been signed by Abbot Nathan Costello, which, in turn, meant that a movie version of the signing of the Pact could be called *Abbot N. Costello Meets a Vampire and a Wolf Man.*

That's terrible, I thought. *But also kind of awesome.* A joke after my own heart, though once again I was forced to wonder why my own world had been so fricking mundane. Both Robur's Jules Verne-inspired world and this one were marvels of imagination compared to mine.

I craved normalcy, I thought. *Robur said I was very quiet when I came to Ygrair's school. What's in my backstory? Will I ever know?*

Every Shaper had attended that school. Robur remembered me. This world must be older than my own, so the Shaper here might remember me, too. Maybe here, maybe somewhere else, I'd find someone who had been my friend, someone I'd opened up to, someone I'd told . . .

. . . well, whatever I'd been so desperate to forget I'd somehow managed the supposedly impossible task of Shaping my own memories.

I sat for a moment, staring pensively into the distance. Since the distance consisted only of Father Thomas' bedroom, it wasn't particularly enlightening, so I took a breath and resumed reading.

There wasn't much more to read. The few pages covering the aftermath of the signing of the Pact were the equivalent of, "and they all lived happily ever after."

That, clearly, had been the intention of the Shaper. But the Pact had failed—ten years ago, Father Thomas had said. As a result, we'd been hunted by vampires, who had taken Karl away and who had battled werewolves who had likely also been hunting us. Zarozje, this village, was walled, and protected by crosses everywhere, not to mention a muscular priest wielding a crossbow with silver-tipped quarrels.

So, what had gone wrong?

Ussher had no answers for me. Any hope of understanding why the Pact no longer held sway—and what that meant for me and Karl and our quest to save the Labyrinth—would have to await the return of Father Thomas.

Where is he, anyway? Just how long does Mass take? Not being Catholic, I hadn't a clue, and even if I had been a Catholic, I doubted twenty-first-century North American Catholicism had much in common with whatever Abbot Costello's Mother Church had decreed for this valley after the Great Cataclysm.

I also had no idea how much time had passed, since my wristwatch hadn't survived my recent adventures (not too surprising, since I'd barely survived them myself), so I shoved the chair away from the table and went out into the now-sunlit churchyard in search of my priestly host.

I entered the church through the back door we had used earlier.

He wasn't in the vestry. Nor was he in the nave, the apse, the choir, the transept, or any of those other gloriously ancient church-parts I remembered from Art History 101 (which, since I'd taken it within the last ten years, I presumably had *really* taken, and hadn't just given myself the memory of taking when I Shaped my world . . .)

I'm going to have to quit worrying about that kind of thing, I told myself. *Sufficient unto the day is the weirdness thereof, as Jesus almost said.*

In point of fact, no one was in the church. Mass was over. So where was Father Thomas?

I hesitated at the front door of the church, wondering if I were allowed to wander around Zarozje. Then I heard something, not behind me, or outside, but to my left—through the side door I had seen Eric take earlier.

Someone was weeping.

SIX

KARL HOPED SHAWNA was having a more interesting and informative day than he. Since he had been unceremoniously dumped onto the balcony of this pleasant prison, no one had come to greet him, interrogate him, torture him, or taunt him—no one had paid him any attention at all.

Why go to all the trouble to seize me and fly me to this castle, and then not even come to talk to me? he asked himself—and had no answer.

He explored every inch of the chamber, fortunately discovering the privy, whose entrance was hidden behind a tapestry, well before *not* discovering it would have been a major problem. The bread and cheese and meat and wine and water he'd found waiting for him would sustain him for that day, but they would not last another. He hoped that meant someone was certain to see him before the day's end. But the day went on and on, and no one came.

He spent some time in silent meditation, searching within himself for some signal from the alien technology in his blood that it had picked up the location of this world's Shaper. He had never entered a world where that signal had failed him . . .

. . . until now.

What that meant, he could not say. He could only wait and hope that eventually, when he had the opportunity to talk to someone in authority in this strangely silent castle, he might tease out some information that could point him in the direction of the Shaper.

If he ever had that opportunity.

He wished for a book, or ink and paper, but found neither, so in the end, he simply sat and stared down at the courtyard to pass the time. He tried shouting at the figures he saw there, who looked like ordinary humans. One or two glanced up at him, but no one responded.

The day passed, but it passed very, very slowly.

I pulled open the door through which the sobbing came, revealing stairs spiraling down. A glimmer of yellow light, too steady to belong to candles or a torch, spoke of a lantern or two at the bottom. And now I could hear, not only the boyish sobs I was certain were coming from Eric, but the soft voice of Father Thomas, providing comfort.

I hesitated, then sat on the steps and listened.

"I know it was a terrible thing," Father Thomas said. "I, too, have killed the creatures of the night, and felt as you do. Just ten years ago, we saw them as our friends, as fellow children of God. We thought God Himself had sent them to us because that was what they told us.

"But that was before the Pact shattered. You were only five years old. You don't remember what it was like, the first attacks on humans. We couldn't believe it was happening. Farm families slaughtered; villages decimated. The emissaries of Mother Church stopped coming. The vampires and werewolves went to war. The queens denied they had anything to do with the attacks on humans, but the attacks continued: clearly, they were lying.

"We had to defend ourselves. We fortified the largest villages, brought everyone into the walls at night, began armed patrols. And in the absence of new instructions from Mother Church, we fell back on the edict written in the Pact itself, the warning to the vampires and werewolves of what would happen if they were lying to us, if they broke their solemn promise not to hunt and feed on humans." Father Thomas paused. "Eric?"

A deep, shuddering breath. "'If the Pact be broken," Eric said in a quavering voice, "it is the duty of every human to kill every were-wolf or vampire they encounter, beneath the moon *or* the sun.'"

Typical parent, I thought. Surrogate parent, anyway. *The poor boy is crying, and he's trying to make it a lesson.*

"And there you have it." Thomas sighed heavily. "There were children of the night I, too, counted as friends, before. But were they to call on me now, I would have no choice. To protect the village, our friends, our *kind* . . . I would have to kill them, though the bolt would pierce my heart, too."

Silence. Then, "May I . . . be excused?" Eric said in a small voice.

"Of course," Thomas said, his voice sympathetic. "Talk a walk around the village, or out by the lake."

"I think . . . I'll just go to my room."

"Or that," Thomas said softly.

I heard the scraping sound of a chair being pushed back across a stone floor, scrambled up, and hurried back into the church. Halfway down the aisle, I turned and waited. The moment Eric appeared, I started forward.

"Hello!" I said cheerfully. "Have you seen Father Thomas?"

Eric started at the sound of my voice. "Yes," he said after a moment. He looked over his shoulder. "Down there. In the library."

"Thanks," I said.

Eric exited through the front doors of the church, flooding the aisle with daylight for a moment before he banged them shut again.

I returned to the spiraling staircase and this time continued down it, the air growing cooler and staler as I descended. I emerged into a larger chamber than I anticipated, the walls lined with books. Two more doors, both closed, presumably led to crypts or storage rooms or janitor closets or whatever else might be in the basement of a medieval church.

Maybe not janitor closets.

Thomas sat, head down, at the table at the room's center, where there were only two chairs, one of which, pushed well back, must have been the one Eric had occupied moments before. Books and papers were scattered across the table, surrounding a single oil lantern.

"Hi," I said, walking up to the table. "I saw Eric in the church. He told me you were down here."

Thomas murmured something, crossed himself, and said, "Amen," and I suddenly twigged to the fact he'd been praying. *Awkward*, I thought, but just bulled on. "A lot of books," I commented, looking around at the surrounding shelves.

"Church records, mostly," Thomas said. "But not entirely." He got up and went to the shelf opposite the bottom of the stairwell, pulling from it a book instantly distinguishable from the others because it was the only one bound in white. He brought it back to the table, pushed aside a couple of other books in front of the chair where Eric had been, put it down, placed his hand on it, and said earnestly to me, "If you want to understand this world . . . this valley . . . why things are the way they are . . . then you must read this next."

I gave it a wary look. It looked . . . thick. "What is it?"

"The Pact."

"You want me to read this whole thing here and now?"

"Of course not," he said impatiently. "The Pact itself is only a few pages. The rest is commentary. Read the introduction, which has additional background information, then read the Pact. It will only take you a few minutes." He returned to the chair he'd been in when I entered and looked at me expectantly.

I sighed, sat, and read.

Abbot Costello (the introduction told me) had not trusted the werewolves and vampires who had appeared at the door of his monastery any more than one would expect a priest to trust such creatures. But he had wanted peace above all, to protect the innocent people living in the valley, and the self-proclaimed prophets, the vampire Barnabas and the werewolf Remus, had professed to want the same thing. And so, the Pact proclaimed peace among all three races . . . but it hedged its bets. Abbot Costello had made it clear that if it were broken by either the vampires or the werewolves, the protections it offered them would end, and humans would not only be permitted to kill them, as was the custom, but commanded to do so. Remarkably (or perhaps not so remarkably, since this was, after all, a Shaped world, and all of this had been made up out of thin air), Barnabas and Remus had agreed.

"Thou shalt not suffer a witch or a vampire or a werewolf to live," the church had long decreed, taking the infamous biblical injunction two steps further. The fact Abbot Costello had been willing to suspend that injunction in the hope that Barnabas and Remus were telling the truth about their desire to live peaceably in the valley with humans also spoke to this being a Shaped world: in my world (which matched, I believed, the First World), I doubted that would have been the case.

Then again, perhaps it would have been. Might makes right, as they say, and no doubt the abbot's remarkable reasonableness had been influenced by the horrifying, undeniable truth of the Great Cataclysm, which lapped up to the edges of the valley literally on the heels of the refugees . . . and then stopped, just as they claimed to have been told it would by God. He had every reason to believe that the humans, werewolves, and vampires in the valley were the only ones remaining in all of the world—and he knew perfectly well that in a straight-up fight, the vampires and werewolves, though few in number, would have made short work of the unprepared humans of the valley.

The introduction of the book told me that the valley was about two hundred miles in length. The Pact gave the vampires the northern end of the valley—fifty miles of lands north of the crag where the vampire castle now perched. It gave the werewolves the southern end—fifty miles south of where the werewolf queen established her court. Humans could choose to live within the realms of either the werewolves or the vampires, or they could live in the one-hundred-mile stretch known as the Lands Between, under the injunction they were not to raise up a king for themselves: their governance would fall solely to Mother Church. (Abbot Costello clearly knew a thing or two about the importance of secular as well as spiritual power; prior to the Pact, each village had had a reeve, but there had been no government above that.) Vampires were not to feed on humans, ditto werewolves, nor were vampires to feed on werewolves or werewolves on vampires. The lion would lie down with the lamb and the peace that passeth all understanding would reign for a thousand years, or something like that.

Under the Pact, humans were only to be changed into werewolves or vampires if they *chose* the change—and if the werewolves and vampires agreed. For those who sought the privilege, it was a great honor to be accepted. (The Church, of course, had a different viewpoint, viewing such people as choosing damnation over salvation, but under the terms of the Pact, agreed to do nothing to stop it, however much it was discouraged.) The changed individuals moved into one of the respective kingdoms.

I pushed the book away. "Fine," I said to Thomas. "Sounds like a great plan. So what went wrong?"

"It is unclear," Thomas said. "But a decade ago, the Pact shattered. Creatures of the night began killing humans, and each other.

Humans were changed without their consent. Mother Church fell silent, providing no guidance, but the Pact's instructions are clear: if it fails, it is the duty of the church to uphold the age-old command to suffer neither witch, nor vampire, nor werewolf to live."

"*Are* there witches?" I asked.

Father Thomas shook his head. "No. The last known witch was executed some two hundred years ago."

Meaning the Shapers had decided they didn't want any around. "And this decree was acceptable to you even though the Lord Himself spoke to Barnabas and Remus and told them to save their people by coming here?"

"Barnabas and Remus *claimed* the Lord spoke to them. Abbot Costello, as the caveats in the Pact make clear, was not entirely convinced they spoke the truth. The breaking of the Pact would seem clear evidence they did not."

I opened my mouth to argue, then closed it again, because what did I know?

I know a few things, I answered myself. *I know I need to find the Shaper of this world. Which means I need Karl. But Karl's been taken by the vampires.*

"I need to find out what happened to my companion," I said. "I need to go to the vampire castle. Will you help?"

Father Thomas stiffened. "No," he said flatly. "It is forbidden to go anywhere near the borders of the Lands Between, north or south."

"By whom?" I said.

"By Mother Church, and by secular law," he said.

"I don't belong to your church or your village," I pointed out.

"We have given you sanctuary. That makes you subject to our laws."

"Why do you care?" I countered. "I'd be risking nothing but my own life." I couldn't believe I was saying that since I wasn't a big fan of risking my life, generally, but I had to find Karl, and if that meant going alone . . .

"If you go to the castle, you will either die or be changed," Father Thomas said. "If you die, well and good. But if you were changed, you would be a threat. You could return and be let through the gates by someone unwary. Or you could tell the vampires details of our defenses against them, perhaps enabling an attack."

"I don't know any details of your defenses!"

"It doesn't matter," he said stubbornly. "It is forbidden. I forbid it, and the reeve forbids it."

I bit my tongue before I gave the two-word response that first came to mind. The fact that it was forbidden for me to travel to the vampire castle meant nothing to me except that it would make it harder for me to do so, since now I would have to somehow get out of the village without being stopped.

How I would do that, I hadn't a clue. Which meant, for the moment, all I could do was bide my time.

"This isn't my world," I said after a moment. "I am still learning." I decided a little buttering up might be in order. "I apologize if I gave offense."

After a moment, the tension in Thomas' shoulders eased. "There is no offense in honest questions. And I know it seems hard. It seems hard to me, too. There were those among the children of the night I counted as friends, who would visit me during the day. I have not seen them since the Pact shattered, and if I did, I would have to . . ." His voice trailed off as he looked down at his hands, folded in his lap. I had already heard him say something much the same to Eric, but I couldn't tell him that. I simply waited.

Finally, he took a deep breath and raised his head to meet my gaze again. "Your ignorance of all these things speaks to the truth of your claim of being from another world." He leaned forward. "And even if you were from this world, there are things you would not know that perhaps you should, to understand why we are so harsh, so determined to kill the creatures of the night when we identify them, though once we thought them friends."

I glanced at the book containing the Pact. That was clearly the world the Shaper had intended. Perhaps Thomas' no-doubt tragic backstory—I could sense one coming—would help explain why it had gone awry.

"My parents died when I was a child," Thomas began, confirming my expectation as to what kind of tale he would tell. "I was raised in the very orphanage I now run, here in Zarozje, where Eric and others live. Father Davin, my predecessor, taught us our letters, and I developed an interest in the priesthood.

"I traveled to Mother Church, to the seminary, took my vows, and returned here to assist Father Davin, who by then was in failing health. Then the Pact collapsed—and Father Davin, who should have died in bed, surrounded by friends and parishioners, instead was torn apart by a werewolf who had slipped inside the village during the day and hid until nightfall. The monster was killed trying to escape, but it changed nothing: at the age of twenty-five, I became the village priest. And ordered the building of the walls that now protect us."

"I'm sorry," I said, unsure if that was the correct response. "What about Eric? What happened to his parents?"

Thomas shrugged. "We do not know. He was placed in a basket in an alcove at the top of the church steps, a basket we keep there, with blankets inside, for just such deliveries."

I blinked. "This village is small . . . you must know . . ."

"There was once much travel among villages, none of which were then walled. Even now, there is travel among the surviving villages during the day," Thomas said. "But there have always been few orphanages. Zarozje has one, and so children have come here from many places and by many torturous paths. No, we do not know his parentage. But from childhood he has shown an interest in the church, a desire to serve her as a priest. And so, as Father Davin guided and taught me, I guide and teach him. The hand of God at work, clearly. He cannot go to the seminary, so I must train him and will, in time, administer his vows."

Though I held my tongue, I did not think God—the God of the First World, if He existed—had much to do with anything that happened in the Shaped worlds.

Thomas replaced the copy of the Pact on the shelf. "It is lunchtime. I can offer only simple fare, but you are welcome to share it."

"Thank you," I said. "You are most generous."

I followed him up from the library, into the church, and out into the sunlight of the village square. With the sunlight came an idea. "On second thought," I said, shading my eyes against the sun and looking across the square, "I would like to explore Zarozje." I lowered my hand and met his gaze. "Unless I am a prisoner."

He hesitated, as if he would have liked to say yes, I *was* a prisoner, but in the end, he said only, "Of course."

I suspected he did not, as the village priest, technically have the right to imprison someone. That kind of power would surely fall to the reeve. The fact that Father Thomas had effectively both arrested me and brought me into the village for testing without me ever seeing the reeve perhaps indicated where the real power in Zarozje lay, but still . . .

And even if none of that entered into his mental deliberations, in truth, there was nowhere I could go. South of Zarozje lay the lake. I hadn't been that way yet, but from what I'd seen up above, it lapped almost at the base of the village wall. What was I going to do? Steal a boat?

To the north rose the cliff face I'd already come down. I could no more climb that without being pursued and caught than I could fly, and since I hadn't been turned into a vampire (*yet*, my mind unhelpfully added), I couldn't do that, either.

To the west stretched the broad flat basin of the valley, open fields where there was nowhere to hide, nowhere to run. I knew there were other fortified villages out there somewhere, but I would face the same questions there as here. No doubt I would be arrested, a message would be sent to Father Thomas, and soon enough I would be returned to him.

To the east, and not all that far away, rose the valley slope, rising to snow-capped mountains. Impassable, everyone said.

And to get to any of those places, even if I wanted to, I'd have to leave through the village gate, which was guarded by people who were unlikely to let me do so.

And so, in the end, "of course" was Father Thomas' answer. He went back inside the church.

I went in search of the orphanage.

SEVEN

AN ELDERLY WOMAN in a cheese shop begrudgingly gave me directions, and soon I stood outside the orphanage, a two-story building of sooty brick that gave off strong *Oliver!* vibes—I half-expected Mr. Bumble to emerge from the door, Eric in tow, singing, "One boy, boy for sale!"

The orphanage leaned against the village wall at the end of a narrow, doglegged street. A crooked sign over the front door bore the words SAINT JEROME'S HOME FOR ORPHANS in faded yellow paint. The whole place had a general air of "go away."

I did not go away. I went up to the door and knocked.

Someone slid aside a piece of wood blocking a small square opening in the door a few inches below my eye level. Suspicious, rheumy blue eyes peered up at me. "What do you want?" said a woman's voice.

"I'm Shawna Keys, a guest of Father Thomas'," I said to the eyes. True enough. Hopefully not *everyone* in the village knew that I'd been suspected of being either a vampire or a werewolf until about, oh, three hours ago. "He asked me to come and check on Eric, to be sure the boy is all right."

The eyes narrowed. The opening closed. For a moment I thought I'd be denied entry, but then I heard a bolt being drawn back. The reason for the low positioning of the peephole became clear as a tiny, rotund woman in a nun's habit, a full head and a half shorter than me but easily twice my diameter, pulled the door inward and stepped to one side, motioning me in. "He's in his room," she said. "He has not spoken since he returned but kneels beside his bed and prays."

I wasn't even entirely sure why I'd come, except he was only a boy, he'd done something that had shaken him to his core, at the behest of his teacher and surrogate father, and my heart had gone out to him when I'd heard him sobbing in the church library . . .

. . . and, okay, yes, it had *also* occurred to me that I'd likely need an ally to escape Zarozje, and he might possibly fit the bill. Of *course,* part of my interest in him was self-interest. My survival, and the survival of my vital mission to gather the *hokhmah* of as many Shaped worlds as I could and take it to Ygrair, was always at the forefront of my mind. That didn't mean my concern for him wasn't real.

At least, that's what I told myself.

I entered the orphanage and looked around. I was in a dark central hall, doors to left and right and a stairway splitting the difference between them. "Up there," said the nun. "Third door on the right."

I nodded. "Thank you, Sister."

"He's a good boy," she said. "He told me what he did, and it had to be done. It was the Lord's work. But he took it hard, poor lad." Shaking her head, she went into one of the side rooms while I started up the creaking stairs.

I listened as I climbed but heard no children's voices. Aside from Eric, the orphanage seemed empty.

The "third door on the right" of the upstairs hallway was also the last. It was closed.

I knocked.

For a moment there was silence.

I knocked again.

"Who's there?" came Eric's voice, guarded and tense.

"A friend," I said. "Shawna Keys."

The door opened a crack. "What are you doing here?"

"I know you're upset. I came to see if I can help."

"I'm supposed to be praying."

"But you haven't been," I guessed.

His breath caught. "How did you . . ."

"Let me in," I said gently.

He studied me a moment longer, then swung the door open.

The room beyond might more accurately have been called a cell. Narrow, it held only a bed, a small round table with a candle on it, and a single chair by that table. There was a window at the end, with nothing to see beyond it but the village wall, whose top was just visible. To the right of the window, between it and the table, was a small, unpadded kneeling bench, a narrow shelf with several half-burned candles on it, and, above that, a wouldn't-have-been-out-of-place-in-a-horror-movie crucifix, one of those particularly graphic and bloody full-color types.

Eric had changed from the clothing he'd worn on the mountainside into a brown, belted monk's robe, feet bare beneath it. He stepped aside as I entered, head down. "I'm not supposed to have girls in my room," he mumbled.

"The door is open," I pointed out. "And I'm not a girl. I'm a grown woman. May I sit?"

Without looking at me, he jerked his arm, palm up, in the direction of the tiny table and chair. The bed would have been more comfortable, but he clearly didn't like the idea of me sitting there. I sat gingerly in the chair and faced him. He remained by the door, as if poised to make a quick getaway if the situation got out of control. "The werewolf you shot," I said. "When she turned into a girl, it shocked you."

He nodded.

"She was pretty."

He nodded again.

"And naked."

His head jerked up, met my eyes, then turned to the floor again. The little bit of his face I could see flushed bright red.

"You didn't feel like you'd killed a monster and maybe saved a life . . . mine. You suddenly felt like you'd murdered a girl your own age, someone you should have been protecting, not killing."

He nodded again.

"I have a confession," I said. "I listened from the stairwell while Father Thomas talked to you in the church library. Did you believe everything he said?"

"Yes . . ."

"But it hasn't made you feel any better?"

"No."

I hesitated then. The course of action that suggested itself to me wasn't nice. But it just might work. It might offer me a way out of the village. And I had to find Karl, and the Shaper of this world. I *had* to.

I took a deep breath. "I was scared when the wolf crouched above me. I thought you'd saved my life. Maybe you did. But the more I think about it . . . I don't think she was going to kill me."

"You don't?"

"No," I said. "I think she was just looking to see if I was okay. Because, after you shot her, and I saw her lying there, I couldn't believe that girl, that poor, dead, naked girl, had meant to do me harm."

He stared at me, horrified. I felt a little horrified myself at what I was doing, undercutting everything Father Thomas had told him to make him feel better about what he had done. But in truth, I *was* beginning to doubt that the wolf-girl had meant me harm. Especially in light of what I now knew about the Pact, and how the Shaper had intended this world to operate. The Shaper would never have given this world's versions of werewolves and vampires any real, unquenchable desire for human flesh and blood. It would make no sense to do that and then also craft the Pact.

What had gone wrong, I didn't know, but if my growing conviction was right, that poor dead wolf-girl had never been a threat, and Eric really had murdered her for no reason.

"Do you remember before the Pact shattered?" I said then. "You were . . . five, I think?"

"I remember a little," he said.

"Did you meet any werewolves and vampires then?"

"A werewolf once. He was nice. He gave me candy. But I never saw him in wolf form."

"Father Thomas even had werewolf and vampire friends, didn't he?"

"I think so," Eric said.

"That girl you shot was about your age. She, too, would have been a child when the Pact still held sway. She would have been raised to uphold it, to never harm a human." If I were right, she would have been *Shaped* to never harm a human. "Do you really think someone who might have been your playmate could have turned into a . . . a mindless killing machine?" The *duh-DUH duh-DUH duh-DUH* beat of *Jaws* ran momentarily through my mind; I squelched it.

"Father Thomas says the Pact failed because they reverted to their true natures."

"Do you believe that poor naked girl was a vicious killer?"

He hesitated. "Father Thomas is my teacher. He told me I have to kill any of the children of the night I encounter. He is the priest. He knows the will of God."

"He *says* he does," I said. "But he's had no contact with Mother Church since the Pact fell apart. What if he's wrong about what he's supposed to be doing?"

"Werewolves and vampires are hunting humans . . . and each other," Eric said desperately.

"All of them? What if it's just a few bad apples? There are humans who prey on other humans. Does that mean all humans should be killed on sight?"

"It's not the same!"

"Isn't it?" I leaned forward in my chair. "I don't believe anyone is responsible for an act of evil except for the person who carries out that act. That girl had done nothing evil. If she had attacked, and you had killed her as she leaped, that would have been one thing. But you simply shot her on sight. And if she was innocent, then her blood is on your hands, and Father Thomas' hands."

And that's when I realized that, no, I wasn't just saying this to get Eric to help me. I really believed it. That poor werewolf had done nothing wrong that I knew of. She'd been killed simply because of who she was.

"I . . . had to do it," Eric said, tears rolling down his cheeks. "Father Thomas taught me . . . I thought I believed, I thought I understood, and shooting the wolf, that was easy, but then suddenly she wasn't a wolf, she was just a girl, a naked girl with my crossbow bolt in her side, and there was so much blood, all over her, all over the ground, and she was staring up at me and . . . and . . ."

His voice choked off. He stepped forward, fell to his knees at the end of the bed, folded his arms on it, pressed his face into them, and sobbed.

I got up and put a hand on his shoulder, useless though the gesture was, thinking black thoughts about Father Thomas, and Mother Church.

No, that wasn't fair. Put the blame where it really lay, where it always lay: with the Shaper. He or she had set up this "perfect" world, but the made-up backstory had come to the fore when something went wrong, the original plot had gone off the rails, and now the people Shaped to live here, each a copy of someone from the First World, were dying, and killing, and *where the hell was this Shaper anyway?*

Now, more than ever, I had to find him or her, and that meant finding Karl.

A part of me still wanted to comfort Eric—but another part of me wanted to rage at him. "Shooting the wolf, that was easy?" He knew it wasn't just a wolf, he knew it was a person in wolf form. He could have refused, even then. Could have made Thomas do it himself. Could have slugged Thomas, talked to the werewolf, and maybe saved her. Maybe even taken a step to restoring the Pact. Maybe it was all just a big misunderstanding. He could have done all sorts of things.

Instead, in the end, he had given in. He had killed the girl in the name of God—or at least in the name of Father Thomas. Thomas believed the vampires and werewolves were already damned, but if this girl had been innocent, if she had never posed a threat to the villagers and indeed had been trying to save me, then Eric had damned *himself* by pulling that trigger.

I found that my comforting hand on his shoulder had tightened, so I forced my fingers to relax. "The girl's people need to know what happened to her," I said. "And I need to meet them. If you feel badly about what you did, if you think you may have done the wrong thing . . ."

He raised his tear-stained face to me. "I do," he whispered. "God help me, I do!"

" . . . then help me escape the village," I said. "I promise I'll tell them what happened. I'll sneak out when it's dark."

Eric gaped at me. "You can't leave Zarozje when it's dark. Something will eat you, or worse . . . change you into one of them."

"My worry, not yours," I snapped. "If you really feel badly about that poor wolf-girl . . ."

"I do," he said, his face crumpling into sorrow again. "I do."

" . . . then you'll help me get out of here so I can tell her people what happened to her." I met his gaze and softened my tone. "Please?"

Eric had already established he was the chivalrous type. I was many years older than him, but perhaps I managed to awake some of that protect-the-female instinct all the same. "All right," he said. "I will." He looked at the open door, then lowered his voice. "There's a door," he whispered. "At the end of Tailor Street . . ."

Fifteen minutes later I descended the creaking stairs. The rotund nun came out of the room she had disappeared into, which had the look of an office. "Thank you," I said. "I believe I was able to offer Eric some comfort."

"Bless you, my child," said the nurse. "What a mercy you came."

I stepped back out into the street, feeling more than a little ashamed of myself. Oh, I hadn't been lying to Eric, or, at least, not entirely. No doubt the wolf-girl's people—pack?—*did* want to know what had happened to her. And maybe someday I'd tell them. But once I was outside the village, my intention was to turn my back on the land of the werewolves, off to the south somewhere, and head straight north for the castle of the vampires, where Karl was held.

Maybe, I thought, he was taken because Queen—what was her name? Patricia, that was it—Queen Patricia was the Shaper, she sensed a Portal opening, and wanted to find out what was going on. In which case, there might very well be more vampire patrols out looking for me. All I had to do was let them scoop me up and fly me off to where Karl waited.

If, of course, I was *wrong* about the vampire queen, and the vampires only wanted me because I was full of fresh blood, then . . .

Maybe a cross wouldn't be a bad idea. And a wooden stake if I could find one. And just in case I encountered werewolves, too, a crossbow with silver-tipped bolts.

As it happened, I figured I knew where to find all of those.

I headed back to Father Thomas' house.

EIGHT

I REACHED THE cottage as Father Thomas emerged from it. He greeted me warmly enough and told me I was welcome to stay there or explore the village further: he had "pastoral duties" that afternoon—visiting the sick, I gathered, not hunting "creatures of the night."

It took me only a few minutes to find a crossbow—he had three, of varying sizes; I took the smallest, which best fit my hand. A cross was easily obtained, too, and as I suspected there might be, there was even a satchel containing nicely sharpened wooden stakes. I found a bag to put the things in and hid it in the churchyard, buried in leaves behind a gravestone near the wall, then set out to see what else I could see of Zarozje.

It didn't take long, and I got suspicious looks from everyone I met, and downright hostile glares from the guards at the village gates, who stepped into my path with spears crossed when I approached, even though the gates stood wide open in the sunlight. I changed direction, after giving them an utterly fake smile instead of the utterly sincere middle finger I would have liked to have given them, then continued my perambulations.

This evidence that, although I had successfully passed Father Thomas' tests to see if I were a werewolf or vampire, I was still effectively a prisoner, only strengthened my resolve to carry out my plan to escape that evening. The difficulty might be in slipping away in the middle of the night from wherever I was sleeping. I currently didn't know where that might be. It seemed unlikely Father Thomas would want a woman in his one-room-and-one-bed quarters overnight. Was there a guest house?

Sort of, it turned out, and when at last I returned to Father Thomas' cottage after having explored every nook and cranny of Zarozje—roughly twelve nooks and maybe fifteen crannies—and he told me where it was, I had to bite my lip to keep from laughing out loud.

"The orphanage is currently empty, but for Eric," he said. (As I'd suspected.) "You may sleep there for now. Starting tomorrow, you must begin earning your keep. Have you any skills?"

"I'm a potter," I said.

His eyebrows raised. "Indeed? Then we can definitely put you to work. We have not had a potter since old Boddington died a year ago. Tomorrow I will show you to his workshop. You will have more work than you can handle."

"I look forward to it," I lied, since I had no intention of still being in Zarozje tomorrow. *Although, to touch clay again . . .* My hands twitched. Maybe I *could* stay a couple of days. Throw a few pots, help out the villagers, and then . . .

No. This wasn't my world, these weren't my people. Their need for new pottery was unimportant. I needed to find Karl and together we needed to find the Shaper, retrieve his or her *hokhmah*, and move on to the next world. This world could iron out its own problems. I was just passing through.

"You may sup with me," Father Thomas said. I sat at the table and watched as he prepared a simple repast of boiled potatoes, stewed tomatoes, and . . . my mouth watered . . . bacon, with a side of coarse brown bread and smelly soft cheese, all washed down with a remarkably not-too-bad, if cloudy, brown ale.

It was my last chance to probe Thomas for more details of the world, so I made the most of it. "So, is every village fortified like this one?" I asked. "Since the Pact failed?"

"Every village that still survives," he said darkly. "Many were destroyed or abandoned in the early days of the Pact's collapse. And even now . . ." He shook his head and stabbed a piece of potato with his fork. "It seems every four or five months another is . . . lost."

"Lost? You mean destroyed?"

"No," he said shortly, pointing the piece of potato at me. "Not destroyed. Just emptied of people. A trader will journey to a place where, just a week before, he had success, only to find unoccupied buildings, open gates, and no sign of the population—not even corpses, or blood."

That mental image chilled me. "Werewolves or vampires?"

"We don't know," Thomas said. "For here is the mystery: not only has everyone vanished, but the *churches* within these villages are missing relics and icons and other holy objects no werewolf or vampire would care—or dare—to carry away." He finally ate the piece of potato and continued. "But whatever the explanation, it doesn't matter. What matters is keeping ourselves safe. Our walls are high, and secure. Every house is warded." He swallowed, then reached for a piece of bacon, crisp, just the way I liked it. "And as you saw today, we do not suffer any werewolf or vampire we find in our vicinity to live." He shoved the bacon into his mouth and chewed with gusto.

I picked at my own food (not the bacon, I'd already eaten *that*), feeling a little nervous now about my plan. "Does no one travel at night, then?"

"Only the suicidal."

"The werewolves and vampires can't be everywhere."

"Nor are they. But it only takes one to ruin your evening, and they can scent a man . . . or woman," he looked at me pointedly, "from a great distance. You and your companion were always doomed to be taken. You are fortunate that you were close to Za-rozje, doubly fortunate the werewolves attacked the vampires and gave you an opportunity to flee. It did not save your companion, but it saved you." He picked up another rasher and pointed that at me, too. "*Eric* saved you. You owe him . . . and us."

If he was trying to make me feel too guilty to plan to escape, he wasn't succeeding. Guilty, yes; but not *that* guilty.

We ate in silence after that, Father Thomas glancing from time to time at the window. As the light dimmed outside, he got to his feet. "Are you finished?" he said, his tone of voice making it clear I'd better be. "The field workers will all be back inside the walls and the gate closed soon."

I got to my feet. "Finished," I said, though I'd left a substantial amount on the plate.

"Come with me on my rounds of the defenses," he said, "and you will understand both why we are secure—and why we *must* be secure. Then, I will take you to the orphanage to find you quarters for the night."

I nodded and followed him out into the darkening churchyard.

I had already seen the village walls, but they had been unmanned during the day. Now, as night descended, there were guards pa-trolling them, men dressed in leather armor (including stout leather collars leaving little of their necks exposed) and simple metal hel-mets, armed with bows and crossbows, with silver-tipped arrows and quarrels, and wooden spears with fire-hardened tips. Also atop the walls, barrels of oil and (Father Thomas told me) holy water stood ready.

"There have been no attacks on Zarozje since the fortifications were completed," Father Thomas said as he led me down the dog-legged street I had already traveled once, unbeknownst to him, to the orphanage. "We are too strong. The monsters seek each other out, instead."

"Why do they fight each other?" I looked up at the stars pricking the sky. The full moon continued to hang in exactly the same place it always hung, day and night. It was the weirdest, most unsettling thing about this world, and the surest sign that it had been Shaped.

Well, that and the vampires and werewolves, I supposed.

"There is bad blood between their queens," Thomas said. "Queen Patricia of the vampires and Queen Stephanie of the werewolves, the heirs to Barnabas and Remus, of whom you read. It is said they were once friends, but they had a falling-out at the same time as the Pact shattered. Perhaps it was their falling-out that shattered it." He shrugged. "It matters not. The Pact has shattered, they are our enemies, they are each other's enemies. The valley is a broken place and the world outside this valley is dead."

"Grim," I said. "Why do you carry on?"

"What else *can* we do? We survive, and we try to do the Lord's will. What more has mankind ever done? 'Fear God and keep His commandments: for this is the whole duty of man.' So wrote Solomon in *Ecclesiastes*, and for all that has passed in the world since he did so, that truth has not changed."

"And God's commandments include killing any werewolves and vampires you come across."

"Yes," he said flatly.

I fell silent. We were almost at the orphanage.

Father Thomas knocked, and the same nun—unless she had an identical twin—who had greeted me earlier swung the door open after a single glance through the peephole. "This is . . ." the priest began.

"Shawna Keys," the nun interrupted. "Yes, we've met."

Father Thomas glanced at me with a raised eyebrow.

"I came to see Eric," I said. "To thank him. And because I thought he might be upset about what happened this morning. I know he had to shoot that girl . . . werewolf . . . but I could tell he took it hard."

Father Thomas sighed. "Yes," he said. "I tried to comfort him, as well. I hope you had more success."

"I think so," I said. "A woman's touch."

"Thank you for that," he said, and I felt another stab of guilt. Then he turned to the nun. "Shawna needs a place to sleep, Sister Benedicta."

The nun nodded.

"We will speak again on the morrow," Thomas said to me.

Not if I have anything to do with it, I thought, but, "Of course," I said out loud.

The room Sister Benedicta showed me to was simple, but clean, twin to Eric's, although its window overlooked the street rather than facing the wall. I took off my boots and sat in my stockinged feet on the straight-backed wooden chair beside the small, round table, and waited until I heard Sister Benedicta make her way to bed, and then another hour. Then, boots in hand, I crept out of my room and down the stairs, which creaked loud enough to wake the dead, it seemed to me, but apparently not loud enough to wake Sister Benedicta. On the front step of the orphanage, I put my boots back on, then hurried through the dark streets to retrieve my bag of weapons from the graveyard. I had to press myself against the wall for a long moment as a sentry passed overhead; then it was back through the churchyard (grateful Father Thomas didn't own a dog), back across the square, back to the orphanage, off with my boots, back up the creaking stairs, and thence down the hallway to Eric's room.

I tapped as gently as if his door were made of eggshell. It opened at once; he'd clearly been waiting.

We didn't speak.

Eric was wearing his monk's robe, not his morning werewolf-hunting garb—perhaps he was still feeling particularly penitent. He was barefoot, carrying a pair of sandals, and so, in as near to silence as the wooden floors would allow, we crept down the stairs, back out through the front door through which I had already passed twice that night, sat on the stoop, put on our respective footwear, and at last started down the cobblestones toward the square. "Am I doing the right thing?" Eric whispered.

"That poor girl's people need to know what happened to her," I whispered back. "Yes, you're doing the right thing."

"Father Thomas . . ."

"Will never know you helped me, unless you confess it." I winced at my choice of words. Eric might be pious enough that he actually *would* confess to helping me escape. *Well, it will be too late for Father Thomas to stop me by then, and that's all that matters.*

We returned to the village square, quiet and dim in the moonlight. To our left rose the church. Eric led me instead to the right, past two darkened shops, to a narrow alley. "Tailor Street," he whispered.

He'd told me, during our conversation in his room earlier, how the ground had subsided at the end of that street, allowing the lake to flood through an old, narrow portal that had once led to the boat piers. The door had long rotted away. "Children swim through it on a dare," he'd said. "Can you swim?"

I'd told him I could.

"Good."

We started down the street, the buildings on either side utterly dark and silent. The ground sloped, and sure enough, long before we reached the wall, we were splashing through ankle-deep water . . . remarkably *cold* water.

Atop the wall, I knew sentries were patrolling, but none appeared on the small section of it we could see. Even if they had, their attention was likely turned outward, not inward.

Fat lot of good it did them. Ahead of us, a large pool of water glistened in the moonlight. As we neared it, it exploded in spray, as a giant wolf with glowing red eyes burst into the village.

NINE

I GRABBED ERIC'S hand and turned to run—and something slammed into my back, knocking me face-first into the shallow water we'd been wading through, Eric splashing down beside me. The bag of weapons I'd been carrying went flying. Gasping, I rolled over, propped myself up on my elbows—and froze.

The wolf stood over us, water pouring from silver fur that shone in the moonlight, eyes as bright and red as coals in a fire. My heart beat a mad rhythm in my chest, as though trying to break out of its boney prison so it could make a dash for safety all on its own.

Another wet wolf ran up beside the first . . . and suddenly, neither was a wolf at all.

The change was nothing like what you see in movies, with long-drawn-out painful reshaping of bones and hair and muscles. It was more like the beasts were made of wax, wax that, in an instant, flowed out of wolf-shape and into human shape.

Naked human shape. A man and a woman, both muscled like Olympic sprinters, the woman pale in the moonlight, the man black as ebony. "This is one of the spies we were ordered to capture," the woman said, pointing to me. "I recognize her smell."

I looked from one to the other. *Wait. What? Spies? Also, "capture"?* "Yes, I'm the one you want," I said, my voice quivering only a little . . . okay, quivering quite a lot. "I was coming to you voluntarily. Take me. Let the boy go."

"Silence," said the woman. "You are not the only one we seek."

"My companion was taken by vampires—"

"You," the woman said to Eric. "We are looking for a girl from our pack. Her name is Elena. Is she in the village?"

I tried to butt in. "We don't know anyone named—"

"I said *silence!*" The woman's eyes flashed hellfire red, and my throat closed on my words.

Eric said nothing. He was pressed against my left side. Like me, he had propped himself up to get his ears out of the water. I could feel him trembling.

I found my voice again. "You've terrified him. He's too scared to speak." *And please, God, keep it that way.*

"We know you send out patrols at dawn," the woman said to Eric. "We last saw her on the other side of the rock face. We traced her trail partway down the path, then lost it. Was she captured? *Do you have her?*"

God was apparently not answering my prayers that night, or if He was, the answer was a resounding "no!" because "She's dead," Eric said.

My heart sank. *Don't say it*, I thought desperately. *Don't say it, don't say it, don't say it . . .*

"I shot her," he finished.

The woman gasped. The man shot her a glance. "Maigrat," he said. "Don't . . ."

He never finished his admonition. Maigrat screamed, a scream that became a howl as she shifted back into a wolf, and then she leaped. She slammed Eric back into the water-covered cobblestones with an enormous splash and, standing astride him with her forepaws on his shoulders, seized his throat in her jaws.

Somewhere on the wall, I heard a shout. Someone had heard her.

I tried to stand, but the man knelt and pushed me back into the water, and I could no more budge him than I could move a mountain. I waited for blood to spray, for Eric to die . . . or me . . . or both . . . but Maigrat, though her wolf-frame trembled, did not close her jaws. Instead, after a long moment, she released Eric's throat, shifted her jaws to his forearm, and bit hard. He screamed. She backed away as, eyes wide, face pale in the moonlight, he stared at his arm. Blood soaked through the torn sleeve of his monastic robe.

Maigrat growled, deep in her throat, then shifted back into woman-shape and stepped back. The man holding me down followed suit. Eric and I both sat up, Eric clutching the wound in his arm. Blood welled between his fingers. "That is a change-bite," Maigrat said.

"No!" Eric cried.

"Yes, boy. A change-bite. You slew one of our pack. Now you *are* one of our pack."

Eric's face had already looked pale in the moonlight. Now it turned positively ghostly. "Please, God, no!"

"Now you must make a choice," Maigrat said. "Come with us, and live, or stay here, and die—slain by your people the way you slew Elena. Which will it be?"

Eric twisted his head toward me. Our eyes met. Then, quick as lightning, he scrambled up and ran as fast as he could toward the village square. Maigrat shifted back into wolf form, dark gray, with a white blaze running down her back, and ran after him.

"Is she going to kill him after all?" I asked my captor, who remained.

"No," he said. "We will kill no one. We uphold the Pact." He hauled me to my feet, gripped my arm painfully tight, and started pulling me after Maigrat and Eric.

"The Pact also forbids changing humans against their will!"

He growled, a very successful wolf sound for having come from a human throat. "Maigrat should not have done that. But the Pact is broken. And not by our doing."

Not the way the humans tell it.

Suddenly, Maigrat was with us again, flowing up from wolf to human shape in an instant. "The brat fled behind the church. Into a cottage by the graveyard . . ."

"Father Thomas' house," I said, and then could have kicked myself.

"The priest," Maigrat snarled. "It would be he who orders the slaying of our kind!" Back into wolf form, and away. We hurried after her on clumsy human feet, across the square, through the lych-gate.

I could still hear confused shouts on the wall. Presumably, the sentries were now staring into the village, looking for the source of the howl they had heard. Also presumably, there would be armed men in the streets very soon. They might rescue me. Or they might die trying.

Just scant weeks ago, I had never seen a violent death. Now they seemed to be following me around. I didn't want any more on my conscience, but I also didn't want to be rescued. Being captured by werewolves hadn't been on my to-do list, but at the least, it would get me out of the village. And perhaps Queen Stephanie would turn out to be the Shaper, rather than Queen Patricia, in whose vampiric clutches Karl currently (presumably) resided. (Although that might be bad news for Karl.) I'd thought Patricia was more likely to be the Shaper because her vampires had captured Karl. But if the werewolves' queen had sent out a patrol specifically look-ing for us, maybe *she* was the more likely one.

In my own world, I'd not made myself anyone important, in-stead opting to be an ordinary potter in an ordinary (if admittedly, in retrospect, suspiciously picturesque) Montana town. But as Karl never tired of pointing out, there was something odd about me. Robur, Shaper of the last world we had been in, had been explicit about his role, styling himself Master of the World. In most worlds, I'd be willing to bet, the Shaper would follow that pattern, and establish him or herself as a great power—perhaps the greatest.

There was Father Thomas' cottage. He stood in the doorway, in a loosely belted robe, clearly just roused from his bed, a crossbow in his hand. Maigrat paced back and forth through the tombstones, growling. I could not see Eric—presumably he was inside the cottage.

Maigrat dared not rush the priest because of the crossbow with its silver-tipped quarrel. Father Thomas dared not shoot into the darkness for fear of missing her and having no time to reload before she was on him.

Stalemate, but one that could not last long. "To me!" Thomas shouted. "Guards! Werewolves in the churchyard!"

Were those answering shouts? I wasn't sure. The distant cries came from the direction of the village gate and could have been nothing more than the guards organizing themselves to search the streets. Enclosed as the churchyard was, I found it hard to believe Thomas' voice had carried much beyond its confines.

Still, sooner or later—probably sooner—the guards *would* be on us. I started to speak, then stopped. What could I tell Thomas that would change anything? If I told him Eric had been given a change-bite, that he was doomed to become a werewolf, would Thomas, though it tore him apart, turn and put that crossbow quarrel right through the boy's heart? He might. And I had no other avenue of persuasion.

Things were abruptly taken out of my hands. From inside the cottage appeared a new wolf, slender, half-grown, pale-furred. He leaped upward, slamming into Father Thomas' back, driving him to the ground. The crossbow skittered out of the priest's hand. He desperately scrambled for it as the young wolf ran over him, and into the darkness—to Maigrat.

"Let's go!" my captor said as he yanked me around and pulled me back in the direction from which we had come. I resisted just for a moment, looking back, afraid I would see Maigrat and

Eric—because the new wolf had to be him—savaging Father Thomas, but in fact, they were both running toward me, and an instant later, past me.

I ran willingly then with my naked captor. We dashed through the village square. Torches shimmered off the walls of the buildings bordering the broad street from the gate, the guards having gotten their patrols in play at last.

Father Thomas shouted behind us, but we were already running around the corner onto Tailor Street, Maigrat and Eric, in wolf form, far ahead. We passed my dropped bag of weapons—no chance to pick it up. The wolves plunged into the water and disappeared. My captor suddenly became a wolf at my side, growling at me, eyes burning. No possibility of running back the other way, then.

I took a deep breath and plunged into the pool just as torchlight came around the corner from the square. I kicked to drive myself down. I couldn't see a thing, but I was close to the wall. I felt its stones, found the opening of the old gate, forced myself through, burst upward into fresh air on the other side, and discovered I could stand, the water neck-deep.

Ahead of me, two dark shapes arrowed through the water, their wakes spreading behind them, glittering in the moonlight. The lake stretched an unknown distance, the far shore only a suggestion of blacker darkness.

My captor surfaced beside me, man-shaped once more. I turned to him. "I can't swim all the way across the lake!" I protested.

"You don't have to," the man said. "Ride me."

This took my mind in an unexpected direction for a moment. "What?"

"Ride me," he said impatiently, and then flowed into wolf-shape. He turned his great head toward me, red eyes blazing. I grabbed two handfuls of black fur, holding on as he plunged ahead into the water with powerful strokes . . . well, a powerful dog paddle, I guess, but whatever you called it, he moved us across the lake with alacrity.

Shouts behind us, on the wall. Light. Could they see us? I heard a zipping sound, a splash. They were definitely shooting in our general direction, but the uncertain light must have defeated their aim, or else they were just firing wildly. Nothing struck me or my wolf-mount.

Now I was free to entertain other thoughts, the first of which was, *Damn, this water is cold. I'll never make it across the lake.* But I did, while that powerful canine body beat the water beneath me, because there's nothing like the threat of imminent drowning to keep your hands in a death grip in the fur of a werewolf's back, no matter how numb your fingers become.

Then came other thoughts. *Queen Stephanie* must *be the Shaper. She sent these wolves to capture us. She must have sensed the Portal opening . . .*

No. She couldn't have *sent* them. When the wolves attacked the vampires on the other side of the rock face, we'd only been in this world a little over a day. Her realm had to be at least a couple of days' travel south.

A message, then, to a patrol already near. Carrier pigeon, maybe?

No, not a patrol, I corrected myself. *A pack. An extended family. And Elena, the teenager, did something impulsive, got separated from the others, and was killed.*

All because I had entered this world.

Once more, I wondered if it was to be my fate to bring death and destruction everywhere I went. *Now I am become Death, the destroyer of worlds . . .*

At last we reached the far shore of the lake. My ride shrugged me off into the shallows, where I fell with an icy splash. I crawled out on my hands and knees and then hunched myself on the shore, knees clutched to my chest. The furry black wolf who had brought me across shook himself (dousing me in more icy water), turned into a naked black man, and stood over me, body shining in the moonlight. I quickly looked away, my head being at an unfortunate elevation, only to find myself surrounded by wolves—clearly, the rest of the pack. I couldn't count them in the dark, but the way they circled me, eyes glowing red, did not inspire a feeling of welcome, unless it was the welcome a Christmas turkey feels when it's brought to the table.

Were Maigrat and Eric among those circling wolves? I couldn't tell.

I turned my gaze toward Zarozje. Fires now burned on the walls and I could see people moving along it, staring out at the lake. A few shouts carried across the water. We had clearly caused great consternation.

"Stay," my guard said, which was pretty rich coming from someone who had been a glorified dog a minute before. I looked up at him again as he turned and strode away. I lost sight of him for a minute or two in the darkness, then he returned, clothed now in a loose robe, cinched at the waist, clearly designed to be discarded in a moment if need arose. His also wore sandals that looked like they could be easily kicked off.

The others took their cue from him, it seemed. All around me, naked people appeared, knelt, pulled robes from hidden packs, dressed. One wolf flowed into a woman-shape I recognized all too well: Maigrat. Beside her, a smaller, pale-furred wolf sat back on its haunches and howled at the moon. A few others remained in wolf-shape, as well. I still didn't have a good sense of how many there were in total.

Someone handed Maigrat a robe. She donned it without hurry, while the young wolf continued howling. "Awoooooooooo! Awoooooooooo!"

"Eric?" I said. The wolf stopped howling, turned his head, and looked straight at me with glowing red eyes. Then he trotted over to me and pushed up against me, and I put my arms around him and hugged him tight.

"Get up," the werewolf who had carried me across the lake said.

I released Eric and stood. "Is the change always so fast?" I said, looking down at the wolf pressed to my thigh, his head raised toward me.

"It happens within a few minutes of the change-bite," the man said. "Something the priest clearly did not know."

"I don't think he knew Eric's wound *was* a change-bite," I said. "If he had . . ." I remembered Thomas standing in the doorway with his crossbow in hand and fell silent.

The man put a hand on the young wolf's head. "Eric is one of our pack, now."

"He didn't ask for this. He didn't want it. You've made him into what he thinks is a monster."

"He no longer thinks that way," the man said. "The change is more than physical."

I was shivering again. I wrapped my arms around myself. "So why is he still a wolf? Why hasn't he changed back to human form?"

"The first change lasts until the next dawn. After that, he will be able to control it at will during the night, as we do." He held something out to me, just a dark shape in the moonlight. "Take this."

"What is it?" I said suspiciously.

He sighed. "A spare cloak."

"Oh." Feeling foolish, I accepted it, pulled it on over my wet clothes, and immediately felt warmer. "Thank you."

"What is so special about you?" asked my ride. I had to stop thinking of him as that, but I had no name for him yet. "Why is the queen so eager to retrieve you? She sent a messenger bird, telling us to find you and bring you to her."

Aha! I was right, I thought.

Maigrat appeared from behind him. "To speak more plainly, what makes you worth the death of my little sister?" she snarled, teeth flashing in the moonlight, and I discovered that the snarl of a werewolf is a threatening thing no matter what form the werewolf is in.

"I'm a stranger," I said. "From outside the valley."

"You lie!" Maigrat spat. "There have been no humans outside this valley since the Great Cataclysm."

"Precisely why the queen wants to see me, I'd guess," I said.

The woman stepped closer, very close, so close I could feel her breath on my face—she was at least four inches taller than me, and I'm not particularly short. "It is fortunate for you she does," she snarled ("snarl" seemed to be her default tone and expression and attitude, at least toward me). "Should the queen decide, after speaking with you, that you are not as interesting as she thinks, I look forward to eating your entrails."

Never having had to respond to such a comment before, I lacked a witty riposte. "Um . . . okay," I said. *I thought you follow the Pact and never kill humans?* I wanted to add, but—probably wisely—didn't.

"Enough, Maigrat," said my erstwhile ride. Growled, really. Maigrat snarled again but stepped back.

I looked at the man. *Alpha male?* I remembered reading that the theory of there being an "alpha male" in wolf packs had been debunked, but maybe the news hadn't made it to this world yet. "The humans will give chase at first light. We must mount and be away. And our new pack member must hunt—he will be starving."

That made me give the newly minted Eric-wolf a second glance, a somewhat worried one. The red-eyed gaze he turned on me was not all that reassuring.

"Can you ride?" the "alpha male" said.

Something other than you? "Yes," I said. "But I'm allergic to horses."

"I do not know what that means."

"It means I will sneeze a lot."

"As long as you don't fall off, you may sneeze your eyes out."

Well, that's an unpleasant image.

He turned away. "Let's go."

We left the lake behind and climbed a low hill. The horses of which he spoke were tethered on the other side. I was surprised they were willing to let werewolves ride them, and even more surprised by how unconcerned they seemed by the unchanged, giant, red-eyed wolves trotting around. A choice of the Shaper's, no doubt: these weren't real horses, they were Shaped horses, like the remarkable horses in some novels that might as well be bicycles, for all the notice the author took of their horsey reality. I was a bit surprised the werewolves intended to ride them wearing nothing but their loose robes—the chafing-and-bruising risk seemed rather high to me—but I guess they were used to it. Maybe they had calluses in unusual places.

Bare legs flashed on all sides as the pack mounted. Maigrat alone took off her robe and turned back into a wolf. She and Eric circled each other a couple of times, then loped away, the white blaze on Maigrat's back and Eric's pale-gray fur shining in the moonlight. *Hunting,* I thought, and hoped it was only animals they sought.

I hauled myself slowly and awkwardly aboard the mare I was offered. Once in the saddle, I promptly sneezed. The mare gave me a reproving look. I shrugged at her, sniffed, and sneezed again.

"Let's move," said Alpha.

Okay, that was enough of that. "What's your name?" I asked.

"Jakob," he said, and then we rode into the darkness.

If I remembered the size of the valley correctly, the northern border of Queen Stephanie's realm lay at least seventy-five miles to the south of us. We clearly would not make that in half a night's ride.

I was right, but not just because of the distance involved: after about four (increasingly miserable, for me) hours, our journey was abruptly interrupted by attacking vampires.

If there was one old adage my journeys through Shaped worlds had so far proved, it was that it never rains but it pours.

Though the sun set, Karl continued to watch the courtyard. In the ghostly light of the ever-present, ever-full moon, he saw a dozen naked people emerge from somewhere below him and, in an instant, transform into the giant bat-like creatures he had seen—and been abducted by—the night before. They flew up and past him, so close he felt the wind of their passage. One glanced at him, its eyes twin sparks of blood-red light.

Karl stared after them, wondering where they were going, and what would happen when they got there.

The moon looked down blankly and blandly, giving no answers.

TEN

THE WEREWOLVES, EVEN in human form, clearly had far sharper senses than I. My first clue vampires were about to attack was when my companions suddenly reined to a halt, leaped from their horses, threw off their robes, and turned into wolves.

This, of course, left me in the unfortunate position of being the sole rider left mounted on a horse surrounded by wolves. I gripped the reins tighter (and sneezed, for good measure), but to my delight, the horse remained unfazed. She just lowered her head to nibble grass from the verge of the path we'd been following between dark, unkempt fields.

I was so happy with the mare's calmness that I leaned forward to pat her neck . . . and something whooshed through the space I'd been occupying a moment before. In the same instant, something else slammed into my side and knocked me from the horse.

I hit the ground hard enough to knock out my breath—one of my least favorite experiences in the world, although I suppose, on a scale that includes being attacked by flying vampires while surrounded by werewolves, it perhaps doesn't rank very high—and rolled, trying desperately to draw breath, only to find a giant black wolf staring down at me, eyes glowing red: Jakob. He took one look at me, as if to be sure I wasn't dead. I wasn't, and at least I was managing at last to draw a little air around the edges of the sharp lump in the middle of my chest, so he twisted away.

I couldn't see much of what was going on. Wolves snapped and howled and leaped into the air at giant black bat-shapes. The battle only lasted a few moments, then the vampires broke off, circling up into the sky and flying back north, the way we'd come.

Several of the wolves shifted back to naked humans. Jakob came over to me, pulling his robe on as he approached. By now I could breathe almost normally, although the lessening of pain in my chest just meant I could feel the bruises on my side where I had hit the ground. I touched my ribs gingerly. Not cracked I hoped but, *ow*. Hadn't broken an arm or a leg, either. All in all, a pretty good fall from a horse, if there was such a thing.

"We were fortunate," Jakob said. He held out his hand and I let him pull me upright. I only groaned a little. "Embry, in lupine form, has been running ahead, then turning to watch behind us. He glimpsed them in the air and gave warning. Carelessness on their part, flying high enough to silhouette against the stars."

"What did they want?" I said. I rolled my shoulders and winced.

"You have to ask? You, of course. And I was a fool to change the moment the alarm came. I had forgotten you are only a human. I should have stayed in human form long enough to pull you down. They almost had you."

"Any casualties?" I asked, feeling subdued. Once again, people—okay, werewolves and vampires, but still people—were fighting because of me.

"Nothing that did not heal when we left wolf form. Some of *them* took worse." He made a face, turned his head, hawked, spat, swiped his sleeve across his lips, and turned toward me again. "And vampires taste terrible."

I blinked. "Not something I ever thought about." Some impulse made me ask, "How do they think *you* taste?"

"I don't know," he said. "I've never let one I've fought live long enough to ask it."

I wanted to ask him how this had all come about, how the Pact had fallen and the vampires and werewolves, once allies, had become enemies, with the humans caught between them—but the middle of the night, after a vampire attack, didn't seem the best time. I filed the question away for later.

The horses, those remarkably placid Shaped horses, had only moved a short distance down the road. We retrieved them, mounted, and continued our journey. The pack didn't talk: no chatter about the attack, or anything else. Just grim, straight-ahead riding.

I found myself slumping in my saddle, only the occasional sneezing fit perking me up. Jakob, riding behind me, trotted his horse up to my side. "Not much longer," he said. "There is a redoubt ahead that we maintain for ranging packs. We will rest there for a few hours."

"Sounds . . ." I sneezed, wiped my nose with the back of my sleeve—nobody seemed to have heard of Kleenex on this world and I hadn't been given a handkerchief—and finished, "wonderful."

"Wonderful" perhaps overstated it, but the "redoubt"—really a cave, its mouth sealed with stone blocks, the only openings in it a narrow wooden door bound with steel bands and two narrow slits perfect (I presumed) for shooting arrows through—was surprisingly comfortable inside. By the time we reached it, dawn was breaking, though the sun would take a while yet to climb above the eastern slope of the valley, in which the redoubt was set. The wolves who had been scouting around the horses had all turned into naked humans who were glad to be given cloaks on our arrival.

Inside, there were a dozen cots, blankets, food (of the dried-this-and-that variety; somewhat to my surprise, considering this was a werewolf redoubt, the this-and-that included fruit and nuts, but I suppose in human form they were no more inclined to eat fresh streaming entrails than I was), fresh water from a spring in the back wall that tumbled noisily into a small pool, and a couple of what I would have called picnic tables, though they probably had a more medieval-ish name I wasn't aware of.

Or maybe not: maybe the Shaper just decided to include picnic tables in her world for some reason, or the world decided on its own that they were appropriate and borrowed them from the First World, as apparently the Shaped worlds were wont to do. The precise rules surrounding such things had yet to be explained to me. I wondered if I had learned them in Ygrair's school, and then forgotten them. Maybe it was just as likely that *nobody* knew all the rules—maybe not even the mysterious Ygrair. Heck, maybe the rules were different for every world. Apparently, physical laws were, since here, humans could actually turn into werewolves and vampires.

I ate, though I couldn't exactly tell you what, and drank water, and then fell into the nearest cot and was asleep in an instant.

Perhaps three hours after they departed, the vampires returned to the castle. Karl had pulled the comfortable chair onto the balcony and had dozed off in it, but he woke to the susurration of wings and peered down into the courtyard to see the bat-things turn into humans. There was much angry discussion, though he could make out none of the words, and then everyone repaired back into the castle, leaving the courtyard empty in the moonlight.

After a few more minutes, Karl left the chair where it was and went to the bed, lying on it fully clothed, in case something happened during the night.

In the end, all that happened was that he slept.

When he woke in the morning, the food and water had been replenished. Someone had come into the room without waking him.

Furious with himself, he sat at the table and ate and watched the door.

Surely, someone would come to him today.

I awoke to dim daylight, finding its way into the cave through the slit windows. I sat up and looked around. The pack still slumbered around me—all except Jakob, who, in his robe, sat on the ground by the door, back to the wall. I went to him. "Good . . ." I stopped. I didn't have a clue what time it was. "Afternoon?" I guessed.

"Almost," he said.

I felt grungy and stinky and generally unappealing, after all the running and swimming and riding on (and falling off of) horses the night before, but there seemed little hope of a bath anytime soon, and clearly, in this world, a shower was definitely out. There was another matter that could not wait, however. I cleared my throat. "Um, where do I . . . ?"

He nodded toward the back of the cave. "Behind that curtain."

"Thanks." Behind said curtain, I found a hole in the ground and a remarkable smell. I emerged feeling relieved in more ways than one. Around me, the rest of the pack still snored. I took a moment to count them: ten, in all, counting Jakob. Of Maigrat and Eric, there was no sign, but they would make the pack an even dozen. Which made me unlucky thirteen.

I found some cheese and dried fruit for my breakfast/lunch and then returned to Jakob. "What happens today?" I asked, sitting beside him.

"We rest until nightfall. We do not travel in daylight if we can help it."

"Why not?"

He looked at me like I was an idiot. "Because we cannot take our superior forms by daylight. In the sun, we are as weak as you humans."

"And you don't like that." I took a bite of cheese.

"It is like having a part of myself amputated."

I thought about that. "And the vampires?"

"They are the same."

"They don't burst into flame or crumble into dust?" Father Thomas had said they didn't, but I wanted a second opinion.

I got the "are-you-an-idiot?" look again. "Of course not. Why would they?"

I couldn't exactly say, "Because they do in my world." Because, of course, they *didn't* in my world, because they didn't exist in my world, other than in books and movies, which I thought meant—though I guess I couldn't be a hundred percent sure—that they didn't exist in the First World, either. So I said nothing, instead sipping water and thinking.

"If the vampires are only ordinary humans by day," I asked after a moment, "then why *not* travel by day? They can't possibly catch you if they can't fly."

"We do not travel by day," Jakob growled.

"Afraid of humans?"

He said nothing. I thought of Eric's crossbow bolt slamming into Elena's side, suddenly wishing I hadn't asked.

Eric was himself a teenaged werewolf now. I asked Jakob where he and Maigrat might be.

"We have other, smaller shelters. Maigrat knows them all. No doubt they are in one of those."

Unless the vampires got them, I thought uneasily. I hoped that wasn't the case. I felt responsible for Eric. If we hadn't appeared, the pack wouldn't have been ordered to capture us, and Elena wouldn't have been shot by Eric, and the werewolves . . .

That way lay madness. Might as well think the Shaped worlds

would all be better places if I'd never existed when, clearly, they wouldn't. I changed the subject. "Tell me about Queen Stephanie." *Tell me if she's the Shaper*, I wanted to say, but I didn't figure that would get me very far.

"What do you want to know?" Jakob said.

"Why does she want me?"

"You will have to ask her that."

Well, that wasn't helpful. "How old is she?"

"I have never asked."

"Older than me?"

"In appearance, yes, although I do not know how old you are."

"Twenty-seven," I supplied.

He raised an eyebrow at that. "You look younger."

"So I've been told." But not in my own world. I remembered what Karl had told me, that in my own world, those around me would have seen me as the age I was supposed to be, but I would not, in fact, have been aging. However that worked. Certainly, the barely-out-of-high-school guy putting up the sign above my pottery studio the day all this began had seen me as too old to be of interest. But in the last world, and this one, I apparently looked younger than I thought I was. It was all very confusing. "How old are you?"

"Forty-one," he said.

"And you've always been a werewolf?"

I got the "you're-an-idiot" look again. Three times in one conversation! A new record. Even Karl hadn't matched it. "What else would I have been?"

"A human," I said. "Like Eric was, until yesterday."

"There are very few changed humans. Within the kingdom, it is seen as a great honor."

"I don't think he thought so."

"Of course he didn't," Jakob said impatiently. "But it is one, all the same. He is part of the pack. He slew Elena. He will regret that all his life. That is his punishment. But he has taken her place in the pack. In that way, he makes right, as much as he can, the wrong he did."

"Vampires can change humans, too. Do they also see it as an honor?"

"I do not know."

"Do they do it more often than you do?"

"I do not know."

"Vampires are undead. So they have to kill someone to change them, don't they?"

"I do not know."

That was just as annoying coming from him as it had been from Karl. Then I remembered something else. "Wait. You said, 'Within the kingdom, it is seen as a great honor.' Why add that caveat?"

Jakob literally growled, a little of his inner wolf seeping into his outer human. "We have heard that the rogues will change anyone, no matter how brutish or violent. They may, in fact, seek out those qualities."

"Rogues?" That was the first I'd heard of "rogues." For a minute, I felt like I was getting somewhere.

But Jakob's lips tightened. "I should say nothing more. I do not know what Queen Stephanie intends for you, or what she wants you to know."

You're not getting off that easy, I thought. "The fields we've passed through are untended. There are abandoned farms and villages everywhere. Is that the work of the rogues?"

"I will not . . ."

"Oh, come on," I said. "I can put two and two together. You've told me your people don't attack humans. But these 'rogues' don't follow that decree, do they?"

After a long pause, he sighed and gave in. "No. They have attacked many farms and small villages, murdering those who dwell there. It began shortly after the Pact failed. In response, the largest villages fortified, and farmers and people from smaller villages fled to them for security, leaving much of the land vacant."

"Father Thomas told me there are also villages that are simply emptied of people, but there's no sign of a struggle—no bodies, no blood," I said. "Is that, too, the work of these rogues?"

Jakob shook his head. "We don't think so. But we have no other explanation for them." His suddenly gave me a sharp, penetrating look. "But *none* of this is *our* doing. Queen Stephanie does not allow the werewolves of the kingdom to attack humans. We believe Queen Patricia has set the same restriction on the vampires of her realm. It is the *rogues* who have been killing humans, attacking any they catch in the night. It is because of the rogues that humans see all werewolves and vampires as the enemy—as they always did, in the world beyond this valley, before the Great Cataclysm, before the Pact. And so . . ." His voice trailed off.

"Elena," I said. I remembered the thump of the crossbow bolt into the flank of the wolf above me, the bolt protruding from the bloody side of the naked girl lying in the dirt when I'd been pulled out of the tree. I swallowed.

"Elena," he said. He shook his head. "The world has become a darker place."

"But how did the Pact break down? Was it the vampires?"

"Yes," he said emphatically. "We do not know why, but Queen Patricia personally led a surprise attack against one of our packs. I saw her myself. Queen Stephanie saw her.

"There was no warning. Among the vampires who attacked were some I counted as friends. None of them spoke. They simply attacked. Queen Patricia herself killed several werewolves." His voice thickened to a near-growl. "One of those was the queen's husband."

Husband? That startled me. Did that mean Queen Stephanie

wasn't the Shaper? She wouldn't marry someone she'd Shaped, would she?

Then I remembered, as if from a long time ago (a fact which made me feel guilty), my own boyfriend, Brent. Hadn't I intended the same thing? The fact I didn't remember Shaping him didn't change the fact I had.

"And there's been no attempt to make peace?" I said.

"Did you not hear what I said?" he said, and for the first time, I heard a hint of Maigrat's default snarl in his voice. "With whom would we treat? *Queen Patricia herself* led the attack. *Queen Patricia herself* murdered werewolves. *Queen Patricia herself* killed Queen Stephanie's husband. *There can be no peace.*"

He got to his feet. "I must tend to the horses," he said, and left me there.

I drank the rest of my water in silence.

The afternoon passed. The werewolves did not confine themselves to the cave. They went out. There were wrestling matches. Nude ones. I retreated to the cave as they began. The werewolves seemed to have no nudity taboo at all, but I was just a small-town girl, and I'd already seen enough naked people to last me quite a while. Although, to be sure, all the werewolves seemed extremely fit and some of the men had impressive . . .

Stop that.

I thought about Karl instead. (Fully clothed, I hasten to add.) The vampires had him. Father Thomas thought they would either kill him or make him one of them. I hoped he was wrong. It was still entirely possible that Queen Patricia of the vampires was the Shaper. If that were the case, she and Karl might even now be planning my rescue.

And then my eyes widened. *Crap. What if that "attack" last night* was *the rescue and failed?*

That would definitely mean Queen Stephanie wasn't the Shaper.

But if she wasn't, what did she want with me? Was I just some kind of exotic takeout?

No, she has to be the Shaper. How else would she have known about our arrival and sent a message to the pack to capture us?

But if she's the Shaper, what does that mean for Karl? And why did the vampires attack—and make a grab for me specifically?

The words in my head went 'round and 'round, like the wheels of the bus in the children's song, but whereas the bus eventually got somewhere, my head got nowhere but achy.

Night fell at last. Five of us changed into giant red-eyed wolves, five of us mounted half of the horses (and led the rest), one of us started sneezing, and we set off by the light of the eternally full moon. I couldn't help glancing up at it, over and over again, searching for the silhouette of a giant bat, but the only thing that obscured it, about three hours into our travels, were clouds.

Shortly after that, it began to rain.

On the minus side, I was cold, wet, and miserable. On the plus side, I quit sneezing. On balance, I rather thought I'd come out ahead.

At least Karl's in a nice warm castle, I thought. *He's better off than I am . . .*

. . . well, you know, if he's still alive.

He is. He must be.

Suddenly, I sneezed again. It had nothing to do with my allergy. It had everything to do with the aforementioned "cold, wet, and miserable."

Drat, I thought.

ELEVEN

NIGHT FELL, AGAIN.

Karl sat in the chair at the table, arms folded, staring at the door, determined that he would remain awake until someone came to replenish the food, water, and wine.

He woke to daylight streaming through the window, lying on the bed, with no memory of how he'd gotten there.

There was fresh food and water.

And still, no one came.

We rode all night. As dawn broke, we camped again, this time in a large house, missing chunks of wall and all of its doors but with a roof over it, which was a good thing, since it hadn't stopped raining. After steaming by the fire for a while, in the company of the pack . . . most of them, though not all of them, had put on their robes, but a few seemed to think bare skin was better when wet and, honestly, I was so happy to be warm, I barely noticed . . . I crawled into one of the cots and fell asleep almost instantly.

I woke around noon. The rain continued to pour down. I mostly spent the afternoon sitting in a rotting old armchair by one of the unshuttered windows, looking out at the gray landscape. I worried about Karl for a while, and then I started wondering about Maigrat and Eric. Almost as though my thinking about them had summoned them, they suddenly appeared, materializing out of the mist, trudging toward the house in the unrelenting rain.

The werewolf-robe Eric wore was almost identical to the priest-in-training robe he had worn in Zarozje, so that he looked mostly unchanged, even though I knew that wasn't true. Maigrat, on the other hand, looked (still) miserable and angry.

Eric walked a few paces behind her, head down. He did not look to me like someone who felt honored to be part of the pack. I wondered what Maigrat had said to him, in the time they had spent apart from us, when he had changed from wolf to boy again. Jakob had said he would no longer think the way he'd thought before he was changed, and certainly he had attacked Thomas without hesitation when we'd made our escape from Zarozje. But it also sounded like Jakob knew very few humans who had been changed—and if it was indeed considered an honor within the kingdom, all of those humans would have *wanted* to be changed. Eric had been changed against his will, in express violation of the Pact these werewolves claimed to still uphold.

I hoped I'd have a chance to talk to Eric, but though he certainly saw me by the window as he approached, he walked by me without meeting my eyes, even when I called his name. Maigrat, however, gave me a malevolent glance that promised she would *love* to talk to me, whether I wanted to hear what she had to say or not.

Which was why—shortly after a lunch of surprisingly savory stew featuring rabbits caught by some of the pack who had remained in wolf form during last night's journey—she found me, once more seated on the old chair by the window, where I'd resumed staring out into the rain. (It wasn't StreamPix, but it was better than staring at a wall, which was the only alternate programming available.)

"How long have you been a spy of Queen Patricia's?" Maigrat said by way of greeting.

"I beg your pardon?" I said, because you have to say *something* when someone says something like that. On the other hand, the last thing she had said to me, back on the shore of the lake, had been how much she was looking forward to eating my entrails, should Queen Stephanie grow bored with me, so perhaps this was progress of a sort.

"I have been thinking about you," she said.

"I'm flattered."

She ignored my feeble sally. "You must be a spy because, otherwise, we would not have been sent to capture you." She leaned forward, *way* forward, hands on the arms of the chair so she could thrust her face almost nose-to-nose with mine, grinning in an entirely nonhumorous fashion. I noticed for the first time that even in human form she had remarkably large and sharp incisors. "I look forward to watching your interrogation," she almost purred. (Wrong species, but right word.)

I pushed myself back into the chair, but it didn't open up nearly enough of a gap between us for comfort. "Not a spy," I said. "I told you. I'm just a stranger. From outside the valley."

"And I told you," she said, "that there *is* nothing outside the valley." To my relief, she straightened.

"Queen Stephanie knows otherwise," I said. *I hope.* "Apparently, she has not chosen to share that knowledge with you."

Maigrat growled, and again I was struck by how adept, even with human vocal cords, the werewolves were at making animal noises. "You keep believing that." She turned away and started toward the door.

"Have you always been a werewolf?" I asked her retreating back.

She spun to face me again. "What?"

"Were you born to . . . this?" I gestured at her. "Like Jakob? Not made, like Eric?" It's a failing of mine to want to push any exposed buttons I come across that are attached to someone I don't like, a category of people into which Maigrat had definitely inserted herself.

She recrossed the space between us with remarkable speed, eyes blazing—literally; sparks of werewolf red glinted inside her otherwise human pupils. "I was not *made*," she snarled. (Again, quite literally.) "I was never *human*. I am of the true stock of the people of the wolf. Your kind . . . you *humans* . . . you long to be us, but very few of you are acceptable to the pack because very few of you are worthy. You, for example," her tone dripped contempt, "will *never* be one of us."

"And Eric was?" I said. "Worthy, I mean? The boy who killed your sister?"

"That is different, and you know it," she said. "He deprived me of my family. He left a hole in the pack. Now I have deprived him of his family and filled that hole."

"He has no family," I pointed out. "He's an orphan. And isn't the pack supposed to be his family, now? You haven't deprived him of his family, you've given him one. He killed your sister, and by your lights, you've rewarded him."

Maigrat's eyes blazed red, as red as they did when she was a wolf, and she bared her unnaturally sharp teeth, so that for a moment I feared I'd find out how effective human-form werewolf teeth were for throat-ripping. Instead, she spun away, robe swirling, and disappeared in the direction of the main room of the house, where the others were congregated.

The pack members, I'd noticed, didn't really like to be apart from one another for very long. I, on the other hand, was quite content to be elsewhere, and managed to keep myself mostly separate from the werewolves for the rest of the day.

The rain let up late in the afternoon, and it began clearing in the west. As the sun set, its final, fiery sliver made an appearance in a gap between two peaks, black silhouettes against the brilliant red sky. I was admiring the view when I caught movement out of the corner of my eye and turned to see Eric standing in the doorway, head down.

I hurried toward him, intending to give him a hug, but he flinched and backed away, and I stopped. "Eric, I'm so sorry. Are you all right?"

"I'm fine," he said. "Better than fine."

"But . . . what they did to you . . ."

"It's a great honor," Eric said. He didn't say it like he meant it. "I'm so strong now when I'm a wolf. I can hear and see and smell things . . . it's amazing." Again, he didn't sound amazed. "I came to say thank you for your help when I was a boy. It was misguided, but I believe you meant it kindly, although Maigrat says you only did it to find a way out of the village."

I winced inwardly. I *had* meant it kindly, but I'd also needed to escape Zarozje.

"Is the pack welcoming you?" I said, remembering what Maigrat had said, and also, conveniently, changing the subject.

"I am part of it now," Eric said, which didn't answer my question.

From the other room came Jakob's shouted, "Time to go."

"Eric . . ." I said, but he had already turned and fled. By the time I emerged from the house, he'd changed into wolf form with the others who would travel in that shape tonight. Jakob sat astride his usual horse, holding the reins of my mare. She gave me a doleful look in the twilight as I approached. I greeted her with a friendly sneeze.

"Tonight, we will cross the border of Queen Stephanie's kingdom," Jakob told me as I mounted.

I sneezed again, wiped my nose, and said, "And then how far to the palace?"

"There is no palace," he said, but didn't elaborate.

The sky had almost completely cleared, the clouds hightailing it before some powerful upper-level wind that did not make it-self felt in the valley. The full moon, locked eternally in its Shaped place in the sky, shone down brightly. We passed two villages where lights blazed atop high walls, staying well clear of them. We also passed three villages that were dark ruins, barely visible in the moonlight.

We passed fields that seemed well-tended, but no lights shone in the associated houses. Presumably, the farmers lived in the near-est walled village.

An hour passed; two. I felt hyperalert, wondering if we would be attacked again, but I was still deaf and blind compared to the werewolves. Maigrat suddenly appeared, naked and pale in the moonlight, in front of Jakob and me. "Rogue," she said. "Feeding. Farmhouse on the right. Two hundred yards."

"Take him," Jakob snapped, and Maigrat flowed back into wolf-shape and loped off into the darkness. Two others accompanied her. I couldn't tell if one of them was Eric. I hoped not.

"Feeding?" I whispered to Jakob. "On what?"

He gave me that "are-you-an-idiot?" look I'd come to know so well, and I knew, as I had already known but had hoped I was mis-taken about, the answer to my question.

Ahead of us, there were sudden snarls, howls, and the most horrible shriek I had ever heard, a high-pitched sound like an entire classroom of third graders scraping their fingernails on a black-board at once. It set my teeth on edge and my body sprouted goose-bumps. "What was that?" I gasped.

Jakob responded by spurring his horse to a gallop. For a second, thinking he had left me alone, I considered trying to escape the pack, but a quick glance around showed that one of them, in wolf form . . . Embry, I thought . . . was behind me. I gave him a wave, sneezed, and trotted after Jakob.

Ahead, as I neared the farmyard, I saw the wolves circling something on the ground. Jakob had dismounted. The other unchanged werewolves were holding the horses.

I reached the yard and saw what the wolves were circling.

It was a naked man, clutching his arm, dark blood running between his fingers and dripping down its length. His eyes glowed red. His lips were pulled back in a snarl as feral as Maigrat's had been earlier, revealing gleaming white fangs.

His arm wasn't the only thing smeared with blood. His mouth was, too, and on the ground . . .

On the ground lay a child, a girl in a white dress, golden hair spread across the ground, sightless eyes staring up at the never-changing moon.

Her throat had been torn out.

I swallowed hard, gorge rising.

Suddenly, Maigrat was human again. "Caught him in bat form," she said to Jakob. "Tried to fly, but I got a mouthful of his wing."

"The girl?"

"Dead when we got here."

"What was a child like that doing out here alone?"

"Wasn't," Maigrat said. She glanced back at the house. "Parents and a toddler, probably her little brother, in there. All dead . . . torn apart. Not just their throats. If I hadn't seen this thing sprout wings, I would have thought it was a werewolf did it." She shook her head. "Don't know what a family like that was doing out here at night. Traveling between villages, maybe, something went wrong, couldn't make it to safety before sunset. Took shelter, but it wasn't enough."

Four dead, I thought. *An entire family. This little girl must have seen her mother and father and brother die, torn apart in front of her, she tried to run, but she only made it this far . . .*

And then I felt anger ... fury ... directed at the person I sought to meet. Who could Shape something like this, a world where unspeakable horror like this was even possible? Who would think of such a world as a place where they wanted to spend the rest of their lives?

Jakob got down from his horse, walked over to the naked man. "Do you serve Queen Patricia?" he said.

The man spat on the ground. "She is nothing to me. I serve the Protector."

Jakob cocked his head to one side. "The Protector? Who is that?"

The man laughed. "You'll find out soon enough." He stood, then, his naked body smeared with blood that looked black as tar in the moonlight, and I saw to my disgust that he was sexually aroused. "The Protector is stronger than your queen, or the vampires' queen. The Protector will rule this valley. The Protector will kill you all."

"Perhaps," Jakob said. "But you will not live to see it."

He nodded to Maigrat. She melted back into wolf-shape—and then the entire Pack leaped at the man.

He changed in an instant into a giant bat-creature, but the werewolves pulled him from the air and ...

I swung myself out of the saddle and dropped to my hands and knees, vomiting into the weeds of the yard as the dying rogue's screams, mingled with wet rending and tearing sounds, echoed from the walls of the farmyard. Jakob paid me no mind, his gaze locked on the pack.

One of whom was Eric. Stomach emptied, I sat on my haunches, and saw him, in young-wolf form, raise his head and look in my direction, muzzle wet and glistening in the moonlight, something long and stringy hanging from his teeth.

Suddenly, the wolves backed away from the carrion, spitting and heaving, like cats trying to rid themselves of hairballs. Maigrat emerged from the pack and turned human. She wiped her hand across her bloody mouth, making a black smear in the moonlight. "There's something wrong with that one," she choked out. "All vampires taste terrible, but that one . . ."

"We've heard that before when rogues are taken," Jakob said. "Pull everyone back. It's time to move on."

I got heavily to my feet. There was a canteen attached to my saddle. I retrieved it, rinsed my mouth, spat, and rinsed again.

"Mount up," Jakob commanded behind me. "We still have a long ride before we reach the border."

I did as I was told, and, as we rode from the farmyard, kept my eyes straight ahead, not wanting to see what was left of the rogue or his child-victim . . .

. . . but it did little good. My imagination filled in the blanks.

The sooner I'm out of this hellish world the better. If Stephanie is the Shaper . . .

She had to be. Why else would she have gone to all this trouble to capture me?

But Queen Patricia had gone to just as much trouble. Stephanie had snared me. Patricia had snared Karl. What if *Patricia* were the Shaper, and I was heading farther away from her, and Karl, with every passing minute?

We'll cross the border tonight. The werewolves will take me to their queen. Then I'll know.

Until then, there was nothing I could do but ride, sneeze occasionally, and try not to think about the dead child in the farmyard . . . the naked man, smeared with blood, aroused by his own human butchery . . . and the sounds the wolves had made as they tore him apart.

I was not very successful.

On his third night as a prisoner, as the mantelpiece clock struck midnight and Karl stood on the balcony, staring up at the moonlit wall of the tower, wondering if he could climb it, someone at last appeared—not through the door, but behind him, hovering in mid-air on black bat-wings, illuminated by the lamplight from his room.

Karl felt more than heard the thing's arrival, spun, and took an involuntary step back. Black-furred and humanoid but with the head of a bat, and prominent fangs, it was a creature of nightmare—and although Karl had seen more than his share of nightmare creatures in his journeys through the Labyrinth, this one exuded an exceptional air of menace. It could hardly do otherwise, with pinpricks of bloody light shining deep within its eyes. Not to mention that faint hint of corruption in the blast of air from its wings, which he had first noticed when flown to the castle.

Karl stiffened his spine and forced himself to hold his ground after that initial involuntary retreat. "Who are you, and what do you want? Why am I here?"

The thing bared its fangs, but the answer to his question came from behind him.

"You are here because Queen Patricia wants you here," said a female voice, and he spun to see the locked door opened at last, and a woman standing in it, framed by torchlight in the corridor beyond. She wore a sleek black dress, the clothing equivalent of the bat-creature's black fur, cut so low her full breasts were barely contained. Her skin was pale as moonlight, her lips red as roses, and Karl felt an unaccustomed surge of desire that shocked him, even though the red sparks in her eyes were proof enough this was just another Shaped creature. The Shaped held no attraction for him. Only one very real woman ever had. And yet . . .

He licked his lips. "And you are here to take me to her?"

"I am."

Karl glanced over his shoulder. The winged bat-creature had landed on the balcony and folded its wings, which made it look rather more Satanic than less. "And why is . . ." he started to say, "it," thought better of it, and instead continued, " . . . *he* here?"

"To ensure you do nothing foolish." The woman stood to one side and swept her hand across her body, indicating Karl should step through the door.

Breathing heavily, trying to tamp down the completely unwarranted lust his body seemed to be committed to and was currently expressing most uncomfortably, he edged past her. She did nothing to get out of his way, so that, unavoidably, he brushed against her breasts. He gasped, the contact almost bringing him to orgasm.

She laughed, a sound that made him want to turn and ravish her right there. And then, like a light switch being flipped, his desire vanished, though its physical manifestation took moments longer to subside. He stepped back from her as though she'd pushed him. "What are you?" he whispered hoarsely, but of course, he already knew the answer: vampire, or this world's version of it.

The ancient legends of vampires did not make them sound sexually appealing in the slightest, but clearly the Shaper of this world—Queen Patricia, perhaps, though he still had no inner sense that the Shaper was anywhere near—was working with more recent source material.

The ability to irresistibly seduce your food source so that it willingly came to you to be drained of blood clearly had advantages to vampires, now that—as his head cleared—he thought of it. Apparently, it could be turned off as easily as it, and he, had been "turned on," to use a phrase he had heard in worlds based on more recent versions of the First World than he remembered.

Not for the first time, Karl wished he was more familiar with the popular culture of the past few decades in the First World, on which many of the worlds he'd already visited had been based. Shawna seemed steeped in it. The last world they had been in had drawn on the works of Jules Verne, whom he had at least heard of. The Shakespearean world from which he'd entered Shawna's had been something of a relief in that regard, although the necessity of framing all conversations in iambic pentameter and ending with a rhyming couplet had become wearying over time.

"What am I?" she said. "I am the queen's lady-in-waiting, sent to bring you to her. My name is Seraphina DeWinter. So if you have quite recovered yourself," her eyes flicked toward his crotch and back again, and his face heated, "we should proceed to the throne room. Follow me."

Karl had emerged from the room onto a landing of a spiral staircase that wound around the tower, both up and down from his prison. Looking back into the room, Karl saw the back of a naked man as he pulled a belted black robe from the wardrobe and put it on. When he turned toward Karl and Seraphina, Karl saw that, like her, his face was extremely pale, and he had remarkably red lips. *If he wanted, could he arouse desire in me, as well?* Karl thought.

Karl had been in many worlds he did not like, in his search for a Shaper strong enough to journey from world to world and gather the *hokhmah* of each to take to Ygrair and save the Labyrinth. A world where the Shaped beings had the power to give the desires of his body primacy over his will and intellect, though, was a new level of horror. He felt disgust, at himself, at the vampires, and at the Shaper who had created them.

Whom, he suspected, he was about to meet—though his body had betrayed him another way, if so, since the Shurak nanotechnology within it had so far failed to recognize his proximity to her.

His eyes narrowed as he thought about that, while following Seraphina down the stairs and then through grand hallways and narrow corridors, in turn being followed by the menacing man. *Perhaps I cannot register her power because she* has *no power*, he thought. *Perhaps she used all of it in creating her world, holding nothing back, and it has not regenerated.*

If that were the case, this could be a world that had spun wildly out of the control of its Shaper. Of all the worlds he had been in that he did not like, those topped the list.

They entered a hall much broader and higher-ceilinged than any they had gone through before. Two men in black surcoats over gilded hauberks, iron-helmeted, wearing swords and holding halberds, guarded a massive double door that stood open. Candlelight spilled from it, brighter than the flickering torches illuminating all the castle's corridors they had passed through thus far.

They reached the door, and despite himself, Karl gasped a little at his first sight of the throne room.

"Candlelit" described it in roughly the way "bright" described the disk of the sun. More candles than Karl had ever seen in one place lit the vast space: candles in tall silver candelabra lining the pillars that held up the vaulted roof, more candles in more candelabra attached to the pillars, candles in wheel-shaped fixtures hanging from the ceiling, and huge candles, as big around as a man's arm and half as tall as Karl himself, between the pillars lining the approach to the throne, and, a dozen to a side, framing the throne itself.

The floor and roof were black and the candles were white, but the pillars were blood-red, as was the intricately carved wood of the throne, on a four-step dais at the far end. Behind and above the tapestry, an enormous Gothic window stood open to the now-night air, the motionless full moon centered within it. Below the window hung a tapestry depicting the castle as Karl had seen it on first entering this world, lit by the moon, windows aglow, black, winged shapes soaring around its towers.

A sculpture topped the throne's high back: a black bat, wings spread, mouth agape to reveal ivory fangs. Its eyes, enormous rubies, glittered red.

The man who had helped escort Karl to the throne room bowed at the entrance and departed, leaving him to approach the throne, and the woman on it, in the sole company of Seraphina, the lady-in-waiting. He could see no one else in all that candlelit space. Perhaps court was not in session, or perhaps all of the queen's retainers had other business this night.

Or perhaps, he thought, *Queen Patricia, as the Shaper, has some notion of who I am, or, at least, that I come from outside her world, and does not wish that information causing confusion and consternation among her Shaped minions.*

He would find out soon enough.

He and Seraphina crossed the black floor, footsteps echoing off of the distant walls. The candles were so numerous he could feel their heat, as though lit fireplaces burned all around, but he could also feel the cool mountain air flowing into the hall through the open window. It made many of the candles flicker, but none, so far as he could tell, guttered out.

The woman on the throne wore a black dress as low-cut as his escort's, but with a high collar that glittered red—inset with rubies, he guessed. She had the same pale-white complexion and blood-red lips, and he felt renewed doubt. Perhaps Queen Patricia was not the Shaper at all, but another Shaped creature. The Shurak technology within his blood, infuriatingly, still gave no clue.

He gathered himself, preparing to speak—only to stumble to a stop as, through the open window, a bat-winged creature burst into the throne room. This one swept down and landed between him and his escort and the throne, the blast of air from its wings making him close his eyes and turn his head. When he turned back, the winged creature was gone and instead a naked man, with skin almost as black as the fur of the creature he had been a moment before, stood before the throne.

The man bowed, straightened, and said, "My apologies, Your Majesty, but there is news."

The queen, who sat askew, leaning her elbow on the right armrest, legs nonchalantly crossed, waved a languorous hand. "Yes, Nicolas?" she said.

"The pack that attacked the village of Zarozje two nights ago has crossed the border into Queen Stephanie's realm," the naked man—Nicolas—said.

"And is the erstwhile companion of this one," she indicated Karl, and Nicolas glanced over his shoulder, "still with them?"

"Yes, Your Majesty," Nicolas said, returning his attention to the queen.

Karl stiffened. Shawna had been taken by werewolves two nights ago?

"You have done good service, following the pack from afar since Antoine's attack on them failed," the queen said. "I give you command of his flight. He will be engaged in . . . other duties."

"Thank you, Majesty."

"You are dismissed."

The man bowed, and then in an instant flowed back into winged shape and flew out through the open window, blowing a blast of warm, fetid, graveyard-smelling air into Karl's face in the process.

"Now," said the queen, straightening in her throne and assuming a more regal air, "who are you, and how did you come into my world?"

Karl walked forward to answer that question, but his mind, for a moment, was elsewhere.

The werewolves had Shawna.

I hope she'll be all right, he thought. *Our quest has hardly begun.*

Then he looked at the vampire queen on the blood-red throne and wondered if perhaps his concern would be better focused on himself.

TWELVE

"THERE IS NO palace," Jakob had told me without explanation, and in between focusing on more immediate concerns like terror and disgust and throwing up and sneezing, my mind had occasionally returned to that cryptic statement as we rode through the night. We crossed the border into Queen Stephanie's realm (or so I was told) an hour or two after midnight, though there was nothing to mark it that I could see.

"This land is well defended," Jakob told me when I asked. "There are patrols everywhere. No rogue could do here what that filthy creature we killed tonight did in the Lands Between."

It was still well before dawn when, exhausted (at least, I was—riding is hard enough, but sneezing every few minutes *really* takes its toll), we finally rode up to the gates of the werewolf queen's royal hall.

"Royal hall" sounds better than "hole in the ground."

Okay, okay, it had a *somewhat* impressive entrance, which might not have looked out of place on a Las Vegas casino. Four columns supported a classical pediment, one column, on the far left, carved into the shape of a nude man, one, on the far right, carved into the shape of a nude woman, and the two inner columns carved into the shapes of two wolves, female to the left, male to the right. A mixture of snarling wolves and handsome human faces also filled the . . . whatever you call the triangular space inside the pediment. (Tympanum, maybe? Or was that the Latin name for ear drum?

Architectural history had been part of my university studies in art, but it had been a while.)

In any event, the message was clear: "Here There Be Werewolves." That would have been more alarming if I hadn't been surrounded by werewolves for the past couple of days. As it was, I was just glad to finally get off that blasted horse.

I sneezed one last time as I dismounted, earning a final scornful look from the mare. She'd flicked her ears regularly when I'd first begun sneezing, but she'd soon stopped, almost pointedly so. I felt she disapproved of me and was as glad to be rid of me as I was to be rid of her. Since her regular rider was undoubtedly prone to turning into a giant, slavering wolf at the drop of a robe, that really put me in my place.

All of the pack members still in wolf form flowed back into human shape and unhurriedly donned their robes. (I looked away as Eric's slim form appeared.) There were guards standing on either side of the closed double doors of smooth bronze, which shone in the light of torches, burning in brackets on the pillars. The guards, a man and a woman, wore flowing white robes they could presumably doff at a moment's notice, but also carried shields and spears and had swords belted at their waists. (I wondered if the sword belts had some kind of special quick-release buckle.)

Their eyes tracked me as I approached, guided by Jakob, who had taken my arm and was leading me forward. Even though the guards were currently human, red sparks gleamed deep in their pupils. Clearly, the Shaper had been a fan of that overly dramatic bit of bioluminescence, although I didn't see it in all the werewolves' eyes all the time. Perhaps they could turn it on and off at will, depending on how intimidating they wanted to appear. "The queen has requested this one be brought to her," Jakob said to the guard on the right, the woman.

She nodded. "Queen Stephanie was apprised of your approach

and awaits you now in the Great Hall." She and her compatriot turned toward the doors, took hold of the upright handles set at the center, and pulled them open. I fully expected them to creak in horror-movie fashion, but they opened silently.

The corridor beyond was carved out of black bedrock—basalt, maybe?—and lit by more torches. Corridors opened to left and right, and, glancing back as we continued, I saw some of the pack peeling off into those alternate passages. By the time we reached the end of the first stretch of corridor, my only companions were Jakob, Eric, and, worryingly, "I-look-forward-to-watching-your-interrogation-and-possibly-eating-your-entrails" Maigrat. I glanced at Eric. He walked with his head down, eyes on his bare feet, and did not meet my gaze.

We came to stairs, which descended . . . and descended . . . and descended some more, one long straight stretch of stairs that, by the time we reached a level floor again, I thought must have taken us the equivalent of a five- or six-story building into the Earth, if you could properly call a Shaped world Earth. Torches provided the illumination, and that puzzled me, just as it always has in me-dieval movies, because honestly, how long does a torch burn? Was there some full-time torch-maintenance werewolf who spent all his time replacing them as they sputtered out, like the workers I'd read about whose entire career was painting the bridge spanning Scotland's Firth of Forth, over and over, reaching the end and then beginning again?

Or maybe, I thought, the Shaper of this world—Queen Stepha-nie, I hoped—had simply decreed that in her world torches would burn all night, just like she'd decreed that the Moon would always be full and always hang in the same place in the sky. Apparently, she'd also decreed that her torches wouldn't coat the walls and ceiling with soot because both seemed to be soot-free. Nor did smoke hang in the air, but I did see openings in the ceiling I took to be ventilation shafts, so perhaps that was why.

The corridor was much wider now, and not quite so basic-black. There were tiles on the floor, black and white, and white sculptures— again, a mixture of naked people and, I suppose, equally-naked-but-not-quite-so-blatant-about-it wolves. "Former rulers and nobles, in both their forms," Jakob explained when he saw me looking at them.

"Ah," I said. In my world, royalty didn't usually go in for being sculpted in the nude, but *O tempora, o mores!* I supposed. I hoped Queen Stephanie would at least be clothed when at last I met her.

We finally reached the end of the corridor, where two more guards, another male/female pair, opened another set of smooth, glowing-in-the-torchlight bronze doors, and there we were, in the Great Hall.

Light from a glowing sphere high above revealed a vast space, the floor tiled in black and white, the vaulted ceiling held up by fluted columns that looked to have been carved out of solid rock. Mysterious alcoves and doors pocked the distant, shadowed walls. It felt a bit like a cathedral, except that, instead of the crucified Christ hanging at the end of it, there was the giant, sculpted head of a snarling wolf, its eyes enormous rubies, its tusklike teeth made of glittering crystal, the rest of it carved, like the ceiling and the columns, from the natural rock.

Beneath that rather arresting sculpture, Queen Stephanie sat on a throne likewise carved from stone. She wore a black robe, trimmed with white fur. A circlet of black stone with a single ruby set in the front served as a crown, and in her right hand she held a golden goblet. Her black hair hung loose around her shoulders, and in her dark eyes, twin sparks of fire burned.

She looked utterly barbaric and werewolfish, and for a moment

I despaired. How could this magnificent creature be a Shaper, some ordinary woman from my own world?

Then she leaned forward, the red light in her eyes faded, and she said, "So. How are things in the old alma mater? Have they ever fixed the air-conditioning in the cafeteria?" and my doubts vanished.

"Um," I said.

Maigrat glared at me. "The queen asked you a question!"

"Um," I said again. "I don't . . . actually remember."

Queen Stephanie smiled. "But you know what I'm talking about."

"Yes," I said.

"Which tells me what I suspected. You're from the First World." She sat back. "I felt your arrival. A 'disturbance in the Force,' you might say. That's why I sent a messenger bird to the pack, told them to look for you, find you, and bring you to me." She put her goblet on the arm of her throne, and came down the steps toward me, silent in bare feet, long legs flashing with each step as the robe parted. "You're young. Early twenties?"

"Late twenties," I said.

Jakob and Maigrat were both looking at us in puzzlement. Even Eric had raised his head.

The queen ignored them. "Those aren't First World clothes, though," she said, walking around me.

"No," I said. "They're from the next world over—the last one I was in."

She'd come around to my front again and stopped. "You didn't come directly from the First World?"

I shook my head. "No. We came through a Portal from another Shaped world."

She frowned. "That's possible?"

I spread my hands. "I'm here, aren't I?"

"And the pack says you were with someone else."

"Karl Yatsar."

She frowned harder. "I don't know that name."

"He's a friend of Ygrair's."

Her eyebrows raised. "Ygrair has friends? Then things *have* changed. Well. We'll talk more about all this in a moment. I have other duties first."

She returned to the throne, turned, sat, and looked at Maigrat and Eric, who had lowered his gaze once more. "I grieve with you over the death of your sister, Maigrat," Queen Stephanie said formally.

"She died in your service, Your Majesty," Maigrat said. "As we must all be prepared to do."

A look of pain flickered across the queen's face. "As so many have, Maigrat. As did Geoffrey." She took a deep breath and looked to Eric. "And this young man is now of the pack?"

"A life for a life, Your Majesty. He slew Elena at the behest of the priest of Zarozje. You forbid us to kill humans . . ."

"The Pact forbids it," Queen Stephanie said, a hint of reprimand in her voice.

Maigrat bowed slightly. "My apologies, Your Majesty. The *Pact* forbids the slaying of humans. The only way he could repay his debt to the pack—and to you—was to take Elena's place. And so I bit him, and now he is one of us."

Queen Stephanie nodded. "I judge it a fair exchange. Well done."

I thought about pointing out that the Pact also forbade making Eric a werewolf against his will, but somehow, I didn't think my input was wanted.

Queen Stephanie descended from the throne again. She stepped close to Eric, reached out, and lifted his chin with her hand. His blue eyes met her brown ones. "You are forgiven, child," she said. "You did as you were told by a man you hold in high esteem. But you are no longer under his sway. From this day forward, you are my creature." She moved her hand from his chin to his forehead.

"Thou art my child, Eric of Zarozje. Thy heart and thy soul art mine to command. Swear it."

"I am your child," Eric said softly, eyes never wavering from her face. "My heart and my soul are yours to command."

"So mote it be."

"So mote it be."

Stephanie lifted her hand. "You are dismissed. The guards outside will point you to quarters."

Eric bowed, turned, and went out without a backward glance, and I was convinced in that moment that the boy I had known and pitied and tried to comfort had vanished forever.

The queen then turned to Maigrat. "There are wine and food in the butler's chamber, but I have dismissed the butler so that I might have a private chat with our new guest. Please take them into the privy council chamber."

Maigrat's eyes kindled red for a moment—so maybe it wasn't entirely under her control—but she bowed and said, "Of course, Your Majesty," turned left, and disappeared among the pillars.

"Jakob, stay with us," the queen said.

"Of course, Your Majesty," he said in his turn.

I glanced at him, then at her. "You don't trust me?"

Queen Stephanie laughed. "Of course, I don't trust you. I don't know how Trish managed it, but I know she's behind your being here. And I'll bet I know why. Somehow, she thinks you can help her seize control." She gestured in the direction Maigrat had taken. "Walk with me."

While I tried to make sense of what she'd just said—"Trish" was presumably Queen Patricia of the vampires, but if Stephanie was the Shaper, how could Trish seize control of the world?—I followed her through the forest of fluted columns. A door in the wall beyond opened into a small meeting chamber, its floor the same black-and-white tile, its walls the same black stone, although they were hung with tapestries showing wolves chasing deer on one side, and wolves chasing elk on the other. At the far end, a blaze burned brightly in a fireplace. There was a second, closed door next to the hearth, made of the same blood-red wood as the oval table at the room's center, around which rested six black chairs.

The queen sat in the chair at the table's head, then gestured for me to sit at the foot. Jakob sketched a quick bow, then exited. The door opened again almost at once (revealing that he was standing guard outside) to admit Maigrat, bearing a tray upon which rested a bottle, two glasses, and a covered platter.

I blanched at the thought of wine at this time of morning. All I really wanted was a bed, preferably one that didn't also involve (as it well might, if I were judged a spy) iron shackles, rats the size of small dogs, a slop bucket, and stale bread and water.

Come to think of it, maybe I *would* have some wine.

Maigrat poured for both of us, looking daggers at me while she did so. The wine, a well-chilled, well-balanced white—sauvignon blanc, perhaps?—went down very easily. Maybe a little *too* easily.

The uncovering of the platter revealed bread, cheese, and sliced ham, and I made the effort to eat, even though I wasn't very hungry, just so I wasn't drinking early-morning wine on a night-empty stomach.

Food served, Maigrat withdrew to the door, no doubt itching to rip me apart if I seemed to pose the slightest threat to the queen.

"So tell me what Trish's mad scheme is," Queen Stephanie said pleasantly. "And how she managed it. And then . . ."

"Then?" I said, taking another sip of wine.

"Then," she said, "you'll tell me how I can make use of it instead."

I opened my mouth, then closed it. I didn't have an answer.

Fortunately, I was momentarily saved from needing one by the arrival, through the second door into the room, of a gangly adolescent wolf with black-and-silver fur, larger than Eric's wolf form but still, clearly, not full-grown, who bounded into the Great Hall, licked Queen Stephanie's hand, and transformed in an instant into a gangly teenaged boy.

A naked teenaged boy. I looked down at the floor. *Nope, still not used to that*, I thought.

"Is this her?" the boy said. I peered up between my lashes. He was donning a robe, red rather than black, but, like the queen's, trimmed in white fur. "Is it, Mom?

My head snapped up. *Wait. What?*

THIRTEEN

KARL TORE HIS mind away from whatever terrors Shawna might be facing in the realm of the werewolves to address the vampire queen lounging on the throne before him, whose eyes, like the eyes of the carved bat that crowned her throne, gleamed blood-red.

"I am a friend of Ygrair's," he said, in answer to her question. "It is in her service that I and my companion entered your world."

"Ygrair?" Queen Patricia leaned forward, eyes narrowed. "You claim to be from the *First World*?"

"I do. I *am*."

"And how was this miracle accomplished?" she said scornfully. "Ygrair never even hinted it might be possible for anyone else from the First World to enter our world. Am I to believe you came through the Graduation Portal?" Her eyes narrowed further. "I believe you are lying. I believe Stephanie has somehow found a way to make me *think* you come from outside this world, in the hope she might worm a spy into my confidence."

"I am not lying," Karl said. "I do not know who Stephanie is. Ygrair sent me into the Labyrinth and gave me the ability to open Portals between the worlds. She did not send me directly into your world, and, no, she did not send me through the Graduation Portal. That no longer exists. The school has been destroyed."

Queen Patricia's eyes widened. "Destroyed? How? Why?"

Karl sighed. "The tale is a long one, Your Majesty." Queen Patricia was not his queen, but there was no point in being provocative.

"Might we discuss it somewhere more comfortable than with you up there and me down here, in the oppressive heat of this most impressive display of candles?"

The queen regarded him for a long, silent moment, unblinking. He supposed it made sense that a creature that could move unnaturally fast could also stand unnaturally still. He found her regard unnerving, as no doubt she intended.

"Very well," she said at last. "We will talk in my quarters." She turned to the lady-in-waiting. "Seraphina, you are dismissed."

Seraphina frowned. "Your Majesty, are you sure that's wise . . ." Her voice trailed off and she visibly wilted—something he would not have thought possible, based on his own experience of the . . . force . . . of her personality—before the queen's icy gaze. "Of course, Your Majesty." She hurried out of the throne room, back through the grand doors through which she and Karl had entered.

The queen stood. "This way," she said, leading Karl to a side door off to his left. Beyond lay a short corridor lit by only two candelabra, instead of a hundred. The ironbound door at the end of that hallway swung open to her touch, and she ushered him into . . .

He looked around. "This is not a medieval room," he commented mildly. Judging from what he had seen in Shawna's world, it was closer in time and design to her era: comfortable furniture, glass-topped coffee table, paintings on the walls, throw rugs on the stone floor. An archway at the back showed a bed that, although appropriately royal-sized, was definitely not the four-poster one might have expected. Nor was there the preponderance of red and black he had seen elsewhere. The walls were pale green, the rugs green and blue and brown. It was, compared to the throne room, soothing.

Not that Karl felt soothed, alone with the vampire queen and Shaper of this world.

"There are times," Queen Patricia said, "that I miss the First World. Sit down." She indicated a comfortable-looking couch upholstered in pale blue, with throw pillows patterned in green leaves.

"Yes, Your Majesty." Karl sat as instructed.

"You don't need to keep calling me that," she said. "Not in here. Out there," she nodded at the door, "yes. But in here, I'm just Patricia Morrison from Salmon Arm, British Columbia." She raised an eyebrow at him. "Do you know where that is?"

"No," Karl said. "But I do know of British Columbia. The westernmost province of the Dominion of Canada. The capital is Victoria, I believe . . . on Vancouver Island."

She inclined her head. "A point in favor of your telling me some version of the truth. Yes. And in British Columbia, I was simply called Trish. You may do likewise."

"All right . . . Trish."

"Wine?" she said then, going to a side table beneath a painting of her castle, lit by the moon, black-winged creatures flying around its high towers, the model, clearly, for the giant tapestry behind the throne. "I only have red." She chuckled. "And, I know, I'm supposed to say things like, 'I never drink . . . wine,'" (for some reason, she said the words in a thick Eastern European accent) "but, in fact, I quite enjoy it. Though not as much as blood, of course."

Karl had no idea what she was going on about, when it came to the wine, but he was happy enough to take a glass of it—even happier it *wasn't* blood—though he only sipped it. It was quite good. "I do not understand that," he said, setting the glass down on the coffee table. "How could you make yourself into a vampire? Shapers cannot Shape themselves." *Except for Shawna, who somehow managed to make herself forget she was a Shaper,* he thought, but set that ongoing mystery aside.

"I didn't," Trish said. She took a rather irritated sip of her own wine.

"Then how . . . ?" Karl began, but Trish waved a hand, the

vampire queen showing through in that imperious dismissal of his concerns in favor of her own.

"I did not bring you in here to tell you my story," she said. "Not yet. I brought you here for you to tell me yours. Explain to me what is going on or, at least, what you *claim* is going on."

"Of course." Karl told her about the attack on the school . . . Ygrair being wounded and forced to flee to her own Shaped world in the Labyrinth . . . the weakening of her hold on the other Shaped worlds . . . the depredations of the Adversary, who was seizing control of worlds not his own . . . the need for someone to go world to world, find those worlds' Shapers, and gather their *hokhmah*, to take it to Ygrair and enable her to save all the worlds from destruction.

He spoke of his discovery and rescue of Shawna in her world, and their success in the last world, though he did not go into detail about Robur's failure to cooperate, and how only his death had released his *hokhmah* to Shawna: he had not been present for most of what had happened there, anyway.

Patricia Morrison listened intently and quietly, occasionally sipping from her wine. "Where is this 'Adversary' now?" she said when Karl had finished.

"Trapped in the world of my companion," he said.

"Are you sure?" She leaned forward as she spoke. "Absolutely certain?"

"As certain as I can be," he said. Now was not the time to mention his concerns about the shirt he had left behind, stained with his blood, blood that contained the Shurak nanotechnology that allowed him to open Portals between Shaped worlds. He frowned at her instead. "Why?"

She sat back with an air of disappointment. "Because, if you are telling the truth, and such a man exists, I thought perhaps his presence here might explain certain things happening in this world. Things that go against everything we Shaped."

Karl blinked. "*We?*"

Patricia poured more wine for both of them. "I am not the only Shaper in this world." For some reason, her mouth quirked, and her voice changed and deepened, as if she were quoting someone else. "'No. There is another.'"

Karl gaped—something he very rarely did. Then he frowned—something he did quite often. "That's impossible."

Patricia matched him frown for frown. "Clearly, it is not."

"Ygrair never suggested . . ." Karl bit off his protestation. He would not complain about Ygrair to an ordinary Shaper.

"Didn't she?" Patricia said. "You claim to be her friend, and yet you do not know this? She certainly taught her students it was possible. Your companion . . . this 'Shawna' . . . should know of the possibility, too, if she attended the school as you claim."

Karl had said nothing about Shawna's lack of any memory of school, or of being a Shaper. He did not say anything now.

"It was Ygrair who placed me and Stephanie together in this world," Patricia continued. "It was she who told us our plan for it would work."

"Your . . . plan?"

"You asked, how did I become a vampire. You noted, Shapers cannot Shape themselves."

"Or anyone from the First World," Karl said.

"So Ygrair taught us all. But she also taught us that we would be subject to the natural laws of our worlds, and she taught us that two people could Shape a world together if they chose. So Steph and I thought, what if we took a world together, and *she* Shaped vampires, and *I* Shaped werewolves, and *she* allowed herself to be bitten by a werewolf, and *I* allowed myself to be bitten . . . killed, in fact . . . by a vampire, and . . ." She spread her hands. "It worked."

Karl nodded, glad to understand what he was dealing with at

last—and impressed despite himself. "A brilliant strategy," he said. "My congratulations."

He studied Patricia. Now, separated from her by only a table's distance, he realized he could at last, though only with intense concentration, detect just the faintest whiff of Shaperhood—Shaperiness?—about her. But very faint. Part of that, he thought, might be related to the rather uncomfortable fact that she was, in fact, dead. Undead, he supposed was the term, but still . . .

But there might be another reason, as well, one he had already considered and now thought even more likely. "But afterward," he continued, "You had nothing left. You can no longer Shape."

"No," Trish said. "Neither of us can. We drained ourselves in the Shaping of the World, and our power has never returned. Perhaps partly because of how we allowed ourselves to be altered." She raised a hand and flexed it. "We thought we would never need Shaping power again, once we were what we wanted to be. I am a vampire. Undead. Undying. Fast and powerful. Able to change into a giant bat and fly wherever I wish. And Steph . . ." She made a face. "Steph is a werewolf. Also fast, also powerful, able to change into a giant wolf whenever she wishes. And, though ordinary werewolves are not immortal, since she is also a Shaper, and Shapers do not age in Shaped worlds, she is as immortal as I, barring accidents."

"And that was enough for you?" Karl said. He did not see the appeal himself.

"It was," Patricia said. "Until it wasn't. Until Stephanie brutally betrayed our friendship and my trust, and the Pact collapsed." She did not look at him as she said that. She had plunged her gaze into her wine, as though she saw something in its scarlet depths he could not see.

"The Pact?" Karl said, thinking, *There has been a falling-out between the two Shapers of this world, and yet, we must gather the* hokhmah *of* both *if we are to take it to Ygrair.* He grimaced. *That could be a problem.*

"We did not Shape a world of terror and bloodshed," Patricia said, raising her gaze once more. "The backstory we crafted for this world was that everyone outside of this God-protected valley was destroyed in the Great Cataclysm, a slow-moving wave of divinely decreed disintegration that spread out from the original site of the Garden of Eden, eliminating all humans, all werewolves, and vampires, and all signs of their existence, returning the world to its untouched wild state. Humans already living in this valley were protected, and then to this valley fled the only survivors of the cataclysm, vampires and werewolves who received a vision from God telling them that here they would find Sanctuary, but only if they swore to live in peace with the humans that theretofore had been their prey.

"The story goes that, in concert with Abbot Nathan Costello," the queen's mouth quirked in amusement again, for no reason Karl could grasp, "of what has now become the Mother Church, they agreed to a grand Pact. The vampires were granted control over the north end of the Great Valley, the werewolves control of the south. Humans could live their lives as they had been, in whichever kingdom they wished, or in the free villages in what is known as the Lands Between. Werewolves and vampires were not to feed on humans or change them into werewolves or vampires without their consent. Peace reigned.

"In the story the people know, Stephanie and I are the children of now-dead kings and queens, born in this valley. I, in the Shaped memory of my servants, grew up here, a vampire from birth—which is possible in this world, as it is possible to be a werewolf from birth, because we Shaped it so. There are servants in Stephanie's underground lair who likewise remember her childhood and youth.

"But ten years ago, for no reason I can discern, Stephanie led an attack on a band of my people in the Lands Between. Without warning. Without any expression of grievances, even though our courts were in regular communication with each other. Completely unprovoked."

"Were you there?"

"No, but my consort was. He saw her, and he knows her well. Others who had met her saw her, too. It was Stephanie. There is no doubt. He also recognized other of the werewolves with her, werewolves he knew personally—many of our people had friends—or so they thought—in the other kingdom. Many of our people were killed, before the werewolves withdrew. My consort barely escaped with his life. Other attacks took place, all through the Lands Between. I expelled her envoys to my court. My own envoys to Stephanie's kingdom never returned.

"Ever since, we have been at war. And as war spread, shortly after it began, rogues appeared, vampires and werewolves who have abandoned the Pact. Whole villages have been slaughtered by them. Farmers have been driven from their lands. From the very beginning of the war, I have forbidden my subjects from attacking humans, and yet vampire attacks continue. I have heard—though how much credence I should give the tale, I'm not sure—that Stephanie has issued similar orders to her werewolves: yet, werewolf attacks continue, as well.

"Now the humans live inside walled villages, like Zarozje, near which you were captured. They hate and fear vampires and werewolves and kill on sight any they come across. And thus, the Lands Between have become a place of terrible violence. And all of it—*all* of it—is Stephanie's fault." She snatched up her glass, gulped more wine, swiped her hand across her mouth, and slammed the goblet on the coffee table so hard Karl was surprised its glass top didn't crack. "Under the cover of the chaos in the Lands Between, I am convinced she is plotting an all-out assault on my realm!"

For a moment, her face turned demonic: angular, pale, terrifying, her eyes completely black except for the hellfire sparks within them. Then she took a deep breath and became fully human once more. She poured herself more wine, took another sip. "In the First World, she was jealous of me," she said moodily. "But I never thought that jealousy could lead to something like this. I thought we had moved beyond it."

"Why was she jealous?" Karl asked. He took another swallow of his own wine.

Patricia shrugged. "The usual reasons. I was the more attractive and had my pick of boys . . . including one or two she had her eye on. I'll admit, I took full advantage of it. But they were just meaningless flings. Long-term attachments were impractical in the school, unless you committed to being a joint Shaper with your loved one. I had fun with the boys, but I never considered Shaping a world with one. In the world Stephanie and I planned, I knew I could Shape the ideal mate, if I chose . . . and I chose." She raised her voice. "Blood of my heart. Reveal yourself. Come meet our guest."

Karl heard nothing, but suddenly sensed something behind him. His heart started pounding, and his breath caught in his throat. Terror gripped him, as unreasoning as the lust he had felt for Seraphina earlier. It took all his willpower to twist his head around.

A tall, elegantly slim man stood there. He wore black—black pants, a black dinner jacket, and a black shirt—relieved only by a diamond stickpin in the shape of a bat, with ruby flecks for eyes, at his throat. He smiled slightly at Karl, revealing the tips of sharp fangs against ruby-red lips. Flecks of bloody fire burned deep within his pupils. His hair was as black as his clothing, his complexion as pale as Patricia's. "Good evening," he said, in a deep voice with the same Eastern European accent Trish had affected earlier. "And welcome." He bowed slightly. "I am Count Dracula."

Bram Stoker's novel had been one of the last books Karl had

read before Ygrair literally dropped into his life. His fear faded away, Dracula clearly withdrawing it deliberately, as Seraphina had earlier withdrawn her carnal influence. It made Karl uneasy to think that he, a creature of the First World—a real man, as opposed to a Shaped one—could be influenced so easily by Shaped creatures. That wasn't supposed to happen.

It's because of the way they crafted the world, he thought. *They* wanted *to be subject to the powers of the werewolves and vampires, so they could* become *them. And so I—and Shawna—are subject to them, too.* He felt an unaccustomed touch of trepidation. *If they chose, they could make me one of them . . .*

He turned back to face the queen as Dracula came around the end of the couch to stand beside her. Trish took the count's hand. "Dracula is my Prince Consort," she said. "My lover, my dearest friend, my second in command."

"I am glad you found a way to make yourself happy," Karl said carefully.

Patricia's lip curled. "But I am *not* happy. I will not be happy—and let me assure you, *you will not, either*—until you tell me the truth: why did Stephanie send you to spy on me?" She leaned forward, and in the same moment, Dracula smiled slightly, and the terror reasserted itself. Karl's mouth opened, and he gaped like a landed fish, struggling to breathe as his racing heart threatened to shatter his rib cage. "I do not believe your story, Karl Yatsar," Patricia said. "I do not believe you are from the First World. I believe you are from this one, and that Stephanie faked your arrival; that she intended for me to capture you and taught you what to say. You played your part well, but I do not believe it is possible to move from one world to another. Ygrair would have told us, if it were. Your queen's scheme has failed. Now tell me, what were you sent to learn? When does she plan to attack?" Patricia's eyes drilled into his, her face going demonic again, the red light flaring deep within eyes that were now all-black. "You will answer my question. *Now.*"

Karl had never felt anything like the terror Dracula projected. He tried to protest that he was not a spy, and neither was Shawna, that everything he had told her about Ygrair, about their mission through the Labyrinth, was true, but he couldn't formulate the words, couldn't fight the paralysis of his throat . . . he felt faint . . .

"Release him," Patricia commanded, and just like that, the fear vanished. Karl slumped back on the couch, panting.

"The terror can return at any moment," the queen said softly.

"Your Majesty," Karl said, when he had regained his voice . . . he dared not call her anything else, not after that . . . "I have not lied to you. I am not a spy. I have not met Queen Stephanie. All I know of her is what you have told me."

He forced himself to squarely meet her eyes, obsidian orbs with glowing red fires deep within. Her fangs had grown and were prominent against her ruby-red lips; her face remained angular, alien. A surprisingly analytical part of his mind noted that there were three forms the vampires could take: human, bat-like, and this demonic one, which looked horribly out of place in her otherwise ordinary chambers. But, of course, the only one truly out of place here was him. He did not belong in this Shaped world or any other, except the one that maybe, someday, if Ygrair kept her word, he would Shape for himself.

Then, to his surprise, Patricia broke eye contact with him, and glanced at Dracula. "He speaks the truth," she said. "Or what he believes to be the truth."

"Thank you for believing me," Karl said to her.

The queen, her face once more human, returned her gaze to him. "It is a simple statement of fact. No human can successfully lie in my presence, if I exert my will to ascertain the truth."

"It is useful for interrogation," Dracula said. "As is my own glamor of terror."

Glamor of terror? Karl shuddered, his face still wet with a sheen of sweat. He nodded without speaking, and for the first time in a long time, took a sip of his wine. His hand shook as he put the glass back down on the table.

"I am sorry for any discomfort you experienced," Patricia said, "but I do not apologize for doubting you. Stephanie is up to something. She means to overthrow me. I am certain of it."

"From what you have told me of the situation, I can understand why you feel that way," Karl said.

"And from what you have told me of the situation, there is nothing you can do to help, even though you are . . . or at least believe you are . . . telling the truth, " Patricia said. "The Pact remains broken. Werewolves and vampires remain at war. Rogues devour humans. Everything we Shaped is crumbling into chaos. And it is Stephanie's doing."

Dracula moved behind Patricia and began kneading her shoulders, so domestic an action Karl thought Shawna would have laughed out loud at it, though he felt no such urge himself. "You are right," Karl said. "There is nothing *I* can do about it. Not on my own. But . . ."

And then he stopped, because what he was about to suggest had nothing to do with his overarching quest, the only thing he was really interested in: helping Shawna—or someone—gather the *hokhmah* of enough Shaped worlds that Ygrair could draw on it preserve the Labyrinth.

He did not care about this specific Shaped world, or any other Shaped world, for itself. The denizens of these worlds were real to themselves, of course, but to him? No. They were nothing but modified copies of people in the First World, golems shaped from the infinitely malleable clay of the Labyrinth. He did not know how long ago Stephanie and Patricia had graduated, but nobody in this world was older than however few decades that had been. This world's "history" had never happened. The heroes and villains of the past had never existed. It was all just fiction. From what he had seen of this world so far, *bad* fiction.

Shawna had not yet fully grasped that truth. For her, the people of her world had been real, even though she had seen them wiped from reality in an instant, had wiped some from that reality herself. She had tried to leave the last world they'd been in better shape (by her lights) than it had been, using Robur's *hokhmah*, which had come to her as he died. Karl had his doubts that the world had in truth become any more peaceful, but he'd never know. Nor did he care.

But Shawna *had* cared. And she would care about this world, too. She would want to use her power, once she had the shared *hokhmah* of Queen Stephanie and Queen Patricia, to make this world better.

And that was something he could use.

"But?" Patricia prompted, eyes narrowed.

Karl pulled his thoughts together. "But Shawna can," he said. "If you share your *hokhmah* with her, and she can likewise obtain Queen Stephanie's, she will have the power to rebuild your world. She can restore the Pact. She can put things back the way they were."

"Stephanie will never allow it," Patricia said flatly. "She started this, and she thinks she can win. She thinks she will be the only ruler once all is done."

"Perhaps," Karl said. "But did you not say that you Shaped her werewolves, and she Shaped your vampires, so that you could each then be transformed into the thing you wished to be?"

Patricia nodded.

"Then giving Shawna your *hokhmah*," Karl said, "will give

her power, not over your vampires—but over Stephanie's were-wolves."

Patricia blinked. And then she laughed. "That," she said, her face flashing again in an instant to obsidian-eyed and angular, "would be sweet." She showed fangs in a toothy smile.

"But your friend," Dracula said, "is being held by the werewolves."

"I am not suggesting an all-out assault," Karl said.

"I'm glad to hear it," said Patricia. "We do not have the forces that would require, and I will not sacrifice my people on such a fruitless attempt."

"Then what *are* you suggesting?" Dracula said.

"Send me to the werewolves alone. I will talk to Stephanie as I have talked to you, convince her to let Shawna go, help negotiate a truce between you. She will give Shawna her *hokhmah*, you will give her yours, and Shawna, who is a very powerful Shaper, will then be able to set right your world before we leave it for the next."

As he said it, he could almost see Shawna's look of surprise at his words, but he ignored it just as he would have had she actually been present. He did not really care if this world were left in better, worse, or the same shape: all he cared about was the quest, and that meant somehow convincing—by any means necessary—the two queens, onetime friends, now enemies, to surrender their knowledge of the world's Shaping to Shawna.

The queen frowned. "Wait . . . if Shawna gaining my *hokhmah* would give her control over Stephanie's werewolves, wouldn't her gaining Stephanie's *hokhmah* give her control over my vampires?"

Karl hesitated, not sure what the queen was thinking. "Yes, I believe so."

Patricia's eyes narrowed. "Then by all means, we must indeed get you to Stephanie's kingdom, and you must retrieve Shawna as quickly as possible, before Stephanie learns what you have told me and uses Shawna to take my kingdom."

Karl started to say he thought that unlikely, then forbore saying anything at all. After all Shawna had accomplished without him in the last world, he no longer wanted to predict what she might or might not do.

The queen turned to the count. "Drac, will you please organize an escort, to leave at the next sunset?"

Dracula nodded. "Of course, my love."

To Karl, Patricia said, "Seraphina will show you back to your quarters."

"I would prefer another escort, Your Majesty."

Patricia smiled sweetly. "Seraphina will show you back to your quarters." She nodded to Dracula, who went out, presumably to fetch the lady-in-waiting, who presumably, was . . . well, waiting, somewhere nearby.

Karl sighed. "Yes, Your Majesty." *Perhaps she will refrain from releasing her glamor. It was only to impress me. It meant nothing more.*

Seraphina appeared in short order, bowed to the queen, smiled at Karl, and turned with a sweep of her hand to indicate he should accompany her.

"Seraphina," said the queen as they approached the door.

Seraphina turned and looked back.

"No drinking."

"Of course, Your Majesty." Seraphina smiled at Karl. "Shall we?"

As they stepped out into the hallway, her glamor came back, full-force, and he groaned. *At least, if she obeys the queen, she won't bite me*, he thought. But after two more steps, he was desperately hoping she would.

And so she did, after a fashion, among a great many other things, once they were back in his tower room, the end result of which left him quite thoroughly drained . . . though not, admittedly, of blood.

FOURTEEN

"HE'S YOUR SON?" I blurted. "How is that possible?"

Queen Stephanie and the boy both looked at me. "How is what possible?" Stephanie asked.

"How can you have a son. . . . in a Shaped world?"

The boy's dark-brown eyes widened, and he gave his mother a startled look. "She knows?"

Stephanie glanced at him. "She claims to be a Shaper, like me."

The boy turned those wide eyes on me. "Wow!"

"Why does this startle you?" Stephanie said, returning her gaze to me.

"Because . . ." I groped for words. "Because . . . you and I are . . ." I didn't want to say "real," not in front of the boy, because that would imply he wasn't. Though he wasn't. Was he? "From the First World," I finished lamely.

"Yes?"

"So . . . did you . . . Shape your son, or . . . ?"

"I had him in the usual fashion," Stephanie said. "I conceived him in the usual fashion, as well."

"Mom!" the boy said. He sounded horrified and embarrassed, like any other teenager who really, really didn't want to think about the unfortunately undeniable truth that his parents, at least once, had had sex.

"Hush, Piotr," she said, and he subsided.

"But his father . . ."

"His father, Geoffrey, was one of the Shaped, yes," Stephanie said. "A fine werewolf, leader of the Briarwood Pack." Her eyes and voice turned dreamy. "I fell in love with him the moment I saw him. So strong, in wolf form, and in human form . . ."

Piotr gave her an imploring look.

"We were married a year after I Shaped this world. Piotr was born the next year."

My mind boggled . . . and my heart ached. Because all this meant that if my boyfriend, Brent, and I had carried through with our plans, and married, I could have been a mother, too.

That dream had crumbled when the Adversary entered my world, stole my *hokhmah*, and made Brent forget me.

And all of this surely put the lie to Robur's claim, in the last world, that the Shaped weren't real, that they were equivalent to the "non-player characters" of computer and roleplaying games. A human woman could not conceive a child fathered by anything other than a human male, could she? Wasn't that the basic definition of being of the same species?

I had come dangerously close to forgetting the reality of the Shaped myself, in my efforts to achieve my quest . . . and my survival. In my own world, I had rewritten people's memories, including my own mother's—or the woman I remembered as my mother—and gotten some of them killed in the process (though I thought, *hoped*, that doing it to my mother had saved her). In the last world, I had not, for most of my time there, had any power, but I had manipulated and used the Shaped anyway, to the best of my ability.

The fact I had survived to come here and try to continue my quest argued that those efforts had been necessary. My quest, after all, was to save all of the Shaped worlds and their (potentially) billions upon billions of inhabitants.

But I should never lose track of the fact that the people whose lives I manipulated were every bit as real as I, however constrained and artificial the world in which they lived—a particularly apt description of this world, with its single inhabited valley surrounded by vast, unreachable wilderness.

Piotr was the son of a woman of the First World, and a man . . . well, werewolf . . . of the world that woman had Shaped. He was real. There he was, in front of me, looking like any other teenaged boy dressed in a fur-lined bathrobe (okay, admittedly, I'd never before seen a teenaged boy wearing a fur-lined bathrobe, but still).

"And now Geoffrey is dead," Stephanie went on, her voice turning cold. "Murdered ten years ago, as I watched, by the woman I thought was my friend. Patricia, queen of the *vampires*." That single word carried as much hatred as I have ever heard two syllables convey. "And so I ask you again: what mad scheme has Patricia come up with? How did she bring you into this world, and how does she think your presence can contribute to her seizing control?"

"My presence here has nothing to do with Patricia," I said.

"I find that hard to believe."

"So let me tell you the story."

She glanced at her son. "Why not? Piotr loves stories. Don't you, son?"

Piotr nodded to her, then turned his big puppy-dog eyes (I know, I know, but honestly, that's what they reminded me of) toward me. "I do!"

So I told them a story. *This* story. The story of me losing control of my world, and fleeing to the next, and gathering the *hokhmah* of its Shaper, and (hopefully) slamming the door in the Adversary's face, and then finding my way through the last world to this one.

Piotr—Prince Piotr, I guessed I should call him—listened with wide eyes, absorbed in the adventure, but his mother's gaze was considerably more skeptical and calculating. "You can take the *hokhmah* of another Shaper?" she said.

"Not forcibly," I said. Although I wasn't sure that was true. After all, the Adversary had taken *mine* that way. But if it were possible, I didn't yet know how to do it. "You have to give it to me freely. I know Ygrair taught you how to do that."

"She taught us how to *share* it," Stephanie corrected. "Which is how this world came to be. Patricia and I shared our *hokhmah*." She grimaced. "To my everlasting regret."

"So share it with me, too," I said. "Your half of it, anyway, if that's how it works."

"That is exactly how it works. There were things I Shaped, and things Patricia Shaped, and a few we Shaped together. Among other things, I Shaped Patricia's vampires, and she Shaped my werewolves. It was the only way I could become a werewolf and she a vampire."

I frowned. "Then why don't you just Shape her vampires to quit attacking you?"

"I would in an instant if I had any power. But I do not. Neither of us has had an iota of Shaping power since we finished the world and became . . . what we became. We used it all." She frowned. "Or so I thought, until now. Patricia must have gathered enough to, somehow, bring you here . . ." Then her eyes widened. "Or make me *think* she brought you here."

"What?"

"I understand it now! She *didn't* bring you here. She couldn't possibly have that much power, or she'd turn the werewolves against me, like you suggested I turn her vampires against her. But she had enough, just enough, to Shape you, tell you what you needed to say to convince me you really came from another world."

She'd just called me a liar. I glared at her.

She ignored it, racing on. "She filled you with this nonsense about being a Shaper, about an Adversary, about a quest spanning all the worlds of the Labyrinth. The mere act of Shaping you was enough to make me feel the presence of a stranger in the world and send someone to investigate. A newly Shaped person, after all these years? Of course, I sensed it!

"She thought I would accept all this at face value and take you into my confidence, so you could spy on me, discover my defenses, and help her launch an all-out assault on my kingdom!"

"Don't be ridiculous!" I snapped (probably not something one should say to a queen, but I was furious). "Everything I told you is true!"

"It cannot be true. Ygrair said nothing of the possibility of travel between the worlds."

"Because she only gave Karl that ability," I said. "And he . . . gave it to me." Slightly accidentally, but still.

"And what makes the two of you special?"

I hesitated, then decided it didn't matter if she knew. "Ygrair is not human. She's an alien. Something called a Shurak. They had technology to access the Labyrinth. That's how she put all the Shapers into it."

A new thought struck me. The Shurak nanomites were carried in Karl's blood. That's how I'd gotten them: putting my cut hand into a pool of his blood. Karl had been taken by vampires. What if Patricia drank his blood? She might *already* carry the technology to open Portals.

Piotr was staring at me wide-eyed again. "An alien? What's an alien?"

"A being from another world."

"So you're an alien?" he said.

"No," I said impatiently. Then I stopped. "Well, yes. In a way, I guess I am. But that's not what I mean. Aliens live on other worlds out among the stars."

"Wow," Piotr said. He looked at his mother. "You never told me that."

"I never told you that because it's not true," she snapped. "She's only parroting what Patricia Shaped her to say. It's all make-believe, to try to fool me."

"Then how *did* Ygrair discover the Labyrinth?" I demanded. "How did she pull you out of the First World and pop you into a world you could Shape as you desired?"

"Magic, of course."

I blinked. "Magic's not real in the First World."

"Of course it is. How else did we end up here?"

"I told you . . ."

"Your story is make-believe."

I fell silent. She thought she knew the truth, and so she rejected my version of it. And, yes, as Arthur C. Clarke famously stated, any sufficiently advanced technology is indistinguishable from magic. But conversely, if you believe in magic, any magic is indistinguishable from advanced technology. She chose to believe it was magic, and because she believed that, she could not believe my story.

Which left me a suspected spy from a vampire kingdom in the heart of a werewolf kingdom. "How can I prove to you I'm not lying?" I said, a little desperately.

Stephanie shrugged. "Shape something."

"I can't," I said. "I have no power here. Not unless you share your *hokhmah* with me."

"Not going to happen."

"If I truly am Shaped," I argued, "that's impossible anyway. But if you try, and it works, then it's proof I'm telling the truth. So what do you have to lose?"

"Sharing *hokhmah* would require us to touch," she said. "Patricia may have Shaped you with some ability to disrupt my *hokhmah* . . ." She stopped, and her eyes widened again. "That's it! She's Shaped you so that, if I try to share my *hokhmah* with you, she can disrupt the bond of loyalty binding my werewolves to me, perhaps even switching their allegiance to her!"

I didn't know what to say. I had no way to prove she was wrong. She thought I was Shaped, and that was that. Her hatred of Patricia was driving her into conspiracy-la-la-land.

She smiled, then. It was not a friendly smile. It was the smile of a dangerous predator with its prey in sight, the showing of teeth in anticipation of some highly pleasurable rending and tearing. "Outside, the sun has risen," she said. "But tonight, beneath the full moon, I will ensure that whatever Patricia intended, it will fail. Tonight, I will ensure your loyalty to me." She leaned forward. "Tonight, you become one of us."

I felt the blood drain from my face, and my heart stuttered. "You . . . you can't!"

"Of course, I can. I can, and I will." Queen Stephanie leaned back. "And once you are absolutely loyal to me, I will compel you to tell me the truth."

"I've told you the truth!"

She looked toward the door. "Maigrat."

"Your Majesty," Maigrat said, coming to the table.

Piotr looked wide-eyed from his mother to Maigrat to me.

"Lock her up," Stephanie commanded.

"With pleasure, Your Majesty," Maigrat said. "Dungeon?"

"No," the queen said. "She will soon be of the pack. In one of the more comfortable rooms. But she is to be guarded."

Maigrat inclined her head. "Of course, Your Majesty."

The queen stood. "Take her away. Piotr, remain with me a moment."

"Yes, Mother," he said, but his gaze followed me as, numbly, I let myself be led from the room by Maigrat.

She told Jakob their orders. Jakob looked at me, one eyebrow raised, then grunted and led the way out of the Great Hall.

Our path took us through a labyrinth of underground passages. I should have tried to memorize the twists and turns so I could find my way out again if I escaped . . . but the truth was, I did not think I would escape. In that moment, I thought all hope was finally gone.

So many times I'd been on the verge of death or failure, and I'd always found a way out. If there was one here, I didn't know what it was.

I had no Shaping power. I was not where I could open a Portal to the next world—I had not even sensed where that would be. My only ally, Karl, had also been captured and might already have been turned into a vampire. I had no friends among the werewolves. Stephanie had rejected the truth and was so convinced that Patricia was behind everything that I could not imagine what I might say to change her mind.

And the course of action she had decided upon . . .

No one from the First World could be Shaped, but this was not Shaping. Stephanie herself proved that. Once in one of these worlds, we were subject to its physical laws, as the not-so-dearly departed Robur had found out so explosively and fatally in the last world. The very Shapers who had made this world had been successfully turned into the supernatural beings they craved—for whatever reason, and frankly, I didn't get it—to be. I had no doubt that I, too, could be turned. And then . . .

In his human form, Eric still looked like the boy I had pitied and wanted to help (*and use for your own purposes*, my always-nagging conscience pointed out), but more than just his body had changed. His allegiance was no longer to Father Thomas and the church, but to Queen Stephanie . . . as mine would presumably be once I became a werewolf. I would belong to her. However much like my current self I might look in my human form, I would no longer be the person I was.

Will I still be a Shaper? I wondered. *Will the Shurak nanotechnology still . . .*

And then, suddenly, I felt a spark of hope.

I was *not* an ordinary human of the First World, or any other world. I carried within my blood the alien technology that allowed me to open Portals, that somehow—though I had yet to learn how to initiate it—allowed me to take the *hokhmah* of multiple Shapers. Would it *allow* me to be changed into a werewolf?

Maybe not.

It was a slim hope, but it was a hope, and I clung to it like a woman swept away by a tsunami might cling to a floating log. I'd never despaired before, and I would not let despair grip me now. I would try to escape, and if I couldn't escape, I would resist the change Stephanie planned to impose on me, and I'd hope that what I carried in my blood would enable me to do so.

And if I *were* changed, I would do everything in my power to resist the bond to Queen Stephanie she expected me to form. That, too, might be weakened or prevented by the Shurak nanotech, by the fact I was from the First World, or by the fact that I was also a Shaper.

And not just any Shaper, I reminded myself. *I'm the most powerful Shaper Karl has come across in his journey through the Labyrinth. I had enough power to set back time in my own world, power to shape the ocean, power to spare.*

Bring it, bitch, I thought then, and it was a measure of how much more positive I was suddenly feeling that my mouth twitched at the appropriateness of applying that particular word to the werewolf queen. Maybe it was just empty bravado, but hey, empty bravado had already carried me through situations I'd never imagined when I was a potter in a small Montana city and thought my cozy dreams enough.

Ahead, the corridor ended in a door. I pulled myself free of Jakob's grasp and strode ahead. I tried the latch; the door was unlocked. I opened it and stepped inside ahead of my guards. It was a minor display of independence, but it made me feel good.

The room beyond, aside from being windowless, was quite pleasant. A fire flickered in the fireplace, and a lantern burned on the mantelpiece. I wondered how a servant had gotten there before us. Perhaps they had their own passages that were more direct than the ones along which I'd been brought.

The bed, broad and four-posted, looked comfortable. The room held an unavoidable underground chill, but the fire would soon take care of that, and in any event, there were plenty of blankets—all red. There were also a small round table with two plain wooden chairs, two comfortable-looking armchairs facing the fire, each covered with what looked like deerskin, a bearhide rug on the floor, and trophy heads of deer and elk and even a moose on various walls. *I use antlers in all of my decorating* ran musically through my mind. Unfortunately, it seemed unlikely animated candlesticks, clocks, and teapots would be coming to my assistance.

Jakob walked across the room and opened the only other door. "The necessary," he said. I hadn't heard that particular euphemism before, but it seemed appropriate, because it certainly was. "There is also a tub, should you wish to bathe. Water will flow from the taps in the wall."

"How civilized," I said.

Jakob frowned, as if he didn't understand why I'd say that, and returned to the main door. I heard footsteps in the corridor outside, and saw an armed and armored man—the first I had seen not dressed in one of the robes that allowed for quick wolf-changes, probably, I thought, because it was now day outside.

"Your door will be locked, and Frederick here will stand guard," Jakob said. "If you need anything, do not ask him. Instead, use this." He gestured me over, and I saw that, in the corner by the "necessary," a curved metal tube descended from the ceiling, something I'd overlooked because it was the same unrelieved black as the stone walls. "Speak loudly into it. Someone will answer, and you may ask for whatever it is you need."

"Except rescue," Maigrat put in. She gave me a sweet smile, with no teeth, which she somehow managed to make even nastier than her usual pointy grin.

Jakob sketched a small bow. "Sleep well," he said, straightening. "Tonight, you will become one of us. I look forward to running beneath the moon with you."

"As do I," Maigrat said. "As do I."

They went out. The door closed behind them, and a key turned in the lock.

I tried to hold on to the flicker of hope and defiance I had managed to ignite in the hallway, but as silence fell, except for the faint crackle of the fire, and I found myself alone for the first time in days, that flicker sputtered.

It did not, however, go out. I still had hope, and I would cling to it.

But first . . . sleep.

I turned down the lamp on the mantelpiece, tossed my pack on a chair, stripped off all my filthy clothes, climbed under the multiple blankets, and despite my fears was dead to the world two minutes later.

I didn't even have time to reflect on what an unfortunate metaphor that might yet turn out to be.

FIFTEEN

KARL HAD NOT been turned into a vampire, but he still felt like something undead, or possibly, just dead, when sunlight streaming through the window of his tower room finally woke him. With the daylight came memories of the night before, of what Seraphina had done . . . had made him do . . . the things they had done together . . .

She was gone, had left even as, exhausted, he had slipped into sleep. He had seen her walk naked to the window, flow into bat-shape, leap into the sky.

Her glamor had vanished with her. She had intoxicated him the night before. He hadn't been able to satiate his desire, no matter how many times he . . . and now, he hurt all over, and felt nothing but shame. She had used him, and humiliated him, and worst of all, she had made him enjoy it. It sickened him.

Yet, he knew if she came back to him and exerted her influence, he would helplessly and happily do it all again.

He felt anger then, anger such as he had seldom felt in a Shaped world. There were many he had passed through he had found unpleasant, but since none of them had had a Shaper with enough power to do what Ygrair had sent him to find a way to do, he had spent little time in them and interacted only enough to obtain food and drink and clothing and shelter as required.

But things had changed. Now, in each world, he had to find the Shaper and help Shawna get close enough to obtain the world's *hokhmah*. Now, he had to engage with the world. The Jules

Verne-inspired one he had come to late, after Shawna had already absorbed Robur's *hokhmah* by being close to the Shaper when he died. Karl had passed through that world as little more than a tourist, observing Shawna's attempts to make the world "better"— by her lights, at least—than it had been when they arrived. He still felt her efforts had likely been wasted. Without a Shaper to ride herd on it, the changes she had made would spiral out of control in unpredictable ways, so that everything she had tried to do to prevent bloodshed and misery might very well produce more of each. But she had done it, and they had come here.

Here, where there were two Shapers. Here, where he could not simply skate through the world, an almost-silent, almost-invisible presence, little more than a ghost, touching nothing and being touched by nothing.

Here, he had to touch . . . and, apparently, be touched. And here, because of the way the world had been Shaped, his status as a "real" human, born in the First World, would not protect him, because the Shapers had designed the world so that its magic would affect First Worlders, because that was what they were, and they *wanted* to be affected!

It left him more vulnerable than he had ever felt in a Shaped world before, even when the Adversary had been pursuing him, first across the Shakespearean world, and then across Shawna's. He felt violated in a way he had never felt before. Unclean . . .

. . . and unfaithful. Unfaithful to the only woman he had ever loved and would ever love, the woman with whom he hoped someday to be reunited, if his quest succeeded and Ygrair kept her promise to him.

He forced himself to push all of that away. The events of the night had happened. He was not a powerful Shaper who could set back time, as Shawna had done in her world, thus convincing him she had strength enough to complete Ygrair's task. He had to live with what had happened. And so he would. But he would not let it affect his duty. If Seraphina came to him again, he would try, again, to resist and, likely, would fail. But the attempt was what mattered. He would be true to himself and to his cause, no matter what this world or any other threw at him, no matter how these Shapers or any other tried to subvert him.

He got out of bed, groaning a little. He used the privy. His clothes were missing—taken to be cleaned, he hoped—but there was one of the ubiquitous robes in the wardrobe. He put it on and then padded barefoot to the table, where breakfast had been placed sometime while he slept. He ate.

And then he waited, for nightfall, and for the vampires who would escort him to the borders of Queen Stephanie's werewolf kingdom, as close as possible to Shawna Keys . . .

. . . and, he hoped, as far as possible from Seraphina.

A scratching sound woke me, far too short a time after falling asleep.

The fire had burned down to coals. At least two or three hours must have passed. It was weird to think, here in this room lit only by dying embers, that outside, it was full daylight. I wasn't a werewolf—yet—but I was already living werewolf hours.

I listened with bated breath for the sound to repeat itself. I heard nothing. I'd almost decided it had been the trailing edge of a fading dream when the sound came again . . . the sound of scratching claws, beyond a doubt. And not from the door, either, but somewhere closer to my head, to the right.

Rats in the walls? I thought, then realized how impossible that was in a lair carved out of solid rock.

And then there was the sound of a bolt being drawn, and a

previously unsuspected door swung inward, letting in a flood of yellow light.

Silhouetted against that light was the unmistakable shape of a wolf, complete with glowing red eyes.

I rolled across the bed away from the door, wrapping myself in the blanket as I went, and was on my feet in an instant, heart pounding. There was nothing in the room I could use as a weapon—not against a werewolf.

Said werewolf came into the room. Its eyes turned away from me, and it nosed the door closed behind it, plunging the room into darkness again. The eyes turned toward me again, two red coals. I thought my heart would explode in my chest. I clutched the blanket closer.

The embers of the fire produced just enough light for me to see the wolf-shape soften, and flow, and extend upward into a human shape, though I could make out no features. "Who are you?" I demanded, my voice considerably squeakier than normal, as though I'd been sucking on helium.

"It's okay, Shawna," said a boyish voice. "It's me, Piotr."

"Piotr?"

Piotr moved, stood for a moment silhouetted against the embers. He seemed to be opening a drawer in the mantel. He walked away from the first. I heard the sound of flint and steel being struck, a spark flew, and a moment later, the lamp on the mantelpiece glowed to life.

Piotr turned toward me. He was, of course, stark naked. I looked away. "Um," I said. "Would you mind getting another blanket off the bed and wrapping it around yourself?

"Why?" he said. He sounded genuinely puzzled.

"You're naked," I said.

"So?"

"It's . . . just please, do it."

"All right," he said. I heard a rustle. "Done."

I clutched my own blanket more securely and turned to face him. "What are you doing here?" I said. "And how did you get in?"

"Servants' tunnel," he said cheerfully. He held the blanket casually closed with one hand. "There's nobody in them during the day."

"But there's a guard outside," I said, nodding to the door. "What if he hears us?"

"I don't plan to shout," Piotr said. "And he's stuck in human form. His hearing is dull, and that's a very thick door."

"Wait," I said. "You came in as a wolf. But it's day outside. How . . . ?"

He shrugged. The blanket slipped off one shoulder. "I'm special," he explained. "Well, me and Mom. When she and Patricia Shaped the world, they decreed that the royal line of the two kingdoms would be able to change whenever they wanted, nighttime, daytime, whatever. All the other werewolves can only change after sunset, and they have to change back with sunrise—not when it clears the mountains, but when it comes up over the actual horizon. Not that I've ever seen the actual horizon," he added, sounding strangely wistful.

I remembered the clock in Zarozje's gatehouse, the one that announced real sunrise and real sunset. "Is that the same for vampires?"

"Not quite," he said. "They can't change until real sunset any more than we can, but they can hang onto their changes in the morning until sunlight actually touches wherever they are."

I filed that information away, thinking it might come in useful later on. "Why did you come as a wolf at all, though?" I said then. "You could have come as yourself." *Wearing clothes,* I added silently.

He laughed. "I did come as myself. I'm as much the wolf as I am the man."

Boy, I thought, but didn't correct him. He was just the age where he would be thinking of himself as a man, and I was just enough older that I couldn't, but I didn't want to hurt his feelings. Boy egos are fragile things. I remembered that from high school . . . or thought I did.

"You still haven't answered the first part of my question," I said. "The important part. Why are you here?"

"Can we sit down?" he said.

"All right," I said. I readjusted the blanket and crossed the room, sitting in the deerhide-covered armchair to the left of the fire. He took the one on the right. I kept hold of the blanket, but Piotr let it fall once he was seated, so that it puddled around his middle. "Now, why did you come?" I asked again.

"Two reasons. First, to apologize."

"Apologize? You haven't done anything to me."

"Apologize for Mom," he said.

Interesting. "You don't agree with what she's planning to do?"

He shook his blond head vigorously. "No! I mean, I love her, but . . . I can't agree with *this*. With turning you into one of the pack. If it even works." He hesitated. "Do you think it will?"

"I don't know. I have some hope that it won't, but I can't be certain."

"I *hate* this world," Piotr said then, surprising me further. "I hate the way Mom and Patricia Shaped it. A single valley. No way out of it. Us at this end, the vampires at the other, Mother Church off to the west, a bunch of villages in between."

"But . . . it's the only world you've known," I said.

"Exactly!" He twisted toward me. "But Mom used to tell me stories about the First World, the world she came from. She told me about huge cities named New York and Paris and London and Hong Kong. She told me about oceans so enormous it took hours to fly across them in magical vehicles called jets. She told me about wagons that run on their own, with no horses pulling them. She told me about something called movies—moving pictures on a screen that tell amazing stories! She told me all about the First World, but when I asked her, when I begged her to take me to it, she told me she couldn't, that I can never leave this world."

I could see where this was going, and my heart broke for him. He might be a werewolf prince, but he was also just a kid stuck in a small town, dreaming of life in the big city. The trouble was . . .

"She's right," I had to tell him. "The Shaped can't leave their own world."

But even as I said it, I realized that wasn't one-hundred-percent true. The Adversary had somehow managed to Shape a handful of his followers into his "cadre," a loyal group of fighters who most definitely *had* left their world, coming into mine and wreaking havoc—including killing my best friend, Aesha. So it wasn't entirely impossible, but *I* didn't know how to do it, and even if I did, it could presumably only work in a world I could Shape—and right now, and for the foreseeable future, I was powerless here.

"But I'm only *half*-Shaped," Piotr said. "My mother is the Shaper. I'll bet I could do it. I'll bet I could enter another world!"

"Maybe," I said. "I don't know." I wondered if Ygrair had covered such things in the schooling I had no memory of. But if she had, shouldn't Stephanie have known?

Ygrair doesn't seem to have suggested to anyone that it's even possible to move from world to world, I reminded myself. And since, without the Shurak nanomites I and Karl carried within our blood, it apparently *wasn't* possible to open Portals between the worlds, why should she?

"I'd like to try. Take me with you when you go!"

"I'm not going anywhere right now," I pointed out. "And there is no 'try.'" I resisted the urge to put on a Yoda voice. "If it doesn't work . . . you'll cease to exist."

"It'll work!"

"You don't know that."

"You don't know that it won't."

Which was quite true. Maybe a compromise was in order. "Karl might know," I said, and, indeed, he might. "But we're separated. I need to rejoin him." And then, though I hated myself for it, I leaned forward and said. "Can you help me do that?"

I knew I was asking him to betray Stephanie, who was not only his mother but his queen. I expected shock, wide eyes, an intake of breath. Instead, he laughed. "I told you I had two reasons for sneaking in here. That's reason number two."

My mouth fell open for a second. "You want to help me escape?"

"Of course, I want to help you escape! You can't lead me to another world if you're locked up in here or my mother turns you into her bitch."

I blinked at that turn of phrase—but it was, literally, what Stephanie intended. "I admit I am not so confident of her inability to do so that I look forward to the experiment," I said. *When did I start to sound so much like Karl?* Mostly to break that stuffy cadence, I added, "Dude, you're on."

"Dude?" he said, looking puzzled. Then he shrugged it off. "Terrific!' he said. He jumped to his feet. Since this meant his blanket fell to the floor, I quickly looked away.

"What's wrong?" he said behind me.

I kept my gaze on the fire. "In my world, we don't . . . we have a . . ." How to explain it? "A nudity taboo."

"What's a taboo?"

"It's a thing that . . . isn't done. In my world, public nudity is frowned on. In fact, it's illegal, most places."

"We aren't in public."

"It's still . . . unless you know someone really well . . ." *and one of you isn't twenty-seven and the other isn't, like, fifteen . . .* "you just don't let other people see you naked."

"But what's the big deal? It's just skin."

"Just put on your blanket, okay?"

"All right." I heard a rustle. "All covered up."

I turned around. He was more-or-less decent again. "Thank you."

"I guess my mother and Trish didn't Shape that into this world," he said thoughtfully. "This 'nudity taboo' thing. It would make it really hard to shift into wolf form in a hurry. And for the vampires, bat form."

"I'm sure that's why they did it," I said. "I'm just . . . it makes me uncomfortable."

"I'll try to remember," Piotr said. "Anyway, here's the plan . . ."

The plan was everything you might expect a fifteen-year-old boy to come up with, if that boy were able to turn into a wolf. It didn't fill me with confidence. But it was my best hope for not being turned into the first werewolf in the kingdom afflicted with modesty, which would clearly be a really unfortunate thing for a werewolf to have, so I agreed to it.

Piotr blew out the lamp and returned to the servants' door. In silhouette, I saw him turn and toss the blanket onto the chair by the fire. Then he closed the door, plunging me into darkness. I heard him slide the bolt back into place, but I'd expected it: he'd told me it would look odd to a servant if the door weren't bolted closed.

I climbed back into the bed. I really needed a good day's sleep before night fell and Stephanie came for me.

I didn't get it. I tossed and turned and worried for a long time before I finally dozed off.

Minutes after that, it seemed, I blinked my eyes open to discover the lamp burning again and flames beginning to crinkle around fresh logs in the fireplace. A servant girl, about Piotr's age, was just uncovering a platter on the table. I smelled bacon, and sat up in bed, clutching the covers to my chest. "Good evening!" the girl said, turning to me. She wore a simple gray robe, belted with white. "The sun has just set." She went to the foot of the bed, and I saw that a gray robe like her own had been laid there. "You are to put this on."

I looked for my clothes. They had vanished. It was the robe, or nothing.

The girl watched me expectantly.

"Would you mind turning around?" I said.

She blinked. "Why?"

"Please?" I said.

She shrugged and did what I asked. I hurriedly pulled on the robe, tying the white rope snugly around my waist. Then I sat down to have . . . supper? Breakfast? Breakfast, I guess, since I was breaking my fast, but it seemed weird to call something you ate just after the sun went down by that name.

The girl watched me eat. "Don't you have other duties?" I asked her.

"No," she said. "Queen Stephanie ordered me to attend to you. I am attending. Is there anything else you require?"

"I'd like my clothes back."

"I do not know where they went."

I sighed. "All right. Then how about instructions on how to find the front gate, and help escaping the kingdom?"

She frowned. "Is that a joke? Why would you want to escape the kingdom?" Then her face cleared. "Oh, of course. You have not yet been honored."

"Honored?"

"With the change-bite."

"No," I said. "No, I haven't been 'honored' yet."

"Once you have joined the pack, you will not want to escape the kingdom."

I sighed. "That's what I'm afraid of."

"It is nothing to fear," she said.

"Were you born a werewolf?" I asked.

"Of course."

"Then how would you know? It may be very painful." It certainly was in every werewolf movie I'd ever seen.

"Why should such a joyous thing be painful?" the girl asked, and I gave up. Unlike Piotr, she was every inch a Shaped denizen— literally the right word, in this lupine labyrinth—and could not imagine anything else. She was utterly loyal to her queen.

Like the close associates of Robur in the last world, I thought. *And look at all the bloodshed* that *led to.*

I finished my meal—which featured eggs, toast, and grape juice as well as bacon—and pushed the platter away, hoping it hadn't been a hearty last meal. "Now what?"

"Now I clear away the dishes," she said. She did. The door closed behind her. I heard the bolt slide shut. Just to be sure, I tried it after a moment to see if it was locked. It was.

After that, there was nothing to do but wait for Queen Stephanie to come for me, and for Piotr to either rescue me or fail miserably, which seemed the more likely outcome.

Within hours, I might be as unthinkingly loyal to the werewolf Shaper of this world as the serving girl.

I didn't relish the prospect.

SIXTEEN

AS DARKNESS FELL, Karl's escort arrived on his balcony: four vampires in bat-shape. Only one of them took human form. It was Nicolas, the vampire he had seen in Queen Patricia's throne room, the one who had reported that the werewolves who had captured Shawna were nearing their kingdom. He carried a strange kind of leather harness. "Are you ready?" he said.

"My clothes are all I have," Karl said. "I lost my pack and all my other supplies when we were first pursued." He nodded at the harness. "I presume that is for me?"

"It is a thing we use when we take human servants hither and yon," Nicolas said. He guided Karl in its donning. It had straps that went around his hips and chest, but the bulk of it, more straps and several large buckles, hung on his back. Then Nicolas turned to one of the other vampires, a huge male, head and shoulders taller than any of the others. "Seth?" he said.

The giant vampire stepped forward.

"Hello, Seth," Karl said.

The vampire only grunted and moved behind him, pushing his body close to Karl's back and buttocks. Nicolas tugged and buckled, then stepped back. "You will find this more comfortable than being hauled around by your arms, as you were on your arrival."

"I suspect you are correct," Karl said. He was very aware of the furred monstrosity pressed up against his back. It was unnerving both because he knew what it was and because it wasn't warm. Any living creature that size should put out heat like a furnace, but the vampire . . . if it hadn't been touching him, he wouldn't have sensed its nearness. Well, except for the faint scent of graveyard corruption . . .

"Then we go," Nicolas said. He flowed back into furred bat-shape, and all four vampires leaped into the sky, driving upward with powerful wingbeats.

Karl gasped as his body sagged in the harness. Below him, the castle courtyard, silvered by moonlight, shrank away. Then they were out over the river, the farmhouse where he and Shawna had sheltered their first night in this world, and the trail beyond, along which they had fled. The cold wind buffeted his face and roared in his ears and made him wish he had something warmer to wear, or fur like the vampire above him . . . who he now had even more reason to wish was warm.

He did not think the temperature low enough he would freeze to death before they reached the borders of the werewolf kingdom, but as his misery mounted, that was, literally, cold comfort.

They flew on through the night, the moonlit world streaming beneath them.

It shouldn't be possible both for minutes to drag interminably and hours to flash by in an instant, but apparently being imprisoned in the underground palace of a werewolf queen, awaiting the bite that will turn you into one of her unthinkingly loyal followers, does weird things to the space-time continuum, because it seemed both forever and no time at all before the door opened—the main door, this time, not the servants' door, which until then had seen more traffic—and the queen herself appeared. She wore the same grand fur-lined robe she'd worn in the throne room. With her were two male guards, robed in white, carrying swords and shields but, I presumed, able to drop them and their loose clothing in an instant and change into wolves.

"It's time," the queen said without preamble. "Once you are mine, you will tell me the truth."

"I've already told you the truth," I said.

"We will soon know for certain." She stepped to one side, and her guards came in, took my arms, and led me out.

With Queen Stephanie in the lead, we made our way through the maze of stone corridors, eventually climbing up a stairway so narrow it forced us into single file, Stephanie in the lead, one of my guards in front of me, the other behind. It was a different route than the one I had followed when I'd first entered the labyrinth with Jakob and Maigrat.

Neither were in evidence. Apparently, turning me into a werewolf did not require their presence. But then, unlike poor Eric, I was not intended for their pack. The queen herself would be my alpha . . . bitch.

I shot a look at the back of Stephanie's head, over the shoulder of my lead guard. The word fit in *so* many ways.

At the top of the staircase, a door already stood open. We stepped out into a moonlit glade: trees on three sides, the rock face from which we'd emerged behind us. I breathed deeply of the fresh air, a nice change from the underground variety, with its faint but ever-present miasma of wolf musk and human sweat. It was also cool enough I erupted in goose bumps beneath the robe, the only thing I wore.

My heart pounded. Would Piotr show?

In the center of the clearing, moonlight gleamed off of a pale stone hexagon, made of smaller hexagonal tiles. I wondered if Stephanie had enjoyed tabletop gaming in the First World. I wondered if I'd be handed dice and given the opportunity to throw a saving roll.

It didn't seem likely.

My gaze darted desperately around the encompassing trees, predominantly birch, their pale trunks only deepening the darkness between and behind them. I saw no glow of red eyes.

My guards pushed me to the center of the hexagon.

The queen looked up at the moon—for what purpose, I didn't know, since it hung exactly where it always had. She had said she would carry out the ritual at midnight, but I didn't know why she'd chosen that time, either. Maigrat hadn't been concerned about the time when she'd bitten Eric.

The guards stepped out of the hexagon, put down their weapons, dropped their robes, flowed into wolf-shape, and began circling me, red eyes locked on mine.

My heart raced even faster. My breath came in short gasps. In all my adventures in the Shaped worlds so far, including my own, I had never been more terrified.

Queen Stephanie stepped forward. "Unclothe yourself," she said.

I clutched the robe to my chest. "No!"

She laughed. "Your modesty will mean nothing in a moment. If you take off your robe now, you will be more comfortable after the change."

"I'll wait, thanks." My voice quavered. I wanted to make a Buffy-like wisecrack, but my wisecrack generator seemed to have seized up.

"Very well." Stephanie reached for the clasp of her fur-lined robe . . .

. . . and a pale, slender shape stepped into the clearing behind her, as though one of the birch trees had suddenly come to life.

It was Piotr, naked. He held something in each hand. "Mother," he said.

Stephanie spun to face him, fur-lined robe swirling. The wolves stopped circling me and locked eyes on him, growling. "Quiet,"

Stephanie snapped, without looking at them. "It's the prince." They subsided, sitting on their haunches.

"What are you doing here?" the queen asked her son. "You told me you weren't interested in attending this ceremony."

"I changed my mind," Piotr said. "But there won't be a ceremony."

"What?" Stephanie said. "Why?"

Piotr's answer was to lob what he held at the werewolves—small packets that burst on impact in clouds of pale dust. The wolves, almost comically, stood on their hind legs, scraping at their muzzles with their forepaws, then turned and ran, howling, as though their tails had been set on fire.

It was my signal. My arms were tied behind my back, but my legs remained free. I charged, driving my shoulder into Stephanie's back. She fell forward and I dashed through the drifting clouds from the bags Piotr had thrown, holding my breath as he'd instructed me. A minute later, I was past him, and in the forest. There, I turned.

Stephanie was already back on her feet, face furious in the moonlight, eyes flickering red. "Piotr, have you lost your mind?" she shouted. "Wolfsbane? You could have killed the guards!"

"Only if they were foolish enough to stand there and breathe it in, which they weren't," Piotr said. "And, no, I haven't lost my mind. You have."

The queen's eyes burned even redder. "How dare you!"

"All my life, you've told me stories of the First World and the Shapers," Piotr said. "You told me about all the wonderful worlds your friends in Ygrair's school intended to Shape. Now there's a chance for me to see some of those worlds. Shawna can take me to them."

My mouth tightened involuntarily. I still had grave doubts about that. On the other hand, I wasn't going to look a gift wolf-boy in the mouth. He was doing his best to keep me from joining the ranks of the periodically hirsute. I'd do my best to give him what he wanted.

"She's lying," Stephanie spat. "She's a Shaping of Patricia's, designed to weaken my hold on my kingdom!"

"If that's true, I'll find out soon enough," Piotr said. "Then I'll bite her myself."

Wait. What?

"You can't get away with this, Piotr. I'll have you chased down."

"I don't think that will be as easy as you think it will, Mother. I've wandered a lot farther than you have."

"Piotr . . ."

"Goodbye, Mother." Piotr flowed from boy-shape to wolf-shape, turned, and bounded toward me. He gave me a quick red-eyed look, and then dashed off into the darkness. Arms still tied behind me, I ran awkwardly after him.

I risked one glance back. Piotr had told me Stephanie wouldn't dare change and chase us herself, and it looked like he was right. I saw her turn and run for the door out of which we'd emerged. Of the werewolves Piotr had hurled his wolfsbane bombs at, there was no sign, but no doubt we'd soon have plenty of pursuers to take their place.

"Piotr!" I shouted. The wolf glanced over his shoulder. "I need my arms freed before I . . . *oof!*"

Before I trip, I'd intended to say. It's hard to run without your arms to balance yourself, and although I hadn't intended to give a practical example of the problem, that was exactly what I did, stepping into an unexpected hollow in the leaf-strewn forest floor, twisting and, unable to use my arms, going down hard.

I lay there, panting. Piotr-wolf looked down at me, red eyes blazing. Then Piotr-boy stood there. "Roll over," he said.

I did, awkwardly—it's also hard to roll over without your arms to help you. It's even harder to stay decently covered while doing so when all you're wearing is the equivalent of a bathrobe, but that concern was secondary. I felt his fingers on the rope binding my wrist, and then I was free. I pushed myself up and got to my feet, readjusting the robe. Piotr was back in wolf form. He gave me one red-eyed look, tongue lolling, then turned and loped away again. I followed, with considerably more agility and stability than before, though I wished my feet were tougher.

We reached a stream. Piotr immediately turned north and began running through the water. Sheets of it, glittering in the moonlight, splashed up around his furry body. I followed him, gritting my teeth against the bite of the bitterly cold water, splashing after him as fast as I could, which wasn't as fast as I would have liked, since the slippery rocks beneath my numbing feet threatened a sprained or broken ankle with every step.

Perhaps half a mile later, Piotr turned back to the same bank from which we'd come. We splashed out onto a shelf of solid rock. Piotr scrambled up some boulders and disappeared. I followed a bit more slowly and found myself looking into the dark mouth of a cave, or at least a space sheltered and overhung by boulders—it was hard to tell in the moonlight.

Suddenly, Piotr the boy was there, his body a pale blur in the darkness. "In here," he said. He dropped to his hands and knees and crawled into the cave. I followed, shivering, teeth chattering, barely able to feel my feet and toes.

My hand felt something rough. Canvas? A bag of some kind . . .

"Your boots," Piotr said. "Socks, too. I returned to your room last night while you slept and brought them here. I knew you would be barefoot. There is also a blanket."

"What about my clothes?" I said.

"They stank. I did not think you would want them."

You thought wrong, I thought, but did not say. The boots were more than welcome—much more running through the forest without footwear and my feet would be hamburger. Oh, sure, they'd toughen up eventually, but I couldn't afford to be slowed down. Still, I would dearly have loved to be making my escape wearing something more than a glorified bathrobe. At least Piotr had brought a blanket. I wrapped it around my shoulders and immediately felt warmer. My feet started to thaw a little, too, once inside both dry socks and the boots, comfortable footwear made specially for me before we left the last world.

"Now food," Piotr said. Something bumped into my knee. I reached out, found his hand, and something in it—a chunk of beef jerky, it felt like. I took it and bit into it, the salty solidity helping to steady my jaw, which was trying to tremble and make my teeth chatter.

"They'll be after us," I said.

"They're already after us," he replied. "But they can't track us through the stream."

"Why is there wolfsbane in a world Shaped to include werewolves?"

"There's also garlic," Piotr said. "For vampires." He laughed. "Well, and for cooking. My mother said she and Patricia wanted to keep as much of the 'lore' as possible."

"Lucky for me. But you're a werewolf. How can you handle the stuff?"

"My mother is the Shaper," he said. "It doesn't affect her, either. It's like her—our—ability to change anytime, day or night. She thought it best if she and her offspring, alone of all the werewolves, were not subject to the usual restrictions. She wears silver a lot, too. It impresses her subjects. I hear Patricia sometimes wears a cross and eats garlic, for the same reason."

Made sense, I guessed—as much as anything in a Shaped world

makes sense. "So what happens next?" With food and proper foot-wear, my shivering was beginning to subside, and for the first time in a long time, my heart rate was slowing toward normal . . . which was probably why I suddenly felt immensely tired.

"We wait for daylight," Piotr said. "Even if someone's after us, they'll be weak and stupid under the sun, whereas it doesn't bother me."

"And once the sun comes up?"

"We leave the kingdom and head north to find your friend. The two of you will do whatever it is you need to do, and then you'll take me with you to the next world you visit."

Do what we need to? What I needed to do was take Stephanie's *hokhmah*. She'd been standing in front of me, close enough to touch, but I'd had no clue even how to begin. And she was just *one* of the Shapers in this mixed-up world. Somehow, I had to get Queen Patricia's *hokhmah*, too.

And even if I succeeded, what Piotr wanted . . . "I told you. I don't know if that's possible."

"Then let us say you will try," Piotr said.

"I can say that," I said. "I will try." *But if I fail, you may cease to exist . . .*

We both fell silent then. I felt a shift in the air. Red eyes gleamed at me. Piotr had gone back to wolf form. Welcome warmth radiated from his fuzzy body.

My internal clock was screwed up, after daytime sleeping and nighttime wakefulness, but I hadn't slept well earlier (the imminent threat of being turned into a werewolf apparently being conducive to insomnia—who knew?) and I'd just done a considerable amount of running for my life, so my exhausted body told my internal clock to stop that infernal ticking, and went promptly to sleep.

I jerked awake.

I sensed at once that Piotr wasn't next to me anymore. I stared around. It wasn't as dark as it had been. Piotr crouched in boy-shape in the mouth of our shelter, silhouetted against the gray pre-dawn light, staring up into the sky.

After a moment, he turned and crawled back to my side. "What is it?" I asked him. "What did you see?"

"The last thing I expected, this far south, this near the border. Vampires. They landed somewhere on the other side of the river."

I opened my mouth, intending to ask him, "Won't your mother send werewolves to drive them off?", but stopped as, deep inside me, something sparked, like a warning light flashing to life on some internal control panel. "Karl!" I whispered.

"What?" Piotr said.

"Karl Yatsar. My companion. He's close." I paused again. "And he's coming this way."

"With vampires?" The air shifted as Piotr became a wolf. His dark, furry shape blotted out the light at the entrance for a moment, then he was gone. I crawled after him and looked out into the chill morning air.

The stream rushed along beneath our sheltering rocks. There were more rocks on the other side of the stream, and then trees. I looked left and right. No sign of Piotr. Nothing else moved, but I could sense Karl's presence, off to my left and on the other side of the river. I clambered out . . .

. . . and froze as Jakob's voice said, above and behind me, "Hello, Shawna."

SEVENTEEN

IF KARL HAD ever spent hours more miserable and uncomfortable than those he spent strapped to the belly of a giant bat winging its way over the moonlit valley, he couldn't remember them. The pressure of the straps across his chest and waist and legs grew intolerable, but he could do little to shift position. The cold settled into his bones and stiffened his muscles. His eyes streamed, so that eventually he had to close them and let his head hang down, but the flight was unsteady enough his skull then rolled from side to side and he had to raise his head again, beginning an endless cycle of looking up as long as he could and then letting his head drop.

He eventually fell into a kind of tortured daze, from which, just as the sky began to brighten in the east, he was jolted unpleasantly by their sudden descent.

The shadowy ground rushed up at him, and he gasped, adrenaline bringing him back to full alertness. Just when he thought he would bounce off the rocks he could now discern below, in a clearing surrounded by spiky evergreens, Seth grunted, pulled up, and slowed their descent with powerful sweeps of his wings. They settled as gently to the ground as though he had stepped from a curb. But as Karl's legs took his weight again for the first time in hours, he gasped in pain. Cramps seized both of them, as though his calves had been clamped in vises.

Suddenly Nicolas, in human form, was in front of him, little more than a pale shadow, but he recognized the voice. "Let me free you," he said, and reached for the straps. As the harness dropped open, Karl fell forward, catching himself on his hands and knees, panting as though he'd run a marathon.

Behind him, air shifted. He glanced over his shoulder to see Seth back in human form . . . although, he reminded himself, they were not human at all, but vampires: dangerously fast, strong, and, literally, bloodthirsty. He took a few deep breaths and then got to his knees and finally to his feet, while his escort donned robes from a pack one of the others had been carrying.

"Where are we?" Karl said. He bent over to massage first one thigh, then the other.

"On the border of Queen Stephanie's land, or as close as makes no difference," said Nicolas.

"Won't they know you are here?"

"The border is largely unpatrolled, and we are quite far from the lair. There is no reason for any werewolves to be nearby."

"Except to prevent vampire infiltration," Karl pointed out.

Nicolas shrugged. "We do not infiltrate the werewolf lands. The conflict has so far been limited to the Lands Between."

"Why?" Karl said.

"The Pact is broken," Nicolas said, "but that much of it remains. For either queen to attack the other's territory would be an escalation neither has yet risked, although that may soon . . ."

Karl quit listening. Inside him, the Shurak nanotechnology had suddenly come to life. "Shawna!" he said.

Nicolas broke off. "Your companion?"

"She's near." Karl looked around at his dim surroundings. The flat, lichen-covered rocks on which they'd landed sloped up toward a forested ridge and down to more forest below. He pointed up the slope and off to the right. "In that direction."

"If she's here," Nicolas said, "then . . ." He looked up at the sky.

"Half an hour until the sun finds us," he said. "Seth! Santano! Change! The rest of you, with me."

Seth and another man dropped their just-donned robes and turned back into bats, then leaped into the sky. Nicolas turned back to Karl. "Lead us."

Karl set off at once, climbing up the treed ridge. On the far side, the trees thinned again on the downward slope. Karl heard rushing water. His view of the stream he knew had to be there was blocked by rocks. More rocks rose on what he judged to be the far bank. His sense of Shawna's presence came firmly from that direction. "She's—" he began, but his voice was drowned out in a cacophony of shrieks and howls as Seth and Santano, the two vampires who had taken to the sky, suddenly swooped out of it again.

From atop the rocks where he knew Shawna waited, wolves leaped up to meet them.

I froze.

"The whole pack is here," Jakob said. "Maigrat, Eric . . . all your old friends."

Two wolves scrambled down to join us. I recognized Eric's pale-gray, half-grown wolf form, and Maigrat, from the white blaze running down her spine.

"It's time for you to . . ." Jakob began, then stopped. His head lifted, and he sniffed. "Vampires!" He turned back into a wolf and disappeared from my sight as two black bat-shapes swooped down and howls and snarls erupted from the bank above the rocks.

Maigrat spun and growled at Eric, clearly telling him to stay with me, then scrambled up the boulders and over the top to join the fray above. I looked across the river. I could sense Karl's presence, stronger than ever. I wondered where Piotr had gone.

Eric growled at me. "Stop it," I said. "The sun will be up in minutes and you're going to turn into an ordinary, weak, naked boy. Mind your manners."

His fur bristled, and he stepped closer. His eyes blazed red, and his lips drew back from his white fangs, and I flinched back despite myself. What I'd just said was absolutely true—but the sun wasn't up *yet*, and he still had plenty of time to rip my throat out, if he lost control, and now that I thought about it, I didn't know just how much control any werewolf had in wolf form, and especially not one who had just changed and was *also* a teenaged boy, a species that itself was not exactly known for self-control.

And then, suddenly, a second young wolf, silver and black, scrambled onto the ledge from the river side. Piotr! He shook himself, spraying me and Eric and the rocks with cold water, then advanced toward Eric, stiff-legged and growling.

Great, I thought. *Two teenaged werewolves squaring up for a fight over a girl. I'm sure this will end well.*

Not that I thought they thought of me as a girl in the, you know, "girl" sense . . .

I cast around for a weapon, but there was nothing on the rocky ledge, not even a loose stone to throw or use as a club.

Above me, snarls and howls and shrieks continued. I couldn't tell whether the vampires or the werewolves had the upper hand. Across the river, I sensed Karl getting farther away, moving upstream. Did he not sense me the way I sensed him? Or . . .

More sounds of combat, now from the *other* side of the river. Some of Jakob's pack must have crossed and attacked vampires over there, too—the vampires in whose company Karl had arrived. And what did *that* fact mean?

Piotr and Eric continued to circle each other—and then, suddenly, with no warning, Piotr flung himself at Eric, snarling. The two young wolves devolved into a single ball of teeth and fur and legs.

The sky had turned from gray to pale pink. I remembered what Piotr had said. Unlike the vampires, the werewolves would lose their power when the sun broke the *real* horizon. Here in the shade of the mountains, the vampires might have a deadly advantage for many minutes.

The werewolves must have known, too. I heard howls and yips rapidly fading, as if the pack were running for the cover of the trees. The vampires who had been above me flew over my head, back across the river to where their kind had also been fighting werewolves, but the sounds of battle had faded there, as well.

A moment later, in the space of an instant, the wolves snapping and gouging at each other shifted and became two naked boys wrestling on the rock. Eric pushed Piotr away and scrambled to his feet, holding his upper arm, blood welling between his fingers. Wide-eyed, he looked at Piotr, then at me.

Piotr stared back. He grinned—or, at least, showed his teeth—and then, very deliberately . . .

. . . he changed back into a wolf.

Growling, he took a step toward Eric. Then another.

Eric, defenseless, bleeding, looked utterly horrified and bewildered. He gave me one final terrified, wide-eyed stare, then spun and scrambled away, up the rocks, over the edge, and out of sight.

Piotr charged after him. I was afraid the werewolf prince would chase him and pull him down to his death, but Piotr only took one look over the top of the rocks, then turned and bounded back down to me. He shifted back into boy-shape the moment he was beside me. "He's gone."

"What about the vampires? The sun hasn't touched us yet . . ."

"They won't take any chances. They'll be gone, too. They won't want to be caught defenseless within my mother's realm. She'll send armed humans who don't care if the sun's shining." He looked across the river. "Is your companion near?"

"Not as near as he was." I pointed upstream. "He ran that way during the fighting."

Piotr nodded. "I'll fetch him. But you shouldn't stay here." He pointed downstream. "Head that way. I'll find you." Then he turned back into a wolf and bounded away.

"Wait—" I started to say, but he was gone.

I shot a nervous look at the top of the rocks. Though the pack might feel enfeebled after dawn, they were still nearby. But maybe, in goose-fleshy human form, they weren't very good at tracking. I took Piotr's advice and started downstream.

The sky grew brighter and bluer, and the sun found me at last. I relaxed a little at its touch. Now the vampires, too, were reduced to mere humans. And the only wolf in the forest should be Piotr.

Well, unless there were also ordinary non-shape-changing wolves. Which there might be. Also mountain lions, bears, snakes . . .

That was not a productive line of thought. I hurried over the shifting rocks along the edge of the streambed as fast as I dared. To my left, the bank became a dirt wall, exposed tree roots dangling from it, a sign the stream sometimes rose much higher than it was now. That meant I could add flash flooding to my list of worries, which—to be honest—was rather a refreshing change from vampires and werewolves.

The rush of water changed tone ahead of me, becoming deeper, more frantic, and I rounded a bend to find myself at the top of a steep hill, down which the river poured in a welter of white water. The dirt wall dwindled to only a couple of feet high where the forest began marching down the slope.

I had a clear view into the valley. A church steeple rose above the trees a couple of miles away, a sure sign of a village, but its slate roof had largely fallen away, revealing bare timbers. It seemed unlikely I would find sanctuary there.

I studied the descent. It looked precarious. I turned left. Maybe among the trees . . .

And there was Jakob, emerging from the forest, no longer a wolf, but a naked, dark-skinned man. Maigrat, pale in the sunlight, stood with him. They might have been Adam and Eve, except for the lack of fig leaves and the fact each of them held a makeshift club.

"You can't change," I said. It was the first thing that came into my mind.

"No," said Jakob. "But we are armed, at least crudely, and both of us are stronger than you. And we are . . . motivated. We will not let you escape."

I shot a look upstream. I could sense Karl back there some-where, getting closer, now on my side of the stream. Presumably, Piotr was with him.

Jakob followed my glance. "Prince Piotr will not save you."

He doesn't know about Karl, I thought. "How can you be sure?"

"Because he is busy."

The rest of the pack. While he fights them, these two plan to drag me back to Stephanie.

But Eric wasn't with them. They might not know Piotr could change even with the sun in the sky. And if that was the case, the poor naked saps of the pack who'd thought they would outnumber an ordinary boy had just found their hands full.

"I won't go with you," I said.

"What makes you think you have a choice?" Jakob said. He moved forward, Maigrat with him.

I backed up but, standing on the edge of the rushing river, there was nowhere to go.

I glanced downstream, wondering what would happen if I flung myself into the stream. The water flowed white and foaming around a number of very large, solid-looking rocks, and it seemed likely that, while my body would definitely escape Jakob and Maigrat's clutches, I wouldn't be along for the ride after the first impact or two.

"Come with us willingly," Jakob said, "or we will knock you down and drag you by force."

"Let's do that anyway," Maigrat growled.

I braced myself . . . and then, in the woods behind them, glimpsed movement. I forced myself to relax. "All right," I said. "Don't hurt me."

Karl Yatsar came into view. He had an armful of rocks. He set them on the ground.

I took a step forward to hold Jakob and Maigrat's attention. "You win."

"You were a fool to think it could be otherwise," Maigrat said. She reached for my arms . . .

. . . and a rock slammed into her naked back. She stumbled forward with a cry, then turned around. Jakob spun, as well. I seized the moment and dashed forward, driving my shoulder into Maigrat, grabbing and twisting the club-branch from her grip as she went down.

Jakob recovered from his surprise in an instant and swung his club at me. The ragged end of the branch tore the left sleeve of my robe and scored the flesh underneath, but then I was out of his reach, just long enough for Karl to throw a second rock. Jakob had to duck, and I gained a few more feet.

I glanced over my shoulder as I dashed for the forest. Maigrat was up again. Both werewolves charged after me. Two more rocks from Karl slowed them as they dodged, but it wouldn't be enough. I could already tell it wouldn't be enough. The dirt of the embankment crumbled beneath my feet. I slid backward, spun to face Maigrat and Jakob . . .

. . . and a young silver-and-black wolf leaped over my shoulder, landed on the rocks, and stood between me and the pack leaders, stiff-legged and bristling.

They looked utterly shocked. "Impossible!" Jakob said. He half-raised his club, but Piotr growled, a deep, threatening rumble, and Jakob thought better of whatever he'd been about to do. As a werewolf himself, he must have known exactly how outclassed he was, an ordinary human beneath the sun, facing a werewolf in lupine form.

"You won't escape," Maigrat shouted, glare slipping from Piotr to me to Karl. "None of you! Beneath the moon, we will find you. And then you will pay for your treachery!"

"That's your prince you're yelling at," I said, admittedly a little breathlessly. "And I'm pretty sure your queen still wants me alive. And, anyway, you'll have to catch us, first."

"We will," Jakob snarled. "We will." He threw aside his club and ran upstream, disappearing around the bend a moment later. After a final, defiant glare, Maigrat followed.

I winced, thinking of running barefoot on the riverside rocks, then turned as Karl Yatsar slid down the bank to stand beside me. "Well met," he said.

"That goes double for you," I said. "Pretty solid throwing arm. Did you ever play baseball?"

"First base." He looked at Piotr. "This . . . creature . . . led me to you. I take it he is with you?"

"Yes," I said. Piotr, after watching Jakob and Maigrat out of sight, turned and trotted back to us. I couldn't help myself. I reached out and ruffled the fur between his ears. He looked up at me and grinned a rather alarming werewolf grin.

"We should go," Karl said. "I was brought here by vampires. They will now be in human form, but they may still be searching for me."

"You really must tell me about your adventures sometime," I

said, and winced, hearing myself once again mimicking his formal style of speaking. "But maybe not right now."

"Perhaps not," Karl agreed. "We should, literally, make haste while the sun shines." He looked upstream, then at Piotr. "Although once night falls, it will be one wolf against many other creatures of the night."

Piotr flowed into boy-shape. "It will not come to fighting," he said. "I know a secret lair where we can hide out overnight. The pack doesn't know about it."

"Why not?" Karl said. "And also, who are you? Shawna called you a prince . . ."

"Prince Piotr," Piotr said. "Queen Stephanie is my mom." He gave Karl a big human grin almost as alarming as the wolfish one he'd given moments before, although with much smaller teeth. "And yes, I know she's one of this world's Shapers."

And then he was a wolf again.

Karl's eyebrows lifted. He turned to me. "This world has surprised me more than any other."

"Since you're supposed to be my all-knowledgeable guide, I find that less than reassuring," I pointed out.

"I never claimed to be all-knowledgeable," Karl said. "Just more knowledgeable than you. Only Ygrair is all-knowledgeable."

Is she? I had my doubts. By Karl's own account, she'd discovered the Labyrinth, not created it. It might hold surprises for her, too.

Well, I thought, *I guess if I survive this quest long enough, I'll find out.*

Out loud, I said, "Let's get out of here. Piotr?"

He gave me another alarmingly toothy grin, then turned and loped downhill, following the tumbling river to the north.

Feeling a bit like I'd fallen into an episode of *Lassie,* I followed, Karl Yatsar—finally!—at my side once more.

EIGHTEEN

WE LEFT THE river when we reached more level ground, following a trail of sorts that Piotr seemed to know intimately but I wouldn't even have noticed if I'd come across it on my own. We moved quickly and, for the most part, silently, since we had no way of knowing what sentries or patrols might be about.

Yet, we saw no one. The sun reached its zenith, and we paused under an overhanging shelf of rock in a narrow space between two forested hills. A spring trickled water down mossy rocks in the shadows. Piotr lapped from the pool it made. Karl and I cupped our hands beneath the stream and drank. The ice-cold water tasted wonderful. I was thirstier than I'd realized.

"Making good time," Piotr's voice said behind us. I turned around to see him sitting cross-legged on the ground. "We'll reach my hideaway by nightfall."

"Surely others of your kind also know about any 'hideaway' you know about," Karl said.

"Nope," Piotr said.

"Why not?" I asked.

He leaned back on his hands, unfolded his legs, and stretched them out in front of him. I sighed and decided I might as well just ignore him being naked from now on. It seemed less stressful. "You'll see."

"Is there food there?" I said. "Because I'm starving."

"Sure, there's food. Although I could run down a rabbit for you right now . . ."

"Could we safely light a fire?"

"No."

"Then I'll wait." Rabbit tartare didn't appeal.

"Let's keep moving, then." He flowed back into wolf-shape and led us out into the woods once more.

As the afternoon passed, we wended our way through the forest, forded the river again at a shallow place, and then climbed the valley slope, higher than I'd yet been, still following a barely-there trail that Piotr alone could see. The climb through thick forest offered no view of anything until, suddenly, as the sun neared the snow-covered peaks to the west, we came out into a clearing, turned, and saw the whole valley spread out before us.

Back the way we came, everything looked wild, but directly below us, and stretching to the north, were the Lands Between, dotted with farms and villages. From here, it wasn't as obvious as it had been below that they were largely abandoned and in ruins. Smoke rose into the declining sunlight from a walled town that was probably miles away—another of the fortified villages like Zarozje, I guessed.

Far to the north, a huge mountain shoulder stretched out into the valley. That had to be the ridge above Zarozje, although we were much too far away to see the village. Another day's journey beyond it lay the castle of Queen Patricia, guarding the southern border of the kingdom of vampires. We'd made it this far without being captured and dragged back, but could we keep it up?

Lost in the view, I didn't realize the others had moved on until wolf-Piotr yipped from behind me. I turned to see him on the far side of the clearing, standing in orange sunset-light, and Karl

Yatsar looking back at me impatiently. I crossed toward them. They didn't wait, plunging ahead into the trees.

We climbed for another twenty minutes, during which time the sun dropped behind the peaks and shadows gathered, though the sky remained bright. The climb became progressively steeper, and then, suddenly, we came out of the trees to find ourselves looking up at a sheer cliff of black stone.

Piotr turned left, trotted along the base of the cliff, turned toward it—and seemed to vanish into thin air. Karl glanced back at me, his face a pale blotch in the deepening twilight, and followed. He, too, disappeared.

I hurried to where I had last seen them and found myself looking into a cave. I put a hand against the cold stone and peered into the darkness. "Karl?" I called softly.

"Just inside," he said. "Waiting for light."

As though he had conjured it into being, a yellow glow sprang to life about twenty feet away, at the end of the tunnel at whose mouth I stood. I followed Karl to where the passage opened into a slightly larger chamber, to find Piotr, in boy form, just placing an oil lamp on a rough wooden table, illuminating his secret den.

Perhaps twenty feet long and a dozen wide, it boasted a pine-wood table, two accompanying chairs, and a low, wide bed, built of peeled logs lashed together with rawhide, gray woolen blankets and two red pillows piled at one end of a cloth-covered mattress. Past the bed was a fireplace, carved into the wall, already laid with wood and kindling. Rough wooden shelves in the opposite wall, next to the table, bore some loose piles of clothing and a few covered woven baskets. At the far end, a long crack, running from ceiling to floor, glistened with running water, which first pooled in a carved stone basin on a pedestal, then, overflowing that, vanished into an opening in the floor.

The whole cozy arrangement puzzled me. Why would a boy

who could turn into a wolf need a bed—especially one of that size? Why would he need a table, and even if he had gone to the trouble to make one—since he certainly couldn't have lugged it up here—why would he need two chairs, in his own private hideaway?

Piotr pulled a dark-green robe from one of the shelves, slipped it on, and cinched it around his middle. Then he took flint and steel from the table where he had set the lamp and knelt in front of the fireplace. A few flicks of his wrist, and a flame appeared and grew.

I expected the air to grow smoky, but it didn't. "A natural chimney?" Karl said, before I could.

Piotr stood and turned toward us, grinning. "Yes," he said. "I told you this place was perfect."

It was. And in a Shaped world, that made me suspicious. "And you just . . . found it?"

"Yes," he said, "but not here." He must have seen my puzzlement, because he laughed. "What I mean is, I found it on a map, tucked away in the palace library. And it's not on any of the maps given to the regular patrols."

"But your mother knows about it," I gently pointed out. "She has to. She's the Shaper. And this cave, with a spring, and a natural fireplace . . . if this wasn't Shaped by her, she must have had it constructed at some point."

"Well . . ." Piotr looked down at the floor. "I think she . . . when she and my father . . . I think they used to come up here when they wanted to . . . um, get away."

A lover's hideaway, for when she didn't want to have to deal with being queen, but just wanted to be a woman . . . werewolf . . . in love. *That explains the perfect-getaway vibe.*

"Then it is not secret at all," Karl said, in the disapproving-voice-of-doom he was so good at. "We should not stay here."

"Mom doesn't know I know about it," Piotr said defensively. "I never told her I found it. There's absolutely no reason she'd send anyone to look for us here."

Karl continued frowning, but he said nothing more. I wasn't particularly sure I trusted Piotr's assurances either, but the fire was already taking the chill off the place, and I was starving and foot-sore, and here there was water, and a bed with blankets and pil-lows, and . . . "You said something about food?"

Piotr nodded. "Human food!" he said. He went over to the shelves. From one of the baskets he pulled out a small wheel of cheese, covered with wax. From another, he took something long and narrow, wrapped in cloth and glistening with what looked like salt. "Cheese, sausages, things that stay good forever," he said.

"A long time, maybe, but not forever," I said dubiously. "How long have they been here?"

He laughed. "Just a few months. I didn't mean they've been here since my parents used to come here. I brought them myself, not that long ago. I like to hunt, but I like human food, too."

From elsewhere on the shelves, he produced a knife and pro-ceeded to cut each of us a good-sized wedge of the cheese and several slices of the sausage. The cheese was solid and sharply flavored, like a well-aged cheddar, and the sausage greasy and salty and absolutely wonderful. Sitting at the table, I ate my share, then ate more, then washed it down with water from the spring.

Then I looked at Karl, seated across from me. "All right," I said. "Now, tell me what happened to you, and I'll tell you what hap-pened to me, and then let's figure out what we do next."

Piotr, who was sitting on the bed, nodded eagerly. "I'd like to hear your story, too."

Karl sat back and wiped his mouth with the back of his hand. "Very well," he said. "When the vampires took me . . ."

As Karl told his tale—minus the deeply embarrassing interval he had spent under the thrall of Seraphina—he studied the werewolf prince, Piotr.

He knew it was possible for Shapers to have children with the Shaped citizens of their worlds, but he had never encountered it in a world like this, where two Shapers had conspired to effectively Shape each other, albeit indirectly. The fact the boy was a werewolf was one thing. The fact he was not constrained by the Shapers' will that the transformation from wolf to boy and back again should only happen at night, beneath the full moon, was another. It implied that he had inherited his mother's Shaping ability: that, given training and offered a place in the Labyrinth, he might even be able to Shape a world of his own.

Ygrair had never suggested to Karl that such a thing was possible. That troubled him. He had been blindsided by ignorance more than once since he had found Shawna and enlisted her help in his quest to save the Labyrinth from the Adversary. What *else* had Ygrair failed to tell him? Or what else, and this notion troubled him even more, did she herself not know about the Labyrinth?

That very day, he had told Shawna that while he was not all-knowledgeable, Ygrair was. He had always believed that to be true. But every time he encountered some situation for which she had not prepared him, it raised these doubts he did not wish to entertain.

To be fair, his preparation for this quest had been, of necessity, rushed. Ygrair had arrived in her Shaped world both seriously wounded and seriously enraged. The physical wounds had healed themselves quickly—Ygrair was not human, after all, no matter how much she might appear to be one. Even if her human body were destroyed, it would eventually reconstitute itself, and she would be reborn. She was, effectively, both immortal and invulnerable . . .

Or so he had always thought. But this time, it quickly became apparent that she had suffered some other kind of wound, not to her human appearance, but to her alien core. The Shurak, her own people, whom she had somehow gravely offended, though he did not know exactly how, had attacked the school in the First World. She had thrown into the Labyrinth the only two Shapers who were still there and sufficiently trained to Shape worlds of their own. One of those had been Shawna Keys. Unfortunately, the other had been the Adversary, because she had not realized then that he, too, was Shurak, and that he had been the spy who had summoned the attackers.

As the school burned around her, she had fled into the Labyrinth herself, but at the very moment of her escape, she had been struck by some kind of weapon that acted upon her like a virus might act upon a human, weakening her, slowly corroding the core of her being—specifically, that part of her which had opened the Labyrinth. As she had explained it to Karl, a thread of her being ran to every Shaped World, but as she weakened, those threads were attenuating. If they snapped, all the Shaped Worlds and all the billions of Shaped people and creatures within them would dissolve back into the extradimensional nothingness from whence they had arisen, and every Shaper would die.

Wounded as she was, she could not rebuild those threads herself, she had explained to him. Instead, she needed someone to gather the Shapers' knowledge of their worlds, their *hokhmah*, and bring it to her. Fortified with that gathered *hokhmah*, she would have both the strength to pour new power into the threads linking her to the Shaped worlds and the strength to fight off the infection of her soul caused by the Shurak weapon.

Karl Yatsar, who had first found her when she crashed on Earth so long ago, who had served her since, and to whom she had long ago given the ability to travel the worlds as her emissary and observer, could not gather that *hokhmah* himself. Though he longed to possess the power (for his own selfish reason), he was no Shaper. But, she said, she could give him the ability to seek out Shapers, to sense them within their worlds. Once he found one powerful enough, he could enlist him or her in Ygrair's great cause.

Do this for her, Ygrair had told him, and when he returned, she would at last make good on her promise to make him a Shaper in his own right.

He had thought long about what kind of world he would create. It would be the world of his youth, for the most part, though with poverty and disease and war eradicated. Within that peaceful world, he would happily take up residence, living his life quietly, thankfully, and joyfully with the woman whose face he still saw in his mind's eye every night as he fell asleep, and every morning when he woke: his long-dead fiancée, Laura.

Of course, she would only be a Shaped copy, and he had worried how that would eat at him over time, should his dream ever come true. And yet, strangely, Shawna Keys had given him new hope. Shawna Keys had somehow Shaped herself (which was not supposed to be possible) to forget that she was a Shaper, to forget her life in the First World entirely. Until Karl had entered her world—and, hard on his heels, the Adversary—she had thought it was the First World, the only world, and the people around her were real friends and family and lovers and acquaintances and strangers. She would have lived on in happy ignorance if circumstances had not conspired to prevent it.

It was now his hope that Ygrair could tell him how Shawna had accomplished her forgetting, so he could copy her feat, and live with his Shaped version of Laura in blissful ignorance of the truth . . . and with no memory of all the horrors he had seen in all the Shaped worlds he had visited, and all those he had yet to visit.

At the conclusion of Karl's recounting of his adventures in vampire land, he fell silent, gazing at Piotr with a contemplative expression. Piotr, as it happened, had fallen asleep, curled up at the foot of the bed. I guess changing back and forth, battling other werewolves, and running through the forest was just as exhausting as being threatened with being turned into a werewolf, rescued at the last minute, and tramping through the forest in the wake of a werewolf prince. While it was true that I, at least, had managed to stay awake during Karl's narrative, it was a near thing.

I yawned, and the sound brought Karl's gaze toward me. He looked almost surprised, as if he'd momentarily forgotten I was there. "So what's the . . ." I yawned again, even more widely. " . . . the plan?"

"We must get the *hokhmah* from both Shapers," Karl said.

"Well, duh. But how?" I shook my head. "I was right in front of Stephanie. Close enough to touch her, like the Adversary touched me in the Human Bean. That's all it took for him to steal my *hokhmah*. But I had no idea how to do that to Stephanie, or even if I could."

"I have been remiss," Karl said. "My assumption has always been that most Shapers, once told the tale and convinced you, too, were at Ygrair's school, would gladly share their *hokhmah* with you so you could take it to her. I have always believed she was universally beloved by her former students. As recent experiences have demonstrated, that is not the case."

"You think?"

"Coercively drawing out and copying another Shaper's *hokhmah* is intrusive and, it has always seemed to me, immoral," Karl continued, ignoring my sarcastic aside "A kind of violation. Equivalent to theft at the least, perhaps even to rape. But it seems we must resort to it."

"*I* must resort to it, you mean." I remembered what I had felt when the Adversary had taken a copy of my *hokhmah*. Had he then succeeded in killing me, he would have had full control of my world. And yes, it had felt . . . well, I didn't know what rape felt like, thank God, but it certainly had been intrusive, obscenely so.

I didn't like the idea of being the one forcibly seizing a copy of someone else's *hokhmah* any more than I had liked having mine forcibly seized. But what choice did I have? It had to be done to, literally, save the world—or rather, save the *worlds*, all of them, all of however-many-there-were Shaped worlds within the Labyrinth.

"Of course," Karl said.

"So," I said. "Can you teach me?"

"No," he said.

I blinked. "Then—"

"However," he continued, "the Shurak technology within me can teach . . . no, program, I think, is the word more commonly used for such things? . . . the Shurak technology within you."

I sighed. "I'll look for a knife."

He looked puzzled. "What?" Then his expression cleared. "Oh, you think you need my blood again. No, this is not like that. You just have to let me hold your hands." He offered his own across the table.

I took them. They were warm and callused.

His fingers tightened on mine. He closed his eyes. "I just have to access . . ." he murmured, then fell silent.

For a moment he stood perfectly still. Then his eyes opened and looked straight into mine, and, in that instant, I felt something like an electric shock, so sharp and sudden I snatched my hands back from his and jumped up, my chair falling backward with a bang.

The sound woke Piotr. He raised his tousled head and blinked at both of us. "What's going on?"

Neither of us answered. Karl kept his eyes on me. I stared at my hands, flexing them.

And just like that, in my mind appeared the knowledge of how to strip a copy of the *hokhmah* from an unwilling Shaper. I could not have put it into words, but I knew how it could be done, what it would feel like, and how to overcome resistance if it were offered.

I could do it. I knew I *would* do it.

And, possibly, hate myself for it.

Piotr was still staring at the two of us, head turning left and right. I took a deep breath. "Nothing important," I said, in belated answer to his question. My exhaustion abruptly redoubled, as if a heavy blanket hovering above my head had suddenly dropped around my shoulders. "I have to sleep."

"You take the bed," Piotr said. He got up, pulled off his monk's robe, put it back on the shelf, and then flowed into wolf-shape. He curled up by the fire, nose to tail, and his eyes closed almost at once.

Mine closed moments later. After pulling off my boots, I stretched out where I was, on the side of the wide bed closest to the cave wall and fell asleep in seconds.

NINETEEN

I WOKE TO find the cave wall inches from my nose, lit pale gray by diffuse daylight rather than by the yellow lantern-glow that had illuminated it when I'd closed my eyes. I'd slept through the night without waking. The new ability Karl had imparted to me still rested uneasily in the back of my mind.

I rolled over and sat up. Piotr was gone, and so was Karl, and I desperately needed to empty my bladder. I got up, pulled on my boots, and went to the mouth of the cave, to find Karl standing there, looking into the woods downslope. "Good morning," he said as I emerged.

"Good morning. Where's Piotr?"

"Hunting."

I grimaced. "I'll take cheese and sausage again, thanks."

"Not for us," Karl said. "For himself."

"Oh," I said. "Good."

"He thought we would prefer the supplies in the cave, and he is able to sustain himself in wolf form just as well as in human form."

"Great," I said. "If you'll excuse me . . ."

"Where are you going?" Karl called after me as I moved toward the woods.

"Think about it," I called back without turning around. "You'll figure it out."

A few minutes later, much more comfortable, I returned to find that Piotr had also returned. He had blood on his muzzle. He flowed into boy-shape, and the blood stayed where it was, now smeared across his face. He licked his lips.

Well, that's disturbing, I thought.

"No sign of pursuit," he said. "I went way down our trail."

"Excellent," Karl said. "We should move out at once, then."

A few minutes later, with Piotr once more a wolf, Karl carrying a bag with the cheese, sausage, and dried fruit that had been stored in the cave, and each of us carrying a rolled-up blanket and a wineskin (filled with water, alas, not wine), we started north again, paralleling the cliff in which the suspiciously convenient cave had been located.

Karl, I noticed, had also taken, and thrust into his belt, the largest knife from the cave, a utensil rather than a weapon, but sharp, and better than nothing . . . against humans. Pretty much useless against werewolves and vampires.

Once the sun cleared the cliff, late in the morning, and began both beating down on us and reflecting off the rock, the temperature climbed steadily toward uncomfortable. Still, we followed the rock face as far as we could, since the trees, not far below, hid the valley floor from us and therefore presumably also hid us from the valley floor. Those trees began to recede as the morning went on, though, leaving us no choice, if we wanted to stay hidden, but to descend.

Back in the forest, our northward progress slowed somewhat. Karl and I didn't talk, in case there was someone unseen within hearing distance, although I hoped Piotr's superior senses would give us advance warning of any threat.

Every now and then, Karl and I paused to rest, drink, and eat a little. Piotr took the opportunity during those short stops to range ahead and behind. Late in the morning, he reported a party of humans, heavily armed, mounted, and in a hurry, on a road far below us. "Caravan from one fortified village to another," Piotr guessed. "And anxious to make it before sunset."

"Shouldn't we join them?" I said. "I wouldn't mind an armed escort. And a horse." *I can't believe I just said that.* My nose tickled and I had to pinch my nostrils to cut off a sneeze. Apparently, I was not just physically allergic to horses, I was psychically allergic, too.

"I wouldn't recommend it," Piotr said. "They could be subjects of my mother."

"How does that work?" I said. "Humans living inside the borders of the two kingdoms, I mean."

"Werewolves and vampires aren't much for farming or raising livestock," Piotr said. "Humans do that for us. We pay well and offer security, and security has become even more important since the Pact broke down. Some of the humans who have fled the Lands Between, rather than join one of the fortified villages, have moved into one of the two kingdoms, instead, for protection from the rogues."

I sighed. "I guess we can't risk it, then."

"Agreed," Piotr said, and turned back into a wolf.

When night came, we were still high up the valley slope. With Jakob's pack, my journey from Zarozje to the werewolf kingdom had taken just two nights. But we had been on horses, and we were following a road. The ins and outs of the valley wall, and the thickness of the forest, meant we were still far from Father Thomas' village, never mind Queen Patricia's castle.

There was no handy, comfortable cave for us this night. We just stopped, in a place where deciduous trees created a canopy to hide us from the sky, and spent a cold, cheerless, and mostly silent night, not daring to light a fire or talk. We spread the blankets we had brought from Piotr's cave and all curled up together, Karl, me, and wolf-Piotr, whose furry body, as I'd noted the night he'd rescued me, put off a gratifying amount of heat.

I missed that warmth in the morning when he trotted off to reconnoiter. It was so cold I almost expected to see frost on the grass around us, and the stupid robe that was all I wore let in annoying blasts of icy air if I wasn't careful to keep it tightly cinched. (Again, I was grateful Piotr had at least provided me with my boots and socks . . . and annoyed he hadn't also brought me my clothes, filthy though they'd been.) Still, once we resumed our hike, I warmed up quickly enough, although it took a while for the aches left over from the previous day's exertions, compounded by sleeping on the ground, to work their way out of my sore muscles.

The second day passed much like the first, until late afternoon. Then, Piotr stopped and raised his head, sniffing. Karl and I stopped, too, and did our own blunt-nosed feeble-senses version of that. "Smoke," we each said, at almost the same time.

Piotr didn't change. He just looked at us with his glowing red eyes.

"We'll stay here," I told him.

Karl glanced at me. "How do you know that was what he was trying to communicate?"

"I speak Lassie," I said, which earned me the patented puzzled-Karl look for the first time in a while. I'd rather missed it.

We sat on the ground and waited for Piotr to return and report, which he did within a few minutes. "Cabin," he said, once he'd turned into a boy. "Smoke from the chimney."

"I don't suppose we can knock on the door and ask to spend the night," I said wistfully.

"No," Piotr and Karl said together.

"There are no trees between it and the cliff, and the land below it is sparsely forested all the way to the valley floor," Piotr said. "As we pass it, we're going to be exposed."

Since he was, of course, naked, I almost made a joke at that point, but restrained myself.

"I don't suppose we could pass you off as a large dog," I said, then shook my head. "No, of course not. I forgot about the glowing red eyes. Can't you do anything about that?"

"Can you change your eyes just by thinking about them?" Piotr said.

I sighed. "That would be cool, but no." *If I had Shaping power in this world, I could change yours*, I thought.

And then I second-thought. Or could I? Piotr was half-Shaper, half-Shaped. Could I Shape him?

Would I? *Should* I? Wasn't he more "real" than the others in this world?

I hoped I wouldn't have to face that particular ethical conundrum.

"We'll wait until twilight," Piotr said. "Poor light for human eyes, but no werewolves or vampires abroad yet."

It was a fine plan, except that, just after Piotr turned into a wolf and trotted off into the forest for another check along our trail, and while Karl and I were sharing a meager ration of our meager rations, a man's voice behind us said, "Stand up and turn around very slowly."

In my experience (no longer *entirely* garnered from TV and movies, but still mostly so), that's a phrase that means someone has a weapon aimed at you. I exchanged a glance with Karl, and then we both did exactly as we had been told.

A man stood at the edge of the clearing, a very large man, dressed in fur and leather, with wild, unkempt black hair and a thick black beard. He carried a basket-hilted sword on his left hip and a dagger on his right, but the weapon that captured most of my interest was the crossbow. It wasn't pointed at either one of us, exactly: it was pointed between us, so he could shoot either of us with equal alacrity.

"Human?" the man said.

"Yes," Karl said. "You have nothing to fear from us."

"I have nothing to fear from you, whatever you are," the man said. Sneered, really. "My weapons are silvered."

"We're just travelers," I said. "If you'll let us go in peace, we won't trouble you again."

"You're not troubling me now. Quite the opposite. Your appearance has saved *me* trouble. Now I won't have to hunt."

Uh-oh. "We'll be happy to share what food we have," I said, although I was pretty sure that wasn't at all what he had in mind.

"I have all the food I need." The man jerked his head over his shoulder. "To my cabin. Now." A wave of the crossbow emphasized the command.

Where's Piotr? I wondered, but then, remembering the man had said his weapons were silvered, hoped, if Piotr were nearby, he had also heard that and understood the danger to him.

Although the dangers to Karl and me seemed substantial, as well.

Our bearded host stayed well clear of us as we passed him, so that even if I were the sort of person to execute some amazing martial arts move—which I most definitely am not—I would have been a pincushion before I got anywhere near him. Karl was apparently no more Jackie Chan than I, and so we meekly walked through the woods to the cabin Piotr had spotted earlier, while I lamented the lost pistol in my lost backpack.

The cabin looked cozy enough, built of pine logs chinked with moss. A steady stream of smoke rose from a stone chimney at one end of the rough-shingled roof. Attached to the back of the main cabin was a kind of lean-to, with no windows and no visible doors.

The bearded man opened the door and motioned us through. To my surprise, there was no bed inside: just a rough-hewn table and even rougher stool on the hard-packed dirt floor, a large fireplace, with a fire crackling in a fashion that, had I been in a made-for-TV Christmas movie, I would have called "merry," but which, under the circumstances, I could only describe as "ominous," a nest of blankets in one corner, some shelves along one wall piled with what looked like a random selection of old clothes, and a really remarkable, nearly eye-watering smell—an animal smell. A musky smell. Like the smell in Queen Stephanie's palace, only more so, and with a different taint to it, a taint of corruption, of rotting meat.

"Dude, haven't you ever heard of air freshener?" I said.

"Be silent." Holding his crossbow on us, he went to the low door at the back of the cabin, which presumably led to the lean-to. He lifted the bar, setting it aside, then pushed the door open. "In!" he commanded, motioning with the crossbow.

I still wasn't Jackie Chan, and apparently Karl hadn't turned into him in the last five minutes, either. We both ducked into the lean-to.

The door closed behind us. The bar slammed shut. We were locked in.

It was very dark in the lean-to, and the smell was so strong now that I almost gagged. It would have been even worse if the room had been air-tight, but slivers of light shone here and there between the logs, and a little clean air made it inside along with the illumination. Thinking I could peek out and see if Piotr had returned, I took a step. My foot kicked something that rolled across the dirt floor. My eyes flicked down to track it. It brought up with a thump against the base of the far wall . . .

. . . and stared back at me with blank black eyeholes.

It was a human skull. A small one. Child-sized.

I gulped and stared around the floor. There were many more bones. Some of them still had bits of flesh clinging to them.

That explained the smell.

It also explained why our host had been so delighted to find us.

I glanced at Karl. "I have a bad feeling about this," I said, but not even my favorite go-to *Star Wars* quip could allay the sinking feeling of dread in the pit of my stomach.

We weren't the bearded man's guests, and it appeared we would only briefly be his prisoners.

We were his dinner.

TWENTY

KARL LOOKED AROUND at the bits and pieces of human corpses scattered around the room and breathed, because he had no choice, the stench of rotting flesh. He had seen worse in some of the worlds he had visited, but he had yet to gain any understanding of why Shapers chose to create worlds where this kind of thing was possible.

"It would seem our host is a werewolf," he said to Shawna. "Presumably one of the rogues we have been told have been troubling the Lands Between."

"I think you mean *eating* the Lands Between," Shawna said. In the dim light, she looked ill. She was staring at the empty eyeholes of the child's skull she had kicked across the bone-scattered dirt floor.

"We are probably safe until the sun goes down," Karl said. "Unless he has Piotr's ability to change under sunlight."

"Not unless Queen Stephanie managed to have an illegitimate son older than herself," Shawna said. "Piotr can only do it because he is half-Shaper."

"Then we must escape before nightfall."

"Thank you, Captain Obvious. Any ideas?"

Karl let the strange expression slide, as he so often did in his conversations with Shawna. "Unfortunately," he said heavily, "I believe our fate rests in Piotr's hands. He is our only hope for escape. If he does not return—or if he does return, tries to rescue us, and fails—and we are still here when the sun sets and our host can change . . . then the only hope, and a faint one it is, is that one of us might escape while the other is being overpowered and devoured. If it comes to that, I will attempt to focus his attention on me, so that you might have that slim chance of survival."

Shawna's eyes went wide and white in the gloom. "You'd do that?"

Karl felt stung by her tone of shock. "Certainly, I would. I am a man of honor, whatever else I might be. Why would you doubt it?"

"First, because chivalry is dead, and second, because you've told me before that if something happened to me, you'd just mourn and then move on in the hope of finding someone else who can complete the quest."

"First, chivalry is not dead," Karl said stiffly, "and second, that was before you were fully . . . activated."

"Activated?"

"You can now open Portals. You can now take *hokhmah* from other Shapers, whether they will it or not. You can succeed at the quest without me. I cannot take *hokhmah* from Shapers, because I am not a Shaper." That truth stung him more than her words. If he were to die here, he would never be a Shaper, and Laura would never live again. *But if I die, at least I will be with her. I have seen a great many strange worlds. If they can exist, why cannot a world where we are reunited after death with those we love?* "If I were to survive and not you," he carried on, after the barest of pauses, "I would, indeed, have to find another Shaper capable of carrying out that task. I might succeed in doing so but I might not. And even if I did, I might have to pass through a dozen more worlds to do so. The Adversary is working even now to find a way to traverse the Labyrinth himself, to enslave as many as he can and ultimately to destroy Ygrair and all the Shaped worlds. We cannot give him the time to do that. *Ergo*, you are more valuable than I."

Shawna shook her head vigorously. "You're wrong. I can't carry on the quest without you. I don't know how to get to Ygrair."

Karl took a deep breath, then said, "True. And it is also true that I had intended to keep the knowledge of how to find Ygrair to myself. But these circumstances are such that I believe I must change my plan." He spread his hands. "It is but another 'program' for the technology within you. And it is the last I have to offer you."

I stared at Karl. He had just shocked me six ways from Sunday, as my mother—my pretend, Shaped mother, at least—used to say. I'd had my doubts about him, and Ygrair. I'd wondered if he had some ulterior motive he wasn't sharing with me. (That went double for Ygrair.) And yet, giving me this gift, this new programming for the nanomites in my blood, would mean I didn't need him anymore. If anything happened to him here, or anywhere else, I could carry on with my quest, working my way ever closer to Ygrair.

It meant, in short, that Karl trusted me implicitly, which was humbling, considering I hadn't trusted him the same way.

"I accept," I said, because what else could I say? There was no way back to my long-lost life. I could only push forward.

"Take my hands," he said. Just as I had in the cave, I did so. He closed his eyes—I could see his face quite clearly now that my own eyes had adjusted to the gloom. His lips moved. And then . . .

Another shock, sharper this time than when he had given me the programming to strip Shapers of their *hokhmah*, as though a nurse had stabbed me with a hypodermic needle. I felt dizzy for a moment, so dizzy I swayed, and Karl had to grab my hands tightly to keep me from falling on my rear end in the dirt. (Considering what else was in that dirt, I was immediately grateful.)

Then the feeling passed. I took a deep breath, and promptly

regretted it, coughing as the stench of our enclosure filled my lungs. I swallowed hard. I was about to say nothing had changed, when suddenly . . . it did.

Within my mind spread a map, a vast map of interconnected dots, the dots glowing green, the lines connecting them glowing gold. At the center of that web glowed a single red dot, present, but not directly connected to any of the others. I closed my eyes to concentrate on the image, brightening and sharpening it by force of will. "That red dot . . . that's Ygrair's world?"

"Yes," Karl said.

"And around it . . . ?"

"The Labyrinth."

"A map to the Labyrinth," I breathed. "Wow." I marveled at it for a moment, but then realized it was less than informative. "Where's the big 'You Are Here' arrow?"

"Concentrate, and you will see . . . well, not that, of course, but where we are."

I concentrated . . . and sure enough, there we were, a blue diamond attached to one of the green dots. I concentrated again, and discovered I could zoom in. There were two golden lines stretching out from the dot our blue diamond was associated with. "Two Portals. But you said we would not be able to return to Robur's world . . . ?"

"Nor can we," Karl said. "The lines lead to two new worlds. Robur's world, as far as I can tell, with no Shaper still within it, has vanished from the map."

"But how can you tell?" My eyes were still closed. "The worlds are just dots. There's no information attached to any of them."

"There once was," Karl said. "I believe its disappearance to be a function of Ygrair's injuries."

I opened my eyes, the map vanishing as I did so, though I knew

I could call it back into being whenever I wished. "What do you mean?"

"She has, because of what was done to her, lost much of her connection to the Labyrinth. Lost the intimate knowledge of the myriad Shaped worlds she once enjoyed. And that will, over time, doom all of the Shaped worlds. Her power is not that of an ordinary Shaper. She opened the Labyrinth, and keeps it open, by force of will—but that will is informed by knowledge. Cut off from the *hokhmah* of all the Shaped worlds, her connection is weakening. Those golden threads you see in the map are already attenuating. Eventually, they will snap. And when that happens, all the Shaped worlds will be lost, even Robur's world, now inaccessible from all others, because that web you see is what gives structure to the Labyrinth, provides space for the worlds. If it collapses, the Labyrinth will return to its normal, formless, primordial chaos."

"'And the earth was without form, and void; and darkness was upon the face of the deep,'" I quoted from Sunday School memories.

"The parallel to the Genesis story of creation has not escaped me," Karl said. "The formless void may yet swallow all the Shaped worlds if you cannot bring the *hokhmah* of enough of them to Ygrair to forestall that fate."

"Ygrair's world is disconnected from all the others."

"You can still get there."

"Any time I want?"

"Not exactly. But from any open Portal . . . yes."

I blinked. "You mean you could have taken me to Ygrair's world *directly* from mine?"

"I could have," Karl said. "But what would be the point, if you are not carrying the *hokhmah* she needs to secure the Labyrinth?"

"What's the point?" I stared at him. "She could tell me about myself. She could tell me why I don't remember being a Shaper. Maybe she could restore my memories!"

"Maybe she could have once," Karl said. "But now she barely clings to life." He shook his head. "No, Shawna. Much as I would like to know the answer to the multiple mysteries surrounding you, to make the journey to Ygrair's world now would be worse than counterproductive. You might anger her, and within her own world, she has power to unmake even those of the First World."

That was new information, piled on top of other new information. Ygrair, the all-seeing woman at the center of the Labyrinth, was at death's door, and yet still capable of snuffing me out like a candle if I angered her? And Karl thought that was a possibility *even after all I had done for her*?

"Why do you serve this bitch?" I said, without thinking.

Karl's eyes narrowed. He jerked back his hands—I hadn't realized until then I was still holding them. "Do not speak so of Ygrair," he said . . . snarled, really, as if he were a werewolf.

My face flushed with anger, but I bit off my reply. "Fine. I won't go to Ygrair until I have a nice big stash of stolen *hokhmah* for her." *I sound like a drug dealer.* "But once I face her, I'm going to have some serious questions for her."

"Once you have delivered your 'stash of stolen *hokhmah*,'" Karl said, "you may interrogate her all you wish. If she unmakes you then, it will not matter."

My opinion of his chivalrousness had taken a definite nosedive in the few minutes since he'd offered to sacrifice himself so I might have a chance, however slim, of escaping and carrying on the quest. I decided to quit before the conversation sank any further into acrimony.

I looked around and found a clean patch of soil to sit on, near the child's skull I had kicked earlier. I turned it away, so it wasn't staring at me, and sank down next to it, my back to the rough logs of the wall.

Karl remained standing. He went to the side of the lean-to and peered out through a crack, back the way we had come.

"Any sign of Piotr?" I said.

"No," he said. But he continued to look out.

We passed the rest of the afternoon in silence. Piotr did not appear. Neither did our host. And Karl and I, it seemed, had said all we could find to say to each other that day, even though it might be our last.

Karl alternated between sitting on another clean(ish) patch of soil next to the door and rising and peering through the cracks. As it grew noticeably darker (and cooler) in the lean-to, he straightened from looking through the wall and said, "Dusk is falling. Our host will be able to change within the hour. I fear—"

Whatever he feared (which was almost certainly what I feared, too), he didn't get the chance to expound on it, because at that moment, I heard the sound of the bar being lifted from the door. A moment later, it opened.

Piotr, wonderful naked Piotr, stood there, grinning. "I think we should go, don't you?" he said.

I wanted to hug him. I scrambled to my feet.

Karl, already standing, frowned. "Where is the man who imprisoned us?"

"He hung around the cabin all day, but he disappeared a few minutes ago," Piotr said. "I've been watching. If we hurry, we can—"

"Can what?" said a booming voice. Piotr spun. I hurried forward so I could see what was going on.

The bearded man stood in the doorway of the cabin, a silhouette against the gray light beyond. "They are mine, pup. I caught them, fair and square. Leave now."

"I am Prince Piotr, son of Queen Stephanie, ruler of the Were-wolf Kingdom," Piotr said haughtily. "The queen has need of these two humans and has sent me to return them to her."

The bearded man laughed. "Queen Stephanie? I know her well." And then . . .

Watching werewolves change back and forth between human and wolf was unsettling enough. Watching that big, ugly man somehow transform himself into the spitting image of Stephanie was the stuff of nightmares. Piotr literally stumbled back from the sight, bumping into me. I grabbed his shoulders.

"I don't give a fig for who you are, or for your mother," the man said. His voice remained unchanged, which made his feminine appearance all the more unsettling. "I bow the knee to neither of your precious queens. I serve the one true ruler of us all, the Protector. And as you can see, I am no mere werewolf."

Piotr gathered himself, pulling free of my grasp. I let my hands fall to my sides.

"Release us," he said.

The man laughed again, and weirdly, his voice changed in the middle of it, becoming feminine—becoming Stephanie's. "You are naked, unarmed, and alone," he/she said. "The sun will not set for half an hour yet. All you have accomplished coming here is to make yourself my appetizer!"

Piotr growled, first in his human voice, then, in an instant, in the deep voice of his wolf form. Suddenly, Stephanie was gone, replaced by the bearded-man, now wide-eyed. "That's not possible!" he cried in his own voice. He backed up, scrabbling for the crossbow slung over his back, but Piotr, like a flash of silver-black lightning, crossed the room and leaped. There was a terrible crunching sound, a gurgling scream, blood sprayed, and the man fell backward. His feet drummed briefly against the ground, then were still. The stench of voided bowels filled the room, which really didn't need any added stench.

Piotr, growling, fully animal, ripped at him, tearing at his throat, at his belly, at his limbs. I turned away, hand to my mouth. Karl grabbed my arm. "We must get away from this place," he said urgently. "There will soon be both werewolves and vampires in the woods and sky, and the smell of blood will draw them here like flies to a carcass."

I could have done without that particular metaphor, but I forced myself to turn back, toward the door.

Piotr raised his bloodstained muzzle from the body on the ground. A loop of intestines hung from his mouth. I gagged—and so did he. He spat the organs onto the ground, and then spat again, coughing like a cat with a hairball. He wiped his muzzle with his foreleg, then turned from the fallen creature and contemptuously scratched dirt over the body with his hind legs.

And then he turned back into Piotr, rising to his feet and turning to look down at the body. Blood smeared his mouth and jaw and body. "There is something wrong with him," he said. He spat again, this time with his human mouth, and wiped the back of his hand across his lips, smearing the blood further. "He tasted . . . wrong."

I swallowed. "How do you know what a werewolf should taste like?"

"I know one shouldn't taste like that."

Vampires taste terrible. I remembered Jakob saying that, after the vampire attack on the pack. "Could he have been a vampire, instead?"

"No," Piotr said. "Vampires have a . . . look. They are always lean. This creature was bulky. And bearded. I don't know why, but no vampires have beards."

"But you saw how he changed . . ."

"Yes." He shook his head. "I don't know anything that can do that. How could he turn himself into someone else?"

"I don't think he did," I said. My brain had been worrying the problem. "If he had truly taken her shape and size—never mind the violation of the conservation of mass and energy—"

"The what?" Piotr said.

"Never mind. The point is, if he had really become a copy of Stephanie, the moment he spoke, he would have sounded different—maybe not exactly like her, but female, at least. But he didn't. His voice didn't change until he *made* it change, and then he made it change to sound *exactly* like Stephanie."

"Ah," Karl said. "He did not change himself, he changed us—he convinced us, somehow, that he first looked, and then sounded, like Stephanie. Not that I have seen Stephanie, but clearly the illusion was to convince you two."

"It was," I said. "But yes, it was definitely an illusion."

"And who is this 'Protector' he spoke of?" Karl said.

"I don't know," I said. "But the rogue vampire the pack killed while they were taking me to Stephanie said he served the Protector, too. Do you know, Piotr?"

"I've never heard of a Protector, no."

Although I was carefully not looking at the body on the floor, looking at a naked boy smeared with blood from the man he'd just disemboweled wasn't exactly an improvement. I decided to look at neither, instead turning my head toward the wall opposite the fireplace. Then I blinked. "Clothes!"

"*Non sequitur*," Karl said.

"Not at all." I pointed at the shelves attached to the wall. "Clothes. Real clothes. Not this monk's robe I'm wearing now." I went to look at them.

"They will have come from victims," Karl pointed out.

"I know that," I snapped. "But they're . . ." I started to say "clean," but then I caught a whiff of them. Even above the noisome stench of the cabin in general, they smelled like the boys' locker room in an un-air-conditioned high school after a week-long basketball tournament, which, believe it or not, was a smell I was familiar with. It might have been one of my fake memories, but it was a vivid one, all the same. "Unbloodied," I finished, instead.

I pawed through them, looking for those that, if not exactly clean, at least smelled least-offensive. I finally settled on a snug-fitting tunic with long sleeves, knit from gray wool, some stout trousers, and a leather vest with a rather fancy belt: men's clothing, no doubt, but protective, practical, warm, and above all, not a drafty robe.

I looked around at my companions. "Turn around. I'm going to get dressed."

Karl raised an eyebrow but turned his back. Piotr looked puzzled. "I don't understand," he said. "I have seen many women without—"

"Not me, you haven't," I snapped. "Nor will you if I have anything to say about it. Turn around."

He shrugged and turned his back.

I quickly skinned out of my robe and into the new clothing. No undergarments, of course, but I still felt far better clad and a little more ready to face whatever the next few horrible days might pile on top of what the last few horrible days had already dumped on us. "All right," I said.

"It will be dark soon," Piotr said, as he turned to face me again. "We must get away from this place. The spilling of blood here will attract both my people and the vampires." He turned into a wolf, jumped over the corpse in the doorway, and trotted into the clearing beyond.

"Go ahead," I said to Karl. "I want one more thing."

He raised an eyebrow at me, but left without comment, carefully stepping over the . . . remains.

I took some deep breaths, and then went over to those remains myself. Doing my best to ignore the gore, I took the crossbow from the rogue's hand, and the quarrel of silver-tipped bolts from beneath his body, though both were sticky with blood. I would wash them later.

Then I followed my companions into the gathering twilight.

TWENTY-ONE

IT WAS, OF course (because this is my life we're talking about), not long after leaving the dead rogue, just after the last of the twilight faded from the sky, that we encountered the werewolf patrol. Fortunately, the wind was blowing toward us down the valley, and Piotr smelled them before they smelled us.

We were in the woods, which had thickened again past the cabin, and much closer to the valley floor than we had yet traveled. We hoped the forest there, with a greater proportion of leafy deciduous trees than the forest farther up, would help shield us from any vampires that might be flying through the night, and toward that end we actually got a break, for once. Thick clouds had rolled in from the west, making the night far darker than it ever could be otherwise in this moonlit world. (A torrential downpour would have been even more helpful—albeit annoying—as a way to keep down our scent, but that fortunate, we weren't.

My first inkling of the approaching patrol was when Piotr became a boy, a pale lump crouching on the forest floor. "Get down," he whispered. Karl dropped at once, and I followed only a second later. "A pack," Piotr barely mouthed. I had to strain to hear him. He glanced at me. "Not Jakob's."

I fumbled for the crossbow, but he put his hand on my wrist. "No. Leave them to me."

Just like that, he was a wolf again, and trotted downhill and out of our sight.

After a moment, I heard the murmur of voices, though I couldn't make out the words. I tensed, ready to run, though I knew I could no more outrun a werewolf in wolf form through the forest than I could take to the sky (which was undoubtedly being patrolled by vampires anyway).

I shifted my weight, and a twig snapped beneath my knee. I froze. It was too dark to be certain, but I would have been willing to bet Karl was glaring at me.

The voices remained low. No one seemed upset or angry.

The conversation ended. Something came back through the trees toward us, announcing its presence first as two red eyes . . . and then changing shape. "They sensed us," Piotr said. "But as I'd hoped, they are traveling *south*. They have heard nothing of what has happened in the palace. I told them the humans with me are loyal servants of the queen, sent as emissaries to Zarozje, and that I am escorting them at my mother's command."

"And they believed that?" I said.

"Why shouldn't they? I'm the Prince." Piotr turned his head away, looking back down the slope. "But now we must move even faster. Sometime soon they may encounter those who have been sent to track us, and once they know the truth, they will lead those trackers here." He looked at the two of us again. "I will change into a wolf. Each of you take hold of my fur, one on each side. I can see in the dark. I can pick the fastest path. Otherwise, we'll be slowed by your stumbling."

A shifting in the air, and two red eyes looked at us. Since his body was largely invisible, it was disconcerting. But I told my primal brain to stop being silly, and as those eyes turned away, reached down, found the fur of his back, and grabbed hold. Karl took hold on the other side—I presumed; I couldn't really see him—and then Piotr started forward.

I'd never before taken a stroll through a pitch-black forest with a werewolf as my only guide. It was like one of the trust exercises they make you do at summer camp to bond with your cabinmates. Piotr moved insistently forward at a speed that terrified me, knowing there were trees and rocks and deadfalls all around. Yet the ground remained relatively level beneath my feet, and though I stumbled once or twice, I just gripped his fur tighter and never fell.

I had no choice but to trust him, but I also had no choice but to remember what I had seen in the cabin, when Piotr had raised a bloody muzzle, eyes glowing bright as coals, guts trailing from his teeth . . . even if he spit them out a minute later and changed into a boy to complain they tasted bad.

Actually, that had made the whole memory *worse*.

Piotr chose that moment to stop and growl, which made my heart jump around in my chest like it was on a trampoline. He held that way for a long moment, his glowing eyes turned skyward. *Vampires*, I thought.

I looked up, but the overcast sky was as dark as the forest. There could have been a hundred vampires circling over us like vultures in a cowboy movie and I'd never have known.

Nothing swooped down at us and either dragged us away or sank fangs into our throats, though, so for all I knew, Piotr had heard geese flying overhead and had enough birddog in him to point.

The thought was silly enough to make me smile, which was what I needed right about then.

Piotr lurched forward again, and I had to grab his fur to keep from losing him. We hurried on through the dark forest for . . . well, I had no way to tell time, but it felt like a week or two.

Then, suddenly, Piotr's fur vanished beneath my hand and I found myself touching naked flesh, which squirmed. It was an extremely disturbing sensation, and I snatched my fingers back. I sensed Piotr rising up on two legs beside me. "Carefully now," he said. "There's a ravine. We must go down the slope."

He turned back into a wolf. I took hold of his fur again, and he led us cautiously down a slope I undoubtedly would have tumbled headlong down if left on my own in the dark. When we reached the bottom, I could hear water running near our feet.

We walked along the ravine a few feet, and then Piotr stopped. He turned back into a boy. "There's a shelter here," he said. "Wait."

He stepped away, where, I couldn't tell; but then I heard the sound of flint and steel. A moment later, light shone inside a . . .

Well, I guess you'd call it a cave, but that seemed to assign an undeserved grandeur to the dank hollow we stepped into. Still, it was, as Piotr had called it, shelter.

I glanced at Karl. Hollow-eyed, he looked as exhausted as I felt (and presumably looked, as well, though I couldn't see myself). Piotr put the glass chimney on the lantern, which I now saw rested on a boulder, behind which was an ironbound wooden chest. He opened the chest and took out blankets and a packet of what proved to be dried meat and fruit.

I took the proffered food eagerly. The only reason I didn't gulp it down was that both the dried meat and the dried fruit took a great deal of mastication. Piotr took a flask from the trunk and slipped out while Karl and I were chewing, and brought it back filled with ice-cold water, presumably from the stream I had heard (but never saw) in the ravine.

"We can only rest here a little while," Piotr said. "Once the sun is up, we need to keep moving."

"How far is it to Zarozje?" I asked.

"With luck, we could reach it by the end of the day."

Karl frowned at me. "We aren't going to the village. We're going to the vampire castle."

"At least a day's travel beyond the village," I pointed out. "In Zarozje, we can get proper supplies. Even weapons. Father Thomas will help." *Maybe*, I thought, but kept that doubt to myself.

Piotr stared at me. Though he was in human form, I thought I still saw flecks of burning red deep in his eyes. "Zarozje," he said. "Isn't that where Elena was murdered?"

I couldn't deny it. "Outside it. Yes."

"I can't go into a place like that!"

I couldn't deny that, either. "No, you can't. But I can."

"You deliberately fled the village," Karl pointed out. "Will that not engender a certain amount of distrust?"

"It probably would," I said, "but Father Thomas doesn't know that. As far as he knows, I was captured by the werewolves against my will, taken from the orphanage along with Eric. I'll tell him I escaped the werewolves, and you escaped the vampires. He'll test us with holy water and silver to ensure we're human, then we'll be fine."

Karl looked unconvinced.

I decided to put my foot down. "I drive this quest now," I said. "I'm the only one who can make it succeed, remember? And I say we go to Zarozje."

Karl's face went . . . frozen. "Very well," he said, and that was that.

In the dark, as I lay wrapped in my blankets (I still had the one I'd brought from Piotr's hideaway, and with a second one from the trunk in this shelter was almost . . . well, cozy would be stretching it, but at least not freezing), listening to Karl breathing slowly and heavily not far away, Piotr's warm wolf-body between us, I was more honest with myself.

I didn't want to go to the village merely to obtain supplies, though those would be nice. I wanted to apologize. To tell Father Thomas what had happened to Eric. To tell him it was, in a way, my fault.

I knew what Karl would say. Father Thomas was merely another of the Shaped, an off-kilter copy of someone in the First World, a computer programmer, maybe, or an insurance broker. I owed him nothing, and indeed, I potentially threatened his existence by doing anything that distracted me from my primary goal of gathering the *hokhmah* from as many Shapers as I could and delivering it to the wounded Ygrair so she could preserve the Labyrinth.

Oh, yes, I knew what Karl would say. But I didn't care. I would do what I felt was right.

No matter what the consequences? some part of me asked the other part.

Yes, I told it . . . me . . . and then tried very hard to fall asleep.

Funny how that never works.

Karl woke, feeling a sudden absence. It took him only a moment to realize what it was: Piotr was gone, hunting perhaps, or patrolling, checking to make sure they remained safe from discovery. It was still dark, so he hadn't been asleep very long.

Now would be the time to wake Shawna and proceed on our own, Karl thought, but he rejected the idea at once. First, because it would be futile. Piotr would track them with laughable ease. Second, because it might be fatal. While both Queen Stephanie's and Queen Patricia's forces were probably under orders to take the two of them alive, their encounter in the cabin with the rogue . . . who had revealed a most interesting ability that Karl thought explained much about how this world had come to its present sorry pass . . . had proved there were many other creatures loose in this world under no such compunction.

But the third reason was the most concerning. Shawna would not agree.

He reviewed his decision to complete the programming of the Shurak technology she carried, to give her the power not only to strip *hokhmah* from Shapers but to find her way through the Labyrinth to Ygrair's secret world. He could not fault his reasoning. Their fates had hung by a thread; ensuring Shawna could carry on without him had seemed the prudent course of action.

In fact, if he were honest with himself, it was a course of action long overdue. He had been in peril many times since he had found Shawna, including the long weeks he was still in her world after she had traveled on to Robur's, and with her programming incomplete, his death would have doomed the Labyrinth. *Her* death might not, since there could still be Shapers to be found as powerful as she (and the late unlamented Robur) somewhere within the Labyrinth, but Karl was increasingly convinced he did not have time to look for them. In the back of his mind, always, was the knowledge of how badly wounded Ygrair had been . . . and the memory of that bloody shirt he had left in Shawna's world, just possibly providing the Adversary, who must certainly have found it, a big enough sample of the Shurak nanotechnology Karl carried to discover how to open Portals between worlds. Once he had that ability, he would not follow in Shawna and Karl's footsteps: he would take another route. They might encounter him in any world, if that were the case, or they might not see him again until they reached Ygrair's world . . . only to discover he had gotten there first, and their quest had already failed.

That risk meant time was of the essence (even though it was also variable, flowing at different rates in different worlds, and flowing very slowly indeed in Ygrair's world, perhaps the only thing that had saved the Labyrinth from collapsing already), and that meant it was quite likely Shawna was the quest's only hope of success.

And so, he would have to acquiesce to her new assumption of leadership. They would go to the village of Zarozje and wherever else she chose to go. His role had been reduced to advising her . . .

. . . and, he feared, trying to save her from the consequences of her own poor choices.

The mouth of their little cave was noticeably lighter than it had been when he woke. Dawn was coming.

He sat up as a wolf-shape blocked the light, then transformed into a boy. "Time to get moving," Piotr said; and so the long day began.

TWENTY-TWO

"THE VILLAGE GATES are still open," I said.

I was lying between Karl and Piotr (who was in naked-human form, which couldn't have been comfortable belly-down in the prickly undergrowth), on a low hill overlooking Zarozje. Off to our left, the lake sparkled in the light of the setting sun. To our right rose the towering cliff face from which Karl had been abducted by giant vampire bats, right after he'd pushed me off of the switch-back path into a handy tree, and the fact that sequence of events was not even close to the most unusual of my recent experiences said a lot about what my life had become.

"They will close soon," Karl said. "The sun is almost down. If you wish to enter, you must approach now." He turned his head to look at me. "Are you still set on this course of action?"

He'd asked me variations of that question several times that day, which was beginning to make me think he didn't fully support my decision. But I'd never wavered. (Okay, that wasn't completely true, I'd wavered internally several times, but I'd never wavered externally, where he could see it.)

"I'm sure," I said. And partly to not give myself one more opportunity to back out, I scrambled to my feet and started down the slope.

Behind me, I heard a scuffling sound, which I knew (because we had discussed it ahead of time) was Piotr sliding back down from the ridge and turning into a wolf, to patrol outside the village while we were inside it. I turned to look at Karl, still lying there. "Coming?"

He sighed heavily, then got to his feet, brushing leaves and twigs from his front. I did the same as he came down toward me, then together, we turned and picked our way downhill toward the village. Very shortly thereafter, urgent shouts provided auditory evidence that someone had taken notice of us.

Visual evidence followed in extremely short order as armed men appeared in the gate, watching us approach. "Hi!" I called out brightly. "I came back! Can I see Father Thomas, please?"

The biggest of the armed men, who boasted a bushy red beard, turned and said something to the man next to him, who happened to be the smallest of them. The little guy nodded and trotted back into the village. Then bearded-giant guy came out to greet us.

I remembered seeing him during my perambulations around the village during my one day there. He carried a cocked and loaded crossbow, aimed in our general direction. (My own crossbow, stolen from the dead rogue, was slung innocuously over my back.) "We thought you dead . . . or changed," he rumbled. Definitely a *basso profundo*. "The latter may still be true. You must be tested—again—before the sun sets."

"Back to the church?" I said.

"No. Outside the gate. Father Thomas will emerge momentarily."

I glanced west. The sun was almost to the mountains. "I hope he hurries."

Big bearded guy said nothing. I watched the sun slip lower. Even after it went out of sight I'd have a few minutes, because it was "true" sunset, below the horizon if we were on the sea or some other flat landscape—southern Saskatchewan, maybe—that controlled the werewolves' and vampires' ability to change.

Just half the sun still showed above the peaks when Father

Thomas finally appeared in the gate. He wore ordinary clothes—brown trousers, brown vest, a white shirt—the only indication of his holy orders the silver cross around his neck. He strode toward us, grim-faced, carrying a flask, accompanied by the smaller man who had been sent to fetch him. Without a word—or a warning—he unstoppered the flask and, rattling off a hurried bit of Latin, hurled holy—presumably—water into my face and Karl's in turn. The water was bracingly cold. I gasped, and heard Karl do the same.

Then Father Thomas gripped the cross around his neck and pressed it first to my forehead, then to Karl's. He pulled it back, studied us for a moment, and dropped the cross onto its chain. He handed the flask to the little guy, then took a silver pin from his pocket. He grabbed my hand and scratched the back of it, then did the same to Karl, who scowled but didn't flinch.

Father Thomas looked from me to Karl and back again, and then snapped at big bearded guy, "Bring them to the church, Simeon. And get those gates closed."

Father Thomas turned and strode away again. Big bearded guy—Simeon—didn't lower the crossbow, despite the fact we literally dripped with holy water and clearly weren't creatures of the night. He gestured with it, though. "In!"

"Thanks," I said. "Zarozje, hospitality capital of the Lands Between, that's what I always say." I strode forward. Karl followed me. I couldn't see it, yet somehow, I could feel his disapproving frown.

Through the gates we went, Simeon and the other guard behind us. "Close them," Simeon snapped to more guards just inside, and as we continued into the twilit village, where yellow light now gleamed through cracks in shuttered windows, we heard the gates creak shut behind us and close with a resounding boom.

Karl stepped up beside me. "They seem *very* happy to see you," he said. "I am *sure* this Father Thomas will *fully* embrace your request for assistance and supply you with *whatever* you require."

"Nobody likes a smart aleck," I said without looking at him.

We reached the square. The front door of the church stood open, and candlelight glowed within. Simeon prodded us up the steps and inside. Father Thomas awaited us in front of the altar, as though about to perform a marriage ceremony.

Not with Karl! I thought. I turned to Simeon. "Thank you so much. You've been a lovely escort," I said, even though I'd just told Karl nobody liked a smart aleck.

Simeon looked at me uncomprehending, then glanced past me at Father Thomas.

"You may go, Simeon." The priest's voice boomed in the empty church.

Simeon grunted, lowered his crossbow, and disappeared back into the square.

I walked down the aisle toward Father Thomas, my footsteps echoing, Karl's slightly out of sync behind me. Father Thomas did not move. Nor did he smile.

I stopped in front of him. "Hello, Father," I said. Karl came up beside me, and I indicated him. "This is my companion, Karl Yatsar. The one who was taken by vampires."

"And yet he lives," Father Thomas said. "As do you, and *you* were taken by werewolves. Neither of you has been devoured or changed. I am most interested in hearing your explanation for this otherwise inexplicable state of affairs." From the tone of his voice, he was already predisposed either to doubt our account or deeply dislike it.

"In a minute," I said. And then, surprising even myself—I hadn't known I was going to do it until that moment—I got down on one knee before him, bowed my head, and said, "Father Thomas, I came here to beg your forgiveness."

I heard a very slight intake of startled breath from Karl.

If I had likewise startled Father Thomas, he gave no indication of it. "An interesting request. For what am I supposed to forgive you?"

My own intake of breath before my answer was considerably larger than the one I had just heard from Karl. I raised my head to look at him. "For my part in what happened to Eric."

The priest had a great poker face, but that elicited something: a blink, a slight compression of the lips. "And what part was that?"

I seemed to need yet another big breath before continuing. "It was because of me he was in the street that night. It was because of me the werewolves captured him. If he had not been with me, he would have been safely asleep in his bed."

Now the priest's eyes narrowed, and his poker face slipped into a frown. "Explain." He made an irritable gesture. "And, please, stand."

I got back to my feet and, with Karl standing rigidly beside me, told him the truth: how I had felt I had to get out of the village to find Karl; how I had played on Eric's guilt at having slain Elena to get him to help me; how he had told me about the sunken door at the end of Tailor Street; how Jakob and Maigrat had gained access through that same door after crossing the supposed barrier of the lake, surprising us; how Maigrat had learned the truth from Eric of who had slain her sister, and given him the change-bite.

"There was no need for you to try to sneak out of the village." Thomas looked and sounded angry now. "I would have let you go. I told you, you were never our prisoner."

"I . . . wasn't sure," I said. "I'm . . . this is not my world, remember?"

"That much you make clear in very many ways." Thomas closed his eyes. "Eric knocked me down and went with the werewolves," he said, his voice little more than a whisper. "What has become of him?"

"This," said a new voice, from the open church door, and I spun, Karl with me.

Eric stood there, naked in the candlelight.

"Oh, Eric," Thomas said, his voice a choked mixture of grief and fear and anger. "My poor boy. You have been damned!"

Eric crossed the threshold. He crossed it as if he were pushing his way through a thick hedge of brambles, but he crossed it, and then came down the aisle toward us. "I have not, Father," he said. "Look. I am here in the church, where you said no werewolf could enter. Here, where I have spent so many hours praying and studying. Here, and not harmed." Then his face crumpled. "Or if I *am* damned," he whispered, "it was because of what I did, because of your teaching. I killed an innocent girl, Father A girl my own age, whose only fault was being different. She was never a threat to Shawna, or to any of us."

With shocking suddenness, hands grabbed me from behind, threw me hard to the stone floor. Father Thomas tugged at the crossbow I still wore across my back, trying to tear it free. Karl shoved him away, and as I rolled over, I saw the priest trip over the step up to the apse and fall onto his rear end in front of the altar. He grabbed the cross around his neck and thrust it out to the end of its chain as Eric moved past me to stand directly in front of him.

"Could you really kill me, Father?" Eric said, still in a whisper. "You raised me from childhood. I am still Eric. I'm still the same boy you knew." He spread his arms. "I am standing here where I helped you celebrate Mass so many times."

I clambered back to my feet. "Listen to him, Father Thomas! Queen Stephanie's werewolves are not evil monsters. They still uphold the Pact. The creatures killing humans in the Lands Between . . . they're rogues. They do not answer to the queen."

"To *either* queen," Karl said.

"The edicts are clear . . ." Father Thomas almost moaned. "Mother Church . . ."

"You have not heard from Mother Church in a very long time," I said. "Not since the Pact broke . . . not since you *assumed* the Pact broke. But if neither Queen Stephanie's werewolves nor Queen Patricia's vampires are attacking humans, then the Pact still holds, at least in some fashion. And if the Pact still holds, then the werewolves and vampires who swear fealty to the queens are *also* under the Church's protection, as they were under God's protection when He led them to this valley as the Great Cataclysm engulfed all the rest of the Earth."

"Father," Eric said. He knelt in front of the priest and held out his hands. "It's me. I'm me. Still me. I've changed in one way, but not in any way that matters."

Father Thomas suddenly lunged forward, the cross in his hand. He pressed it to Eric's forehead. The boy took a breath yet held firm. Thomas dropped the cross, fumbled in his vest, and pulled out the flask of holy water. Hands shaking, he unstoppered it and flung its remaining contents—just a few drops, it looked like—into Eric's face. Another intake of breath, but still Eric did not move or cry out.

"You see, Father?" Eric whispered. "I am not a creature of evil."

Something seemed to break inside Thomas. He drew a ragged breath and then lurched up and to his knees and almost fell forward to embrace Eric.

A deep growl sounded behind us, and I turned to see Piotr, in wolf form, fur bristling, standing behind Karl and me. Apparently, it was werewolf night at the church. I wondered if there'd been an announcement in the bulletin. "It's all right," I called out quickly. "Everything's all right."

Piotr growled again, and then flowed into boy-shape. "I followed that one," he said, jerking his head at Eric. "He entered through an opening in the wall below the water, at a place where the lake laps against the wall. I would never have known about it."

"He grew up here," I said.

Thomas' eyes, closed as he hugged Eric to him, opened. He stared at Piotr. "Another?" he said.

"I am Prince Piotr," Piotr said. "Son of Queen Stephanie. We uphold the Pact. You have nothing to fear from me."

"I know that now," Thomas said. "Eric . . ." He pushed the boy away, gently, and looked into his face. Tears glistened in his eyes. "Eric proves that. I should have understood, the moment he entered the church. The Pact holds, for at least some of the creatures of the night. If it did not, Eric and . . . Piotr . . . could never have entered this holy place at night."

I remembered him telling me that the first time he tested me, though he hadn't mentioned then that it was contingent on the existence of the Pact, which I hadn't known anything about at the time, so I wouldn't have understood if he had.

He glanced at Karl and me. "Which could also mean that these two have, in fact, been changed, but also uphold the Pact . . . ?"

"No," I said. "Still human."

"As am I," Karl said.

Thomas took a deep breath and actually managed a small, shaky smile as he looked from Eric to Piotr. "While I am happy to learn you are not evil monsters, being naked in a church is . . . frowned upon. Let's go into the vestry. I'll give you robes, and then we will go to my cottage and talk further. There is much I need to know."

He got up and held out his hand. Eric took it, and Thomas led him toward the vestry, with me and Karl and Piotr following.

"Why should being naked in a church matter?" Piotr said behind me. "This obsession with clothing you humans have puzzles me."

"We can't sprout fur at a moment's notice," I said. "We get cold."

That seemed to satisfy him for the moment, and in another moment, he and Eric were pulling on white, scarlet-belted robes in the vestry. Then we all went out the back door into the churchyard.

The only light came from the full moon: the previous night's clouds had blown away during the day, the wind that removed them bringing with it considerably colder weather, so that our breath puffed white in the moonlight. *Surely even Piotr is happy to have clothes to wear in this*, I thought.

In his cottage, Father Thomas lit a lantern, then the fire. He invited us to sit, which in practice meant two at the table and two on the bed. He poured wine for all of us. Eric looked surprised, but he took it. Piotr didn't look at all surprised, and also took it. I definitely took it. It was a rather sweet white—a German-style Riesling, or something similar. It occurred to me I'd had a variety of wines, all of which had have come from this single valley, even though there couldn't be that much climate variability within it. *One or both Shapers must be an oenophile*, I thought.

"I want to know what's going on in the valley," Father Thomas said without preamble. "What have you seen? What do you know?" He looked at Karl and me. "What are you trying to do?" He looked at Eric. "What are *you* going to do?"

Piotr, surprisingly, spoke first. "Before we say anything," he said, "I want to know why *this* one is here." He looked at Eric.

"My name is Eric," Eric said.

"Very well," Piotr replied. "Eric. How can you be here, without the pack?"

"Your mother ordered the pack not to pursue you."

Piotr blinked at that. "What? Why?"

"The queen said you would soon be captured anyway, because she will rule all the valley."

Piotr froze. "You mean . . . ?"

"Her anger at Queen Patricia, after the skirmish with the vampires that brought this one to our borders," he nodded to Karl, and I was struck by how his use of "this one" echoed Piotr's use of it when he was referring to Eric, "was intense."

I looked from one to the other of the boys. "Okay, so *you* both know what's going on. Care to tell the rest of us?"

"I cannot," Eric said. "My loyalty to the pack forbids it."

"I can," Piotr said. He met my eyes. "My mother's forces are moving south in force. They intend to attack Queen Patricia's castle. They intend to end the war between us once and for all and restore the Pact."

Karl frowned. "How will that restore the Pact?"

"Queen Patricia will be hostage," Piotr said. "She will command her vampires to stop their attacks on werewolves. It may be a reluctant peace, but peace will reign."

Karl shook his head. "It won't work."

Both Piotr and Eric glared at him. "How do you know?" they said together, then exchanged surprised looks. For his part, Father Thomas stood silently, eyes flicking from speaker to speaker. I suppose mine were, too.

"I have spoken to Queen Patricia," Karl said. "Her fury at your mother is every bit as great as the anger your mother directs toward her. Even if you take her hostage, she will not command her forces to stand down. The war will not end. It will explode into a bloodbath that will continue until one side or the other is exterminated."

"Her vampires won't attack if they know their queen could be killed," Piotr protested.

"Would the packs stand down if Queen Stephanie were taken hostage, if she did not order them to?"

Eric answered. "No. The packs obey the queen, but if she did not order them to stand down, they would continue to fight, to try to free her."

"And if she were killed?"

Eric showed his teeth in what was definitely not a boyish grin. "They would not rest until every vampire had been torn limb from limb and their entrails steamed upon the ground."

Oh . . . kay, I thought. I glanced at Father Thomas. That little outburst didn't seem very helpful to the "convince-the-priest-I'm-not-an-evil-monster" effort. On the other hand, the torn limbs and theoretically steaming entrails *(would they steam? Considering vampires are already dead? And I can't believe I just thought that)* in question belonged to vampires, so perhaps he saw that as a net good.

In any event, Father Thomas seemed unfazed. He looked from the boys to me. "This quest you say you are on. What exactly do you need to do?"

"I just need to get close enough to each queen to touch her," I said.

"To take their *hokhmah,*" Piotr said. I glanced at him, surprised. I kept forgetting he knew all the details of how this world had come into being—that he was, in fact, half-Shaper himself.

The word meant nothing to Eric, though. "The what?"

Father Thomas frowned. "I know that word. It is Hebrew. It means . . . wisdom." He looked at me with narrowed eyes. "How can you take 'wisdom' from someone merely by touching them?"

I hesitated. I looked at Karl. He shrugged. Clearly it was up to me to figure out how to explain what was going on. Part of me wanted to simply tell the truth, the whole truth, and nothing but the truth, and let the chips fall where they may. Except . . . Father Thomas was a man of faith, and to tell him that his Mother Church was imaginary, put in place by two women crafting a place where they could play at being werewolves and vampires, might destroy him. Nor could Eric hear the truth.

"It is a power I have by virtue of being from another world," I said, and winced a little as I said it, because I immediately saw myself as a wizened alien with a glowing finger touching Elliot's cut and making it vanish. But it fit the tale I had already more-or-less convinced Thomas was true. "The wisdom I need to gather is . . . a deep understanding. If I can fully understand both of the queens, I believe I can mediate a peace between them."

"It sounds like witchcraft," Father Thomas said, and I remembered him telling me the last witch had been executed two hundred years ago.

"Only because it comes from another world," I said. "Any sufficiently advanced . . . knowledge and practice . . . is . . . indistinguishable from witchcraft." *With apologies to Arthur C. Clarke.* It was the second time his law had sprung to mind since I'd been in this world.

The priest's fingers tightened on his mug of wine, but when he spoke, it was not to denounce me. "You have convinced me already that my view of good and evil is . . . simplistic." He looked at Eric. "You have led Eric back to me when I thought he was lost to evil forever, and he himself has proved to me he is not a monster." He closed his eyes and bowed his head. "And may God have mercy on the soul of that poor child who died because I believed otherwise." He murmured something, a prayer, no doubt, crossed himself, then lifted his gaze to me again. "If you say you need to get close enough to Queen Patricia to touch her, so that you can bring peace to our world once more, then I am willing to accept that, even if I don't fully understand it." He smiled a little. "'Lord, I believe; help thou mine unbelief.'"

"Your faith does you credit," Karl said, "but you need not rely merely on belief."

I shot him a surprised look.

"If you help us get Shawna to Queen Patricia, she either will, or will not, take the queen's *hokhmah*. Once she has it, she can . . . call it 'influence' . . . this world, at least in some fashion. Exactly how much she will be able to do, I am not certain. But she will be able to do something, and if she is able to do *anything*, that will be proof that she tells you the truth now."

Not bad, I thought. And absolutely true. Well, maybe. Because *would* I be able to Shape—"influence"—this world in "some fashion," with only half the *hokhmah*, drawn from only one of the Shapers? I had no idea, and I was willing to bet Karl didn't, either. But if it helped me get close enough to Queen Patricia to try, maybe the slight fib was worth it.

Oh, I thought. *Situation ethics. What would your Sunday School teacher have had to say about* that?

Well, that bird had flown. I'd been situationally ethical all over two worlds now, and while I had clung to my principles enough to apologize to Father Thomas for my role in getting Eric captured by werewolves, I still had to survive. I still had to complete my quest. I could not go backward, only forward. And to go forward, I needed all the help I—we—could get.

And then I remembered something else. "We may also have a better idea of why the Pact failed—which might help restore it," I told Father Thomas. "Have you ever heard of someone or something called the Protector?"

He raised an eyebrow. "No," he said. "Why do you ask?"

I told him about the rogue we had encountered. "He said he served the Protector, not either of the queens. At first, we though he was a werewolf, but Piotr thought he . . ." (I decided to avoid the word "tasted") " . . . seemed odd. And he had an ability that surprised all of us."

Father Thomas looked intrigued. "What sort of ability?"

"Just before he died, he took on the appearance of someone else."

"My mother," Piotr said.

Eric looked startled. "What?"

"Did he literally change, or was it an illusion?" Father Thomas said intently.

"Illusion," I said. "First his appearance changed, but not his voice; then his voice changed, too; then, instantly, he was himself again."

"It sounds like you know something of this," Karl said.

"Not this specific ability," the priest said, "but the ability to throw what is called a glamor is native to vampires. There are vampires who can project fear, others who can make themselves hard to see, not invisible, but difficult to focus on. Some authorities believe there are even vampires who can engender lust in their victims, so that they willingly open themselves to the vampire's fangs. There may be other glamors we don't know about."

"But he looked nothing like a vampire," I said, giving Karl a puzzled look; he'd turned away suddenly and gone to poke at the not-particularly-in-need-of-poking fire while the priest spoke. I turned back to Father Thomas. "He looked like a werewolf . . . and then he looked like Queen Stephanie. And the sun was not yet set."

"I cannot explain it," Father Thomas said. "Do you think this rogue and others of his kind had something to do with the collapse of the Pact?"

"Without a doubt," Karl said, returning from his strangely flustered poking of the fire. "Queen Patricia told me that Queen Stephanie in person led an attack on vampires. That attack, as she saw it, precipitated the outbreak of hostilities between the two kingdoms."

"And Queen Stephanie," I said, "told me that Queen Patricia personally led the attack that killed her husband, which *she* saw as the reason for the Pact's collapse."

"The face-changing glamor of this rogue you killed—and probably others—at work," Father Thomas said. His face lit up. "Then, you might not even need this otherworldly power of yours to restore the Pact! If we can prove to the queens that they have been duped, that they are the victims of someone else trying to sow dissent and destruction, they will surely join forces once more to root out this 'Protector' and make him pay for his crimes!"

Pretty big if, I thought. I forbore pointing out that restoring the Pact wasn't actually my goal at all—I still had to use my "otherworldly power" on each of the queens if Karl and I were going to fulfill our questly responsibility. As far as the Protector went . . . not my problem.

Thomas turned his back on us, gazing into the fire while he sipped his wine. I looked at Karl again, but his eyes were locked on Thomas. So were Eric's. Only Piotr met my gaze. He gave me a small, knowing smile. I smiled back, though the smile fled as I looked back at Thomas and reflected on the fact that Piotr thought he could follow me into the next world . . . and I was not at all sure he could, or that he should.

Sufficient unto the day is the ethical dilemma thereof, I thought.

Father Thomas took a final sip of wine, straightened his shoulders, and turned to face us. "I will help you," he said. "I will provide supplies and weapons."

"Thank you," Karl said.

"But more than that . . ." His gaze flicked to each of us in turn. " . . . I am coming with you."

TWENTY-THREE

FATHER THOMAS' DECLARATION, while unexpected, was certainly not unwelcome. He took us out into the village, gathering for us, as the evening progressed, additional food and water, fresh clothes (undergarments! yay!), warm cloaks, extra clothes, packs, daggers, and sturdy staves (even for Eric, who, since we would be traveling by day, would be a normal boy; Piotr, of course, while he suffered to wear the white robe he'd been given by Father Thomas around the village, intended to travel in wolf form), and then showed us an empty-but-furnished house where we could sleep in actual beds. The owner, he said, had died recently—victim of neither rogue nor plague, he assured us—and had had no heirs to claim his worldly possessions, which would soon be going to those in need. For the moment, those in need were us.

We rose in the predawn darkness and made our way to the gate. Father Thomas had spoken the day before to the reeve (a man I'd never met, which said something about where the real power in the village lay), and also to Simeon. Neither, apparently, had been happy about his decision, but no one had the authority to tell the priest he could not travel on what he said was business of the Mother Church—which, I suppose, it was.

Father Thomas had also offered to assemble an armed escort for us, but neither Karl nor I thought that a good idea. We needed to travel with some stealth, and we also needed to travel quickly.

However many werewolves might be making their way north to attack the castle, they could not be far now. We might have very little lead on them.

Simeon joined us as we waited in the chill air outside the brick building where I'd been temporarily ensconced under Eric's guard when I'd first come to the village. Through the open door, I heard the musical four-note chime of the little clock Thomas had told me announced the time of real dawn every day of the year. Simeon stepped forward as those notes died away and unbarred the gates. He pushed open one side. "God speed," he said to Father Thomas.

"Worry not," Father Thomas said. "I will be back within days."

Simeon said nothing to that, but even in the still-dim light, I saw doubt on his face.

Our little party left the village. The sun had not yet touched it, so, theoretically, there could still be vampires about, but Father Thomas had said they only risked staying out past real dawn, even in the shadow of the mountains, in extraordinary circumstances; Piotr had told me something similar, after the battle on the border.

I looked up at the switchback path that would take us to the top of the cliff that loomed over the village, remembering when I'd been brought down it, just a few days before—remembering, too, poor Elena. I glanced at Eric. He stood staring up at the cliff, tears glistening on his cheeks.

The moment we were out of sight of the gate, Piotr doffed his robe and shifted into wolf-shape. Then he loped along the path ahead of us, disappearing over the top of the cliff while we were still toiling up it, to scout out the forest beyond. By the time we reached the top, the sun shone full force across the valley floor. I looked out at the overgrown fields and abandoned farmhouses. The only living things I saw were herds of sheep and horses, unre-strained by fences that seemed mostly to have fallen.

"There's really a werewolf army out there?" I said to Eric.

"There's supposed to be," he said. "They hadn't set out yet when I left."

"Maybe they didn't."

"Maybe," he said, but not as if he believed it.

I didn't really believe it, either.

Piotr reappeared. He didn't bother turning into a boy, instead just giving a deep "woof," which clearly meant, "All clear." We set off through the woods I had last passed through in the misty, moonlit night while running from a party of vampires. Sunshine made a nice change.

We saw no one all day. All the werewolves and vampires were presumably holed up somewhere, hidden from the sun. Eric himself looked deeply unhappy to be out in it. "I feel so weak," he said at one point, as we labored up a slope. I didn't reply since I was busy gasping for breath.

As the sun passed the zenith and began its descent, I looked ahead and tried to judge how much farther we had to go to reach the vampire castle. I really didn't want to reach it after sunset.

Unfortunately, as Mick Jagger famously sang, you can't always get what you want. We reached the cottage where Karl and I had spent our first night just as the sun touched the saw-toothed peaks of the western mountains. There, we parted ways with Father Thomas. "Wait here," I told him. "Watch. If things go badly . . . get back to your village and warn them."

He frowned. "I had intended to enter the castle with you."

"Not a great idea, since if we're wrong, and they no longer uphold the Pact, you're literally food on feet," I said bluntly.

"They claim Stephanie is the one who no longer upholds the Pact," Karl said.

"I wouldn't recommend Father Thomas enter Stephanie's lair, either," I said.

Father Thomas nodded reluctantly. "Very well. I will tarry here. If things go badly, I will return to Zarozje and try to ensure its safety. But if things go well, I want to talk to the queens."

"If things go well, you can," I said.

Eric went to the priest. "Be safe," he said.

"You, too, son." Father Thomas embraced the boy.

We left him there, staring at the castle, and descended along the white-stone path that had been the first thing I'd seen when I'd opened the Portal.

I frowned. And which had had a werewolf on it. Why had a werewolf been this close to the castle?

Probably scouting, I answered myself. *Stephanie was already planning this assault, long before we popped up.*

We were at the bottom when Eric said, "Sun's down." He stripped, packed his clothes into the pack he carried, tucked the pack under a handy bush, then changed into a wolf. Piotr was behind us, watching our back trail. Eric now trotted forward, to use his sharper senses to try to minimize surprise.

Above us, the castle loomed on its rocky outcropping, spires and battlements silhouetted against the darkening sky. Lights began to glow in its many windows. I remembered how lit up it had been when we'd first seen it: for creatures of the night, the vampires seemed to love a brightly illuminated fortress.

Just for effect, it seemed, a clammy ground mist like the one that had bedeviled us the night before Karl was taken by the vampires rose up around us, given an unearthly (literally) glow by the ever-present moon. I pulled up short. "Not ideal timing," I said to Karl as he stepped up beside me. "What do we do?"

He shrugged. "We march up to the gate and demand to see Queen Patricia. I'm known in the castle, and they know I was sent south. She will want to see me. And she knows about you, so she'll want to see you, too."

"And the boys?"

"I think they'd better stay out here," Karl said. "And stay hidden."

I nodded. I whistled. I'd felt bad suggesting it as a signal for the boys, once they were in wolf form, but neither of them had understood why. "It is a sound that carries and that we can easily hear above other sounds," Piotr had said. "An excellent choice."

"But it's like . . . calling a dog."

Piotr had laughed. "No, it's like calling a wolf."

So, whistle I did, and the wolves came bounding through the mist, red eyes blazing. They didn't change. They could understand me fine in wolf form, though they couldn't talk. "We're approaching the castle," I said. "You two lie low. Don't get caught by vampires. Watch for any sign of Stephanie's attack."

Piotr did change then. "And if we see werewolves?" he said.

"Warn us," Karl said. "However it seems best."

Piotr nodded, and returned to wolf form. He and Eric ran off together, vanishing into the mist and darkness. The last of the daylight had faded from the sky, leaving only the looming moon. Karl and I set our eyes on the castle and began climbing the path to its gates.

I was wondering if there'd be a bell to ring, like at the gates of the Emerald City, but I never found out. We were still a hundred yards away when fetid air blasted me from above and behind, and sudden terror gripped me. I froze, trying to breathe, certain that death stood at my back.

"Karl Yatsar," said a strangely sibilant voice as cold as the grave. "How unexpected."

"Re . . . release us," Karl choked out, and just like that, the fear vanished.

I turned to see what had engendered it. A man-shape stood there, tall and slender, but a man-shape with the demonic eyes of the vampires in bat form. He was not clothed, but shadows seemed to wrap his naked form like a cloak.

Behind us, up the hill, I heard the sound of the castle gates swinging open. They gave off such a stereotypical haunted house groan I would have been tempted to laugh if there was the slightest chance I could have while facing the thing before us. Dim torchlight spilled down the path from the opened gates, just enough to show me the thing's face, too angular to be entirely human, with gleaming, slicked-back hair above the hell-pits of those glowing eyes. Fangs showed over lush lips.

"Shawna," Karl said, "allow me to introduce the Prince Consort of Queen Patricia. I believe you know of him."

I had to swallow before I could speak. "I . . . don't think so."

"My name is Dracula," said the vampire. "You must be Shawna Keys."

Dracula? I wanted to give Karl a withering look but didn't dare turn my head. He'd mentioned the queen's consort but somehow hadn't thought it important to mention the vampire's name. "*The* Dracula?" I said.

Dracula smiled. "I know of no other. The name means 'son of Dracul,' and I was an only child."

"We need to see the queen," Karl said. "Immediately."

Dracula's smile vanished. "You do not have the right to demand such a meeting."

"I am not *demanding* it," Karl said. "But I am *urgently requesting* it. I have returned with Shawna Keys, whom I went to retrieve from the kingdom of the werewolves. She escaped from the very presence of Queen Stephanie. We have reason to believe that Queen Stephanie is approaching with a large force of werewolves, to execute an assault aimed at capturing this castle. If we are correct in that belief, do you really think Queen Patricia will be pleased if our appearance before her is unnecessarily delayed?"

Dracula's eyes blazed bright, like embers fanned by a bellows. "An attack? Impossible. Our patrols would see any approaching force."

"Maybe it's still on its way," I said. "All we know is what we were told by someone from Stephanie's court. Don't you think we should pass that along to Queen Patricia?"

Suddenly, Dracula was back in bat form. He hissed, almost like a snake, the sound directed over our heads, and I turned to see two more winged vampires behind us. They had approached without the slightest sound; it felt like they had appeared out of thin air.

Werewolves were beginning to look not-so-bad. At least they were warm and fuzzy. These things were cold and dead.

As vampires are wont to be, I reminded myself. The Shapers had kept many traditional aspects of their creatures intact, even as they had warped others. These vampires, for example, could apparently reproduce like normal humans. I wondered how that worked. What did baby vampires drink? Did they nurse? Did they . . . ?

There are some things, I thought then, *I'd really rather not know*.

With a blast of wind, Dracula leaped into the air, winging up and over us and the castle wall, heading for a huge open window, ablaze with light, high up the side of the keep. Our silent guards pointed us toward the gate.

We climbed up that last hundred yards, our feet crunching on the path's crushed white stone. We passed between the ironbound doors into a torchlit courtyard. We paused there while our escorts closed and barred the gate behind us. Overhead, I saw Dracula—I presumed—emerge from the open window. Somehow, he must have communicated with many more of the castle guard in the few moments he had had to do so. The creatures streamed over us, at least two dozen of them, maybe more, winging their way from various parts of the castle, where large windows capable of accommodating them seemed to the be the norm. If hordes of werewolves were indeed somewhere out there in the valley, the vampires would surely see them.

But then, *No*, I thought. *Stephanie knows about the vampire patrols. She understands their abilities. Somehow, she will have hidden their approach.*

She's out there, for sure. But how close?

Not as close as the other queen, Patricia. In short order we entered the keep, climbed steps, walked down a hallway, turned left, turned left again, and strode along another long hallway, at the end of which light glowed through the open doors of what had to be the throne room.

We entered it. Just as Karl had described, it blazed with candles, so many they turned the air oppressively warm: and there on the black throne sat Queen Patricia, accompanied by two other female vampires, both dressed in long, flowing black robes trimmed with red fur, their feet (and presumably the rest of them) bare beneath. "Seraphina," Karl muttered under his breath. I glanced at him. His eyes were locked on the vampire to the queen's right, who looked like she'd stepped right out of the pages of an old comic book I'd seen once . . . *Vampirella*, that was it. *Seraphina, Vampirella. Pretty close . . .*

"Welcome back, lover," said Seraphina, and my eyes, which had drifted to her, slashed back to Karl.

Lover? He hadn't mentioned *that*. He hadn't mentioned *her*.

I wasn't jealous—there was nothing like that between us—but I was surprised he could be attracted to a . . .

My eyes suddenly turned back to Seraphina. *She's gorgeous. How did I miss that?* My breath quickened along with my pulse. I'm not gay or bi, but right then, if she'd asked me to, I would have . . .

"Seraphina," the queen said. "Stop it."

Just like that, just like Dracula's terror before it, the desire I felt vanished. I gasped, then swallowed, and very carefully did not look at Karl, who I was pretty sure was also very carefully not looking at me, although obviously I couldn't be certain without looking at him, in which case, he might look at me . . . so I didn't.

"I see you succeeded, Karl Yatsar," Queen Patricia said. "A surprise, since your escort returned with tales of a werewolf ambush and your disappearance."

"Our arrival coincided with a scheme of Stephanie's to turn Shawna into one of her werewolves," Karl said. "Fortunately, I was able to rescue her."

A lie, of course, but we had decided Piotr would not make an appearance in our tale. Nor would Eric. We didn't want vampires wondering where they were now and perhaps going in search of them.

"And you return with a wild tale of Stephanie planning an assault on this castle," the queen continued. "Unlikely in the extreme. Impossible, even, given our patrols."

"Yet we saw those patrols flying out in force as we entered," Karl said. "Surely at your command."

Patricia shrugged. "It costs nothing to check your story, and confirming it as a lie is worth some minimal effort. The question I have is, *why* would you lie about such a thing? Is this supposed intelligence coup intended to sway me to your side?"

"I did not lie. I told you what we were told," Karl said.

"Of course, you did," Patricia said. She turned her attention to me for the first time. "I presume you are this Shawna Keys of whom Karl spoke—the companion my followers saw him with but were unable to capture, due to the interference of the werewolves. Karl says you claim to be a Shaper."

I felt a surge of annoyance. "I don't *claim* to be a Shaper," I said. "I *am* a Shaper. Like you."

"Who lost her world to this . . . Adversary . . . Karl speaks of?"

"Yes," I said (perilously close to snarled, actually).

"When were you in Ygrair's school?"

"I left ten years ago."

"Some fifteen years after Stephanie and I graduated, then," she said. "Tell me, did Ygrair ever build that new girls' dorm she talked about, or did you have to freeze in the winter and swelter in the summer in old 'Heartbreak Hotel' like we did?"

I didn't say anything for a moment. Karl was looking at me. It sounded like a test. I could assume she'd made it all up, I could try to be vague, or . . .

To hell with it. "I have no idea," I said. "I have no memory of being in Ygrair's school."

I heard a sharp intake of breath from Karl, but I kept my eyes on Patricia.

Her eyebrows raised. She turned her gaze to Karl. "She remembers nothing of Ygrair, and yet you would have me give her my *hokhmah*?"

"I don't know why I don't remember," I said, forestalling any comment from Karl. *Talk to me, Queenie. I'm the Shaper, not him.* "But I *am* a Shaper. If you try to give me your *hokhmah* and it fails, you'll know I'm lying. But if it succeeds, it proves I'm telling the truth." *And let me get close, and I'll take it from you whether you want to give it to me or not. Because I can do that now.*

Patricia glanced back at me with a slightly surprised look, as though my speaking for myself was unexpected. "It might prove that, but it will not prove that you are an ally."

"I am not your ally," I said. "Nor am I Queen Stephanie's. I serve Ygrair. I want to save this world, and all the others in the Labyrinth. And to do that, I need your *hokhmah*."

Queen Patricia leaned back again. She steepled her fingers under her chin. "This needs consideration." She turned to the other vampire at her side, the one who wasn't Seraphina and who hadn't tried to magically seduce me. "Escort them to . . ."

To where, we never found out. A woman's voice rang out behind us, a voice I instantly recognized, but could not, for a moment, believe I was hearing: the voice of Queen Stephanie, queen of the werewolves.

"Hello, Trish," she said. "Long time, no see."

TWENTY-FOUR

QUEEN STEPHANIE STOOD in the doorway to the Great Hall, flanked by four giant wolves: one as dark as night, one dark gray with a white blaze on its back, one white as snow, one silver as . . . well, silver. Their eyes burned red above their snarling muzzles. They echoed their queen's announcement with rumbling growls.

I recognized all four of them: Jakob and Maigrat were the black-and-white-blazed pair in front. The white wolf and the silver one were two other members of the pack that had escorted me to Stephanie's kingdom.

Stephanie wore a simple belted robe; clearly, she hadn't wanted to make her grand entrance naked, but she also wanted to be prepared to change at a moment's notice.

Queen Patricia's head had jerked around at the sound of Stephanie's voice: now she leaped to her feet, face suddenly angular and alien, eyes black and blazing. "That's impossible!"

"My presence in your castle?" Stephanie turned and closed the doors into the hall, then walked to the side, where an iron bar leaned against the doorjamb, and placed it in brackets built into the door. Door sealed against any further intrusion, she turned back. The werewolves had never moved, their fiery eyes flicking back and forth among the queen, her attendants, Karl, and me. "Do you remember our Shaping of this world?"

Patricia stood still as a statue, hands clenched. "Of course, I remember."

"Do you remember how we decided each of us would Shape some pleasant surprises for the other to find, so that there would be things in the valley for us to discover with no preknowledge of their existence?"

"I remember," Patricia said. "The waterfall at your end of the valley was one of mine."

"And it is beautiful," Stephanie said. "As is the crystal-filled cavern I gave you."

"It is. Get to the point."

"There was another surprise I Shaped you've never found." Stephanie walked toward us, the wolves padding at her side, spreading out as they came. I saw Seraphina and the other attendant watching them. Both had likewise shifted into the non-bat vampire form, their black eyes burning as red as the wolves' and their fangs visible on their lush red lips. I felt nothing of Seraphina's seductive aura, or whatever glamor the other vampire might have. I suspected they would not work on the werewolves, anyway.

"I thought it would be amusing, on some special occasion—a birthday, perhaps, or the anniversary of our Shaping—to surprise you," Stephanie continued. "And so I Shaped, into your castle, a secret entrance, and a tunnel, and a staircase, and a hidden door, just outside your Great Hall. The appropriate time to use it never came, but I kept it secret from you, as I presume you have kept secret some of the surprises you Shaped for me . . . ?" She cocked her head, inviting Queen Patricia to respond.

Patricia only . . . smoldered, I think would be the word. Like Karl, I was swiveling my head back and forth, as if we were spectators at a tennis match who had somehow found ourselves on the court, the balls whizzing past our ears. This particular volley, Patricia did not return. To continue the metaphor, Stephanie had the advantage . . . although "love" was not the word I would have used to apply to Patricia's lack of scoring thus far.

Stephanie stopped a few feet away, glanced from me to Karl, but then spoke between us, to Patricia. "Of course," she said, "none of the surprises I Shaped for you could hold a candle . . ." (she took a sardonic look around at the plethora of candles in the hall) " . . . to the ultimate surprise you gave me: your decision to shatter the Pact by attacking one of my packs." And just like that, the mocking tone in her voice vanished, replaced by pure fury and hatred. "The pack my Geoffrey belonged to. *Whom you murdered*."

This time, Patricia returned the serve. "A lie," she spat. "*You* shattered the Pact with your unprovoked attack on a group of my vampires. My Dracula barely escaped."

"We attacked no one!" Stephanie shouted.

"Nor did we!" Patricia shouted back.

I cleared my throat. "We think we know how—"

"Silence!" both of them shouted at me, and suddenly one of the pack was at my feet, crouched and growling, red, burning eyes locked on mine. I swallowed. The face-shifting rogue explained how these two erstwhile friends had become enemies. But exactly how I was going to get them to listen to me, I wasn't sure. It seemed clear my next word might be my last.

They turned their blazing eyes from me back to each other. Stephanie took a deep, shuddering breath, clearly fighting to regain her composure before speaking again. "You know the truth," she said at last, coldly. "You lie now for only one reason—to maintain your cover of innocence in front of these spies, especially this woman," she jerked her head toward me, "whom you have Shaped with knowledge of the First World in a vain attempt to worm her into my confidence, so that you could launch an assault on my kingdom."

That was too much. I opened my mouth to protest. The werewolf guarding me growled, a growl full of murderous intent. Fuming, I closed my mouth again and pressed my lips together.

"*My* spies?" Patricia spat. "They're not mine, they're yours! The man allowed himself to be captured, lied to me, tried to sway me to his side, so he could spy on *me*. You cannot deny it."

"I do deny it!" Stephanie turned to face me. "And this woman will tell me all the details, once I complete what was interrupted three nights ago, and she becomes one of mine."

I froze. "Wait . . ." I said.

"Silence!" Stephanie shouted for the third time. She looked at her werewolves. "Keep the vampires where they are. Kill them if they try to interfere."

She reached for the belt of her robe, undid it, and slid it from her shoulders. She stood naked for only an instant, before her pale body reformed into wolf-shape. It was the first time I'd seen her in that form. She was not the largest wolf I'd seen, but she was the only one I'd seen with golden fur—not yellow, or orange, but pure metallic gold. And her eyes, of course, blazed brighter and redder than any other wolf's. *Well*, I thought inanely, *I suppose just because you've chosen to gain the ability to transform yourself into a ravening monster doesn't mean you can't look good doing it.*

She took a stiff-legged, threatening step toward me, golden fur bristling, burning-ruby eyes locked on mine. I tensed. Karl tensed. The werewolves tensed. They were all crouched, ready to spring in an instant at the vampires, who were also tensed.

It was, in short, a tense moment all around, which suddenly got even tenser, because two vampires in bat-shape burst in through the open window above the throne, each carrying a squirming young wolf. They pulled up short a few feet above the floor, clearly startled by the tableau before them. Their furry prisoners seized the moment, both managing to break free, twisting and snapping, dropping and landing easily on their powerful legs. I recognized them instantly: Piotr and Eric.

"Get reinforcements!" Patricia shouted to the flyers, who swung around the hall, wingbeats extinguishing a fair number of candles as they did so, and flew back out into the darkness, trailing beeswax-scented smoke.

Stephanie snarled, and leaped.

Not at Patricia. At me.

"*Hokhmah!*" Karl cried.

He needn't have bothered. I'd already realized what I had to try to do. The knowledge of how to do it now nestled inside me, a part of me, like a muscle I could move at will. Stephanie's paws slammed into my shoulders, driving me backward to the hard stone floor, but even as I slammed against it, wincing in pain, I was pulling her *hokhmah* into me.

The transfer was instantaneous, just as it had been when the Adversary took mine in the Human Bean in those horrific moments after the attack in which Aesha died. I had it!

And it did me no good, because a) I couldn't Shape someone from the First World, and b) Stephanie was only *one* of this world's Shapers. I might be able to Shape *vampires* to help me, since Stephanie had Shaped them originally, but I could do nothing to tell either Stephanie or her werewolves to stand down.

I realized all of that in one horrible instant, as Stephanie's slavering jaws spread and she prepared to either give me the change-bite that would turn me into one of hers, or possibly, if I had angered her enough, rip my throat out . . .

And then, a furry rocket slammed into her from the side, and she rolled off me, yipping in a surprisingly small-dog fashion.

Karl, suddenly at my side, hauled me upright. I gulped and stared at Stephanie, who had regained her feet but was glaring, motionless, at a smaller, more slender, silver-and-black werewolf, who matched her glare for glare: Piotr.

"Patricia," Karl said urgently.

"Right." I spun toward the vampire queen and started toward

her. Seraphina's eyes narrowed. I felt the start of her carnal aura, but I yelled "Stop!" with a touch of Shaping behind it, and just like that, it vanished.

The other vampire attendant released a taste of the terror Dracula had exuded, but it was pitiful compared to his, and a glance and push of Shaping from me erased it.

The success of both those Shapings was a huge relief, not just because they stopped the vampires from possibly sucking me dry, but because they showed I *had* Shaping power. I hadn't been certain I would. In Robur's world, I'd gained an enormous burst of power from the open Portal into my old world, but it had waned quickly. It had been days before my own power had reasserted itself.

On the other hand, in Robur's world, I'd received his *hokhmah* in a single, overwhelming blast when he died next to me. Maybe it had stunned my own power, driven it down deep. Here, I'd taken the *hokhmah* using the Shurak technology Karl had awakened inside me: a controlled extraction, rather than a hammer blow.

The werewolves surrounding me snarled, baring their teeth, a literally pointed reminder that this was, perhaps, not the best time to try to puzzle out the finer details of the working of alien technology. Jakob took a stiff-legged step toward me . . . but suddenly, Eric was between us, in boy form. Naked but defiant, he faced Jakob. "Leave her alone! This is what must be."

Jakob stayed a wolf, but Maigrat rose up in female form. "How dare you defy your pack leader!" she shouted. "Stand aside!"

"No," Eric said.

While they glared at each other, and Piotr and Stephanie glared at each other, I completed my approach to Patricia, who (there seemed to be a theme) was glaring at *me*. Her burning eyes narrowed. "What have you done?"

"Just what you were told I would do," I said. "I have Stephanie's *hokhmah.* Let me have yours, and I can end this battle, and restore the Pact, the Pact you were both misled into breaking. I can mend your world."

Patricia stared at me a moment longer. Then, "No," she said.

Vampires, I discovered, are fast. Far faster than werewolves. I barely registered her final word before she was on me. I gasped as her teeth plunged into my neck . . .

. . . but she had touched me.

I seized her *hokhmah,* but it did not stop the pull on my throat, the blood being sucked from me, the lassitude gripping my limbs . . .

And then she, like Stephanie before her, was slammed aside by a furry body, her fangs ripped from my throat. I spun around and sat down, hard, on the nearest surface—which happened to be Patricia's throne. Raising a shaking hand to my bleeding neck, I saw Eric, now in fur-shape, standing over the fallen queen, growling. But he was only one young werewolf. *She'll kill him . . .* I thought faintly.

Except, suddenly, he wasn't alone. Jakob and Maigrat and the others from his pack stood with him, staring down at Patricia, protecting him despite facing off against him moments before. Patricia looked furious, but she was outnumbered, and her attendants remained where they were, still in my thrall.

I felt weak, and my heart pounded hard in my ears. I lived, but I would not have much longer, had Patricia continued feeding. I pulled my hand away from my neck, staring at the scarlet staining it.

Karl came to my side. "Are you all right?" he said, which, considering the aforementioned bleeding neck, was perhaps not the most perspicacious question of the day.

"I'm alive," I said. I took another deep breath, and forced myself to my feet, pushing against the arms of the throne. Karl took my left arm to steady me as I wavered. "Piotr!" I called. "Stephanie! Quit growling at each other and try talking, instead!"

Piotr didn't look at me. He kept his gaze firmly locked on his mother. But Stephanie glanced my way, then at the vampire queen, held in place by the pack surrounding her, and stood up in human form. As Piotr continued to watch her, she walked to her robe and drew it on again. Only then did Piotr turn into a boy.

Stephanie glanced at me, but then turned her attention to him. "Why, Piotr?" she said.

"You were making a mistake, Mom," he replied, voice trembling. "You can see that now, can't you? Shawna really is what she says she is."

"I felt . . . something," Stephanie said. "My *hokhmah* . . ." She cocked her head. "I have no power," she said, turning to me. "I have not had any since we Shaped this world. But I can tell . . . it's still there. And yet I felt it leave."

"We share it," I said. I nodded at Patricia. "And I share hers, too. I now have the complete *hokhmah* of this . . ."

And then I faltered, because I realized, suddenly, that somehow, impossibly, that wasn't true. It wasn't complete. There was . . .

I turned my head and stared off into the southwest corner of the hall.

"Yes," Karl said beside me. "I feel it, too. That is the nearest place where a Portal can be opened . . . and somewhere near there, there is a third Shaper."

TWENTY-FIVE

"**WHAT ARE YOU** talking about?" Patricia said. "Stephanie and I Shaped this world together. No one else." I thought her choosing to participate in the conversation was pretty impressive, considering one werewolf had her pinned and four others were staring down at her, growling.

"She's right," Stephanie said.

"You're both wrong," I said. "I can feel her—or him—and so can Karl." I glanced at the wolves surrounding Patricia. "Let her up."

I didn't put any Shaping power into it, so as one (except for Eric) they glanced at Stephanie for confirmation. She nodded. "Let her up," she repeated.

They stepped back. Eric looked at me over his furry shoulder. I nodded, too. He backed away.

Patricia got to her feet. Her face smoothed into her normal human appearance. She eyed Stephanie warily. Just as warily, Stephanie eyed her back.

Karl continued to gaze off into the southwest corner. "It is very odd," he said, his voice troubled. "I cannot explain it. But I can feel the place where a Portal can be opened. And without question, close to it, there is another Shaper."

"First things first," I said. I looked up at the open window behind the throne. "Since Patricia called for reinforcements, I would expect, any minute now . . ."

Right on cue, a dozen winged vampires poured in. They swooped down . . .

. . . and I shouted, "Hold!", with Shaping power poured into the word.

The vampires landed. They shifted into naked-human shape.

I sighed. I'd seen more naked people in this world than I'd seen in ten years of watching that Home Theater Ticket series *Contest of Castles*—and that was saying something. *And now*, I suddenly realized, *I'll never see the final season. Bummer.* It seemed unlikely, with the dour and authoritarian Adversary now running my world, it had even aired. *Probably sucked anyway.*

The pack shifted into human form, too. A whole room full of naked people eyed each other suspiciously.

The immediate threat taken care of, I closed my eyes and concentrated. *Peace*, I thought, and Shaped. Without the *hokhmah* of that mysterious third Shaper, I could tell I couldn't make the kind of Shapings I had managed in my own world, creating quarries out of nothing, resetting time by three hours, conjuring fog, accidentally stirring up hurricanes—that kind of thing. But I could influence the Shaped vampires and werewolves within this hall . . . no, within the entire valley. I had the power.

I used it. *The Pact is restored*, I thought, and I felt that truth take hold.

I opened my eyes again, looked around the room of naked people, closed them for a moment, Shaped, and opened them again to see robes lying at everyone's feet. (And that, I could tell from how it had made me feel, was about the greatest act of physical shaping I could hope to manage with the *hokhmah* I currently possessed.) "Get dressed," I said, and put a little Shaping into that command, too.

As the werewolves and vampires covered up, Stephanie turned to stare at me. "You really are a Shaper," she said.

"Duh," I said.

Patricia's eyes were also wide. "I don't know what to say."

A new vampire flew into the room. He carried a struggling Father Thomas.

"Leave him alone!" Eric shouted.

The vampire landed and shifted into human form without releasing Thomas. It was Dracula. The Pact might have been restored, but that did nothing to influence individuals who felt their loved ones were threatened. "Harm the queen and this one dies," he said. Eric dropped his robe he had barely donned and turned back into a wolf.

"Eric! No!" I shouted.

Fur bristling, he held where he was, crouching.

"Vlad," Patricia said. "It's all right. Let him go."

Dracula hesitated. He stared around the room, clearly trying to make sense of what he saw.

"Vlad," Patricia said. "Please."

With a kind of hissing grunt, Dracula shoved Thomas to the ground. He fell to his hands and knees and stayed there, taking deep, shuddering breaths. In Dracula's grasp, the aura of terror must have been utterly paralyzing. But at least the priest hadn't been harmed.

Eric turned back into a boy and ran to Thomas' side. Dracula's clad-in-shadows routine didn't really work in a bright room, I realized with a sigh. *Keeping people clothed around here is like playing whack-a-mole.* I Shaped him a robe, as I had the others. "Get dressed," I ordered, and he obeyed.

Patricia's eyes shifted from him to me to him again, and I realized what she had just seen: I'd Shaped her consort, just a little, but still.

Piotr, meanwhile, scooped up Eric's robe and took it to him. Eric dressed, then they both knelt beside Father Thomas. All three spoke in low voices.

Dracula hurried to the queen. "Are you all right, blood of my heart?" he said.

"I'm fine," Patricia said. She took his hand in both of hers and held it to her breast. "I'm fine." She kissed him, then turned to face me, keeping his right hand clasped in her left. Her eyes shifted to Karl, still at my side. "Karl Yatsar," she said. "I must apologize for my doubts. You were telling the truth."

"I was," Karl said. "Were you?"

Her eyes narrowed. "I don't understand."

"There is a third Shaper. You said you Shaped this world with Stephanie, alone."

"And so I did," Patricia said.

"As I Shaped it with her, alone," Stephanie said. "With my best friend . . ."

She walked toward Patricia then, her eyes locked on the vampire queen's. "Tell me the truth," she said. "Did you kill Geoffrey?"

Patricia let go of Dracula's hand and reached out to Stephanie. "How could you ever have thought it? I knew . . . know . . . how much you loved him."

"I saw you do it," Stephanie said. "Or I thought I did. And the ones who attacked were recognized by those who survived on my side . . ."

"As you were seen," Patricia said, "by Dracula." She nodded to her consort. "And those of mine who survived the attack recognized other of the werewolves, as well."

Both queens looked at me. "You started to say you could explain this," Stephanie said.

"I think you'd better," Patricia added.

I nodded and told them about the rogue who had so convincingly altered his appearance.

"That sounds like a form of glamor," Patricia said, frowning.

"Glamor is a vampire trait . . . but none of my vampires have that particular ability."

"Because I did not Shape it into any of them," Stephanie said. She frowned in her turn. "Yet you say he looked like a werewolf?"

"Yes," I said. "Whatever he was, it seems clear his kind are behind the breaking of the Pact. And he told us he followed someone he called the 'Protector.' Whoever that is, he—or she—must be behind everything that's gone wrong."

Stephanie turned to Patricia, then, and pulled the vampire queen toward her. They embraced. I saw tears on Patricia's face. I felt a slight burning in my own eyes, but I put it down to the lingering smoke from the candles, more of which had sputtered out in the blast of Dracula's whirlwind entrance.

I looked at Karl. "So, are you thinking what I'm thinking?"

"I imagine I am. Obviously, this third Shaper must be the called the Protector."

"But why would he or she . . ."

Karl shook his head. "I do not know."

Oh, great, that phrase again, I thought.

"What I do know is, we must find him . . ."

" . . . or her," I put in.

"Or her," he agreed, "and take this Shaper's *hokhmah* as well. Only then will this world be protected from the Adversary, and only then will we have the full knowledge of it, which Ygrair must have."

I remembered thinking, back in Zarozje, that the Protector wasn't my problem. Clearly, I'd been wrong. "Great," I muttered. "Here I thought I'd just beat the final boss, and it turns out there's a whole 'nother level to go."

"Your words," Karl said, "make no sense to me. As usual."

I laughed. I still felt a little woozy from the blood Patricia had drained, and maybe from the Shaping of the cloaks. "Keep hold of me," I told Karl, and he gripped my arm, steadying me, as I walked down from the dais to where the two Shapers had just separated. They turned to look at me, like everyone else in the room, as I approached them.

"We're going to have to seek out this previously unsuspected Shaper," I said. "We're going to need an escort. And supplies."

"Where do you believe this . . . impossible person is?" Stephanie said. She and Patricia had stopped hugging, but they were still holding hands. I thought Dracula looked a little jealous.

I remembered something from the Jules Verne world. "Do you have a map of the valley?"

"Of course." Patricia glanced at Seraphina.

"Yes, Your Majesty," she said. She hurried off to a side door.

I looked around at the silent, almost frozen vampires and werewolves all around us, and raised my voice. "Talk amongst yourselves! Get to know one another! Does anybody know any good team-building exercises?"

Stephanie and Patricia laughed. No one else did. *At last!* I thought. *Someone who gets my jokes!* Karl, of course, just shook his head.

"Seriously, though," I said to the queens. "Maybe take charge here a bit? Yes, I can Shape things a little, but it's your world, and you rule."

They exchanged glances, then broke apart. Stephanie went immediately to her small pack. "Embry," she said to one of her men, "unbar the door, hurry out to our forces, and tell them that what they feel is true: the Pact is restored. Tell them to stand down. There will be no attack."

"Yes, Your Majesty." Embry hurried to the door, unbarred it, opened it, disrobed, changed into a white wolf, and dashed out past a large group of rather confused-looking vampires in human form, these clothed and armed in conventional fashion. Clearly, my restoration of the Pact had taken hold, however; they made no move to stop the werewolf.

"Vampires, gather before the throne!" Patricia cried. As the vampires in the hall and those Jakob had just revealed outside the door began to move, she took Dracula's hand and returned to her accustomed place of honor.

Dracula looked relieved. *Well*, I thought, *if your consort is also kind of a goddess, and she suddenly starts making eyes at another goddess, I suppose that* could *be threatening to a male ego.*

I rubbed the wound on my neck. The punctures seemed to have closed with alacrity, part of the original Shaping, no doubt. Karl was still supporting my other arm, but I felt stronger, so I smiled and told him to let go. Somewhat doubtfully, he did so.

With him close beside me, clearly afraid I might still keel over, I went to join my own little group, Piotr and Eric and Father Thomas, who now sat on the edge of the dais. The priest's breathing had returned to normal, but he still looked pale. "He came out of the sky," he said. "I barely knew he was there until . . . the terror . . . it drove me to the ground . . . I thought my heart would burst. Then he picked me up, flew me . . ."

"I'm sorry," I said. "I really thought you'd be safe in the cottage."

"I did not stay in the cottage," he admitted. "I was worried. I saw Eric and Piotr snatched away. I went down into the valley, looking for a way into the castle."

"Oh." I felt a surge of annoyance at his disobedience, then slapped it away. Father Thomas was his own man. He had accompanied us here for his own reasons, not because I had any right to command him. *Although he would have been better off if he'd obeyed me . . .*

I slapped that thought down, too. *I'm hanging out with too many princes, tyrants, and queens. It's starting to rub off.*

Power corrupts, as they say. And absolute power . . . like the power of a Shaper . . .

No. That isn't happening to me.

Not yet.

Shut up.

"The Pact is restored," I said out loud to Father Thomas.

His head jerked up, eyes wide. "The story of the rogue who could make himself look like one of the queens . . . it convinced them?"

"It helped," I said. "But no, I had to use that power of mine we told you about. I touched each of the queens, and took their *hokhmah*, their wisdom. And with it, I was able to influence them. I convinced them to restore the Pact."

"God be praised!" Father Thomas cried.

"God?" I said. "Not that long ago, you were worried my ability sounded like witchcraft."

"Witchcraft isn't used for good," he replied. "Therefore, this isn't witchcraft. And as to whether or not God was involved . . . I don't believe that's for you to say."

I smiled. "Touché."

Seraphina reentered the hall, carrying a map. She went first to Patricia, who said something to the vampires gathered around her, then rose from her throne and approached me with Seraphina and Dracula in tow. I caught Stephanie's eye across the room, and she disengaged herself from her cadre of werewolves and joined the rest of us off to one side of the dais, Piotr with her.

The remaining vampires suspiciously eyed the remaining were-wolves, whom they now greatly outnumbered. The werewolves attempted to make up for their small numbers by eying the vampires even more suspiciously in return. The Pact might be restored, but trust apparently remained in short supply.

Seraphina spread her map on the floor. For the first time I saw a complete representation of the valley. I was surprised how many villages were marked north of the castle and south of Stephanie's lair. There, presumably, something like more ordinary life continued. In the rogue-plagued Lands Between, however, there were far more villages marked. I wondered how many had been destroyed or emptied, and which remained intact, but heavily fortified.

"What are you looking for?" Thomas said.

"It's hard to explain," I said. Of those around us, Piotr, Stephanie, Dracula, and Patricia—well, and Karl, of course—knew the truth of the Shaping of this world. Eric, Seraphina, and Father Thomas did not. "Please. I have to concentrate."

I closed my eyes to better get in touch with my inner alien technology, which was less fun than getting in touch with my inner child but more fun than getting in touch with my inner demons. I could sense the mysterious third Shaper, and the potential Portal, practically in the same place, and that place was . . .

I opened my eyes and pointed at the map. "There. That's where we have to go."

Everyone leaned forward to see where I was pointing.

Father Thomas spoke first. "Mother Church," he said reverentially. "You're going to Mother Church, at the end of the Sacred Vale!" He looked at me. His face was alight with joy. "And if the Pact is restored then I can come with you!"

TWENTY-SIX

I LOOKED AT the spot on the map I had pointed to. It was far off to the west, down a long side valley—the Sacred Vale, apparently.

"Four or five days' travel on foot from here," Father Thomas said. "But if the Lands Between are no longer beset, it will be an easy trip."

"But they *are* still 'beset,'" Karl said. "By the rogues."

"Followers of this 'Protector,'" Stephanie said, frowning.

"Some of whom have the ability to change their appearance," Patricia said, also frowning.

"The restoration of the Pact will mean nothing to them, because they bear no allegiance to the queens," Karl said.

"But what are they, exactly?" Patricia said. "Again, this illusion-casting ability sounds like something a vampire would have, yet you said the one you encountered looked physically more like a werewolf."

Piotr nodded. "And he tasted . . . wrong."

I looked around the group. Only Father Thomas seemed the slightest bit surprised or disturbed by that last sentence. The vampires and werewolves just frowned.

"Wrong how?" Stephanie said. As opposed to, say, a horrified, "You ate him?" which, you know, an ordinary mother might have said if her son had confessed to cannibalism.

"He tasted . . . of old blood. Dead blood. He looked like a were-wolf, but he tasted like a vampire."

Jakob, though he was standing some distance away, reacted to that, coming forward. "The rogue we killed, the one who devoured the farm family, who also professed to be ruled by this 'Protector,' also tasted wrong."

"But you also said 'Vampires taste terrible,' after the attack on us," I blurted, which perhaps was not the most diplomatic thing to say at that moment, considering we were in the throne room of the vampire queen and the vampires outnumbered the werewolves by a considerable number.

"It's true," Jakob said, eying the assembled vampires, who eyed him back. "All vampires taste terrible. But this one tasted terrible in a different way; like Piotr said, a *wrong* way."

"Werewolves taste terrible, too," Dracula said.

"We Shaped it that way," Stephanie murmured to me. "We didn't want them to develop a taste for each other."

"So these bad-tasting rogues are not something you two Shaped," Karl said. "They are the work of the Third Shaper, who styles him-self the Protector." He tapped the map. "Whom we will find at Mother Church. I feel him there."

"Or her," I said.

He inclined his head. "Or her."

I glanced around the gathered group. Those not in the know were looking puzzled, especially Father Thomas, at this talk of "Shaping" and "Shapers."

"But how can there be a *third* Shaper?" Stephanie demanded. "How could Patricia and I not know of such a person until now?"

"We will not know until we confront the Protector," Karl said.

"Four or five days?" I said to Thomas.

He nodded.

"It does not have to be four or five days," Patricia said.

Karl, for some reason, winced.

I frowned. "I don't . . ." Then I realized what she meant. I should have twigged sooner—I'd seen it often enough. "Your vampires can fly us there?"

"In a single night."

"It is not a pleasant way to travel," Karl warned.

"But it is fast," Patricia countered. "And it will keep you clear of any—as Karl put it—bad-tasting rogues. With the Pact restored, Stephanie and I and our forces will work jointly to clear these monsters out of the Lands Between, so they can be repopulated, the villages and farms restored. But that will take time. Months. Years, perhaps."

"It will, indeed," Karl said. "And if this third Shaper has already sabotaged your intentions for this world once, I think you can be certain he, or she, will attempt to do so again. And if some or all of these rogues share the power of illusion demonstrated by the one we encountered . . ."

"If they're like vampires," Patricia said, "there will be a variety of powers we must beware of—and we have no way of knowing what they are." She shook her head. "This is *infuriating*. We Shaped the world we wanted. How dare this interloper interfere with that? And at the cost . . ." She took Stephanie's hands again and finished in a whisper, " . . . of so much misery."

Stephanie smiled a little moistly.

Karl cleared his throat, apparently more uncomfortable with all this display of naked emotion than he'd ever indicated he was with this world's frequent display of naked flesh. "So," he said, "the sooner we confront this person, the sooner your world will be restored to the way you want it."

I wondered about that. I was sharing *hokhmah* with Stephanie and Patricia, as the Adversary had shared mine when he had touched me in my world. He had needed to kill me—or drive me out of the world, which is what actually happened—to have unfettered control over the Shaping of my world. If I took this third Shaper's *hokhmah* but he or she survived, wouldn't he or she still have at least some limited power to act against Stephanie and Patricia? Especially since this "Protector" seemed to retain some Shaping ability, while they did not?

Father Thomas suddenly spoke up. "I do not understand this talk of Shapers. Of which there are, apparently, three."

Surprisingly, it was Piotr who jumped into the breach. "It is just another word for 'ruler,'" he explained . . . okay, lied. "Someone who shapes a realm to his or her liking, as rulers have done throughout history."

Oh, well done, I thought.

"But where does it come from?" Thomas said. "I am, if I may be slightly immodest, a well-educated man, and it is not a word I have ever heard."

I gave his mind a push.

"Oh!" Thomas said, interrupting himself. "Of course! I just remembered. An old text, one I have not thought of in years. Pre-Cataclysm. That was, indeed, a word used for ruler."

And then I realized what I had done. I hadn't even thought about it. His unretouched memories seemed likely to be inconvenient, and so I'd simply rewritten them. Why not? He wasn't real, was he? Just a Shaped person. A copy . . .

All my agonizing about the morality of that kind of modification apparently had no effect on my actions. *Is this who you've become?* I asked myself.

And if so, given time, and more worlds, what *else* would I become? The absolutely corrupt tyrant I'd already reflected absolute power might produce?

No! I vowed. *I just I have to think before I Shape. I have to.*

Because every time I Shape someone else without thinking, I'm Shaping myself, too; maybe into something I do not want to be.

"We queens tend to be somewhat archaic in our thinking and speech," Stephanie said.

"Yes," Patricia said, "we do."

They must have guessed what I had done, but neither made an objection. Why should they? Certainly, the only other Shapers I'd met so far—the Adversary and Robur—had had no qualms about Shaping the denizens of these worlds. Nor did Karl.

Only me. And my qualms were quite quickly becoming quiescent. Perhaps the only reason I still had any at all was because I couldn't remember Ygrair's training. A far as I could tell, in her school, concern for the Shaped was not only not part of the curriculum, it was actively discouraged.

Which, once again, raised my never-far-from-the-surface doubts about Ygrair, the spider at the center of the Labyrinth's web, the one Karl insisted was the epitome of goodness.

I took a deep breath. Once more, I had no choice but to drive on, despite the fog of ignorance and doubt shrouding the highway ahead. "Well, if that's settled," I said briskly, "let's get to planning. Who will come?"

"I have already said I will," said Father Thomas. "I will serve as the representative of all of the priests remaining in the Lands Between. We must know the will of Mother Church."

"Mother Church may no longer be in the church's hands," I said carefully.

"Then I must know that, too."

"The members of the pack who are here now," Stephanie said, "are those I chose to protect me. They can certainly protect you." She nodded to them. "Jakob, Maigrat, Zikmund, and Embry, when he returns from delivering my message to my forces outside."

"And me," said Eric.

"*You* left the pack without permission," Jakob said, with one of his remarkably-good-for-being-in-human-form imitations of a wolf's growl.

Eric neither cowered nor backed down. "I disobeyed no orders, and I had good reason. You ripped me from my home and family. Yes, I admit, that, too, was for good reason—but all the same, I could not leave that wound unhealed."

Jakob growled again, but he said nothing more. Maigrat looked like she would have liked to, but Stephanie gave her a queenly look, and she, too, subsided.

Then Piotr looked his mother in the eye. "And I am going, too."

She stiffened. "Piotr. You are the prince. You cannot—"

"You can't stop me, Mom. I think I've already proved that."

I winced, waiting for the parental explosion, but Stephanie, after glaring at him for a long moment, suddenly relaxed and lowered her gaze . . . which among werewolves, I guessed, as with dogs, was the equivalent to a surrender. "Yes," she said. "I guess you have, at that." She sighed. "Just please be careful."

Piotr said nothing. Only I, of those present, knew he had no intention of returning to his mother's side. I wondered if I should say something. I decided I should not. He had earned the right to make his own decisions and his own mistakes.

"Dracula will come with you, as my representative," Queen Patricia said. "And Seraphina."

Karl reacted to the choice of Seraphina with a visible start. "Your Majesty," he said, eying the lady-in-waiting, who raised an eyebrow at him and smirked in return, "I would prefer . . ."

"I do not care what you prefer," Queen Patricia said.

"Will Dracula and Seraphina be among those carrying passengers?" I asked, while Karl subsided into silence.

Dracula and Seraphina's icy return gazes were answer enough. *I could Shape you to force you to carry us*, I thought, but then recoiled from the idea, my second thoughts after Shaping Thomas fresh in my mind.

Instead, I said, "Well, then. We need vampires to carry . . . um . . ." I did a quick count. "Nine of us."

Dracula surveyed the various vampires in the candlelit hall, standing with the unnatural stillness that seemed to be one of their abilities. In fact, I had almost forgotten they were there. "I will select . . ." he began.

"Not tonight," I said hastily. "I can't speak for everyone, but I'm exhausted. A day's rest. Even two. If I'm going to face this third Shaper, I need to be at full strength, and right now I'm more at the end of my rope." I touched my neck. "You might say I'm feeling a little drained."

Patricia didn't apologize. I didn't expect her to. Instead, she said, "I don't like leaving this usurper in place one minute longer than necessary."

"Nor I," said Stephanie.

"Two days won't make any difference," I said. "And . . . well, not to put too fine a point on it, but I insist."

The queens exchanged glances. "Very well," Patricia said, after Stephanie acquiesced with a nod. She turned to Dracula. "My heart, will you look after gathering supplies, as well as choosing which vampires will provide transportation?"

"Of course," said Dracula. "We will depart from the tower room the night after next. With the additional load, it will be easier to launch from a height."

"We cannot go straight to Mother Church," Father Thomas said. "Please. I must first go to Zarozje and tell them what has transpired."

"They cannot let down their guard," Karl warned. "The gates must still be closed at night; the guards must still patrol the walls. The murder of humans found abroad after sunset has been entirely the work of the rogues. The reforging of the Pact we have achieved here will have no effect on the rogues' reign of terror."

"They might think about blocking that underwater door, while they're at it," I put in, wondering if the cliché about closing the barn door after the horse was gone existed in this world.

"I do not expect them to lower their guard," Father Thomas said. "But I can give them hope that in the not-too-distant future, they may be able to. And hope is something we have not had in a very long time."

"Very well, we'll go to Zarozje first," I said quickly, forestalling any possible objections from anyone else, and reemphasizing the fact that I was now the one in charge.

And then I felt a surge of wonder at that thought. *It's true. I am the one in charge. I decided we would take time to rest before we continue on the quest, and the others agreed. I'm the only one who can carry the* hokhmah *of other Shapers to Ygrair—and now I can not only open Portals, I can find Ygrair on my own. I can already Shape this world. I'm the most powerful person in this room.*

Yes, I answered myself, *and remember what you were thinking just a few minutes ago: power corrupts.*

"Thank you," Father Thomas said.

"Would you and Karl join Steph and me in my private quarters?" Queen Patricia said.

"Of course," Karl said.

I saw Piotr staring at us, and knew he longed to come, too, but I ignored him.

Patricia's quarters proved to be disconcertingly non-medieval. If it had had a few modern appliances and a big-screen TV, it wouldn't have looked out of place in my own town of Wind River, Montana.

"You've redecorated, Trish," Stephanie said as she gazed around the room. "I like it."

"Thanks!" Patricia said. She busied herself retrieving wine-glasses from a cabinet at one side of the room, and then drew a bottle of wine from another. She uncorked it with a very modern-looking corkscrew (an easy way to open wine bottles would definitely have been something I'd have Shaped into my own world if I'd decided to go historical, so I approved the anachronism), and poured each of us a glass of, appropriately, blood-red wine: far too rich a wine to have come from the kind of grapes that would grow in this valley's climate in my world, reinforcing my suspicion that one or both queens were long-time wine snobs.

Karl and I took the couch and Stephanie and Patricia took the chairs. Dracula loomed by the fireplace. Clearly, Patricia had no secrets from him. I remembered Athelia, in the previous world, whom Robur had likewise Shaped to accept the truth of her world with equanimity and to have unbreakable trust in her Master. But the two of them hadn't been lovers . . . though Athelia might have wished they were.

"How can there possibly be a third Shaper in this world?" Patricia said without preamble, the moment she had seated herself.

The question was directed at me, another sign, perhaps, that my being-in-chargeness had been recognized. All the same, Karl answered: totally fine, I decided, since he'd been to far more worlds than I had.

The insight he had to offer, though, was less than scintillating. "I do not know," he said. Again. "I have never encountered such a thing. But neither have I previously encountered a world with *two* Shapers. I would suspect the one is somehow a function of the other."

"We were the only two Shapers who entered this world," Patricia said, emphasizing each word. "You know what that process is like. There's no way a third Shaper could have entered surreptitiously because there was nowhere to hide. The primordial world initially exists as a featureless plane extending only a few feet in diameter from the Shaper. Or in our case, Shapers. There is nothing outside that small circle until the Shaping is begun."

Stephanie nodded her agreement.

Karl may have known what that was like, but I did not. And yet, just for a moment, I had a mental image of standing in just such a blank, featureless place, then reaching out and . . .

It was gone. Memory, or imagination?

Stephanie glanced at me. "The two of you entered our world surreptitiously. Could this other mysterious Shaper have entered the same way?"

"No," Karl said flatly. "The ability to open Portals is jealously guarded by Ygrair. She gave me that ability, and I, in turn, passed it on to Shawna. No one else has it."

Delicately put, I thought, since I'd gotten it by sticking my hand into a puddle of his blood on an altar dedicated to human sacrifice.

"Then *how*?" Patricia demanded.

Karl spread his hands. "I do not know."

I grimaced. Karl had now used that previously rare statement so many times since we'd entered this world it risked becoming his catchphrase . . . you know, if someone ever made a TV series about our adventures. Not knowing what was going on had become the theme of this entire adventure.

I jumped in. "Well, then, I guess we'll just have to ask her . . ." (I flicked a smile at Karl) " . . . or him."

"Not very satisfying," Patricia said.

"Not satisfying at all," Stephanie said.

I couldn't argue, so I sipped my wine instead. Unlike our situation, it was *very* satisfying. And suddenly, I felt completely exhausted—so exhausted, my head dropped forward, and I jerked it back, blinking.

"You're falling asleep where you sit," Stephanie said to me, in a Mom-like tone I was pretty sure Piotr would have found familiar. "Trish. She's right. She needs rest. She's only human."

That stung a little. *Better a human than a shapeshifting or undead monster*, I thought, but wonder of wonders, stopped myself from saying out loud. I had the queens' *hokhmah*. I understand how they had Shaped this world. I just didn't understand *why*. What about werewolves and vampires had appealed to them?

Well, it could have been worse. It could have been zombies. And then I mentally shuddered. *And in some other world, it may be!*

Patricia studied us. "Karl in the tower room, again, I think. Shawna in the east wing? The werewolves can make their own arrangements, can't they, Steph?" she added, glancing at her fellow Shaper.

She nodded. "They'll return to the camp."

"Great," I said, stifling a yawn. "Somebody, show me the way."

Twenty minutes later, I was sound asleep in a very comfortable bed in a room with all the charm of a funeral parlor, all heavy velvet drapes, dark tapestries, and black furniture.

I did little for the next two days except sleep and eat and talk to the queens. It was nice to chat with someone with some of the same cultural references as me, even if they'd left the First World some fifteen years before I had. Karl had no opinion on the best *Star Trek* episodes, the best Beatles tunes, or the failings of *Return of the Jedi* compared to *The Empire Strikes Back*.

Unfortunately, neither Patricia nor Stephanie were huge musical theater fans, so the work of Stephen Sondheim still wasn't up for discussion.

I hadn't realized how deeply exhausted I was until, at last, I was able to relax. I slept many, many hours. I also ate huge amounts, Patricia having Shaped her vampires so they could enjoy food despite being undead. (I now had within me the knowledge of how

their digestive systems worked to eliminate the food they ate simply for pleasure, since they took no sustenance from it and thus it
was never digested, but I tried not to think about it. And that went
double for the having-babies thing, which I also understand in every revolting detail.)

Two nights later, Karl, Stephanie, Father Thomas, Piotr, Patricia, and I were in Patricia's quarters, waiting for Dracula to tell us
all was prepared, having (speaking of food) a final, and very fine,
dinner. As I washed down a delectable baklava with, alas, water
(drinking alcohol before embarking on our journey seemed a bad
idea), the door opened, framing Dracula. "All is prepared," he said.

"Thank you, my heart," Patricia said. She drained the last of her
wine (she wasn't coming, so it didn't matter if *she* drank, I thought
a little sourly), then stood. "There is no reason for delay, is there?"
she asked the rest of us.

"No," said Stephanie.

"None," said Karl.

"Let's mount up," I said, because who else was going to insert
the appropriate movie-dialogue clichés into the conversation?
"Let's do this thing," I added, for good measure.

Karl ignored me, of course, but Patricia and Stephanie gave me
identical exasperated looks. It was nice to be appreciated.

Karl seemed to know where we were going; he took the lead,
and a few minutes later, we stood in a comfortably appointed room
high up one of the towers. "My cell when I was first brought here,"
he said to me by way of explanation. "And my chamber, these last
two nights."

"Not bad, as prisons go," I said. "Very comfortable-looking bed."
I womanfully refrained from looking at Seraphina as I said it.

"Still a prison," Karl said shortly.

The vampires Dracula had assembled waited on the balcony,
which curved around a large portion of the tower's circumference

and thus was big enough to hold us all. Each of them wore a leather harness I saw immediately would hold us tight to their bodies.

Dracula pointed me to one of the vampires. I smiled at him as I approached, because clearly, we were about to be intimate. "Hi," I said. "I'm Shawna. You're . . . ?"

"He is Vasili," Dracula said. "He cannot speak in this form."

"Vasili," I repeated. "Well, Vasili, shall we take a flight together?"

Pact. Solid. Shaped it that way, I told myself firmly—but my heart still pounded as the bat-winged, blood-drinking, weirdly cold monster strapped me to his chest. And it's just possible, Shaper-in-charge though I might be, that I screamed like a little girl as we leaped off the balcony into thin air.

TWENTY-SEVEN

FLYING STRAPPED TO the belly of a vampire, it turns out, is even worse than flying jammed into economy class on a budget airline with a sweaty fat man next to you, a seat-kicking toddler behind you, a screaming baby across the aisle, and a I'll-recline-my-seat-whenever-the-hell-I-feel-like-it jerk in front. No in-flight services were provided, not even a handful of tasteless peanuts, and restroom facilities were completely lacking.

Also, the environmental controls were sadly inadequate. The air was already chill. Whipping past my ears at however-many-miles-an-hour a vampire could fly ("An African or European vampire?" asked an English-accented voice in my head) made it considerably chillier. I was numb with cold and my teeth were chattering when we swooped down outside the gates of Zarozje, and it took considerable effort (and help from Vasili) to unhook myself.

Then, rubbing my arms vigorously, I walked up to where Father Thomas stood, staring at the village, frozen in a way I didn't think had anything to do with the cold. "What's wrong?" I said—and then I looked up the road.

Zarozje was dark. No torches flickered on the walls; no lamps burned. The ever-present moonlight provided more than enough illumination to reveal that the gate stood wide open. No sentinels guarded it. Nothing moved.

Father Thomas broke out of his momentary catatonia and ran

toward the gate. I ran after him—I needed the warming-up, anyway—and was passed a moment later by the wolves of the pack. I glanced back. The vampires were following more sedately, clearly not understanding the priest's urgency. Several of them carried dark bundles—it took me a moment to realize they were the robes of the werewolves.

At first, I didn't understand Father Thomas' urgency, either, but as we neared the open gates, the hairs on the back of my neck stood up. The village was utterly silent—and, so far as we could tell, utterly deserted. Piotr and Eric raced into it. Father Thomas slowed enough so that Karl and I caught up with him.

"Where have they gone?" he said, staring around in the moonlight. "What has happened to the people?"

"You said other villages have been mysteriously emptied of people," I said.

"Yes, but I never thought . . . our walls were strong, our people prepared. How is this possible?" He broke into a run again, and I hurried after him, Karl a few steps behind.

We burst out of the narrow street into the courtyard in front of the church. Its doors, too, stood open, but the interior was utterly dark, not even the ever-burning lamp meant to indicate the presence of Christ still alight. Christ, it seemed, had left the building.

Father Thomas hurried up the steps, then turned right in the darkness. I heard him fumbling in the dark, then the sound of flint on steel. A lantern on a pedestal just inside the door glowed to life. He lifted it up and hurried down the aisle into the church's cavernous interior.

I followed. He stopped at the transept and raised the lantern high to illuminate the apse. "The altar vessels are gone," he said. "All of them." He turned this way and that. "Just as in the other villages that have been emptied!"

I looked at Karl. "The third Shaper?"

"It seems likely," he agreed.

"But how is such a thing possible?" Father Thomas cried. He came back to us. "Where are my people?"

"That," Karl said, "is what we must discover."

I heard claws on stone, and I quickly turned to see Piotr and Eric skidding to a halt. They shifted into boy-shape. Behind them, I saw the outlines of the vampires at the entrance to the church . . . but they did not enter. *Oh, right,* I thought, glancing up at the giant crucifix above the altar. *Some* parts of traditional lore remained intact.

"We have been over the entire village," Eric said. "There is no one here. No people. No animals. Nothing but empty houses."

"Stripped of anything portable," Piotr added.

"Any signs of a struggle?" Father Thomas said.

Both boys shook their heads.

"The vampires have your cloaks," I said. "Get dressed."

They nodded, turned as one, and headed toward the door.

I looked at Father Thomas. "What do you suppose happened?"

"I do not know," he said in an anguished voice. "As your companion said, that is what we must discover." He looked up at the crucified Christ. "The people of this village are my flock," he whispered. "It is my responsibility to protect them. But in their moment of need . . . I was absent."

"You sought knowledge of events that might impact them," Karl said. "You were absent *because* you wanted to protect them."

"That was only an excuse," Father Thomas said bitterly. "I accompanied you primarily because of selfish curiosity. I should have been here when . . ."

"If you had been here when whatever happened happened," I said, "you might be as mysteriously missing as they are, and we wouldn't even know—we'd have flown straight to Mother Church. Don't beat yourself up."

"Your words are kind, but they do nothing to assuage my guilt."

"In my experience," Karl said, "guilt can be a useful emotion."

I shot him a startled glance.

He ignored it. "There is no reason for us to linger here," he continued. "There is still time to fly to Mother Church before dawn, if the distances on the map were accurate, and if I have judged the flying speed of the vampires correctly. Shall we go?"

Now he *did* look at me, and I realized, with a slight start, that the question was addressed to me. This being-in-charge thing was going to take some getting used to.

"We should," I said; and we did, leaving the cold, empty church as we had found it, except that Father Thomas relit the sanctuary lamp, so that, at least for a time, the metaphorical light of Christ's presence once more glowed within his church.

The vampires waiting outside, all in winged form except Dracula, watched us emerge, their glowing red eyes even more demonical than usual, given the lack of light in the village other than the moon. "And were any insights to be found within *this place*?" Dracula said. Clearly, Pact or no Pact, backstory including a revelation from God to the vampires and werewolves or not, he still didn't like churches or crosses or holy water. *Probably not big on garlic toast, either,* I thought.

If you ate enough garlic before you were attacked by a vampire, would it keep them from drinking your blood? I wondered then. *Or would your garlicky sweat keep them from even coming close?* I thought about asking Dracula but decided maybe this wasn't the time.

"The altar vessels are missing," Father Thomas said shortly. He had warmed to werewolves but still seemed to have as little use for Dracula as Dracula had for his church. I suppose Dracula being the one who had terrorized and captured him had something to do with that. "Whether that is the work of robbers—or whoever drove the people from the village—or whether the people took them, or hid them somewhere, we cannot tell."

"This village's people have presumably been taken where we intend to go, into the Sacred Vale," I said.

"So . . ." I sighed. "Let's get flying." *Could be worse*, I reminded myself. *Could be horses.* Then I thought of something else. "But first . . ." I turned to the priest. "Father Thomas, would the church happen to have a store of warm clothing intended to help the poor this winter?"

He actually smiled a little. "As it happens, it does! This way."

A few minutes later, the humans in our strange troupe were all more warmly attired. I still wore the knit top, black trousers, and leather vest I'd taken from the rogue's cottage, but now I had a proper coat to go on top of it, a scarf, a fur hat, and some fur-lined mittens. The wind in my face remained icy cold as Vasili's wings beat the air, lifting us up above the courtyard and church, but the scarf across my mouth and nose cut the worst of it, and in general, the flight we embarked on now, across the silvered fields and cottages and streams and ponds and woods of the valley floor, was far more comfortable than the one we'd taken to the village . . .

. . . right up until, with no warning at all, just as we reached the mouth of the Sacred Vale, still forty miles from Mother Church, Vasili screamed and, like a buckshot goose, tumbled from the sky into the forest below, taking me, likewise screaming, along with him.

Karl was not accustomed to feeling like baggage, or how he imagined baggage might feel, but there was a definite air of "Not Needed on the Voyage" about his journey strapped to the belly of a vampire—whose name he had not been given—first to the abandoned village, and then west across the valley toward Mother Church.

By giving Shawna the tools she needed to continue the quest even if something happened to him, he had abdicated his position as sole arbiter of what their next actions should be. It had been, and continued to be, a conscious decision. It had made no sense to leave the possibility of achieving their goal dependent upon his survival. Of course, he had every intention of surviving—and, if Shawna fell, he would have to find someone else to attempt to do what she had failed to do—but this way, if either of them died or was otherwise prevented from continuing, there was still some hope, however faint, of success.

All of that he knew, *rationally*. All of that he had accepted, *rationally*. *Rationally*, he was at peace with the decision.

Emotionally, however, it galled him to no longer be the one who decided what they should do, and where they should go, and who should or should not accompany them. It galled him to be reduced to nothing more than a clumsy bundle carried by a taciturn flying monster . . .

. . . and it terrified him when that taciturn flying monster suddenly fluttered from the sky like a moth caught in a rainstorm. He could do nothing but hang there, helpless, while his ride fought to gain control, which she did just a little too late, so that, although they did not crash into the trees below them with *fatal* impact, they still crashed into them with *painful* impact. Karl threw his hands in front of his face to spare his eyes as branches and twigs lashed against him as they crunched and slithered down to the forest floor. There, he unbuckled and almost leaped away from the vampire, who slumped and shifted into a naked woman trembling on the ground, pale in the moonlight flooding the clearing in which they had finally landed.

Around him, more vampires came crashing down through the trees. Their burdens freed themselves. The vampires all shifted into ordinary human form. Two of them threw up. Seraphina turned human, pulled her knees up to her breasts, and sat there, shivering, head down. Even Dracula looked ill, as he clung to a tree trunk for support; nor was he "clad" in the shifting veil of shadows in which he had appeared the first time Karl saw him, outside the castle.

The werewolves looked every bit as shaken. They huddled like the pack they were, Eric clinging to Jakob and Maigrat as though they were his long-dead parents.

Father Thomas limped over to Karl. "What happened?" he cried.

"I have no idea," Karl said, staring around the clearing. "Where is Shawna?"

"She's not . . . ?" Father Thomas peered around, as well.

The combination of moonlight and tree-cast shadows made it hard to be certain for several minutes, but in the end, Karl had to face the truth: Shawna and the vampire carrying her, Vasili, were both missing.

Piotr suddenly appeared from the edge of the clearing, supporting the vampire who had been carrying him, a dark-skinned woman whose name Karl had not learned. She sank down with her back to a tree, and Piotr, who alone among the werewolves seemed unaffected by whatever had just happened, came to join Karl and Thomas.

"We need to find Shawna," Karl said to him. His thoughts of just a few minutes before, of having to somehow carry on if Shawna fell, came back to haunt him. He had not meant it as a prophecy. If he had been a Shaper, he would have worried he had somehow made happen the very thing he'd been thinking about.

Piotr just nodded once. He slipped off his robe, turned into a wolf, and loped away into the darkness.

Karl, with Father Thomas following, went to Dracula and Seraphina, who were side by side. "Do you know what happened?" he asked them both.

"A barrier," Dracula snarled. "In the air. As though . . ."

"As though it were a wall of crucifixes, or a cascade of holy water," Seraphina said, raising her head. "I cannot pass through it. None of us can pass through it." She hugged her knees, shuddering. "I feel defiled."

As I felt after you exerted your glamor against me, Karl thought, but did not say. "I would think it some influence of Mother Church, except the werewolves felt it, too," he glanced in the direction of the huddled pack, "and they—or, at least, Eric, who clearly is as ill as you—had no trouble entering the church in Zarozje." He frowned. "And Piotr seems entirely unaffected."

He is half-Shaper, he did not add out loud. *Perhaps that is why. But what does* that *say of this mysterious barrier?*

That it is the work of the third Shaper, he answered himself. *A protective barrier. The ordinary werewolves and vampires Shaped by the two queens cannot enter this side valley, where he holds sway.*

That the rogues could enter it, he had no doubt at all.

Piotr suddenly returned, rising up into boy form. "I found her," he panted. "She's hurt." And then he was a wolf again, and Karl and Father Thomas hurried after him into the darkness of the forest.

TWENTY-EIGHT

WE HIT THE trees in a confusing welter of blows and lashes and scrapes and tumbles and breaking sounds. Then, suddenly, all was quiet.

I found myself hanging from the harness just as I had when we were flying, but we weren't flying; we were suspended several feet above the forest floor—how many feet, I could not tell in the uncertain light.

Something cold and wet dribbled down my left cheek, and then dripped toward the floor below. I raised a hand. It came away covered in a dark liquid.

Blood?

For a moment I panicked. But nothing hurt. Surely if I were bleeding that much, I would hurt.

Which meant . . .

"Vasili?" I said.

No answer.

I twisted my head, trying to see him, but to my right, all was dark, and to my left, my view was blocked by a branch that glistened wetly in the moonlight . . .

. . . and, I could just see from the corner of my eye, disappeared into Vasili's chest.

A stake to the heart. Another bit of ancient lore Stephanie had kept when crafting Patricia's vampires.

I actually thought, *At least he didn't poof into dust*, which would have sent me crashing to the ground, and then hated myself for it. Had I become that callous? I'd argued with Karl and Robur that the Shaped were real people. Did that only apply to the *human* Shaped? Even the vampires and werewolves of this world were copies of individuals from the First World. If *any* of the Shaped were real people, then Vasili, too, was a real person, and my selfish response to his death was as horrific as the manner of it.

All of which went through my mind in about two minutes, and none of which did anything about my immediate problem of being harnessed to a deceased—twice-deceased, I guess—vampire a deadly distance above the unforgiving ground.

The branches around me suddenly gave an alarming crack and creak, and I and Vasili's body both dropped several feet. The top of a smaller tree seemed to lurch toward my head, and I yelped and turned my head before it could poke out an eye.

It didn't hit me. We'd stopped again.

Vasili's thick, cold blood continued to run down my cheek and drop into the darkness below. Helpless, I hung.

After, approximately, forever, I heard something pushing its way through the bushes, then a pronounced snuffling sound—and then a wolf burst into view below. It lowered its head and sniffed at the blood on the ground, then raised its glowing red eyes and looked up at me.

In the uncertain light I didn't know if it was one of the pack or a rogue, so I closed my eyes and played dead. It barked, a strangely dog-like sound, and then I heard it rushing away again.

I opened my eyes and stared after it. *If it was one of the pack, there'll be help here soon*, I thought. *But if it was a rogue . . .*

If it was a rogue, I was about to be someone's late-night—or early morning—snack.

The tree branches supporting us shifted again, and I suddenly found myself pointing almost straight down. If I dropped from there, I'd break my neck. I held my breath.

"Here!" said a boy's voice, and the question of the whether the wolf I'd seen had been a rogue or from the pack was answered by the appearance of Piotr below me, his pale, naked form foreshortened by my head-down orientation.

Crashing through the woods behind him came Father Thomas and Karl, who stared up at me. "Are you all right?" he called.

"I think so," I said, a little breathlessly. "But Vasili is dead."

Another crack, another shift downward. I was still far too high to survive a head-first fall.

"I need down," I added (possibly squeaked), probably unnecessarily.

"Have you tried Shaping?" Karl said.

I instantly felt like an idiot. *Of course,* I thought. *All I have to do is Shape the tree a little, so that we're safely deposited on the ground.*

I closed my eyes. I concentrated.

Nothing happened.

I tried again.

Even more nothing.

I opened my eyes. "It's not working," I said. "I . . . oh!"

Vasili's body suddenly started sliding, but not straight down. It twisted as it dropped through the tree branches, and I twisted with it, so that I was suddenly on top of him, instead of head down or hanging beneath him. Accompanied by Rice Krispies sounds—snap, crackle, and pop—we completed our descent in short order, slamming into the ground so hard I might well have broken ribs or something else had not Vasili's corpse acted as a cushion . . .

. . . a squishy cushion that made an awful sound as we hit.

I stared up at the moonlit sky. The jagged, broken end of the branch that had killed Vasili, and remained in his chest, extended up past my left side. "Get me off of here," I said. "Please."

It was a struggle, but I managed to avoid throwing up until Piotr and Karl had freed me from the harness, and I had rolled off of Vasili's corpse onto the needle-strewn ground. *Then* I threw up.

I sat back on my haunches and spat. Karl silently handed me a canteen, and I rinsed my mouth. "What happened?"

"A barrier of some kind," Karl said. "Invisible and undetectable to us," his glance took in Father Thomas, Piotr, and me, "but utterly impassible to the ordinary vampires and werewolves."

"Not quite right," Piotr said. "I felt it, it just didn't affect me the way it did them."

"Is it only in the air?" I said. "If we could get past it on the ground, and then resume flying . . ."

Piotr shook his head. "It extends all the way to the ground." He pointed west. "I can feel it, not twenty yards away."

I glanced at Vasili. He still had not crumbled into dust, but he looked . . . smaller. His body, I realized, was collapsing in on itself, as though months of decay were happening in hours, though there was no smell of corruption except for that faint whiff of it that seemed to accompany all the vampires. He was just withering away. The process must have begun the moment he was staked by the tree branch.

"Poor Vasili," I said sadly. I looked at the others again. "We don't have any choice, then. We have to continue on foot." I glanced at Karl. "Do you agree?"

"Yes," he said.

"Let's go tell the others." I took about three steps, then stopped. "Um. And they would be . . . where?"

"I'll lead," Piotr said, and folded back down into wolf-shape. We three humans followed him through the trees (in a completely different direction than I'd have chosen).

The werewolves and vampires were all in human shape, the vampires naked, the werewolves in the robes they'd worn in flight, all huddled with their own kind. Dracula turned toward us as we emerged from the trees into the glade where they'd gathered. "We have tested the barrier," he said. "We cannot pass it." He looked angry. "It is unacceptable! I am the consort of Queen Patricia. How dare anyone forbid me entry to any part of the valley?"

"You couldn't enter Father Thomas' church," I pointed out. "Perhaps this is something Mother Church erected in response to the apparent collapse of the Pact." I'd made that up on the spot, but it sounded pretty good to me, and had the advantage of not going anywhere near the concept of Shaping.

"Forty miles from the church itself?" Dracula said. "How is that possible?"

"I would have said it was not," Father Thomas said, "and yet, that would seem to be the most likely explanation." He glanced at me. "And if it is true, it is good news, is it not? It means that Mother Church is still in control in this valley, not this renegade ruler you keep speaking of, this Third Shaper."

"But it does not explain why your villagers, and so many others, vanished from their homes," Dracula said.

"Perhaps it does," Father Thomas said. "If the disappearance was occasioned by the rogues, there would be signs of struggle and violence. Whereas, if someone from Mother Church came and offered sanctuary within the Sacred Vale, where, as we have just discovered, no vampires or werewolves can enter . . . perhaps they were persuaded."

I had thrown out the idea of Mother Church being behind the mysterious barrier more as a barrier of my own, an obfuscation of the truth that, of those on the expedition, only Karl, Piotr, and I knew. But Father Thomas' suggestion actually made a lot of sense, and the third Shaper might even be the explanation for how

Mother Church had been able to accomplish such a thing: he or she had simply willed it into existence.

But that didn't explain the rogues. They *also* had to be the work of the third Shaper since neither Stephanie nor Patricia had Shaped them. I had the *hokhmah* from both of them, and I knew that beyond a shadow of doubt. The question was . . . why?

We'd get no answer until we met the third Shaper face-to-face—and what had been a short flight had just turned into a long walk.

"We have to get moving," I said.

"Humans?" said Seraphina. There was an undeniable tinge of contempt in her voice. "How far do you think you will get? If you encounter a rogue . . ."

"Then I will deal with him," said Piotr's voice behind me.

Dracula and Seraphina glared at him as he stepped forward to join me and Karl. "You are a werewolf," Dracula said, more than a little contempt in his voice. "You cannot pass the barrier. It affected your comrades as it did us." His eyes flicked past me, and I glanced back, discovering the werewolf pack had moved in behind us. When I turned back toward Dracula, I saw the vampires clustering in around him, which meant everyone we had brought on the expedition—except poor Vasili—could now hear what was being said.

"It's true," Jakob said. "None of us can go through this barrier, either."

"It doesn't bother me," Piotr said.

"Maybe it's a question of youth?" Father Thomas said. He turned toward Eric.

Eric shook his head. "No, Father. I can't pass it either."

"I don't know why," Piotr said, which was a lie, of course. "I just know it's true."

"Then it's settled," I said. "Karl, Piotr, and I will go on, and discover what has been happening in Mother Church's neck of the valley."

"And I!" Father Thomas snapped. "I will not be left behind now."

I looked at him. "Are you certain, Father?" I asked. I knew he was, but it would make things a lot easier if he could be dissuaded, since the other three of us knew about Shapers and he didn't.

Of course, I could Shape him not to come with us, but the thought filled me with disgust. No. I wouldn't do that to him, just for my convenience. He deserved the chance to find out what had happened to his people.

"Of course, I'm certain! My villagers have disappeared into this valley. I must make sure they are safe. And then, I will present myself at Mother Church. We have been too long cut off from her guidance." He looked at Eric and the others of the pack. "I . . . am sorry for what happened to the girl, to . . . Elena," he said quietly. "The depredations of the rogues led us to believe that the Pact was truly broken, that the old ways, from before the Great Cataclysm, had returned. Mother Church fell silent. I interpreted church law as best I could. But now . . . I feel I was overzealous. I did not understand then." He glanced at Eric. "Now I do."

"Nice sentiments," Maigrat said contemptuously. "But they do not bring back Elena."

"No," Father Thomas said. "They do not." He had not taken his gaze from Eric. "Thank you for coming to find me," he said to the boy in a low voice. "But now your life is with your pack. Your new family. Go with them. And . . . I'm sorry."

Eric nodded once, then suddenly almost leaped forward and enveloped the priest in a hug. I found myself blinking away tears. And this time, there was no candle smoke to blame them on.

Eric stepped back, raised a tentative hand in farewell, then turned and rejoined his packmates. "Let's go," Jakob said. They stripped off their robes, let them fall, turned into wolves, and vanished into the dark forest.

Dracula still looked peeved, as did Seraphina. I tentatively reached inside myself to see if I thought I had the Shaping power to order them to leave, but I could tell I did not. It was as if the mysterious barrier were affecting me, as well, and *that* I did not think had anything to do with Mother Church, even if Father Thomas' Pollyannaish explanation for what might be going on proved true. The power of the third Shaper was clearly interfering with mine, here in the part of the world that he or she had Shaped, a world described in *hokhmah* I did not yet possess.

Fortunately, Shaping was not needed. "Very well," Dracula said. "We will report back to Queen Patricia. No doubt she will be anxious to hear your final report."

"No doubt," I said noncommittally.

"And there is no doubt in my mind," Seraphina said, "that no such report will be forthcoming. I think you go to your deaths." She turned her burning gaze to Karl. "Pity."

"If we do," I said, "it is our choice."

Seraphina snorted.

"We fly," Dracula said, and the vampires shifted into bat-shapes and flung themselves into the sky, the blast of their wings chasing fallen leaves around our feet.

I looked at the robes the wolves had left scattered around the glade and sighed. *What a waste of a good Shaping.* Then I turned to my companions. "Well," I said. "Let's go find out if Seraphina was right, shall we?"

Piotr grinned, and flowed back into wolf-shape. He loped ahead, the silver in his fur shining in the moonlight, and Karl, Father Thomas, and I followed.

The Fellowship has sundered, and now we march on to face the dark lord, I thought. Not for the first time, I wondered how I'd fallen into a fantasy novel, and if I could count on a happy ending.

We trudged through the woods, the only sign when we passed through the mystical barrier a kind of shivering sigh from Piotr. Since he was in wolf form, I couldn't ask him what he'd felt, but the hair on his back was visibly erect for several minutes.

"It occurs to me," Karl said after we had walked for twenty minutes or so, "that there is no longer any reason for us to travel at night."

I stopped dead, feeling like an idiot. "Oh, good grief, you're right. We were only traveling at night because we were being flown by vampires. If there are rogues in these woods, this is the most dangerous time to be abroad." I winced at the unintentional pun, since, technically, I *was* a broad. "Out and about, I mean." Now I sounded stuffily English. "My circadian rhythms are a mess."

"Not being behind solid stone walls at this time of night has been causing me a considerable amount of anxiety, I admit," Father Thomas said mildly.

"The difficulty," Karl said, looking around at the endless trees— only the ever-shining moon, and possibly Piotr's nose, had kept us from going in circles—"will be finding a place to shelter."

Piotr trotted back from ranging ahead of us. His eyes glowed red. He gave one of his Lassie-barks, incongruous coming from a red-eyed lycanthrope. I resisted the urge to ask him if Timmy had fallen down a well, and instead said, "You know of a place?"

He woofed again, then turned and trotted off in a slightly different direction from the one we'd been trending. He looked over his shoulder, red eyes burning. They gave me the shivers, even though I knew he was friendly.

"It appears he does," Karl said.

"I will be glad of it," said Father Thomas. "Although I suppose stout village walls are not likely to be on offer."

They weren't, but neither was the shelter Piotr had found just a damp, drafty cave. Instead, he led us into a farmyard. The thatch-roofed cottage looked intact, as did the shed, although its doors were open and if it had ever held animals, they were no longer present. The garden to the cottage's south was not overgrown, and there were even flowers in pots on either side of the front door. It looked like a family should be sleeping inside it, but when we opened the door . . . which was latched but not locked . . . the interior, just visible in the moonlight through the windows, was empty of everything but a table, two chairs, and the frame of a cot in the corner. There were no pots, no bedding, no curtains, no poker for the cold hearth, nothing but a clean wooden floor that looked as if it had just been swept.

"It is like the village," Father Thomas said, staring around. "The people left, with no intention of coming back, apparently of their own free will."

"Well," I said, "we'll take it for the night."

"Whatever convinced them to leave may well show up before morning," Father Thomas pointed out.

"Then at least we'll have a wall between us and it," I said firmly.

We dared not light a fire. By some unspoken male agreement, I found myself the unquestioned occupant of the cot. The blankets from my backpack, spread out on the netting that spanned the space made by the wooden frame, made for a fairly comfortable bed, so I womanfully refrained from taking the opportunity to rail against the patriarchy.

Father Thomas and Karl stretched out on the floor. Piotr, without ever changing into a boy, slipped outside.

I fell asleep almost at once.

Karl had a most unusual dream.

In his dream, a voice he did not recognize and yet trusted completely called sweetly to him.

In his dream, he got up from the floor, packed up his blankets, and set out into the night, joined by Piotr, in wolf form, and Father Thomas.

In his dream, they walked quietly to a clearing, where they were lifted up into the sky by vampires, and flown swiftly the rest of the way to Mother Church herself, a giant cathedral-like church and associated side buildings atop a cliff grander than the one on which rested the castle of Queen Patricia, though this one had no waterfall. At its base stood an impressive town of stone buildings, several times larger than Zarozje, walled about on three sides, with the fourth protected by the cliff itself.

Still in his dream, Karl and Piotr and Father Thomas were gently deposited atop the cliff, then guided by a powerfully built man wearing a black robe to a cell in the crypt beneath the church, where they were shown to cots. Piotr jumped up onto one, turned around a few times, and lay down with his tail across his nose. Father Thomas and Karl reclined in the more usual manner.

Oh, Karl thought, in his dream. *This is one of those unusual dreams where you sleep a second time within it*, and it appeared he was correct, because, in the dream, he slept.

Then, in the morning, he woke in a dark and stony cell alongside Father Thomas and Piotr and realized it had not been a dream at all.

He waited for someone to come and demand answers of them.

He waited a very long time.

TWENTY-NINE

I WOKE TO morning light and a strange feeling of silence and solitude.

I sat up and stared around.

The little house was empty of priest, mysterious guide, and teenaged werewolf alike. Not only that, their packs and blankets had vanished, too.

I was alone.

I got up and went to the door. The clearing around the farmhouse was as empty as the house. So was the shed.

I raised my hands to my mouth, intending to shout the names of my companions—then thought better of it. I didn't know who or what else might be in earshot. That *something* was, I had little doubt, because it seemed to me that whatever had caused the original inhabitants of the farmhouse, and Father Thomas' village, and who knew how many other villages, to simply gather their belongings and march peacefully away had come again during the night and spirited away the other members of my party.

The question was, why had I been left *un*-spirited, and the answer seemed obvious: because I was a Shaper, and had the *hokhmah* of the rest of this world tucked away in my head, or my bloodstream, or wherever the Shurak nanotechnology stored it. Whatever power had been exerted on the others simply had not worked on me.

My nighttime thoughts about the sundering of the Fellowship returned. If I were this story's Frodo, it seemed I had been left without even my faithful Sam (a comparison I was pretty sure Karl would have hated, had he ever read the books). There might well be a metaphorical Mount Doom waiting at the end of the Sacred Vale . . . and yet, it was to the end of the vale I had to go. I could feel the pull of the potential Portal in that direction and sense the third Shaper. I only hoped I'd find my spirited-away companions there, too.

I went back into the cottage, pulled some dried meat and fruit out of my pack, and ate a meager breakfast while I considered my course of action. My hand shook a little as I raised a piece of pemmican to my lips. *Stop that*, I told myself. *This isn't the first time you've been on your own in a strange world. You succeeded in Robur's world. You can succeed here, too. You're better prepared, and you have an ability you didn't have there—you can seize another Shaper's* hokhmah *just by touching them. You don't have to wait for someone to blow them up while you're standing next to them.*

All of which would have been more reassuring if not for the memory of being locked in the rogue's larder just a few days before. If not for Piotr and his unexpected (to the rogue) ability to take wolf-shape during the day, our clothes might now be on that shelf in the rogue's cabin, our bones part of the interior decoration.

So, travel by day, take shelter by night. I finished eating and packed up my blankets. There was a pump in the farmyard. I pumped it hard a few times and then let the ice-cold water cascade over the back of my head before filling the wineskin I was using as a canteen. After shouldering my pack, I slung the wineskin on its thin leather strap over one shoulder, so it hung at my hip, made sure my knife was loose in its scabbard on my belt and my little crossbow was cocked and loaded, took a deep breath, and started west.

A trail led in the right direction from the farmyard. I hesitated before taking it, but given the thickness of the underbrush, I really had no choice. Reasoning that no monsters would be around in the daylight—or at least, if they were, they'd be ordinary people, and I was armed—I set out along the path.

I had, not surprisingly, slept in, so the sun reached its zenith only an hour or so later. I didn't stop for lunch, gnawing more pemmican and a wedge of hard, strong-flavored cheese as I walked, washing it down with water from my wineskin-canteen. More trails joined mine from elsewhere in the woods, so that my path soon began to widen and look more like a proper road . . . which I guess it was, because in midafternoon I topped a low rise and saw in front of me a village, or the remains of one. It had an untended air, and nothing moved on its narrow streets. I approached it cautiously. Sure enough, it was as empty as Zarozje had been. I poked my head into a few shops and houses but saw nothing useful. Like Zarozje, like the farmhouse, it had been stripped of pretty much anything portable.

There was no church—perhaps the village was too small for one to have been built, and a circuit-riding priest had once ministered to the needs of the people. I looked around uneasily at the black, gaping, unshuttered windows, the cracked walls and falling-in thatch, and was glad to leave the place behind.

Every so often, as I walked, I would try to reach out with my Shaping ability, but it remained utterly blocked. I might have the *hokhmah* of the original Shapers of this world, Patricia and Stephanie, but I could make no use of it here.

What's the point of godlike powers if they're always being blocked by this or that? I wondered petulantly.

Since I was heading west, the setting of the sun in front of me was rather like the play clock on a football field, warning me I only had so much time before I'd be assessed a penalty—which in this case might involve being eaten (a penalty like that in football, I reflected, would probably greatly reduce the number of time-count violations).

I started looking for possible shelter, and didn't have to look very hard, because as I came around a bend in the road, I found myself at the top of a substantial rise. Down at the bottom of that rise stood another village, but this one bustled with life—human life.

Smoke rose from chimneys, children ran and played in the square, men and women moved hither and yon, carrying this and that, and the sound of laughter and talking carried to me in the still, chill, almost-evening air. Although on this side of the village the forest through which I'd been trudging came up close to the buildings, on the other side, of which my elevation gave me a clear view for several miles, I saw sizable and, as far as I could tell from that distance (and with my limited knowledge of any agricultural activity not involving apples, the *raison d'être* of my hometown of Appleville, Oregon), well-tended fields of ripe wheat. Farmhouses nestled among those fields. The road I was on emerged from the village's far side and continued on through the fields to the dark, distant line where the forest resumed and another ridge rose, blocking my view further west . . . except for the giant, snow-covered peaks that Patricia and Stephanie—as I knew from their *hokhmah*—had Shaped to be literally impossible to cross, and which the lowering sun was about to touch.

I also knew this valley would end in a cliff, at the top of which, on a plateau, stood the ancient edifice of Mother Church, and behind which had once been (in the fictional history of this world) the beginning of a pass through those mountains and a road to the world outside.

And somewhere up there, near the church, behind it, possibly—maybe even likely—in the mouth of the closed pass itself, I would be able to open the Portal to the next world and leave the vampires and werewolves of this one behind forever.

First, though, I had to survive another night. I studied the village again. It looked safe enough. Lights were beginning to glow behind windows. It had no wall, so clearly the people did not feel threatened by whatever might haunt these woods by moonlight.

But like the abandoned village I had seen earlier, this one had no church, even though this village was larger, with proper stone buildings here and there and a sizable cobblestoned square with a pump at its center. Within that square, toward the western end, there were new cobblestones that did not match the old ones, made of a paler rock . . . and they limned a suspiciously cross-shaped area of considerable size.

Clearly there *had* been a church. Now, there wasn't one.

This is Sacred Vale, I thought uneasily. *Why is there no church?*

The sun slipped behind the mountains. The sky remained bright, but the temperature dropped precipitously. I shivered and made up my mind. I'd risk the village.

I was seen, almost the moment I started down the path between the towering trees that had been my companions all day (I would rather have had my old ones back). A small boy playing by a tree stump gaped up at me, then turned and ran into the village, crying, "Stranger! Stranger!"

Stranger danger, I thought. I felt like someone should praise him for being so careful, except since I was the stranger in question, the danger was more likely to be coming at me than from me.

I kept walking, but I kept my left hand on the hilt of my dagger and the index finger of my right hand on the trigger of my crossbow though I also made sure to keep it pointed at the ground.

By the time I reached the edge of the village, there were about twenty adults waiting for me, with a fringe of small children behind them, peering around and in some cases between their legs. I stopped and waited for someone to say something, which someone, in the form of a rotund man with a beard that was only slightly too brown to make him a perfect Santa Claus, did.

"Greetings," he said. "I am Reeve Gregory Krause-Snow. Who are you?"

"Shawna Keys," I said. "I'm . . . a traveler."

"A traveler?" He raised eyebrows which, unlike the beard, not only had the requisite Santa Claus bushiness, but were also bright white, matching the second half of his surname. "From where?"

That was easy. "The village of Zarozje."

"Really?" said the reeve. "A late arrival, then?"

I blinked. "What?"

"Your fellow citizens passed this way two days ago," Reeve Krause-Snow said. "By now, they are in their new homes in Abrahmville, the Protector's city."

"Their new homes." *Go with it*, I told myself. "Yes," I said. "I was away when they left but am anxious to rejoin them." And as much to satisfy my own curiosity as because I knew Father Thomas would want to know, if I ever found him . . . "Who was leading them?" I asked.

"A priest," the reeve replied. "Father Thomas, I believe his name was. Accompanied by a very large young man."

A rogue. No, two rogues. One to take the appearance of Father Thomas, to lure the villagers out of Zarozje. But what was the purpose of the second one?

The reeve turned and spoke in a low voice to a young blonde-haired woman standing next to him. By now the sun had descended far enough behind the mountains that stars pricked the twilit sky and the ever-present moon grew ever brighter. Since I knew what kinds of things might be roaming the forests very soon, if not already, I awaited their decision with bated breath.

Reeve Krause-Snow turned back to me. "You are welcome here," he said. "And on the morrow, my daughter, Emma," he indicated the young woman, "will personally guide you."

"Um, thanks," I said, startled by the offer. "I don't want to be trouble."

"It is no trouble," said the young woman. In my own world, I would have pegged her as college age. She smiled. "I have been Chosen. I must make the journey anyway."

"Indeed, you must," said the reeve. "We are all so proud of you."

"Thank you, Father," Emma said.

"I accept," I said brightly.

"You will stay with us tonight," Emma continued. She held out her hand. "Come! I will show you the way."

The others dispersed, their curiosity satisfied and, no doubt, suppers to get and bedtimes to arrange. They moved away in leisurely fashion, not at all like people who feared ravening creatures of the night might come loping and/or flying into their village at any moment to rend them all limb from limb. It made a nice change from Zarozje, to tell the truth.

It was a short journey to the reeve's house, a substantial two-story structure with diamond-paned windows, through which glimmered candlelight. Emma Krause-Snow led me up the steps and through the front door—which was not locked or armored and had no crosses hammered into it, I noted, unlike every door in Zarozje—and into an entrance hall. Stairs rose directly in front of us. To the left, a fire burned merrily in a flagstone hearth, inside a large room whose ceiling was spanned by dark wooden beams. Down the short hall, copper pots gleamed in what could only be the kitchen, from which wafted the most mouth-watering smells. *No pemmican tonight!* I thought.

Emma led me up the stairs. "We will share my room," she said, opening one of the two doors in the upstairs hall. "There is a second bed. It belonged to my sister, Tabitha."

I glanced in. Two narrow cots, each covered with red woolen

blankets, shared the tiny space, clearly meant for sleeping and nothing else. "I don't want to take your sister's bed," I said.

Emma laughed. "Oh, there's no need to worry about that. She doesn't need it. She was Chosen last year. I was so jealous. But now it's my turn."

There was that term again: "Chosen." I tried to damp down the bad feeling I was getting. *Probably picked to attend a prestigious school or something*, I told myself, but it was hard to make myself believe it, since I knew that, however pleasant and pastoral this little slice of late medieval life might seem, mysterious disappearances and a known population of rogue werewolves and vampires did not seem an auspicious combination.

"What exactly does being 'Chosen' entail?" I asked carefully.

Emma gave me a surprised look, eyes wide and white in the dimming twilight from the windows at each end of the hall and the faint, warm yellow glow now shining up the stairs from the main room below. "You don't know?"

"It is not something we have in the Lands Between," I said, which was true, as far as I knew. "And I have just arrived."

She laughed again. "Of course, I'd forgotten."

You forgot I just arrived, when I just arrived? There was something off about everyone I had so far met in the so-called Sacred Vale. It worried me.

"The Chosen are those young people selected to serve the Protector in his great house at the head of the valley," she said. "Every six months, ten young people are Chosen from across the Sacred Vale. From some villages, no one has ever yet been Chosen. The fact *two* have been Chosen from our village, in succession, is a great honor. And two from the same family? First Tabitha, and now me? Unheard of. My parents are beside themselves with pride."

Alarm bells were going off in the part of my head that remembered reading Shirley Jackson's "The Lottery."

"How long do these young people stay in service to the Protector?" I asked.

"Oh, a while," Emma said vaguely.

"So Tabitha will come back?"

"Of course," she said. "Eventually." She turned away. "Supper will be ready soon. Let's go downstairs."

The evening was pleasant, but, like the people, odd. Reeve Krause-Snow and his wife, Jacqueline, seemed supremely unconcerned about the fact that within six months both their daughters had been taken from them by the Protector. "We are thrilled," the reeve said. "And honored. Aren't we, my sweet?" He took his wife's hand.

"Of course, dear," she said.

They were equally unconcerned about the fact their village was completely unprotected from any marauding vampires or werewolves that might pass their way.

"There's nothing like that to fear here," the reeve said. "The Protector protects us."

"Is that not why you and the other villagers of Zarozje came here?" Jacqueline inquired. "To escape the depredations of such monsters in the Lands Between?"

Not exactly, I thought, but I smiled and said. "Yes, of course."

Jacqueline put her hand on mine. "Then please relax, Shawna. You are safe in the arms of the Protector, and safe in this house." She sat back. "Now eat up. You, too, Emma, before your meat grows cold."

My concern was not enough to keep me from eating. It *was* enough to keep me awake for a while in the narrow bed, with Emma breathing deeply and contentedly just a few feet away, but eventually I, too, slept, and woke to enjoy a hearty breakfast of eggs and bacon and bread before my new friend and I set out on the next leg of my journey to what she called the House of the Protector and I knew from the Shapers' *hokhmah* within me should be Mother Church.

I'd tried to raise the subject of the missing village church at supper the night before and had gotten nothing but blank looks. The word "church" seemed to have no meaning for the people of the Sacred Vale: they'd clearly been Shaped. There was no longer any doubt in my mind that the Protector was the third Shaper I sought.

But what was he playing at?

And I knew for certain it was a "he," now. I even had a name. Emma had confirmed it that morning over breakfast, calling him "Protector Abrahm" as she enthused again about how wonderful it would be to serve the great man in his own house.

We left as the sun cleared the trees, Emma bidding a surprisingly—to me—cheerful farewell to her parents, who embraced her with big smiles on their faces and whose tears seemed more related to overwhelming pride than sadness at her departure. I carried my pack but had, at Emma's urging though against my better judgment, tucked my dagger away in it, along with the crossbow and its quiver of quarrels. Instead, I held in my right hand a stout walking stick, a gift of the reeve. Emma carried her own pack, just a leather pouch slung over one shoulder, and her own walking stick, twin of mine.

The sun warmed our backs as we walked west, the birds sang, the air held a pleasant autumnal crispness, and if not for the fact my companions had vanished, I knew this world was plagued with man-eating monsters, and I still had to gather the *hokhmah* of the Protector, find Karl, open a new Portal, and escape to another world where I might face even worse dangers, I'm sure I would have enjoyed the walk.

And, in truth, those concerns were distant enough that I did enjoy it, a little . . . okay, more than a little. Emma was a pleasant traveling companion/tour guide. "That's Emma Lake," she said, pointing to water glittering through the trees to our left. She giggled. "No relation."

We passed other lakes, interesting rock formations, and, of course, villages, walking through the center of half a dozen over the course of the day, each of which had a suspiciously vacant spot right where I would normally have expected to see a church. No one seemed suspicious of us, though, unlike when I'd appeared at Emma's village. (Maybe the crossbow I'd been carrying that first night had had something to do with that.) Instead, they just cheerily greeted us. "Chosen!" Emma would call, and the villagers would grin and clap and shout congratulations.

All of them.

Without fail.

The Sacred Vale seemed to be vying with Disneyland for the title of "The Happiest Place on Earth." Not that this was Earth. Or, at least, not the original Earth. But then, neither had my world been, and unlike this one, it had actually *had* Disneyland.

The thing was, I couldn't really see why everyone was so happy. The suspiciously churchless villages were pleasant enough, but primitive. A lot of backbreaking work seemed to be going on, and a lot of animal husbandry involving a lot of manure, and, in general, just a lot of the sort of thing that I'd always tried to avoid. So why was everyone so happy?

"Tonight we will rest in the hostel at Goodwater," Emma told me as we left behind one of the villages (which had the unlikely name of Eyebrow; her own village, she'd told me, was called Elbow, for no reason she knew). The sun, now in front of us, was dipping once more toward those towering snow-covered peaks. "We will reach the House of the Protector late tomorrow afternoon."

"Is it a nice place, this hostel?" I said. A comfortable bed and a good meal sounded appealing after a day of walking.

"Oh, yes," Emma replied. "One of the nicest. All the Chosen from the eastern part of the valley stay there while traveling to the Protector's House. We will journey the rest of the way tomorrow in their company."

"Are only young people Chosen?" I asked.

"Occasionally an elder will be so honored," Emma said, "but, in general, yes, it is the young people. Young people are stronger workers!"

"And what kind of work will you be doing, exactly?"

Emma shrugged. "I don't know. Cleaning and serving and suchlike, I guess."

Just how many cleaners and servers and "suchlike" does one house need, no matter how big it is? I wondered. *And why would it need a fresh batch every six months?*

I didn't ask. But my Spidey-sense . . . Shaper-sense . . . was tingling.

It tingled even more when, after reaching the hostel in Goodwater—a comfortable, sprawling, one-story building of wood and wattle—we sat down in the common room with three young women and two young men, all likewise Chosen from various villages, though none came from the villages we had passed through on the road. Not one of them expressed the slightest doubt about whether or not being Chosen was an honor, or what might await at the end of the road, or why a fresh batch of Chosen were needed every six months.

"I'm not Chosen," I said to them, "but I would love to serve the Protector. Do you think, if I present myself with the rest of you, they might accept me as a . . . volunteer?"

Much discussion ensued. No one had an answer, but no one

seemed much troubled by it, either. "I say give it a try," Emma said, finally and cheerfully.

There was a general chorus of agreement to that from the cheerful . . . always cheerful . . . almost annoyingly cheerful . . . young people.

"What's the worst that can happen?" a young man named Zachariah said (cheerfully). "They won't let you serve the Protector and you have to get a job in the town instead."

"Good point," I said (also cheerfully, although my cheer was considerably more forced than theirs). I kept to myself what I thought the worst that could happen would *really* be.

After a comfortable night and a hearty breakfast, we were on our way again, the whole party from the hostel traveling together. We passed through several more villages, and picked up another two Chosen, so that as the sun once more touched the now much-nearer-and-thus-higher western mountains, there were nine of us trudging along the road, along with other traffic—drovers of sheep and cattle with their flocks or herds, wagons laden with cabbages, itinerant knife-sharpeners, that kind of thing.

For some time now I'd been able to see our destination, atop the cliff capping the western end of the valley. A path switchbacked up the mass of stone to what looked like an enormous Romanesque church from my own world.

The big double doors between those towers were shut. Light glowed through the rose-shaped stained-glass window high above those doors, and through windows in each of the towers. It had an almost fairytale appearance in the twilight, but I was pretty sure it wasn't deserved. Patricia's castle had had a similar glittering look the first time I'd seen it, and it hadn't been welcoming at all when I finally got there.

As we drew nearer the cliff, I could no longer see the church. The cliff itself was separated from us by the stone wall of the

Protector's city, aka Abrahmville. When we'd first seen the town, from atop a ridge now far behind us, we'd been high enough I'd been able to glimpse, over the top of the wall, the town's rather impressive (by this world's standards) stone buildings, topped by bright-red roofs. Now, though, the wall formed a formidable barrier, battlemented and forbidding.

Two-story doors of black wood stood open at the end of the road we had followed for so long. Guarding it were armed and armored men, two on either side, silhouetted against torches in sconces behind them.

Extremely aware I was not, in fact, one of the Chosen, I held back for a minute, stepping behind a tree to take my crossbow out of my pack, load, and cock it. I slipped it back into the pack, out of sight but still easy to grab in a moment, then ran to catch up with the others.

Running with a cocked and loaded crossbow in a backpack probably violated all kinds of best practices in the safe handling of pointy medieval weapons, but I'd been feeling increasingly naked without some kind of weapon. I would have liked to have put my dagger back on my belt, too, but none of the Chosen were wearing weapons, and I had a feeling I really, really didn't want to stand out.

I tensed as we approached the gate, but the guards waved us through with what looked like bored contempt. I wasn't about to take offense. With my new companions, I hurried through the forbidding gate into the town beyond.

There, in a small courtyard with brick buildings on all sides, lamps on their corners casting yellow light across the cobblestones, and only one exit, an archway revealing nothing but a narrow street, we were met by a big, bearded man wearing a black robe with a scarlet belt. His feet were bare beneath it, and I was willing to bet the rest of him was bare beneath it, too, so he could transform in an instant . . . into what, I wasn't sure, but he looked enough like the appearance-shifting rogue Piotr had killed to have been his brother, which worried me.

"Chosen?" he rumbled. "To me."

We crowded over to him. My heart was pounding. While Emma and the others thought I'd be welcomed, I didn't share their confidence. Patricia and Stephanie had both sensed the opening of the Portal and my entry into their world. What if this mysterious third Shaper, this "Protector," had sensed it, too? What if he could sense my presence, and knew I was near?

If he did, he apparently hadn't ordered black-robed guy to keep an eye out for me. "My name is Thaddeus," he growled. Literally. "You will follow me."

And just like that, the young people around me changed. They'd been laughing and pointing at things, joking and commenting and goofing around and generally acting like a group of high-school kids on a field trip. But now, as though someone had flipped a switch, all that stopped. They went quiet. Quiescent. Dull-eyed. After a second's shock, I tried to emulate them.

"Single file," said Thaddeus, and they complied without a word, and so did I, though my heart was pounding harder than ever. I made sure I was the rearmost person in line as we followed him through the archway deeper into Abrahmville. I remembered the terror I had felt when Dracula had surprised us, the seductive pull of Seraphina, the illusion of Queen Stephanie . . .

And suddenly I knew how it had been done—how all of it had been done. Including the spiriting away of Karl and Piotr and Father Thomas.

At Zarozje, two rogues. One to take on the appearances of Father Thomas, another, like Thaddeus here, to exert another kind of glamor . . . call it the glamor of obedience. The villagers of Zarozje had quietly packed up their belongings, including the treasures of the church, and followed their new leaders into the lands of the Protector, without question or suspicion.

This same coercive power explained what had happened to Father Thomas, Karl, and Piotr the night they vanished from the farmhouse. From outside, a rogue had called everyone inside to come to him, and they had responded. Presumably because I now had the *hokhmah* of the original Shapers of this world within me, I was immune. Fortunately for me, the rogue had been so arrogantly sure of his power he had not checked to make sure everyone had emerged.

It seemed I was immune to Thaddeus' glamor, too—unlike the Chosen, who had suddenly become mindless cattle, entirely in his thrall.

And cattle, it occurred to me, suddenly and sickeningly, were food.

THIRTY

YOU KNOW HOW pleased with yourself you feel when you solve a mystery that has been puzzling you? This was not one of those times. I felt absolutely certain I now understood what was going on . . . and absolutely sick about it.

I was keenly aware I had a crossbow, cocked and loaded with a silver-tipped bolt, tucked away in my backpack. I was also keenly aware that taking it out now, as we walked through the dark, deserted streets of Abrahmville, only an occasional corner lamp or spill of light through windows alleviating the gloom, would likely accomplish nothing but getting myself killed.

If the moment arose, though . . .

After a few minutes of trudging over the cobblestones, we reached the base of the cliff. Looking up, I saw that the path I had seen from a distance consisted of steps cut into the rock. The cliff recessed just enough as it rose (Shaped that way, of course) to make it possible to continue the staircase to the top. Lamps lit those steps or were beginning to—a dark figure ahead of us was lighting each in turn, then returning it to the hook or shelf on which it rested.

The steps, comfortingly broad and even, had been built/Shaped with ornament as well as purpose in mind: beautifully carved balusters supported the handrail. I stayed as quiescent as the young people in front of me, who spoke not a word as they climbed—

who hadn't spoken a word since the moment Thaddeus said, "Follow me."

Of that ascent, the less said the better. I'm not afraid of heights, but I'm also not keen on falling from them, and as the height increased, I was less and less keen. I couldn't hold on to the balustrade because no one else did, and it seemed a little low to me, anyway—not nearly high enough to ensure I wouldn't topple right over the top of it if I tripped. It reminded me uncomfortably of the path above Zarozje that I *had* fallen off of, albeit with Karl's help and for, I'm sure he thought, a good reason.

The lamps cast pools of illumination around themselves, but they weren't nearly frequent enough for my taste, serving mostly to ruin my night vision for the stretches in between where only the moon lit the way. And we never stopped to rest: trudge, trudge, trudge, step by step, switchback by switchback, up the cliff face, while the lights of Abrahmville dropped away below us and the valley of the Mother Church opened up to the east, bodies of water glimmering here and there beneath the gibbous moon. The top of the cliff never seemed to get any nearer.

Of course, that was just a nasty illusion. We eventually stepped from the stairs through an archway into a courtyard paved with massive white stones. The not-quite-high-enough balustrade repeated along the edge of the cliff, not that I had any intention of going anywhere near it.

It was all I could do not to drop to my hands and knees and take some deep, gasping breaths. None of the others did, though (although everyone was panting except for Thaddeus), so I didn't dare. Nor had they made the slightest protest at the brutal pace of the climb or commented on how glad they were it was over, so deeply were they enthralled by Thaddeus' glamor.

It was he who now stopped us, with a single, sharp, "Stay!", as if we were pet dogs. He strode away. I wiped night-chilled sweat from my face and looked around.

The dark bulk of Mother Church loomed over the western side of the courtyard, light glowing through the rose window above the doors. More lamps had been lit since I'd seen the church from down below: giant ones hung on each side of the towers, and others flickered on poles around the courtyard. *That bare brick façade looks so wrong*, I thought. I knew, from the *hokhmah* within me, that it should be covered in white-and-green marble, like the Duomo in Florence. Statues of saints should have looked down from multiple alcoves; colorful paintings of religious scenes, bright with gold leaf, should have filled the semicircular spaces above the three doors, one in each tower and the double one in the center; the doors themselves should have been covered with ornate bronze reliefs. But all of this had vanished, as if it had never existed. There was only brick.

It's not the Mother Church anymore. It's the House of the Protector. And he clearly doesn't hold with churches—he's had them torn down, and Shaped the people to forget they ever existed, in all the villages of this valley.

And then, a thought struck me.

He had indeed, in the villages, *had the churches torn down.* Physically torn down, by the villagers. At the Shaper's behest, no doubt, but he hadn't simply Shaped them out of existence: if he had, all physical traces of them would have vanished. And here, on Mother Church herself, the bricks were chipped in places, missing in others, the mortar ragged. The ornate façade had been physically, forcefully removed.

Why do that, if he was truly a Shaper? Unless, unlike Patricia and Stephanie, he had some power left . . . enough, perhaps, to Shape humans to his will, but not enough to make the kinds of changes in the environment a more powerful Shaper could?

Someone like, for instance, me?

An encouraging thought. He might not expect me to be able to do what I might be able to do once I had all three *hokhmahs* of this world, and he might be limited in what he might be able to do to try to prevent me from getting close to him.

Might was a word doing a lot of work in that sentence, though.

The courtyard was embraced, if that was the right word, by long, low buildings, fronted by colonnades, that ran out from the sides of the church a short distance, then turned at right angles and extended straight to the edge of the cliff. I was reminded a bit of the colonnades of St. Peter's Basilica in Vatican City, though these were nothing like their size, they were straight instead of curved, and they weren't topped by religious statues—okay, they weren't very much like St. Peter's at all. Still, that's what I was reminded of. And for all I knew, these colonnades had once also been topped with statues of saints and apostles, but they had been stripped of them just as the church itself had been stripped of its religious symbolism.

This third Shaper clearly hated the works of the original Shapers, Patricia and Stephanie, and the peaceful, Pact-protected world they had set up, where they could play at being werewolves and vampires without any of that nasty eating-the-peasants stuff. The epicenter of the wrongness that had invaded their world was definitely this hulking, naked ex-church.

Thaddeus disappeared into a low wooden building near the left tower of the church—just a hut, really, which looked incongruously out of place in the grand courtyard—and I suddenly realized this was my chance—maybe my only chance—to prepare for whatever might come next. I pulled off my pack, knelt, opened it, pulled out the crossbow and one of my blankets, set both on the ground— all the time keeping an eye on the door Thaddeus had entered— closed the pack, put it on, wrapped the crossbow in the blanket, and stood up, holding my new bundle to my chest, just as Thaddeus emerged again, looking down at a clipboard.

He raised his head and glanced at our line as he moved to the front of it but didn't react to the fact I was now carrying something I hadn't before. Perhaps it wasn't as unusual as I feared. Perhaps he'd never noticed what I was carrying before we set off up the cliff—he hadn't looked back once, clearly confident we could do nothing else but follow him, and the entire journey had been made in the dark, after all. Even here, though there were lamps on the ex-church, more lamps visible between the columns of the colonnades, and, of course, the brilliant, too-large moon hanging in its eternal place in the sky, the light wasn't exactly conducive to noticing details.

Or, possibly just as likely, he was so certain of his superiority, so sure we were under his control, that he noticed but it didn't alarm him in the slightest.

Whatever the reason, Thaddeus simply shouted, "Follow me," and set off again, leading us not to the massive (and closed) front doors of the ex-church, but past the out-of-place log-cabin-like wooden hut to the end of the colonnade to our left nearest the church wall. He led us up the three steps and between the columns, beneath one of the lamps hung on chains down the length of the colonnade. In the building attached to the colonnade was a series of closed doors, all plain, pale, unweathered oak. Someone, clearly, had recently replaced all the old doors with new ones. *Probably had religious emblems on them*, I thought.

Thaddeus opened the door closest to the church. "In here," he said, and barely stood aside as, one by one, we entered, which forced me to brush past him so close I felt his breath on my cheek. I kept my eyes straight ahead and did my utmost to look hypnotized rather than terrified.

I found myself, with the others, in a long, narrow room, with another door to our right, which had to lead into the former church. The room had a floor of red tile and walls of plain white plaster— again, with a fresh, new look. I wondered what religious frescoes that plaster covered.

Thaddeus went to the second door in the room and swung it open, revealing a square landing with brick walls. To the left, stairs descended. Yellow light flickered up them. "Down," Thaddeus said, and one by one, we brushed past him again.

He was clearly counting us. He glanced at the paper in his hand, looked up, looked down, frowning all the time . . . until I, still at the end of the line, approached. Just as I slipped by, he suddenly smiled— with teeth. Very pointy teeth. Vampire teeth, or werewolf teeth, I couldn't tell, but definitely not just human teeth.

Heart hammering again, I followed the others down the stairs past flickering torches, a long way down, farther than I would have expected. Only one thing could lie this deeply under a church: the crypt.

Thaddeus closed the door after I passed through and followed us. His bare feet made no noise, so I had no idea how close behind me he was, and I didn't dare turn around and look. When at last we reached the larger chamber at the bottom of the stairs, dark and dank, I walked farther in than I might have before, hoping to min-gle with the others.

There was no illumination in the room itself, but light followed me into it. Thaddeus had plucked the last torch from the stairwell. He walked around the room and lit two more torches already in place, then put his in an empty sconce next to another door made of bright, fresh-looking oak, set in what looked to me like an equally new wall of smooth stones, the mortar joining them smooth and uncracked—unlike the decaying mortar in the other walls.

I still thought this should be part of the crypt, but if it was, the Protector must have done some spring cleaning—presumably hauling out a lot of dead monks, doing I-didn't-want-to-know-what with the bodies (although, since many of those bodies must date to the entirely fictional past of this Shaped world, had they ever been alive, or were they just stage props? That pesky conundrum again)—and then a little subdividing, with the goal, I had a suspicion, of transforming crypt to dungeon.

Or, possibly, if my nasty suspicion was true, larder.

Thaddeus turned toward us then. Eight people stared at him with dull, disinterested eyes. One person stared at him with extremely interested eyes that she was desperately trying to make *appear* dull and disinterested.

The Chosen closest to Thaddeus was my companion from the road, Emma Krause-Snow. She did not react as he reached out and cradled her chin in his hand. I did: I tensed.

"Lucky number nine," he crooned to her. "I'm only supposed to have eight. That's what the paper says. One to be changed, seven for feasting. One extra, not on the paper, never missed . . . for me!"

His face suddenly writhed and shifted. He stayed humanoid and stayed clothed, like I'd seen the vampires do, but he didn't look like them; he looked like a horrible, bipedal wolf, like a Lon Chaney-style Hollywood werewolf. He reached out, grabbed Emma, pulled her toward him, bared his teeth, leaned down to rip out her throat—

—and my crossbow bolt slammed into the side of his head before the blanket that had been concealing my weapon finished tumbling to the floor at my feet.

Thaddeus dropped like the bag of meat he'd suddenly become, dragging Emma down with him. I ran to them both, set the crossbow aside, pulled the dead thing off her and stared down into her face. I saw her eyes come back to life, the spell he'd been exerting on her gone. I heard indrawn breaths behind me from the other Chosen. Though I was shaking, and horribly aware of Thaddeus' dead eyes staring at me, wide and puzzled, and the growing pool of blood beneath his head, I managed a smile. "You're all right now," I said. "He's dead."

Emma stared up at me, then glanced left, saw Thaddeus, and sat up so suddenly I had to jump back to keep from getting cracked on the jaw by the top of her head. "What have you done?" she whispered, horror in her voice. She scrambled to her feet and backed away from the corpse, her eyes locked on it. Then her head snapped up and she stared at me, wide-eyed. "What have you done?" This time, she screamed it. Shrilly. "You've killed one of the guards of the Protector!"

Uh-oh, I thought. I grabbed the crossbow in my left hand and backed toward the door Thaddeus had been about to usher everyone through. All of the other Chosen watched me, their faces grim with righteous indignation, I guess. One-handed, I pulled off my pack and dropped it on the floor in front of me. Still they stared.

I knelt, keeping my eyes on them, opened the pack, reached in, and by feel found what I most wanted at that moment—the hilt of my dagger. I stayed kneeling, gripping the dagger but keeping it out of sight. Only then did I reply. "He was going to eat you."

"It was a test," Emma cried. "We were told there would be tests. It was a test of our loyalty, of our willingness to serve, and you . . ."

"You killed him!" one of the boys shouted.

"Murderer!" screamed a girl.

"Monster!" "Monster!" "Monster!" "Murderer!" "Evil!" "Betrayed . . ." I kind of lost track of who was saying what, but I sensed the moment when their shock flipped to anger, and jumped to my feet, dagger in my hand. They flinched back.

It had occurred to me that if I were going to Shape people to be ever-cheerful cattle, I'd make sure to squelch the part that made them fighters. And it looked like I was right: though they could easily have overwhelmed me, none would close with my blade.

"Now what?" I said. I looked at the girl I'd thought was becoming my friend. "Emma? I saved your life."

"Saved it?" she spat. "You ruined it!" She turned to the others. "We must go and tell someone what has happened. She is trapped here. That door is locked."

"Yes," said another girl. "If we close the door at the top of the stairs and hold it, she won't be able to get out. Then more of the Protector's servants will come and capture her."

A chorus of agreement followed. I remembered that old dismissive word "sheeple," which conspiracy-minded types like to apply to anyone who stubbornly refuses to grasp the truth of the shadowy forces arrayed against them. This was the first group of people I thought I could actually apply it to. *Baa! Baa!* I thought.

And just like that, they turned and headed back toward the stairs, leaving me alone with the body of Thaddeus. Emma was the last. "I liked you, Shawna Keys," she said from the doorway. "I thought you were a friend. How could you have betrayed me?"

I said nothing.

Shaking her head, Emma climbed out of sight.

I took a minute to resheathe my dagger and reattach it to my belt, and to cock and reload my crossbow. Then I cautiously took hold of the door handle behind me and turned it, just to be sure it was, indeed, locked.

And, of course, it was.

But Thaddeus had been about to usher everyone through it. Which had to mean . . .

Grimacing with distaste, I knelt beside him, avoiding the spreading pool of blood and trying not to look at the crossbow bolt protruding from his temple. *I should pull it out*, I thought. *I might need it later.* But that was a gross-out too far. I left it.

Instead, I rummaged through his pockets, finding what I hoped for, a ring with five keys on it, which, ickily enough, was underneath his body. I stood up in a hurry, breathing hard, and turned back to the door.

I tried the first key. Nothing.

The second. No good.

Were those distant shouts, up the stairs?

I took a deep breath and tried key number three.

This time, it turned. I grabbed the knob, swung the door open, dashed through, turned, slammed it shut, locked it again. Only then did I look around.

More suspiciously fresh-looking masonry stretched in the corridor from left and right, punctuated, on the opposite side from which I'd entered, by new-looking doors with tiny, barred windows in them. Torches spluttered here and there.

I thought for a minute. In a church, stairs down to the crypt often descended from somewhere in the middle, which had to be to my left. It seemed brighter in that direction, too.

So to the left I went, running, expecting that at any moment the door I'd come through would open and guards would come pouring through, the Chosen having summoned them from the courtyard. But the door did not open, and after a fairly short dash, I stopped, breathing hard, and looked back.

Nothing. And, come to think of it, we hadn't exactly seen a lot of guards in the courtyard. Someone had been in that little log hut, and he might well have shut up shop for the night after the Chosen arrived. Maybe the Chosen were wandering around looking for someone to tattle to, or maybe they were hurrying back down that long staircase to Abrahmville.

I suddenly felt bad for holding them in such contempt. They'd been Shaped to believe the Protector could do no wrong, Shaped to believe being Chosen was an honor. Even Thaddeus' attack on Emma hadn't shaken that baked-in belief.

My anger at the yet-to-be-met Abrahm, the unwelcome,

unexpected, and so-far unexplained third Shaper of this over-Shaped world, burned hot in me at that moment. Since I wasn't being chased, I double-checked my crossbow. The dead Thaddeus was proof silver worked just fine against these weird vampire/werewolf rogues. (Although a bolt to the brain, silver-tipped or not, might have killed even an ordinary werewolf—after all, it supposedly worked on zombies.)

Then I headed down the corridor, listening hard for any sound of pursuit.

I didn't hear it. Instead, I heard the scrape of footsteps ahead of me, where there was a change of the light, from the flicker of torches (very occasional torches, so that most of the corridor was in darkness, which suited me fine), to the glow of much brighter, steadier light, streaming down spiraling stairs.

The exit from the crypt, leading up into the church proper. It had to be.

But there were figures between me and it, shadowy silhouettes, six human shapes. The light was too dim for me to make out details, other than the fact one was naked, but then one of the non-naked ones spoke, and his voice rang clearly back to me.

"Where are you taking us?" he demanded.

Karl!

THIRTY-ONE

FOR TWO DAYS, Karl waited.

No one answered his shouts, but three times, bread and water appeared, slid through a small square opening in the bottom of the door. Whoever brought it was nothing but a brief silhouette against the flickering torchlight.

A couple of times, that torchlight went out, but it always came back: torches being renewed and relit, Karl thought. He tried shouting, but no one answered.

Nor did they talk much amongst themselves, after the first moments when they had all awakened from the strange, dreamlike state in which they had been ensconced.

Piotr had immediately changed into boy form. "What happened?" he asked, his young voice tense with worry.

"My guess," Karl said, "is that we have been victimized by another kind of vampiric glamor. Like the terror Dracula exudes, or the seductiveness of Seraphina, but one that engenders blind obedience."

"I didn't experience either one of those," Piotr said. "What do you mean, the 'seductiveness of Seraphina'?"

Karl started to answer, reflected on how young Piotr was, and changed direction slightly in his response. "She was able to deflect my suspicions of her," was all he said.

"I have never heard of a glamor of obedience," Father Thomas said. "Nor had I heard of a glamor of illusion like the one you ascribed to the rogue you encountered in our valley. There are clearly more things in heaven and earth than are dreamt of in my philosophy."

Karl raised an eyebrow. Had Shakespeare existed here before the Great Cataclysm, or was that just another of the odd echoes of the First World one tended to encounter in the Labyrinth?

"I felt all was happening in a pleasant dream, until I came fully alert here," Father Thomas concluded.

"Me, too," Piotr said.

"My experience, as well," Karl said.

"But then, why isn't Shawna with us?" Father Thomas asked. "She was in the cottage, too. Was she taken elsewhere?"

"I suspect she was not affected," Karl said.

Father Thomas' face was only a dim, pale oval in the darkness, but Karl sensed him frowning. "Why should she be immune?"

"You know she is from a different world."

"Yes," Father Thomas said. "I accept that. But so are you, and you were affected."

Karl said nothing. Father Thomas remained ignorant of the true nature of his world, and he did not think either Shawna or Patricia or Stephanie would appreciate him attempting to enlighten the priest. It could destroy the man's faith, and what purpose would that serve? Karl and Shawna, if all went well, would eventually depart this world. Father Thomas had no choice but to continue to live in it, and his place in it was priest and protector of his village. He was here to save his villagers, if he could, and return them to their homes. Knowledge of the Labyrinth, of the existence of myriad worlds, of the fact that his world was only a couple of decades old in reality, that everything he thought he knew about it was a make-believe, a fiction concocted by the queen of the vampires and the queen of the werewolves out of scraps of romantically nonsensical tales they had heard in the First World . . . such knowledge would destroy him, if he accepted it, and likely turn him against Karl and Shawna as blasphemous liars if he did not.

Karl had argued with Shawna about the reality of the Shaped citizens of the world they entered, claiming they were not real in the same way as citizens of the First World, that their fates were nothing they needed to be overly concerned with as they pursued their quest. And yet, faced with Father Thomas, a flesh-and-blood man in whose company he had now spent several days, he did not want to hurt him.

"Maybe it's just because she's a girl . . . a woman, I mean," said Piotr.

"That is most probably correct," Karl said immediately, even though he knew it absolutely was not.

Father Thomas still sounded dubious. "Perhaps. I hope you are right, and she was not affected. Might she be able to rescue us?"

"One woman against the Protector, his forces, and this rather secure structure?" Karl said. "It seems . . . unlikely."

But once again, he was saying something he did not believe. Because if there was one thing Shawna Keys had shown, since he had identified her as the Shaper of her world, approached her, and seen how much Shaping power she could bring to bear, it was that she was surprisingly resourceful.

After that, they had little to talk about. Piotr, complaining of being cold, returned to wolf form and remained that way. Father Thomas went back to sleep. Karl sat on his cot, his back to the wall, and stared at the door, as if by sheer force of will he could cause it to open and the mysterious third Shaper to summon them.

His exerted will, of course, had not the slightest effect. As Shawna continued to drive home to him as her own abilities grew and she moved beyond needing his assistance to complete their quest—or, at least, his assistance to open Portals, find Shapers, and take their *hokhmah*—he was not a Shaper.

Succeed in the quest, and Ygrair had promised he might yet become one. But sitting in the dark dungeon, ignored for that first day and then a second . . . for one of the few times in his journeys so far, he almost despaired.

Then the door opened.

Piotr tensed and crouched, growling. Father Thomas, who had been dozing, sat up. Karl got to his feet.

Two guards stepped in. They carried drawn swords, but wore no armor, garbed instead in black robes with scarlet belts. "Lord Abrahm wants to see you," growled the first. "Up." He pointed his blade at Piotr, and from the glint of it in the torchlight, Karl could tell it was silvered. "None of that. Human shape, now."

Piotr growled again, but then flowed up into his boy-shape. Father Thomas got to his feet, too.

"Let's go," said the first guard. The second guard stepped to one side, and Piotr, Father Thomas, and Karl stepped into the corridor. A third guard awaited them there.

One for each of us, Karl thought. An honor, I suppose.

To the right glowed honest lamplight, steady and bright, unlike the flickering light of the torches that illuminated the corridor to the left. The light poured down a winding, spiral staircase. "Move," said the first guard, who seemed to be in command, and they all started toward the stairs.

"Where are you taking us?" Karl asked.

"Into the presence of the Protector," growled the commander. "And mind your behavior. Now be silent."

Karl clenched his jaw and held his tongue. He followed the guard up the stairs. Father Thomas and Piotr trailed him, and the other two guards brought up the rear. He could feel the presence of the third Shaper somewhere up above . . . and the place where the Portal to the next world could be opened.

Shawna Keys, he thought, *where are you? Because this is where you need to be.*

They climbed toward the light.

"Into the presence of the Protector," one of those other shadowy figures answered Karl. "And mind your behavior. Now be silent."

Karl and the Protector! I thought. *A twofer.* Or a fourfer, actually, since now I knew one of those figures was Karl, I recognized another as Father Thomas and a third—the naked one, of course—as Piotr. And the place of the potential Portal was close, too. Very close. If I played this right, I could seize the *hokhmah* from Abrahm, open the Portal, grab Karl, and get the hell out of Dodge in the next few minutes . . .

. . . and leave the Protector to continue "choosing" young people from the villages of his private valley. "One to be changed, seven for feasting," Thaddeus had said. One to be changed into a rogue. The others food, maybe even for the one who had been changed, who, in his or her first famished frenzy, would gorge on someone who, moments before, had been a friend.

Perhaps my thought that Abrahm could not Shape the physical world to any great extent was true. Perhaps he only had the power to influence and control the Shaped. But that word, "only," held immense possibilities for evil.

I remembered Emma unprotestingly letting her head be tilted back so Thaddeus could rip out her throat and how she had then screamed at me for killing Thaddeus and saving her life, unshakable in her belief in the goodness of the Protector, in how much she had been honored in being Chosen to "serve" him. I remembered that and felt something I hadn't felt in a long while: something I hadn't felt even for Robur, who had crafted his world as an endless wargame; something I hadn't felt for anyone except the Adversary, who had stolen my world from me and murdered my best friend before my eyes: hatred.

Not fiery, all-engulfing, lava-hot hatred, but the cold kind, the icy kind, the kind that freezes all emotion except for itself.

I took a deep, shaking breath, gripped my crossbow, and let that hatred drive me down the corridor, toward the steps Karl and the others had just climbed.

Though the shape of the enormous space into which Karl ascended in the company of Piotr, Father Thomas, and the three guards was unmistakably that of a church, no religious iconography remained within it. Instead of the crucifix that must have once adorned the back of the apse—which, Karl saw, was part of the mountain itself, bare gray granite—there was a double door, twice the height of a man, made, apparently, of gold, bearing intricate carvings. He could not see them clearly from where he was. The light that had poured down the stairs came from a single, wheel-shaped fixture far over their heads, in which at least two dozen oil lamps burned, but its glow barely reached the apse, where candles flickered but more confused the eye than illuminated.

In any event, Karl did not really care about the decorations on the door. What interested him the most was the sudden certainty, flowing through the Shurak nanomachines in his bloodstream and delivered like a punch in the gut, that it was through those doors that a Portal into the next world could be opened.

In front of those golden doors and potential Portal, where once the altar would have stood, there was, instead, a throne. It, too, was made of gold.

On it sat a young man. To his right, on a lower chair, sat a young woman.

Urged forward by his captors, Karl could see that the throne, like the door, was intricately carved. As he neared it, he identified some of those images: stars, the moon, lightning bolts, and oak trees, and above the man's head, a rising sun, its rays of light rendered in crystal, sticking up like icicles from the throne itself.

The smaller chair on which the woman sat was comparatively plain: gilded, upholstered in red, but otherwise unadorned except by the young woman herself. She was, Karl had to admit, quite a striking adornment, being clad in a flowing, sleeveless white dress with a golden collar, the dress slit far enough up her side to make it arrestingly clear she wore nothing beneath it. Her hair, as gold as her collar and the chair, was piled into an intricate mass on her head, held there by combs that glittered with emeralds and topazes.

By contrast, the man on the beautiful throne was . . . underwhelming.

Though his height was hard to be certain of, since he was seated, Karl had the distinct impression that, standing, he would be considerably shorter than Karl himself. He also looked considerably pudgier, although to be fair, short rations and a great deal of walking over the past few months of his life had left Karl far leaner than he had been when he had lived in Ygrair's palace.

The man's hair was an unremarkable shade of brown. His face was average, the only distinguishing characteristic being a nose that seemed too small for the broad jaw and forehead. His ears stuck out. He had freckles.

His clothing, on the other hand, echoed the over-the-top opulence of the throne. He wore a tunic and trousers of sparkling white, adorned with gold braid and a red sash and a diamond pendant. He wore a gold collar and a gold crown. He had rings on each finger. His high boots were bright red.

He looked, to Karl, like a man playing at being something he was not. And yet, this surely had to be . . .

"Kneel before Protector Abrahm, Lord of the Sacred Vale, Creator of Good, Scourge of Evil," said the commander of the three guards, and pressed hard on his shoulder to emphasize the point. Karl knelt on the first of the four steps leading up to the once-apse. Beside him, Piotr and Father Thomas were likewise forced to their knees.

Abrahm gave a languid shooing motion with his hand, and the guards stepped back from the three kneelers. The woman looked at them as though they were spots on her immaculate dress.

Father Thomas was staring around him, his face anguished. "What have you done?" he said, his voice choked with emotion. "You have desecrated Mother Church! You have violated the holiest—"

"Quiet," Abrahm said, with no heat in his voice, but with something else, something that made Father Thomas cut off in midspeech.

He Shaped him, Karl thought. And so it was confirmed, not that he had had any doubt: the Protector, Abrahm, was the third Shaper.

"I brought you here," Abrahm said, his female companion turning her gaze to him adoringly as he spoke (a sure sign, Karl thought, that she was also Shaped, because Abrahm did not appear to him to be adorable in the slightest) "because of the curious manner of your arrival. It has been a long time since anyone journeyed into the Sacred Vale from the Lands Between without being guided here by my followers. And the last ones who did, some months ago now, certainly did not enter the vale hard on the heels of my Veil of Protection being activated by an incursion of the Imperfect.

This leads me to believe that originally you three were traveling in the company of the Imperfect. Such a thing has not been known since I successfully shattered the precious Pact of the Imperfect Queens. This concerns me. You will now tell me exactly how you traveled here, and more importantly, why."

Karl said nothing. He was working through what Abrahm had just said, extracting what he could from it to better understand how Abrahm viewed the world he had at least some limited ability to Shape. In any event, he certainly had no intention of telling the man the truth. Piotr stayed silent as well, possibly fuming at hearing his mother, Queen Stephanie, described as "Imperfect."

Abrahm glanced from Karl to Piotr, then turned to Father Thomas. "I am now your ruler, and you will obey me in all things."

"You are now my ruler, and I will obey you in all things," Thomas said dully. "Of course, Protector."

Karl, though he had seen the work of Shapers many times, still felt chilled at the ease with which Abrahm stripped Thomas of the core of his being—his unwavering belief in God and the Church—and instantly replaced it with unwavering belief in Abrahm.

"Now answer my questions."

Thomas proceeded to do so, telling Abrahm of their journey to the Sacred Vale in the company of werewolves and vampires, how those companions had been prevented from entering, how they had continued on foot, how he had come to try to find out what had happened to his village and other villages, but how Piotr and Karl and Shawna had come for reasons he found obscure. As he spoke, the woman yawned, looking bored, but Abrahm listened intently.

Thomas revealed, of course, that Piotr was the werewolf son of Queen Stephanie, and that caught Abrahm's attention. He looked at the boy with one eyebrow raised. Piotr, with remarkable self-control for one so young, Karl thought, had as yet said nothing.

"And yet you made it through the Veil of Protection?" he said. "Interesting . . . but I will examine that later." He looked back at Father Thomas. "It is this 'Shawna Keys' who interests me most. Tell me more."

Obligingly, Father Thomas told him how Shawna Keys had come to his village, how she had claimed to be from outside the valley—from another world, in fact—how she and her companions had managed to restore the Pact, and how she had strange abilities to influence others and had even performed miracles: with his own eyes, he had seen her conjure clothing out of thin air.

"But she is not with you," Abrahm said, narrowed eyes glittering in the candlelight.

"When we felt the call in the night," Father Thomas said, "and in a dream approached your holy presence, she did not come with us."

"Indeed?" Abrahm sat back. "Immune to the call and capable of making things out of thin air?" There was an unmistakable thread of excitement in his voice. "And claims to be from outside the valley . . ."

His eyes focused on Karl and Karl braced himself for whatever questions were about to come. Abrahm might try to Shape him, as he clearly had Father Thomas. It would not work, because he was of the First World. But if he could convince Abrahm it had worked, he might be able to . . .

But then, a disturbance. From far back in the hall came the sound of a door opening and closing again. The young woman brightened, peering into the distance as though hoping something more exciting was about to happen than had happened so far, as footsteps hurried the length of what had once been the nave.

Abrahm looked up from Karl, frowning. "What is this?" he called, his voice booming in the vast space.

"My apologies, Protector." Karl turned his head to see another guard in a red-belted black robe—a woman, though a particularly tall one, this time—come up beside him. She bobbed her head by way of salute. "There may be an intruder in the House."

"An intruder?" Abrahm's eyes flicked to Father Thomas, to Karl, then back to the female guard. The young woman beside the throne straightened, clearly intrigued. "Tell me more."

"Thaddeus, of the First Company, was murdered by a woman who infiltrated a party of food," the guard said. "The food, of course, reported it. We are searching the grounds, but it is possible she was able to enter the crypt—Thaddeus' keys were taken."

"A party of food?" Abram said. His eyes flicked to the young woman at his side. "The one arriving tonight?"

"Yes, Protector."

"Were any of them harmed?"

"Who?" the female guard said, sounding puzzled.

"The food!" the Protector snapped. "One of them is *not* food. She was Chosen to be changed. Were any of them harmed?"

"No, Protector."

"And you think this mysterious, murderous woman could be in the crypt?" Abrahm's eyes moved again, as did the young woman's, over Karl's head, to the stairwell in the floor. "I presume you are searching it."

"Yes, Protector. A squad has just entered it. If she is down there, she will be forced . . ."

"Nobody forces me to do anything," a woman's voice said, and Karl closed his eyes and took a deep breath. *End game*, he thought.

Shawna Keys had arrived.

THIRTY-TWO

WHILE I HAVE not exactly spent my life treading the boards, my brief forays into theater—a middle-school production of *The Sound of Music*, a high-school attempt at *Fiddler on the Roof*, a disastrous venture into the world of student-written-and-directed-avant-garde-plays in university, and, of course, my time touring with the Worldshapers Theatrical Troupe in the last world I'd passed through—had at least taught me how to make a grand entrance.

I'd listened to Father Thomas spill the beans, and knew it was because he had been Shaped by the loathsome slug on the throne. I had felt the Shaping power exerted, and the hate I already felt for the so-called Protector redoubled. It tripled when I heard the guard refer to the Chosen—seven of them, at least—as "food." Emma and the others had been stripped of their individuality by the ruler of this abhorrent house, made to accept whatever fate he decreed for them: one to be changed into a monster, the others to be fed to monsters.

And, yes, in my hatred I reached for my own Shaping ability, but I was still blocked. Here, Abrahm's *hokhmah* held sway, and the only way I was going to be able to set anything right was to get it from him. Which meant touching him. Which seemed pretty loathsome in its own right, but a girl's gotta do what a girl's gotta do.

The announcement that there was a party of guards searching the crypt coincided with my hearing voices and the clank of arms and armor down at the bottom of the stairs where I was crouched, listening to the voices in the hall above echoing down to me from the high, vaulted ceiling. And that, clearly, was my cue.

I still had my crossbow in hand, but I kept it pointed down as I rose and walked up the stairs into what had once been Mother Church. "Nobody forces me to do anything," I said.

I heard Karl heave a sigh, though it sounded more like exasperation than relief. I ignored him. My eyes widened a little at the sight of the girl seated on the lower chair beside the throne—I'd had no idea she was there, since she hadn't spoken—but I gave her only a glance before focusing on the three male guards standing behind the kneeling trio, and the female guard who had just announced my "infiltration," who likewise stood behind the kneelers but in front of the other two. They all turned to look at me.

I raised the crossbow, and the four on the floor converged instantly in front of Abrahm, hiding him and the surprise girl from me and my weapon . . . and hiding something else, something I knew was there but couldn't see: the location, burning in my mind like a beacon, of the place where I could open a Portal into the next world.

I smiled. "The name's Keys. Shawna Keys. First one who rushes me dies."

Shouts echoed below me in the crypt. In a minute, more guards would be swarming up the stairs, and I only had the single crossbow.

"But that's not what I'm here for," I said. I moved onto the floor, a vast checkerboard of red-and-black squares, so I couldn't be grabbed from behind. I lowered the crossbow, knowing I could bring it back up in a minute. "I'm here to talk to Abrahm. I want to know how he's able to do the things he can do—the same kinds of things I can do."

I stopped, halfway between the stairwell in the floor and the throne, and waited.

"Put down your weapon, and you may approach," Abrahm's voice came from behind his trio of human shields. "Jael, call off the guards in the crypt. I am adequately protected. They may return to their duties."

"Protector?" The female rogue who had just warned her boss about me sounded peeved.

"Jael," Abrahm said softly, and the rogue turned without another word and hurried past me to the stairwell, though the look she gave me was hot enough to fry me on the spot had this been a world with superheroes and she'd had heat vision, which, it occurred to me, could totally be a thing.

Carefully, though with some regret and not a little trepidation, I placed the crossbow on the floor, followed by my dagger. One of the remaining guards hurried over and picked both of them up, then escorted me toward the throne . . .

. . . but not, alas, *all* the way to it.

"That's far enough," said the Protector when I was still behind the three kneelers. The young woman with him, who had yet to speak a word, stared at me avidly, as though I were the most interesting thing she'd seen in ages.

"You could let them up," I said. "Their knees must be killing them."

Abrahm ignored that. "You are their leader, I presume."

I guess I am, I thought. "Of course."

"I thought so. You clearly have some of the same powers I have, though of course they do you no good in my presence."

He was, unfortunately, correct.

"The fact you were immune to the call, while these three," he indicated my companions, "were not, is another indication that you are no ordinary woman. But there is, of course, another test."

I frowned. "A test? I don't . . ."

"I am now your ruler, and you will obey me in all things," he said, and I *felt* it: I felt the Shaping power he put into those words, flowing around me like water around a boulder in a mountain stream—but just like that boulder, I was unmoved.

"Um, no," I said. "That won't work on me. We're two of a kind." *Build trust. Get close. Touch him. Game over.* Eight words that described my entire plan of action.

"I knew it," he breathed. He actually stood up, proving my first impression, that he was short.

"Protector," Karl said. "If I may . . ."

"You may not. I am now your ruler, and you will obey me in all things." I felt the power of his Shaping flow over Karl with no more effect than it had had on me.

The Protector must have felt that, too. His eyes narrowed. He glanced at Piotr. "I am now your ruler, and you will obey me in all things," he repeated.

"Never," Piotr said. It was the first word he had spoken since he'd been brought to the foot of the throne, at least that I'd heard, and it dripped with hatred to match my own. "My loyalty is to my mother, Queen Stephanie of the Werewolves, and the Pact she upholds."

I'm sure your mom would be surprised to hear that, considering how much you've disobeyed her in the last few days, I thought, but I wasn't about to undercut his moment.

The young woman's eyes had grown wider and wider as each of us rejected Abrahm's Shaping power in turn. I stared at her. There was something familiar about her face, but how could there be?

"The werewolves are imperfect," Abrahm said coldly. "Your mother is imperfect. Her Pact is an abomination. I will sweep the wolves, and the vampires, and both queens away when I am ready to lead my forces out of the Sacred Vale. I will rule, and I alone, with my splendid creations at my side, while humans take their proper place as artisans, servants . . . and food."

Piotr snarled, leaped to his feet, changed . . .

And, just like that, stopped. A young silver-black wolf stood motionless on the steps where the boy had been a moment before. I looked at Karl. His head had dropped forward, as though he had dozed off. So had Thomas'. Abrahm looked at the three of them with contempt. "Whatever protection two of you may have against my creative force, it is clear you are still inferior beings who can be easily swayed by my perfected creatures." He glanced at the young woman. "Well done, Tabitha."

The young woman inclined her head, "Thank you, my love."

I stared at her and felt suddenly ill. *Tabitha?*

No wonder she looked familiar. That young woman, clearly Abrahm's consort, was Emma's sister, who had been Chosen six months ago. And that meant . . .

"You had Emma Chosen because Tabitha wanted her here," I heard myself say out loud. "Wanted her changed."

Abrahm raised an eyebrow. "You know Emma?"

"You know my sister?" Tabitha said eagerly.

"Yes," I said. I looked at Tabitha, not Abrahm. "Your parents welcomed me to your village. I slept in your old bed. And I traveled with Emma all the way here." Then I turned my gaze to Abrahm. "And saved her from Thaddeus. He was going to kill her, because there was one more Chosen than was on the list, which he thought gave him a free snack."

Tabitha gasped. "Is she all right?"

"She was fine the last time I saw her."

Abrahm reached out and down and took Tabitha's hand, drawing her to her bare feet. "I promised you," he said fiercely to her. "You will change her yourself, and then you and your sister can both serve me."

There was something about the way he said "serve" that made me think he had more in mind than just some light housework and a little cooking, and my hatred for him—which I wouldn't have thought could wax greater—waxed greater.

Tabitha gave him a look of Shaped adoration that sickened me, especially considering what I was sure he was proposing. "Thank you, my love!" Then she turned her blue eyes on me. "And thank you for saving her."

"She's a friend," I said. *Or was.*

Jael, who had gone below to call off the search in the crypt, re-emerged up the staircase. She took in our small group in front of the throne in a glance. "If you would like me to stay, Protector . . ."

"Unnecessary," Abrahm said. "Matters are well in hand. Secure the food—tomorrow is feast day. Take the one to be changed to my wife's chambers." He glanced at Tabitha. "Would you like to wait for her there?"

Tabitha clapped her hands. "Oh, Abrahm, may I?"

"Of course," he said indulgently. He looked past me to one of the three guards remaining. "Samuel?"

"Yes, Protector?" Samuel, who was cut from the more typical big, burly, and bearded rogue-cloth, came forward. He was the one I had heard talking to Karl in the corridor below.

"If you would be so kind as to take over from Tabitha?"

"Of course," Samuel said. He looked at Father Thomas, Piotr, and Karl, frozen in place. "I'm ready."

"Release them, Tabitha," Abrahm said.

She smiled radiantly. "Done!"

My three companions lurched in place, then froze again as Samuel stared down at them.

"You may go," Abrahm said to Tabitha. She squealed like a puppy and ran off, disappearing through a door to the left of the apse.

To Jael, Abrahm said, "Carry on."

"Yes, Protector," Jael said. "I will take the one to be changed to the Lady Tabitha's quarters, and secure the food." She turned sharply on her heel and strode off into the gloom, back to the main doors, while I fought with all my might to keep my horror, disgust, and rage from overflowing. *Secure the food.* The young people with whom I had traveled up the valley, laughed and joked and sung songs with. *The food.*

Somehow, I managed to keep a disinterested look on my face, smiling an (I hoped) inscrutable Mona Lisa smile. Abrahm sat back down. "Now," he said. "Tell me where you really came from." He flicked his hand at Father Thomas. "The priest said you told him you came from another world. There are no other worlds, so clearly you lied. Why?"

"I did not exactly lie," I said cautiously. Abrahm obviously had some explanation of his own in mind, and I wanted him to lead me to it. "As you can clearly tell, I come from outside this valley."

I waited for him to tell me there was nothing outside the valley, as Father Thomas had so vehemently claimed—which had led to me learning about the Great Cataclysm—but Abrahm only smiled, the self-satisfied smile of someone who had been proved correct, at least in his own mind. "I have never believed the myth of the Great Cataclysm," he said. "It has always seemed to me a flimsy make-believe taught to the inferior creatures to hide some greater truth. Over the years, as I realized the power I had over everyone else, as I molded them to do what I wanted, to give me what I desired, to fulfill my every whim . . . I realized I was not of their race at all, that I must come from some superior race not evident within the valley—which could only mean, from outside the valley." He sat back, folded his hands over his ample stomach, and smiled at me. "And now here you are, a woman with the same powers to change things around her—at least, when that power is not, understandably, overwhelmed by proximity to my far *greater* power—who also came from outside the valley, who *admits* to coming from outside the valley. Tell me the truth: the Great Cataclysm was merely the cleansing of the outside world so that those of our race could enjoy it unimpeded, was it not? And this valley is merely an isolated backwater no one bothered with until now."

That, I thought, was perhaps the most conceited backstory anyone had ever crafted out of thin air to justify their feeling superior to those around them. I could totally work with it.

"Your perspicacity is impressive," I said, and gave myself bonus points for using "perspicacity" in a sentence. "You have it exactly right. The true rulers of this world—those with the power to . . . shall we say, Shape it . . . drove the lesser creatures away so we would not have to interact with them. The process was not without controversy, and war has raged since. But many years ago now, peace returned at last, and it was decided that it was time to track down the last remnants of the . . ." I hated myself for using the expression, but needs must, " . . . inferior races, hiding here and there in, as you say, backwaters like this one. I and my servant . . ." I glanced at Karl, somewhat surprised his outrage at what I had just called him didn't snap him out of whatever trance first Tabitha and then Samuel had put him into, " . . . entered this valley as explorers. We were caught up in the chaos in the main part of the valley, but with judicious application of my powers—far more limited than yours, as my inability to use them here bears witness—we were able to extract ourselves from the clutches of the imperfect queens and head to the passage out of the valley. We knew there was something strange happening here in the Sacred Vale, but we had no idea we would find another of the . . ." (God forgive me) " . . . master race holding sway."

"Your companion is of our race?" Abrahm gave Karl a doubtful look. "While it is true I cannot mold him, he fell easily under the sway of Samuel. Yet you seem to be immune."

"He is one of us," I said, "but his power is stunted. He is allowed to serve, but he can never hope to rule."

Abrahm nodded. "Of course." He had the gall to smile at me in a conspiratorial fashion. "So now that you know of me and my power . . ." he waved his hand, encompassing what had once been Mother Church and now was simply his pretentious house, " . . . what is your responsibility to your superiors?" He didn't say, your *other* superiors, but the implication was clear.

"I have no standing orders covering such an occurrence," I said. "It is unprecedented. I have no idea how you can even be here."

"I do not remember my infancy, of course," Abrahm said, "and it was not until puberty that my powers manifested. However, I was raised in the orphanage of Mother Church—the late, unlamented Mother Church," he added with an infuriating smile, spreading his hands to indicate the stripped building around us. "I have therefore always assumed I was a foundling."

"It should be possible," I said thoughtfully, "to determine your true heritage once you return to civilization. There are . . . magical tests that can be conducted." I'd almost said, "DNA tests," but this was entirely the wrong world for that.

" 'S'truth?" he said, eyes widening, and I was jarringly reminded of Father Thomas using that same archaic expression when I'd first told him I came from another world. *Both raised by the church,* I thought, *one seeking only to serve . . . and the other to destroy. To rule.*

I hid my gritted teeth behind a big smile. "Absolutely," I said.

Abrahm glanced at Samuel, who showed no interest whatsoever in what was going on, then at my three entranced companions, and then at the two remaining guards behind them. "You two," he said abruptly, "are dismissed."

"Protector?" said the man who had taken my crossbow and dagger.

"Dismissed!"

There was no further argument, if you could even count the

saying of a single word with an interrogative uptalk at the end as an initial argument. The two guards saluted. Rather than make the long trek to the main doors of the hall and out, like Jael, they descended into the crypt. My crossbow and dagger, alas, went with them. In my pack, still on my back, there were another dozen or so silver-tipped quarrels, but unless I wanted to pull one out and stab Samuel with it, which would probably prove difficult since he would likely be trying to kill me at the same time and was bigger, stronger, and faster, they didn't seem to offer any offensive capabilities.

When the guards were out of sight (though I doubted they were out of earshot—if I were a guard who took his duties seriously, I would be lurking at the bottom of the crypt stairs just in case I was needed at a moment's notice), Abrahm said, "This valley is of no permanent interest to me. I will come with you."

I could see why he didn't want the guards hearing that. I wasn't quite as sure why he didn't care if Samuel heard it. Or maybe I was. I remembered how Robur, in the last world, had spoken openly about how he viewed the Shaped as less-than-real, even with his chief intelligence officer, Athelia, sitting there listening. (It gave me no end of pleasure to reflect that she was the one I had left in effective charge of that world after our departure.) Robur had Shaped Athelia to be unconcerned about such things. I thought Patricia had done the same with Dracula. Clearly, the same held true for Samuel.

"But I'm puzzled," Abrahm continued. "You entered the valley somewhere near the castle of the so-called queen of the vampires, Patricia, did you not?"

I nodded.

"There is no pass into the valley there. In fact, it is a long way from there to the high mountains. The only way into the valley I know of is—was—that one." He jerked his thumb over his shoulder.

I looked past him at the big golden doors set in the living rock of the mountainside, the doors where I knew a new Portal could be opened, and almost laughed. Of course. "That's where Barnabas Ross and Remus Gailbraith and their followers entered the valley, isn't it?" I said. "When they were greeted by Abbot Costello and hammered out the Pact. That's the secret pass into this valley."

"Not a pass," Abrahm said. "A tunnel. Or rather, a series of great natural caverns that lead beneath the mountains to the lands beyond. Once the werewolves and vampires came through those caverns and told their scary stories of the so-called Great Cataclysm, the way was blocked, millions of tons of rocks brought down with blasting powder to ensure no one could ever enter this valley again . . . or leave it." He sounded angry. Clearly, he would be out through those caverns in a flash if he could.

Wait . . .

"And every year," he went on, while I was still trying to grab onto the slippery guppy of a thought that had flitted through the dark aquarium of my mind, "when this was still Mother Church, they would hold a solemn Mass celebrating the day those caverns suddenly disgorged a ragtag band of vampires and werewolves, supposedly led here by God." He twisted around to look at the golden doors, then turned back to me. "And I have always been told that it is the *only* entrance into this valley. Yet, you somehow entered the valley in a place where there is no tunnel, where there is nothing at all."

"Not quite true," I said. "We entered through an old barn."

Abrahm frowned, and I held up a placating hand. "I'm telling the truth. You see, we entered magically."

"I do not believe in magic."

"Poor choice of words," I said, backpedaling freely because I really needed to allay his suspicions. "Magic is what the inferior races call what we do. You and I. The others of our race. The re-making of the world. The . . . Shaping of it."

"Oh, of course," Abrahm said. "The priest called what you did, summoning cloaks for the vampires and werewolves in the vampire queen's castle, 'magic.'" He nodded. "So, you created a door-way into this valley in an old barn?"

"Exactly," I said.

"Then why didn't you leave the same way?"

"Well, first, because we needed to find you," I said. "And second, because we could not go back the way we'd come."

"Why not?" Abrahm said.

I shrugged. "You would have to ask a . . . a . . ." *Scientist? Theologian? Wizard?* " . . . my superiors," I settled for. "I am a fairly low-ranked official of the . . . Exploration Corps." God, if I piled up the make-believe a little deeper, I'd lose myself in it. I already wasn't sure I could remember everything I'd claimed. What if I contradicted myself? How did authors of fat fantasy novels keep it all straight? "All I know is that we could not exit the way we entered. There is a separate exit. And," I paused dramatically, "it is here!" And then I pointed, not at Abrahm, but past him, at the golden doors.

He twisted around again. "But that is an actual exit," he said, staring at the doors. "Not a 'magical' one. And as I told you, long sealed."

"Have you ever tried to reopen the tunnels?" I tried to make the question sound guileless, but it was anything but. The fact he had not opened that pass, the fact this church had been physically stripped of its furnishings but not remade into something less obviously a church, the fact that, although the Shaped in the so-called Sacred Vale had never even heard of the church, every village we'd passed through had had a church-sized hole in it . . . it all pointed to me being right about his limitations as a Shaper, limitations that, if I got hold of his *hokhmah*, I did not believe I would share.

Abrahm, I was now very nearly certain, could not Shape anything physically on a large scale. He could play with the Shaped to his heart's content, erasing their memories, changing their beliefs, ensuring their loyalties, even melding werewolves and vampires together into one repulsive whole and crafting new "glamors" for them. But he could not unblock the caves that would have led him to the world outside, even though it was the one thing he most longed to do, because he had utterly convinced himself he belonged out there among the entirely fictional superior race he fancied himself a part of.

"I would if I could, but I cannot," he said. I was almost surprised he admitted it. "Are you saying you can?"

"Not physically," I said. "No. But I can open a way out, a . . . call it a Portal . . . which will lead directly somewhere else. Somewhere outside the valley." Since I had no idea what might lie on the other side of the Portal, I didn't want to be any more specific than that.

"How?" he said. "My power overwhelms you here, you said so yourself."

I doubted very much that that was what was really going on—I thought my current powerlessness more likely had something to do with the fact that his weird, twisted, inexplicable hunk of *hokhmah* was incompatible with what I had brought with me, the *hokhmah* of the true Shapers of this world—but the last thing I wanted to do was undercut his well-honed sense of superiority. "It has nothing to do with my power," I said, and in fact, that was true: my ability to open Portals derived entirely from the alien technology of the Shurak. "It is simply something I was trained to do."

"Well, then," said Abrahm. "We have come to the most straightforward test of someone's truthfulness I believe I have ever encountered. If you are telling the truth, you can work your 'magic' and, if we open the golden doors, we will find behind them a passage into the outside world, not the millions of tons of jumbled rock I know are there currently. Is that the gist of it?"

"I guess so," I said, while my mind whirled, trying to figure out how to work this. He would surely get close enough for me to touch him if we both went up to the doors. That was all it would take. Just a touch. I would have his *hokhmah*, and with it, the complete *hokhmah* of this world, and then I could turn the tables on Abrahm and his monstrous rogues, free Karl, and we could leave this world behind forever.

All I needed was that single touch . . .

Abrahm, however, remained frustratingly out of reach as we approached the doors. *For someone who has Shaped all of his citizens to be unquestioningly obedient, he seems awfully paranoid*, I thought. He hung back, instead ordering Samuel to accompany me. Karl, Father Thomas, and Piotr remained frozen even after Samuel turned his back, his power over them intact though he was no longer focused on them.

I looked up at the doors, gleaming in the candlelight. They were magnificent works of art, but the most astonishing thing was, I recognized them—or *almost* recognized them. My art history class in university had, not surprisingly, focused quite a lot on Florence during the Renaissance, and these doors, though gold instead of bronze, were clearly based on Lorenzo Ghiberti's Gates of Paradise, the bronze doors of the eastern portal of the Battistero di San Giovanni, the baptistry located in front of Florence's cathedral, the Duomo. Karl had told me that the Shaped worlds filled in details with things drawn from the First World, and here was a clear example. *But how does that work?* I wondered, as I stared at those magnificent doors, soon to be, I hoped, a magnificent Portal. These weren't identical to the Gates of Paradise—Ghiberti had not, I was pretty sure, included vampires and werewolves in his imagery. And yet, the relationship was unmistakable. Surely such borrowing had to be the work of some vast intelligence. Ygrair? Or someone—or something—else?

I mentally shook myself. *Not the time*, I thought, and instead reached out to touch the gold. It was cool under my fingers. I reached inside myself, found the knowledge that now came readily to mind, moved my hands in the requisite patterns. Blue light flashed. I stepped back, then seized the handles of the doors and tugged them open.

They must have weighed a literal ton, but they opened smoothly. And beyond . . .

. . . a dark alley, rain pouring from a sky that glowed in a way familiar to any city dweller: the glow of low clouds illuminated by streetlights. *Electric* streetlights.

The alley ended, maybe twenty feet away, in a T-intersection: a blank brick wall with a cross-street cutting in front of it. There was not a hint of color. The alley, the sky, the wall, everything was as black and white as though it belonged in an old movie, one starring Humphrey Bogart, maybe, or Edward G. Robinson.

"At last," I heard Abrahm breathe behind me.

"Come, take a closer look," I said, turning toward him. Surely now he would walk over, I could grab him, I could end this . . .

But, instead, he turned to Samuel. "Go through," he said.

Samuel walked forward. I admit it; I froze for a moment. This was the last thing I expected. "Wait!" I managed to call as he approached the open doors.

Samuel didn't even glance at me. He stepped forward, reached a hand through the Portal . . .

. . . and vanished.

He didn't explode, or turn to dust, or scream, or stumble back clutching the stump where his hand used to be. He simply disappeared: there one second, gone the next, with an audible *pop!* of displaced air.

I turned toward Abrahm. "I don't—" I began, but he was backing away, eyes wide.

"Guards!" he screamed. "Guards!" And then Abrahm, whom I had to touch, whose *hokhmah* I had to have, turned and ran away from me.

"Shit!" I said and ran after him.

THIRTY-THREE

FOR A SHORT, pudgy guy wearing big boots, the Protector was remarkably fast. Apparently, seeing his henchman disintegrate in front of him had given him an incentive to get the lead out.

Also, he didn't have far to run: his goal was clearly the door that once, when this was still a church, would have led to the vestry and now presumably gave access to his private chambers since that was the way Tabitha had gone.

Shouting, "Guards! Guards!" at the top of his voice wasn't slowing him down, either. He was going to get through that door before I could catch him . . .

But then, from my left, came a silver-black streak, Piotr in wolf form. He leaped and bore the Protector to the ground. The Protector screamed, an almost girlish sound, and rolled over onto his back, arms across his face, as Piotr stood over him and slavered, lips drawn back from his fangs, growls rumbling deep in his chest.

I resisted the urge to say, "Good boy," and approached, ready to reach out and take the Protector's *hokhmah* . . .

. . . only to be knocked down in my turn by Father Thomas. He sat astride me, holding my arms pinned. I struggled, but I couldn't break free. I tried to Shape him, but Abrahm's blasted shouldn't-even-exist Shaping remained firm, since I didn't have his *hokhmah*.

"What should I do, Protector?" Father Thomas called, but Abrahm was too busy fending off Piotr's snapping jaws—I knew

Piotr was only keeping him in place, not really planning to devour him, but presumably, the Protector didn't—to answer.

For the moment, both Abrahm and I were pinned to the floor like butterflies in a museum display . . . but only for a moment. Now Karl hit Father Thomas from the side, driving him off me. *Took you long enough*, I thought. Ordinarily, I would have needled him out loud, but there wasn't time. As he and Father Thomas wrestled and Piotr growled and I got back to my feet, Abrahm's guards finally responded—but not in human form.

The rogue the pack had found feasting on the farm family had looked like a regular vampire, but maybe that was partly appearance-changing glamor, because the two rogues that now exploded up from the crypt stairwell clearly showed their mixed vampire/were-wolf heritage. Winged like vampires, but with the snarling canine visages of wolves, they were bigger than any vampire I'd seen, and dove at me with murder in their blazing red eyes, howling.

I gasped, turned, ran, and, as the first came literally screaming out of the air, flung myself on the floor like a baseball player sliding into home . . .

. . . except, I slid into Abrahm.

Jaws snapped so close above my neck that spittle sprayed me. A blast of hot, fetid air swirled around me, extinguishing the nearby candles, as the rogue pulled up and swung around for another pass. The second one was diving in now and wouldn't miss . . .

. . . but I had touched Abrahm, and I had stripped the *hokhmah* from him in an instant—stripped it and, I knew with sudden certainty, taken *all* of it. I did not share it, as the Adversary had been forced to share mine after he had touched me in the Human Bean, as I knew I shared the *hokhmah* of Patricia and Stephanie, though they no longer had sufficient power to use it to Shape their world. I had stripped it from him, *ripped* it from him as though I were ripping down an offensive poster from a wall, an ability I had not known I had until that moment—an ability Karl had not even hinted at.

Abrahm's *hokhmah* exploded into me like a Molotov cocktail, set alight, perhaps, by the burning rage I had suppressed, but never extinguished, as I tried to sweet-talk my way close to him. Shaping power flooded me. I reacted instinctively to the diving threat. The rogue exploded into red mist, gobbets of flesh, and splinters of bone, which sprayed the onetime chancel with gore and extinguished the remaining candles. The other rogue grabbed air with his wings, shock readable even on his monstrous features. I reached out and made him change—not into an ordinary human, but into the movie-style werewolf Thaddeus had turned into just before I killed him. Then I put the rogue to sleep. He crashed to the tile floor like a marionette whose strings had been cut. I did not think the fall would have killed him, while he was changed. I did hope it hurt like hell.

That done, I got to my feet, sticky and stinking, my fury now fully unleashed. Father Thomas and Karl, painted as red as I by the blood that was everywhere, had stopped struggling. The priest looked confused, Karl . . .

Karl looked grim. He watched me as I stepped toward the two of them. I didn't say anything, but I reached out and touched Father Thomas' head. It took only a tiny application of Shaping to return his mind to the way it had been. He gasped and jerked away from me, then his eyes widened in horror as he remembered what had happened to him. "I'm sorry . . ." he said, but I had already turned my back on him as I faced Abrahm, wolf-Piotr still crouched over his supine body.

The Protector looked shocked. Undone. He must have sensed the loss of his power, and his bewilderment showed on his face. He really was a young man, younger than me, and his slight pudginess and small stature made him look almost childlike in that moment.

I didn't care. I didn't care at all.

"Let him up," I told Piotr.

Piotr gave me a look I interpreted as questioning, even though it was delivered by a wolf with glowing red eyes.

"Let him up," I repeated.

Piotr stepped back.

The Protector got to his feet. The spray of blood and meat and bone from his messily deceased guard had turned his sparkling white clothing mottled pink, flecked with darker bits. "Go on," I said. "Run to your sanctuary." I pointed to the door into the vestry. "Go!"

He gulped air, turned, and ran. Even as he did so, I was Shaping . . . not him, but the room beyond the door. He would find it unchanged, except for two things. One, it no longer had a second door, leading to his quarters, through which Tabitha had gone. Two, the one door it did have, the one he would enter by, could no longer be opened from the inside.

He reached that door, jerked it open, passed through it. It closed behind him.

He was trapped.

"Shawna," Karl said quietly, "what are you doing?"

I ignored him. My anger still burned inside me, unquenchable. I walked over to the sleeping rogue. I touched his forehead. I Shaped. I healed.

I woke him.

He blinked up at me, then got to his feet. "You have done well," I said.

"Thank you, Protector," he said.

I heard Karl's sharp intake of breath, but I ignored it.

"Are you hungry?" I said.

He grinned, showing wolflike teeth, though his face was nearly human. "Very, Protector."

"I have food for you," I said. I pointed to the vestry door. "In there."

He licked his lips, eyes glowing an even brighter red in anticipation.

"Go on," I said. "Enjoy."

He needed no further encouragement. He dashed to the vestry, threw the door open.

"Shawna!" Karl snapped. "What are you—"

"Shut up, Karl," I said.

The door closed behind the rogue. Abrahm shouted frantically though I couldn't make out the words. There weren't any words after the first few seconds, anyway. There was only screaming—high-pitched, agonized screaming. It went on a surprisingly long time.

Only when it was done did I reach inside myself for the full and compete *hokhmah* of that moonlit world.

Stephanie and Patricia had carefully crafted a world populated by monsters that did not kill. Abrahm, however he had come by his power, had corrupted it. His Shaping of it was like a cancer, eating away at the healthy tissue of the world. And so I excised it.

Shaping power exploded out of me, so much that I dropped to my knees, and then to my hands, breathing hard. I'd reached my limit . . .

. . . but it was enough. I knew it had been enough. I could feel it.

Every rogue, every evil vampire/werewolf monster Abrahm had Shaped, every vile monster preying on humans and Stephanie and Patricia's subjects alike, ceased to exist in that moment. They could no longer exist in this world, under its natural laws, any more than Samuel could exist in the world beyond the Portal, and so, they were undone.

Including, I knew, Tabitha, Emma's sister. I did not spare her, for one simple reason: in the *hokhmah* I had taken from Abrahm I discovered a terrible truth, that every rogue, upon being changed and without fail, devoured a human, willingly, eagerly . . . and worse, Abrahm had decreed that human must be someone they knew, to prove they had left their humanity behind forever.

Had Emma been changed, she would have fed on one of the Chosen who had come with her to the end of the Sacred Vale . . . as Tabitha must have fed on one of her companions.

I could not bring her back to her humanity after that. I did not want to.

In the same moment the rogues vanished, all of the Shaped within the Sacred Vale returned to themselves, the selves they had been before Abrahm seized control.

The churches would be rebuilt. The villages would be repopulated. Peace and prosperity would reestablish themselves. Stephanie and Patricia's vision was restored.

But the dead were still dead. The murdered stayed murdered. The devoured remained devoured. I could not return them to life, any more than I'd been able to bring Aesha back from the dead when she vanished from my world.

My reaction, after all that was done, surprised me. I burst into tears. Curled up like a baby on the cold tile floor of what would once again be Mother Church, I wept.

I heard footsteps approach, booted ones, and the click of canine nails on a hard surface. I tried to regain my composure, but it was several minutes before I could pull myself together enough to sit up. I swiped my sleeve across my face. "It's done," I said, to Karl, Father Thomas, and Piotr, who sometime in the last few seconds had turned back into a naked boy. "The world is back to what it was meant to be."

Karl looked grim. "What did you do?"

"I undid Abrahm's handiwork," I said.

"After having him horribly murdered," Karl said.

"Are you saying he didn't deserve it?" I snapped.

"No," Karl said. "But it is not him I am worried about."

"I don't have the strength to argue with you right now," I said. "You can tell me what a horrible mistake I made later. In the next world, maybe." I glanced into the apse. Through the open golden doors I could still see the dark, rainswept alley. It gave no hint of what kind of world it belonged to, other than the electric-light glow in the clouds.

"The next world," Piotr repeated, following my gaze. "You'll be leaving soon, then?"

"Not right this minute," I said. "I don't know about the rest of you, but I'm exhausted. And I think we need to go back to the main valley and tell Stephanie and Patricia what's happened." I smiled at him. "Your mother will be proud of you."

"Maybe," he said. "I guess you'll find out."

"I guess . . ." I said. And then, "Wait. *I'll* find . . . ?"

Piotr was already changing. In an instant, he was a wolf, streaking across the floor toward the open Portal.

In horror, I scrambled to my feet. "Piotr, no! You can't—"

He leaped through the Portal, into the rainswept alley—and kept going, charging to its end and around the corner, out of sight.

He hadn't disintegrated.

"We have to go after him," I said. I turned to Karl. I stopped, but weirdly, the Great Hall didn't. It whirled around me. "We have to . . ."

Everything faded away. I dimly felt arms catching me as I toppled, and then I felt nothing at all.

THIRTY-FOUR

KARL STUDIED SHAWNA'S face as she lay unconscious in the bed in the same tower room in Patricia's castle where he had once been held prisoner.

Her collapse, in the wake of such a sudden and massive outpouring of Shaping power, had not surprised him. Her actions before the collapse had.

The unmaking of the rogues . . . they were monstrous, to be sure, but no more monstrous than the vampires and werewolves Shaped to inhabit this world to begin with. They could have been Shaped, like those creatures, to adhere to the Pact. Each of them, no matter how evil they had seemed in the moment, were, at the core, copies of real people in the First World, as all the Shaped were. Until that moment in the former Mother Church, that had mattered to Shawna. But given the opportunity to take revenge, this time, she had taken it.

Yes, the rogues had killed untold numbers of the ordinary humans of the vale—but those humans were no more, or less, real than they were. All were Shaped. All could be re-Shaped. All were thinking, feeling beings.

Karl did not consider the Shaped real in the same way he and Shawna and the Shapers they encountered were real—the fact the Shaped could not pass through a Portal (except, somehow, the Adversary's cadre, and how he managed that, Karl was not entirely sure) provided sufficient evidence of that for him.

But again, Shawna had always considered the Shaped real, or more real than Karl had. She had always felt bad about Shaping them to her own ends. And yet, now . . .

Genocide, without thought, committed in the heat of anger.

And more. Shawna had discovered an ability he had not known the Shurak nanomachines would give her. She could strip the *hokhmah* entirely from another Shaper, against that Shaper's will, not just taking a copy, as the Adversary had done to her.

He had himself given her the ability to travel through the Labyrinth without him, the ability to find Ygrair's world, the ability to take a copy of a Shaper's *hokhmah* with a touch and without permission. This new, frightening ability made her even *more* capable of carrying out her quest without his assistance. But her actions made him wonder what *else* she was capable of doing, as she traveled through the Labyrinth.

She had said she wanted to leave Robur's world better than she found it. Perhaps she had felt the same way here. But that was not her role, nor did he think it was one Ygrair would countenance. Ygrair wanted variety, diversity, an endless series of worlds of every conceivable type. Imposing control on the worlds, shaping them as she thought fit, had never been something Ygrair had considered. That, in fact, was the *modus operandi* of the Adversary . . .

. . . and now, perhaps, of Shawna. So, when Shawna reached Ygrair, with all of the new power and knowledge she was amassing, with this new dark and dangerous edge she had displayed honed razor-sharp after who knew how many other encounters with Shapers in who knew how many more worlds, would she then meekly do what Ygrair needed her to do? Or would she, in the end, reject the quest and challenge the wounded and weakened Ygrair for control of the Labyrinth?

In carrying out Ygrair's wishes, had he inadvertently planted the seed of Ygrair's destruction?

And if Ygrair were destroyed, what would become of her promise to him, to make him a Shaper and give him his own world?
What would become of the dream that was all that had kept him
going, all that had kept him living and serving Ygrair, for so many,
many years?

And so Karl sat and studied Shawna as she slept. He found no
answers, only questions. *All I can do is stay with her and watch her.
Closely. And if the time comes . . .*

He pushed away that thought.

*Watch her. Try to guide her. If it comes to that, try to save her.
She must carry out the quest. She must carry the* hokhmah *of as
many worlds as possible to Ygrair. Ygrair must be revived and em-
powered once again to save the Labyrinth and defeat the Adversary.*

She must so that she may reward me at last.

Shawna stirred. Karl gathered himself, smiled, and leaned forward to greet her.

I admit it. The first thing I said, when I woke in that nice soft bed
and saw Karl smiling at me, was, "Where am I?" I'm not proud of
it, but it's surprisingly hard to be original when you come out of a
days-long stupor.

And it had been days long. There'd been no Vampire Air option
to get back to the main valley. I'd apparently been taken, unconscious, on a stretcher down to the Protected City, loaded onto a cart,
and hauled back to the Great Valley proper like a prize side of beef.
There were implications to the fact I woke clean, bathed, and wearing a simple shift that I had no intention of asking about, but Karl
told me without prompting that Emma Krause-Snow, no longer under the sway of the rogues or the influence of their Shaped loyalty
to the Protector, had nursed me all the way to Patricia's castle.

She had already gone back to her parents' village, so I wouldn't be able to thank her. She would never know what her sister, Tabitha, had become, or what I did to her. But perhaps that was best, both for her and for me.

"What about the Portal?" I said. "Piotr is in the next world! We have to go after him!"

"And we will," Karl said. "But with your collapse, there was no possibility of following him immediately. And we need to replenish supplies before pressing on to the next world, anyway."

"But he's alone . . ."

"His choice," Karl said.

"What did you do with the Portal?"

"I closed it," Karl said. "It wouldn't do for some poor Shaped person on the other side to blunder into it and unmake himself."

"No," I said. I remembered the abrupt disappearance of Samuel. "No."

Assured I felt well enough, Karl left me so I could get dressed, in the same leather vest and tough black trousers and warm knitted long-sleeved tunic I'd worn during the climactic battle in Mother Church. Someone had done a marvelous job of cleaning them. I didn't find a single bloodstain.

Then, accompanied by Karl, I descended to the castle proper. Those we passed in the halls—vampires or werewolves or humans, I couldn't tell, since it was broad daylight outside, and in the sunshine, in this world, all the Shaped looked the same—looked at me curiously, but showed no indication they had a clue what I had done.

That made sense, I guess, but I admit I felt a pang when I thought of what might have been—something along the lines of the medal-presentation scene at the end of *Star Wars: A New Hope*, with me in the Luke Skywalker role and Princess Leia replaced by the Queens Stephanie and Patricia. Karl would have to be Han

Solo. Piotr would have made a reasonable Chewbacca, in wolf form, but of course, he was gone.

Given the varying dietary requirements of werewolves, vampires, and humans, even a celebratory feast would have been problematic. Instead, I, Karl, Patricia, and Stephanie met in Patricia's very First World-seeming private quarters. Dracula was off on an inspection tour of the Lands Between, apparently. I didn't miss him, even though, with the *hokhmah* of the world tucked away inside my head, I was now immune to his fear-glamor.

Seraphina, Patricia's lust-inducing lady-in-waiting, was not invited. I didn't miss her. I wondered if Karl did.

Karl had, of course, told the queens what had happened. Patricia and Stephanie thanked me for restoring their world. "But what about my son?" Stephanie said, her tone pleading.

I looked at Karl. He shrugged. I looked back at her. "He survived the transition," I said. "That's all we know."

"But he's just a boy," Stephanie said. She shook her head, and I saw tears in her eyes. "He's all I have left of Geoffrey," she whispered. "What will I do without him?"

Patricia reached out a hand to her. "I know I can't replace him," she said, "but you are welcome here anytime. I've missed our friendship. It's a poor substitute for a son, but . . ."

Stephanie laid her hand on the vampire queen's. "I've missed our friendship, too," she said. "And right now, it means more than I can say."

I blinked hard and cleared my throat. "All I can say is, we'll find him," I said. "And as long as we're in the next world, he can return to this one through the Portal we've opened. But we don't know what's waiting for us in there. Or for him. I can't promise anything."

"I know," Stephanie said sadly. "It's my fault. I should never have told him the truth. He's always dreamed of leaving this world. He said it was too small for him."

Teenagers are teenagers, I thought. *Even if they're werewolves.*

"At the very least," she went on, "when you find him, tell him I love him. Tell him I always will."

I had to clear my throat again before answering. "I promise."

"I still do not understand," Patricia said after a moment, "how Abrahm could have existed. How could there be a third Shaper in our world?"

"I have a theory," Karl said, which hardly surprised me. "I have been thinking about it a great deal while waiting for Shawna to wake." He looked from queen to queen. "It has been, I believe, twenty-five years since the Shaping of this world?"

They nodded.

Karl looked at me. "Would you say," he said, "that Abrahm was perhaps twenty-five years old?"

"No way to be certain," I said, "but that seems reasonable. He was very young."

He turned to the queens again. "Here is my theory. The Shaped are copies of people from the First World. A small percentage of people from the First World have, like the three of you, the innate ability to be Shapers."

"So?" I said.

"So," he said, "a certain number of the Shaped should also have that ability."

"Maybe," Stephanie said. "But Ygrair had to awaken it in us before we could use it."

This was news to me, the Shaper amnesiac . . . although, just for a moment, on the edge of my memories, something nibbled, like a mouse at a piece of cheese, an image, a feeling, a . . .

No. It was gone.

"Exactly," Karl said. "It is awakened through exposure to an act of Shaping. Each of you was taken through the Graduation Portal, and Ygrair Shaped, for one moment, an entire world . . . and then erased it again. Exposure to that amount of Shaping power woke your own power."

"I remember," Patricia said. "It was like an explosion of light. A big bang, but it only lasted a second. Then darkness again. And when it was done, I felt different. I wanted to do what she had just done, but keep the light shining. I wanted to Shape."

"I remember, too," Stephanie said.

Once again, I had nothing to add.

"But hold on a minute," Patricia said. "If you're saying that some Shaped person who carried over Shaping ability from their original in the First World turned into a Shaper because they were exposed to our Shaping of this world . . . that makes no sense. The Shaped appear in an instant. They're part of the Shaping. It can't waken their power, surely."

"Ordinarily, no," Karl said. "But your Shaping of this world was a more drawn-out affair because there were two of you. It was awash in Shaping power—and more of it—longer than any ordinary Shaped world. And Abrahm's age is a clue, as well. Twenty-five. The same age as this world.

"I believe he was in the womb, or even literally being born, while this world was being Shaped. That, I believe, is what woke his Shaping power. A stunted form of it—he didn't have training, he didn't know what he was, and he was already in a Shaped world. But enough. Enough for him to do what he eventually did, leading him to piece together an entirely fanciful—and, ultimately, malignant—explanation for that power. He saw himself as superior because of his abilities. He developed a hatred for Mother Church and for you two, because he saw you as rivals he had to eliminate to become the unquestioned ruler he was convinced he was destined to be."

"I've heard that smart people are more likely to fall for conspiracy theories because they can reason themselves into anything, by teasing entirely spurious patterns out of random data," I said, which earned me a Spock-like raised eyebrow from Karl and surprised looks from both queens. "What?" I said defensively. "I read a lot."

Karl sighed and continued his explication. "While still a teenager, no older than Piotr and Eric, he acted: Shaped the Sacred Vale. Created the rogues. Gave them the power to change their appearance and cause the Pact to come crashing down. He was sowing chaos, working toward the day—which would have come soon—that he could seize all power for himself."

He shrugged. "There is no way to prove my theory. But it fits the observed facts. And if it is correct, you need not worry about another renegade Shaper suddenly appearing in your world. The circumstances that produced this one were unique. They cannot be repeated here, and in truth are unlikely ever to be repeated anywhere in the Labyrinth."

After that, it was just a matter of refilling our packs with as much food and water as we could carry. I also got a new dagger to carry on my belt. I was offered one with a golden hilt, encrusted in jewels, but remembering the plain, colorless world beyond the Portal, I opted instead for something sleek, black, and deadly.

I mean, it would have been deadly if I'd actually known how to use a dagger. "Stick 'em with the pointy end," was pretty much the alpha and omega of my knowledge on the subject of knife fighting. All the same, I felt better for having it.

Karl and I bid a final farewell to the queens, then flew back to Mother Church via Vampire Air, with the full moon shining on the land below our feet. We made one brief stop on the way, swinging into the churchyard of the repopulated Zarozje. Father Thomas had been told of our coming and was waiting for us.

He clasped Karl's hand, then turned to me. "So much has happened since you first came to me with your wild tale of being from another world," he said. "I did not know then that you were a miracle worker."

"Don't put me up for sainthood," I said. "I don't think I've lived quite the life expected of saints."

Father Thomas smiled sadly. "There is no one to declare saints," he said. "None of the hierarchy of Mother Church survived the Protector's interregnum. It will be months before the remaining priests can convene to choose a new leader."

"I would not be surprised to see you ensconced in Mother Church someday," I said. "You strike me as a worthy successor to Abbot Costello."

He laughed. "If that happens, it will be God's punishment for my failings."

We bid him a final goodbye, and climbed once more into the air, circling Zarozje once before setting out for the Sacred Vale. Though it was close to midnight, the village gates stood open. Father Thomas had said that, over time, the walls would be dismantled, the stone used to rebuild some of the area farmhouses, to which citizens were returning now that the Pact had been reestablished. It seemed a worthy repurposing to me.

In the early hours of the morning, we finally reached Mother Church. Cold and stiff, I stepped away from my escort. He and the larger vampire who had carried Karl raised hands in farewell and flew off into the night, silhouetted briefly in best horror-movie fashion against the moon.

Mother Church was dark except for the sanctuary light, burning once more on the altar that had replaced Abrahm's gaudy throne. Its soft red glow showed the towering golden doors that had once marked the long-blocked entrance to the Great Valley, and now marked the location of a Portal to another world.

Once we stood before those doors, Karl gestured to me to do the honors. I nodded and stepped forward. A quick pass of my hands, a flash of blue, and the Portal returned. Together, we pulled open the heavy doors, and there was the alley. It was no longer raining in the next world; instead, thick fog almost hid the cross street, around the corner of which Piotr had disappeared.

We stepped through, turned, and saw that on this side, there were no doors: the Portal appeared in a brick wall topped with outward-leaning spikes strung with barbed wire. I gestured, blue light flashed, and the Portal closed.

I turned back to the foggy alley. "Where now?" Karl said quietly.

I was about to say that was a stupid question, since there was only one way to go, but before I could say a single snarky word, in the distance, a wolf howled.

"Follow that sound," I said, and Karl and I set off together into yet another strange new world.